Special Deliveries

A Baby with Her Best Friend

MAUREEN
CHILD

CAROLINE
ANDERSON

KATHIE
DENOSKY

Special
Deliveries
COLLECTION

August 2016

September 2016

October 2016

November 2016

December 2016

January 2017

Special Deliveries

A Baby with Her Best Friend

MAUREEN
CHILD

CAROLINE
ANDERSON

KATHIE
DENOSKY

MILLS & BOON

First Published in Great Britain 2016
By Mills & Boon, an imprint of HarperCollins*Publishers*
1 London Bridge Street, London, SE1 9GF

A BABY WITH HER BEST FRIEND © 2016 Harlequin Books S.A.

Rumour Has It © 2013 Maureen Child
The Secret in His Heart © 2012 Caroline Anderson
A Baby Between Friends © 2012 Kathie DeNosky

ISBN: **978-0-263-92691-0**

24-0916

Harlequin (UK) Limited's policy is to use papers that are natural, renewable and recyclable products and made from wood grown in sustainable forests. The logging and manufacturing processes conform to the legal environmental regulations of the country of origin.

Printed and bound in Spain
by CPI, Barcelona

RUMOUR HAS IT

MAUREEN CHILD

To Rosemary Rangel Estrada
We really miss you, neighbour!

Maureen Child writes for the Harlequin Desire line and can't imagine a better job.

A seven-time finalist for a prestigious Romance Writers of America RITA® Award, Maureen is an author of more than one hundred romance novels. Her books regularly appear on bestseller lists and have won several awards, including a Prism Award, a National Readers' Choice Award, a Colorado Romance Writers Award of Excellence and a Golden Quill Award. She is a native Californian but has recently moved to the mountains of Utah.

One

Amanda Altman's back in town.

It was all anyone could talk about and Nathan Battle was getting pretty damn sick of it. Nothing he hated more than being at the center of a gossip tornado. He'd already lived through it once, years ago. Of course, he'd escaped the worst of it by moving to Houston and burying himself in the police academy and then his job.

Wouldn't work this time. He'd built his place here. He wasn't going anywhere. Mostly because Nathan Battle didn't run. So he'd just have to ride this mess out until the town found something new to chew on.

But that was life in Royal, Texas. A town too small to mind its own business and too big to have to repeat the same gossip over and over again.

Even here, he thought, in the hallowed halls of the Texas Cattleman's Club, Nathan couldn't escape the talk—or the speculation. Not even from his best friend.

"So, Nathan," Chance asked with a knowing grin, "you see Amanda yet?"

Nathan looked at the man sitting opposite him. Chance McDaniel owned McDaniel's Acres, a working dude ranch and hotel just south of town. The man had built the place from the ground up on property he'd inherited from his family, and he'd done a hell of a job.

Chance's blond hair was cropped short, but he still couldn't get the wave out of it no matter how he tried. His green eyes were amused and Nathan shook his head, knowing that *he* was the source of his friend's amusement.

"No." One word. Should be concise enough to get his message across. And maybe it would have worked with anyone else. Of course, Nathan told himself wryly, it wouldn't be nearly enough to get Chance to back off. They'd been friends for too long. And nobody knew how to get to you better than a best friend.

"You can't ignore her forever," Chance mused, taking a sip of his scotch.

"It's worked so far," Nathan told him and lifted his own glass for a drink.

"Sure it has," Chance said, muffling a laugh. "That's why you've been such a cool, calm guy the last couple of weeks."

Nathan narrowed his eyes on his friend. "Funny."

"You have no idea," Chance agreed, lips twitching. "So, Sheriff, if you're avoiding the Royal Diner these days, where are you getting your coffee?"

His fingers tightened on the heavy, old crystal. "The gas station."

Now Chance didn't bother to hide his laughter. "You must be desperate if you're drinking the swill Charlie brews down there. You know, maybe it's time you learned how to make decent coffee yourself."

"And maybe it's time you let this go," Nathan told him. Irritating is what it was, he thought. His whole damn routine had been splintered when Amanda moved back home to Royal. Used to be he started off his day with a large coffee and maybe some eggs at the diner. Amanda's sister, Pam, always had his coffee ready for him when he walked in. That was a routine a man could count on. But since Amanda blew back into his world, he'd had to make do with Charlie's disgusting coffee and a packaged sweet roll.

Even when she wasn't trying, Amanda found a way to screw with him.

"Seriously, Nate," Chance said, lowering his voice a little so the other members of the TCC couldn't over-hear, "from all reports, Amanda's here to stay. Seems she's been making some changes to the diner, settling in. Even talking about looking for a house of her own, according to Margie Santos."

Nathan had heard all the same talk, of course. Hard not to, when everyone in a ten-mile radius was more than eager to talk to him about Amanda. Margie Rice was the top real estate agent in Royal and one of the biggest gossips as well. If she was spreading the word that Amanda was looking for her own place, then Nathan had to admit that she was here for the long term.

Which meant he couldn't ignore her for much longer.

Too bad, because he'd finally gotten good at not think-ing about Amanda. Wasn't always the case. Several years ago, Amanda was *all* Nathan thought about. The pas-sion between them had burned hotter than anything he'd ever known. She'd filled his mind, waking and sleeping.

Of course back then, they'd been engaged.

He scowled into his glass of scotch. *Times change.*

"New subject, Chance," he muttered and let his gaze slide around the main room of the TCC.

While his friend talked about what was happening at the ranch, Nathan's mind wandered. Over the years, it seemed like inside the TCC, time stood still. Even the fact that women were now officially members of the long-standing, males-only club hadn't affected the decor. Paneled walls, dark brown leather furniture—sofas and club chairs—hunting prints on the walls and a big-screen TV so you didn't miss a bit of any Texas sporting event.

The air smelled of lemon polish and the wood floors and tables gleamed in the lamplight. The TV was on now, but muted so that members could sit and brood behind newspapers or chat without having to shout to be heard. The soft clinking of crystal against gleaming wood tables underlined the hushed conversations surrounding them.

A woman's laugh pealed out just then, shattering the quiet and Nathan grinned as he noted that Beau Hacket actually cringed at the sound. At nearly sixty, Beau was short, thick around the middle and with a lot more gray in what was left of his dark red hair. He had a big laugh and a narrow mind—he believed women belonged in the kitchen and didn't care who knew it.

Now, Beau fired a hard look around the room as if to silently say, *Did you all hear that? That's just wrong. Women don't belong here.*

No one said anything, but Nathan read the tension in the room and noted more gritted jaws than usual. Women were members, but they still weren't really welcome. Everyone was gathered for the weekly TCC meeting and none of the old guard were happy about having women included.

"Sounds like Abigail's enjoying herself," Chance muttered into the stillness.

"Abby always enjoys herself," Nathan mused.

Abigail Langley Price, married to Brad Price, had been the first female member of the club. And, of course, she was having a good time now, since she had women to talk to in here. But it hadn't been easy on her, gaining acceptance at the TCC. Even with the support of Nathan, Chance and several of the other members, she'd had to fight her way in—and Nathan admired that about her.

"Does it feel weird to you," Chance asked, "to have women in the club now?"

"Nope." Nathan finished off his scotch and set the empty glass down on the table in front of him. "Felt weirder when they weren't allowed in here."

"Yeah," his friend said. "I know what you mean." Leaning forward, he braced his elbows on his knees. "But men like Beau over there aren't happy about it."

Nathan shrugged. "Men like Beau are always complaining about something. Besides, he and the others are just gonna have to get used to it." Then he added what he'd been thinking a few minutes ago. "Times change."

"They really do," Chance agreed. "Like, for example, the vote we're taking tonight."

Relieved to be off the subject of Amanda, Nathan turned his thoughts to the upcoming vote. It had been the talk of the town for days. Once Abigail and the other women became members of the TCC they'd had some ideas of their own to put forth and tonight marked the vote for one of the biggest items.

"The child-care center?" Nathan asked and Chance nodded.

"It's a big deal and only going to make the hard-line members more irritated than ever."

"True," Nathan agreed, imagining the fireworks that would soon take place over the vote. "Only makes sense if you think about it, though. A safe place for the kids while their parents are here. Probably should have done it years ago."

"Right there with ya," Chance told him with a shake of his head. "But I'm not sure Beau's going to agree with that."

"Beau doesn't agree with anything," Nathan said with a chuckle. As town sheriff, Nathan had to deal with Beau Hacket on a regular basis. The man had a complaint about everything and everyone, and didn't mind taking up the sheriff's time with them. "A more contrary man has never lived."

"True."

The clock over the river-stone fireplace began to chime the hour and both of them stood up.

"Guess it's time to get the meeting started."

"This should be good," Chance told Nathan and followed him down the hallway to the official meeting room.

An hour later, the arguments were still being shouted out. Beau Hacket had some support for his Neanderthal opinions. Sam and Josh Gordon, the twins who owned and operated Gordon Construction, were getting to be just as hardheaded as Beau.

"Is it just me," Nate whispered to his friend Alex Santiago, "or is Sam Gordon starting to become more and more like Beau Hacket?"

Alex shifted a look at the twin who was spouting all the reasons why children didn't belong in the TCC.

"It's not just you," he answered quietly. "Even his twin looks surprised at Sam's arguments."

Alex hadn't lived in Royal very long, but he'd made lots of friends in town and seemed to already have a handle on the town and its citizens. A venture capitalist and investor, Alex was wealthy and had become, in his short time in Royal, very influential. Sometimes Nate wondered why a man as rich as Alex would choose to settle down in Royal. But at the same time, he told himself with a smile, people probably wondered why Nathan Battle chose to be the town sheriff. Since he owned half of the Battlelands Ranch, Nate was rich enough to not have to work at all.

But then what the hell would he do?

Shaking his head, Nate gave a quick look around the long table at the members gathered. Not all of them were present, of course, but there were more than enough for the voting. Ryan Grant, former rodeo star, was attending his first official meeting and Nate saw the bemusement in the other man's eyes. Dave Firestone, whose ranch ran alongside Nathan's family spread, was lounging in a chair, watching the goings-on as if he were at a tennis match. Beau was nearly purple in the face, shouting down anyone who argued with him. Chance was sitting beside Shannon Morrison, who looked as if she wanted to stand up and tell Beau Hacket exactly what he could do with his outdated opinions.

And then there was Gil Addison, the TCC president, standing at the head of the table. His dark eyes flashed and Nate knew that his friend had about reached the limits of his patience.

Almost at once, Gil slammed his gavel onto its pedestal until he had quiet. The echoes of arguments and recriminations were hanging in the still air like battle flags when Gil said, "Enough talking. Time for a vote.

All in favor of the child-care center being added to the TCC, say 'aye.'"

All of the women, including Missy Reynolds and Vanessa Woodrow, spoke up, but Nathan, Alex, Chance and several of the others were quick to contribute their votes.

"All opposed," Gil added, "say 'no.'"

A few loud voices were heard.

The gavel slammed down again sharply. Gil nodded at the group and smiled. "Motion's passed. A child-care center will be added to the Texas Cattlemen's Club."

Beau and a few of the other members, still bristling over the fact that women were now included in their group, were practically apoplectic. But, there was nothing they could do about it.

As Beau stormed out of the meeting, Nathan watched him go and almost felt a flicker of sympathy. He could see the other side of the situation, but you couldn't stay locked in the past. The world moved every damn day and you moved with it or you got steamrolled. Tradition was one thing, being stuck in the mud was another.

Change happened whether you liked it or not, so the best way to handle it was to hop on board the train as opposed to stretching your body across the tracks and being run over. Which was, he told himself, a good way to think about how to deal with Amanda.

"This is great," Abigail Price said with a wide smile for her friends and those who had supported them. "And our Julia will be the first child enrolled as soon as we're up and running."

"You bet she will, honey." Brad Price gave his wife's hand a squeeze. "Shame Beau and the rest are upset, but they'll get over it."

"You did," Abigail reminded him with a smile.

True enough, Nate mused thoughtfully. Not too long

ago, Brad and Abby were butting heads every chance they got. He'd done his best to keep Abby out of the TCC and now just look at them—in love, married, and with a great little girl.

While everyone around them talked, Alex suggested, "Why don't we head over to the diner and get some coffee and pie?"

"Good idea," Chance agreed and flicked a glance at Nathan.

Friends could be a real pain in the ass sometimes, Nathan told himself. These two were trying to maneuver him into a meeting with Amanda and it just wasn't going to work. He'd see her. In his own time. In his own way. And damned if he was going to put on a show for the folks in Royal.

"No thanks," he said, pushing up from the table. He didn't even look at the other members in the room. "I'm headed back to the office to finish up some paperwork, then I'm going home."

"Still in hiding?" Alex murmured.

Nathan bristled. "Pretty hard to hide in a town the size of Royal."

"You should keep that in mind," Chance told him.

Irritated, Nathan just gritted his teeth and left. *No point in arguing with a jackass,* he thought.

Amanda was so busy she almost didn't have time to worry about Nathan.

Almost.

Turns out, even running the family diner, looking for a new house and arranging to have the transmission in her car replaced *still* left her brain enough room to plague her with thoughts of Nathan Battle.

"Bound to happen," she reassured herself for the fortieth time that morning. Just being in Royal had brought the memories rushing back and, there were a *lot* of memories.

She'd known Nathan most of her life and had been nuts about him since she was thirteen. She could still remember the sharp, bright thrill of having Nathan, then an all-powerful senior, taking a lowly freshman to the senior prom.

"And, if we'd just stopped it right there, it would be all sunshine and roses," she murmured as she refilled the coffee urn with water, then measured in fresh coffee grounds.

She pushed the button to start the brewing process, then turned to look out at the diner. Even with the changes she'd made in the last couple of weeks, being in this place was as good as being home.

She'd grown up in her parents' diner, working as a busgirl, and then a waitress when she was old enough. The Royal Diner was an institution in town and she was determined that it stay that way. Which was why she'd come home after her father's death to help her older sister, Pam, run the place.

As that reminder rolled through her mind, Amanda squared her shoulders and nodded briefly to herself. She hadn't come home because of Nathan Battle. Even though a shiver swept through her at just the thought of his name, she discounted it as sense memory. Didn't mean a thing. Her life was different now.

She was different now.

"Amanda, my love, when're you going to marry me and run off to Jamaica?"

Startled out of her thoughts, Amanda smiled at the familiar voice and turned to look at Hank Bristow. At eighty, Hank was tall and thin and his skin was craggy from a lifetime spent in the sun. Now that his sons ran the family ranch, Hank spent most of his time in the diner, talking with his friends. His blue eyes twinkled as he held out his cup for a refill.

"Hank, you just love me for my coffee," she told him, pouring a stream of the hot, fresh brew into his cup.

"A woman who can make good coffee?" Hank shook his head and said solemnly, "Worth her weight in gold."

She smiled, patted his hand, then carried the carafe along the length of the counter, chatting with her customers, freshening coffee as she went. It was all so familiar. So…easy. She'd slid into life in Royal as smoothly as if she'd never left.

"Why did you order new menus?"

Okay, not completely smoothly. Amanda turned to face Pam. As usual, the shorter woman didn't look happy with her. But then, the two of them had never been close. Not growing up. Not now. Even though Amanda had primarily come back to Royal because Pam had needed help running the diner. But, she supposed, *needing* help and *wanting* it were two different things.

Amanda walked the length of the counter again, and set the coffeepot down on the warmer before she answered.

"Because the old ones needed to be replaced," she said. "The laminate was cracked and old and the menus themselves were outdated." Catching the look of interest on Hank's face, Amanda lowered her voice. "We don't even serve half the things listed anymore, Pam."

Her sister's chin-length brown hair was tucked behind her ears. She wore a red T-shirt and jeans and a pair of scarlet sandals wrapped around her feet. She was tapping the toe of one sandal against the shining linoleum floor. "But our regular customers know that. They don't need fancy new menus, Amanda."

She sighed, but stood her ground. "They're not fancy, Pam. They're just not ratty."

Pam hissed in a breath.

"Okay, sorry." Amanda dug deep for patience and said, "We're in this together, right? You said you needed help and I came home. The Altman sisters running the diner. Together."

Pam thought about that for a long second before finally shrugging. "As long as you remember I didn't ask you to come in and take over."

"I'm not taking over, Pam. I'm trying to help."

"By changing everything?" Pam's voice spiked, then she seemed to realize that everyone in the place was no doubt listening because she spoke more softly when she continued. "There's such a thing as tradition around here, you know. Or did you forget, living off in Dallas for so long?"

A small twinge of guilt nibbled at her insides. Amanda hadn't been around much the last few years, it was true. And she should have been. She knew that, too. It had been just Amanda, Pam and their father, since her mother had died years before and the three of them had sort of drifted apart. For the rest of her life, she knew she'd regret not spending more time with her dad when she had the chance.

But she had grown up in the diner just as Pam had. Changing things wasn't easy for her, either. A part of her hated getting rid of things that her father had put in place. But times changed whether you wanted them to or not.

"Dad told us himself that when he took over the diner from *his* father, he made lots of changes," she argued, defending the new, still red—but unscarred red—counter and tables.

Pam scowled at her. "That's not the point."

Amanda took a deep breath and inhaled the aroma of fresh coffee, eggs and bacon. "Then what is the point, Pam? You asked me to come home and help, remember?"

"Help, not take over."

Okay, maybe she had been a little quick with changes. Maybe she hadn't taken the time to include her sister in decisions being made. That was her fault and she was willing to take the blame for it. In her defense, Pam had made herself scarce since Amanda got back to town. But, if she mentioned that, it would only start a new argument, so she let it go.

"You're right," Amanda said and watched surprise flicker in her sister's eyes. "I should have talked to you about the menus. About the countertops and tables and I didn't. I just…" She paused to look around the diner before adding, "I guess I didn't realize how much I'd missed this place. And when I got home, I just dove right in."

"I can't believe you missed the diner," Pam muttered.

Amanda laughed. "I know. Me, neither. You and I spent so much time working here as kids, who knew that I'd look forward to working here again?"

Pam sighed and leaned against the counter. She shot a frown at Hank, who was still listening in. The old man rolled his eyes and looked away.

"It's good you're here," Pam finally said. "And between the two of us, we should be able to both run the diner *and* have lives."

"We will," Amanda said, smiling a little at the tiny bridge suddenly springing up between the sisters.

"But it *is* the two of us, Amanda," Pam told her firmly.

"You don't get to make all the decisions and then let me find out later when the new menus arrive."

"Absolutely," she said. "You're right. I should have talked to you and I will from now on."

"Good." Pam nodded. "That's good. Now, I'm heading out. I've got a line on a new supplier of organic vegetables and—"

Amanda smiled and let her mind wander while her sister rattled off information on local farmers. Her gaze slid across the familiar faces filling the diner, then drifted out to the street beyond the wide glass windows. Main Street in Royal. Sidewalks crowded with early shoppers. Cars parked haphazardly along the curb. The sheriff stepping off the sidewalk, headed for the diner.

Sheriff. Headed for the diner.

Amanda's heart jumped in her chest. Her mouth went dry and her gaze locked on the one man in the world she couldn't seem to forget.

Nathan knew it was past time to face Amanda.

He left the sheriff's office with his deputy, Red Hawkins, in charge and stepped out onto Main Street. The morning was clear and promised another red-hot day. Summer in Texas was already off to a blistering start. The sun was a ball of fire looking to combust.

God, he loved it.

Walking down the sidewalk, his boots clattering out a sharp rhythm, Nathan nodded at those he passed and paused to hold a door for Macy Harris as she struggled to carry a baby and cling to her toddler's hand.

This was his place. Where he belonged. He'd actually had to leave and spend a few years in Houston as a city cop to figure that out. But now that he was back, Nathan knew he'd never leave Royal again. He'd found his place and damned if he was going to let Amanda Altman make him uncomfortable in it.

He loped across the street, dodging the occasional car, and headed straight for the Royal Diner.

The place was a landmark in town. He could remember going there as a kid with his folks and then later, as a teenager, he'd gathered there with his friends after football games and on long, boring summer afternoons.

It was the unofficial heart of town, which meant that at any time during the day, there would be a crowd inside. A crowd that would watch his and Amanda's first meeting with interest.

"Well, hell," he muttered as he marched up to the glass door. "Might as well get it done and let the gossips loose."

He pulled the door open, stepped inside and stopped, letting his gaze slide over the familiar surroundings. *Mostly* familiar, he corrected silently.

The walls had been painted. No longer a bright white that seemed to sear your eyes on a hot summer day, the walls were now a soft green, dotted with framed photos of Royal through the years. The counter had been changed, too—the old chipped and scarred red was now a shining sweep of a deeper, richer red. The black-and-white checked floors had been polished and the red vinyl booth seats had all been revamped. There were new chairs pulled up to the scatter of tables and sunshine streamed through the windows lining Main Street.

But none of it really mattered to him.

How could it?

He was too focused on the woman standing behind that new counter, staring at him.

Amanda Altman.

Damn. She looked way too good.

Nathan took a breath, forcing air into lungs suddenly

starving for sustenance. He hadn't really expected to feel
the rush of heat swamping him. He'd convinced himself
he was over her. Had forgotten what it had been like to
be with her.

Big mistake.

"Hello, Nathan."

"Amanda," he said and ignored the swell of whis-
pers sliding around the room as if carried along by a
west Texas wind.

She moved toward the end of the counter, position-
ing herself behind the cash register. Defensive move?

Oddly enough, that eased him some. Knowing she
was no happier about this public meeting than he was
took some of the pressure off. In fact, he thought, it sort
of tossed the power back into his lap.

She was new here. Okay, yeah, she'd grown up in
Royal, just as he had. But Nathan had been here for the
last three years and she'd been back in town only a couple of weeks. He'd made his place here and she was still
treading water.

With that thought firmly in mind, he walked toward
her and noted her chin came up defiantly. Damned if he
hadn't missed that stubborn move of hers.

"Morning, Nathan," Pam chirped loudly. "We've
missed you in here lately."

"Been busy," he said and ignored Hank Bristow's
snort of derision.

"You want your usual?"

"That'd be good, Pam, thanks," he said, his gaze never
leaving Amanda's.

She looked the same and yet…different. Maybe it was
just that she was older now. Maybe it was the fact that her
eyes weren't shining with adoration when she looked up

at him. Didn't matter, he assured himself. Amanda was his past, in spite of his body's reaction to her.

"So," he said, knowing everyone in the diner was holding their breath, waiting to hear what might happen next, "you back to stay or this just a visit?"

Pam walked up to him then and handed him a to-go cup filled with black coffee. He didn't even glance at her as he took it and reached into his pocket for cash.

"On the house," Amanda told him.

"Not necessary," Nathan said and laid a couple of dollars on the counter. "You didn't answer the question, Amanda. You here to stay or just blowin' through?"

"I'm home to stay, Nathan," Amanda said. "I hope that won't be a problem for you."

He laughed shortly, and took a sip of coffee. Deliberately then, he said loudly enough for everyone to hear, "Why would that be a problem for me, Amanda? You and I are long since done."

He could almost *see* every customer in the place perking up their ears and leaning in closer so as not to miss a single word.

"You're right," Amanda said, lifting her chin even higher. "We're not kids anymore. There's no reason why we can't be friendly."

Friendly? His entire body was jittering with heat and she thought they could be friends? Not a chance. But he wasn't going to give her the satisfaction of knowing that.

"None at all," Nathan agreed tightly.

"Good. I'm glad that's settled," she said.

"Me, too."

"Oh, yeah," Hank muttered with a snort. "We can all see that this has worked out fine."

"Butt out, Hank," Nathan told him and turned for the door.

"Walk me to my car, Nathan?" Pam blurted and had him stopping for one last look behind him. But instead of seeing the woman headed toward him, his gaze darted straight to Amanda and he felt a surge of heat zap him.

The past might be dead and gone, but whatever hummed between them had just enough life left in it to be annoying.

When Pam threaded her arm through his, Nathan led her out and didn't bother looking back again.

Two

"That went well," Amanda told herself as she entered the tiny apartment over the diner that was now home.

All day, she'd been thinking about that brief, all-too-public meeting with Nathan. Which was, she thought grimly, probably exactly what he'd been hoping for. Nathan had always been the kind of man to assume command of any given situation. He was the take-charge type and so it was like him to make sure their first meeting was just the way *he* wanted it. That's why he'd come into the diner during the morning bustle—so that there would be so many witnesses to their conversation, neither one of them could really *talk*.

Honestly, the man hadn't changed a bit. Still stiff-necked and hardheaded. She'd seen that familiar, stony glint in his eye that morning and known the minute he opened his mouth that nothing between them would be settled. But then, she thought, why would it be?

She dropped onto an overstuffed, floral sofa that was older than she was, and propped her feet on the narrow coffee table in front of her. The romance novel she was currently reading lay beside an old ceramic pitcher filled with daisies and bluebells. Their scent was a soft sigh of summer in the too-warm room and, not for the first time, Amanda wished the apartment boasted more than a thirty-year-old air conditioner with a habit of shutting down every now and then for no particular reason.

The sofa held bright, boldly colored accent pillows and the two chairs in the room were more comfortable to look at than they were for sitting. There were pictures on the walls, a few throw rugs across the scarred wooden floor and the walls were still the dusty sand color Amanda's mother had preferred.

Folding her arms over her chest, Amanda stared up at the lazily spinning ceiling fan. A tired breeze of air sulkily drifted over her. This little apartment above the diner was like a security blanket. Her parents had lived here when they first married and opened the diner. Then later, they'd rented it out, furnished, to different people over the years. Pam had lived here for a while, then it had been Amanda's turn while she was in college. Having her own place had given her the chance to find her independence while staying close enough to home to feel safe.

Plus, she and Nathan had met here a lot back in those days. Those memories were imprinted on the tiny apartment, with its outdated, yet cozy furniture. If she tried, Amanda thought she'd be able to hear his voice, whispering to her in the dark.

She didn't try.

Instead, she concentrated on what he'd had to say that morning. Or rather what he *hadn't* said.

"He didn't want to talk anything through," she said to

the empty room and paused, as if waiting for the shadows to agree with her. "He only wanted to let me know that seeing me again meant nothing. He was trying to lay down the rules. Just like before. He tells you what things will be like, lays out his orders, then steps back, giving you room to follow them."

Well, he was in for a shock. She didn't *take* orders anymore. In fact, looking back at the girl she had once been made her nearly cringe. Back then, she'd been young enough and in love enough, that she had never once argued with Nathan—at least until that last night. When he announced his choice of a movie, she hadn't said she hated action movies. She'd never told him that she didn't like going to car shows or that she found fishing to be the most boring activity in the world.

Nope. Instead, Amanda had sat through countless movies where the only storyline revolved around demolition. She'd spent interminably long days watching Nathan fish in local streams and rivers and she didn't want to think about the hours lost staring at car engines.

Looking back now, Amanda couldn't believe how completely she'd given herself up to Nathan. Then, he was all she had cared about. All she thought about. And when everything fell apart between them…she'd had no idea what to do with herself.

It had taken a while to find her feet. To find *Amanda*. But she'd done it and there was no going back now— even if she wanted to, which she *so* did not.

Lifting her chin, she narrowed her eyes on the fan blades as if facing down Nathan himself. "I'm all grown up now, Nathan. I'm not going to roll over and speak on command. I don't *need* you anymore."

As her own words rang out in the room, Amanda

gave a tight smile. Good words. Now if she could just *believe* them.

Oh, she didn't need Nathan like she had then. Like she had needed air. Water. No, now what she needed was to get rid of the memories. To clear Nathan Battle out of her mind and heart once and for all, so she could move on. So she could stop remembering that when things were good between them, they were *very* good.

What she had to concentrate on, she told herself firmly as she leaped off the couch to pace the confines of the small living area, was the bad parts. The times Nathan had made her crazy. The dictatorial Nathan who had tried to make every decision for her. The man who had insisted they marry because she was pregnant, then the minute that pregnancy was over, had walked away from her so fast, she'd seen nothing but a blur.

That was what she had to remember. The pain of not only losing the baby she'd had such dreams for, but also realizing that the man she loved wasn't the man she'd thought he was.

If she could just do that, she'd be fine.

She walked to the galley-style kitchen and rummaged in the fridge for some of yesterday's leftovers. Working with food all day pretty much ensured that she wasn't hungry enough to cook for herself in the evening. But tonight, pickings were slim. A bowl of the diner's five-star chili, a few sandwiches and a plate of double-stuffed baked potatoes that hadn't sold the day before.

None of it looked tempting, but she knew she had to eat. So she grabbed the potatoes—and a bottle of chardonnay—then closed the fridge. She pulled out a cookie sheet, lined the potatoes up on it and put it in the oven. Once the temperature was set, she poured herself a glass of wine and carried it with her to the doll-sized bathroom.

It only took her a few minutes to shower and change into a pair of cutoff jean shorts and a tank top. Then she took her wine and walked barefoot back to the living room to wait for dinner.

The crisp, cold wine made the waiting easier to take. Heck, it even made thoughts of Nathan less...disturbing. What did it say about her, she wondered, that even when she was furious with the man, she still felt that buzz of something amazing?

Sad, sad Amanda.

In the years since she and Nathan had broken up, she hadn't exactly lived like a nun. She'd had dates. Just not many. But how could she think about a future when the past kept rising up in her mind? It always came back to Nathan. When she met a man, she waited, hoping to feel that special *zing* she had only found with Nathan. And it was never there.

How could she possibly agree to marry someone else if Nathan was the one who made her body burn? Was she supposed to settle? Impossible. She wanted what she'd once had. She just wanted it with someone else.

Heck, she had known Nathan was there the minute he'd walked into the diner. She hadn't had to see him. She'd *felt* his presence—like the electricity in the air just before a thunderstorm. And that first look into his eyes had jolted her so badly, it had been all she could do to lock her knees into place so she wouldn't melt into an embarrassing puddle of goo.

No one else had ever done that to her.

Only him.

She took a sip of her wine and shook her head. "This is not a good sign, Amanda."

It had been *years* since she'd seen him, touched him, and it might as well have been yesterday from the way her own body was reacting. Every cell inside her was jumping up and down, rolling out the red carpet and putting on a party hat.

But there weren't going to be any parties. Not with Nathan, at any rate. She'd never get him out of her system if she let him back in.

Trying to distract herself from the hormonal rodeo going on inside her, she walked to one of the windows overlooking Main Street and looked out at Royal. Only a few cars on the road and almost no pedestrians. The silence was staggering. Streetlights dropped puddles of yellow light on the empty sidewalks and, above the town, a clear night sky displayed thousands of stars.

Life in a small town was vastly different than what she'd known the last few years living in Dallas. There, the city bustled with life all night. Shops and clubs and bars glittered with neon lights so bright, they blotted out the stars overhead. Tourists flocked to the city to spend their money, and the nightlife was as busy as the daytime crowds.

It had been so different from the way she'd grown up, such a distraction from the pain she was in—Amanda had really enjoyed city life. At first. But over time, she had become just another nameless person rushing through the crowds, going from work to an apartment and back again the next day. Nights were crowded with noise and people and the gradual realization that she wasn't happy.

Her life had become centered around a job she didn't really like and a nightlife she didn't actually enjoy. She had a few friends and a few dates that always seemed to end badly—probably her own fault since she never had been able to meet a man without comparing him to Nathan. Pitiful, really, but there it was.

Then her father passed away and, a few months later, she got the call for help from Pam. Even knowing that she would have to eventually deal with Nathan again, Amanda had left the big city behind and rushed back home to Royal.

And she had slid back into life here as easily as if she'd never left. The truth was, she was really a small-town girl at heart.

She liked a town where nighttime brought quiet and families gathered together. She liked knowing that she was safe—without having to have two or three locks on her apartment door. And, right now, she liked knowing that she wouldn't have to talk to anyone until at least to-morrow morning.

She could have stayed at her family home, where Pam was living. But Amanda had become accustomed to having her own space. Besides, as evidenced by her sister's behavior today, just because Pam had needed her help didn't mean that she wanted Amanda around. She'd never been close with her sister and, so far, that situation looked as though it wasn't going to change any.

She took another sip of her wine and let that thought, along with all the thoughts of Nathan, slide from her mind. She wasn't going to solve everything in one night, so why drive herself nuts?

Her gaze slid to the darkened sheriff's office. No one was there, of course. In a town the size of Royal, you didn't need an on-duty police presence twenty-four hours a day. Besides, Nathan and his deputy were only a phone call away.

She wondered if Nathan still lived out on his family's ranch, the Battlelands. Then she reminded herself firmly it was none of her business where Nathan lived.

"Thinking about him is *not* the way to stop thinking about him," she told herself aloud.

The scent of melting cheese and roasting potatoes was beginning to fill the air and her stomach rumbled. Apparently she was hungrier than she had thought.

When the knock sounded on her door, she was more surprised than anything else. She took a step forward, then stopped, staring at the door leading to the outside staircase at the side of the diner. A ripple of something familiar sneaked across her skin and she took a gulp of her wine to ease the sensation. Didn't really help. But then, nothing could. Because she *knew* who was knocking on her door.

When she was steady enough, she walked to the door and asked unnecessarily, "Who is it?"

"It's me, Amanda." It was Nathan's voice, low and commanding. "Open up."

Wow. Skitters of expectation jolted through her. Amazing that just his voice could do that to her. After all these years, he could still stir her up without even trying.

She put one hand flat against the door and she could have sworn that she actually felt heat sliding through the wood. She took a breath, smoothed out her voice and tried to do the same for her racing heart. It didn't work.

"What do you want, Nathan?" she asked, leaning her forehead against the door panel.

"What I want is to not be standing out here talking through a door where anyone in Royal can see me."

Not that there were a lot of people out there at night. But all it would take was one busybody happening to glance up and word would fly all over town. *Nathan was at Amanda's doorstep last night!*

Okay, she thought, straightening, *good motivation for opening the door.* So she did.

Under the porch light, his brown hair looked lighter, his shoulders looked broader and his eyes…too shadowed to read. But then, she thought, it wasn't difficult to guess what he was thinking, feeling. His stance was stiff, his jaw tight. He looked as though he'd rather be anywhere but there.

Well, fine. She hadn't invited him, had she? "What is it, Nathan?"

He scowled at her and stepped inside.

"Please," she said, sarcasm dripping as she closed the door against the hot, humid air, "come in."

"We have to talk," he said, striding across the room before turning to face her. "And damned if I'm going to do it in the diner with everyone in town listening in."

Her fingers tightened on her wineglass. "Then maybe you shouldn't have come into the diner this morning."

"Maybe," he muttered and stuffed both hands into the pockets of his jeans. "But I needed some decent coffee."

She hadn't expected that. But he looked so disgusted, so…frustrated, Amanda laughed. His head snapped up, his gaze boring into hers.

"I'm sorry," she said, shaking her head as another laugh bubbled out. "But really? Coffee is what finally brought you in?"

"I've been getting mine at the gas station."

"Poor guy," she said, and he frowned at the humor in her voice.

"You can laugh. But I don't think Charlie's so much as rinsed out that coffeepot of his in twenty years." He grimaced at the thought and made Amanda smile again.

Shaking his head, he nodded at the wine in her hand. "You have any more of that?"

"I do. Also have beer, if you'd rather."

"Yeah, that'd be good." Some of the tension left his shoulders and one corner of his mouth tilted up into what might have been a half smile if it hadn't disappeared so fast.

She walked to the kitchen, opened the fridge and pulled out a beer. Amanda paused for a second to get her bearings. The moment she'd been dreading for years was finally here. Nathan and her were together again. Alone. And there was just no telling what might happen next. But whatever it was, she thought, at least it would be *something*. Better than the vacuum they'd been in for the last few years. Better than the rigid silence that had stretched between them since she came back to Royal.

With that thought in mind, she walked to the living room, handed him the cold bottle, then took a seat on the couch. Mainly because her knees felt a little wobbly.

Looking up at him, she watched as he opened the beer and took a drink. He looked so good it was irritating. His skin was tanned and there was a slightly paler line across the top of his forehead where his hat usually rested. His brown eyes were watchful as he glanced around the apartment, no doubt taking in everything in that all-encompassing sweep. She wondered if he was remembering all the nights they'd been together, here in this room. Could he still hear the whispered words between them? Probably not, she thought. Nathan wouldn't want to be reminded of a past that had no bearing on his life anymore.

She studied him as he studied the apartment. He wore scuffed brown boots, blue jeans and a short-sleeved, dark green T-shirt with Battlelands Ranch emblazoned on the shirt pocket. He stood stiff and straight as if awaiting a military inspection.

He was off-duty and yet everything about him screamed *police*. Nathan was just that kind of man. Devoted to duty, he preferred order to chaos, rules to confusion. He would take a road trip and stay on the highway, where Amanda would prefer the back roads, stopping at everything interesting along the way. No wonder they had clashed.

And even knowing all of that, she still felt the rush of attraction that she couldn't deny. She *wanted* to be immune to him and, clearly, she wasn't.

But this was exactly why she needed to be here. Because until she *was* immune to Nathan Battle, she'd never be able to move on. Instead, she'd go on being haunted by memories, by thoughts of what might have been.

He took another drink of his beer and looked down at the bottle in his hand. "I was sorry about your dad."

She blinked against the sudden sting of tears. The one thing she hadn't expected from Nathan was kindness. It was…disarming. "Thanks. I miss him."

"Yeah, he was a good man."

"He was." Safe ground. Talk about their families. Don't mention the tension coiled so tightly between them.

"Why did you come back?"

And *there* was the Nathan she knew best. So much for the pleasantries—it was on to Round One. "Excuse me?"

"Well, hell, Amanda." He frowned down at her and looked a little surprised that she didn't seem affected by his displeasure. "You were gone for years. Why come back at all?"

"Are you in charge of Royal's borders now, *Sheriff*?" she asked. "Do people have to check in with you before they move in?"

"I didn't say that."

She pushed to her feet. Even though she stood five foot ten, she was forced to tip her head back to meet his gaze, but she did it. "Royal's my home as much as it is yours, Nathan Battle."

"Couldn't tell from how you acted," he said, completely ignoring the hard glare she fired at him.

"I seem to recall you living in Houston for quite a while. Were you interrogated when you moved back home?"

"I'm not interrogating you, Amanda," he countered. "I'm just asking a damn question."

"That you already know the answer to," she shot back. "Pam needed help with the diner. I came home. That's the story. None of this concerns you, Nathan. This is my business."

"Damn straight it is, but now that you're back, it's *my* business, too." He stood as still and cold as a statue.

"How do you figure?"

"I'm the sheriff here. This is where I live. For you to come back now and start stirring things—"

"What am I stirring, Nathan?" she interrupted, and saw with a jolt of glee that he still hated being cut off. It infuriated her to remember that in the old days. She'd have shut her mouth so he could keep talking. Well, that time was gone. "I'm working at my family's diner."

"And getting tongues wagging again," he pointed out.

"Please. People in Royal gossip about everything. I didn't have to *be* here to have them talk about me."

"They're not talking about you," he elaborated grimly. "They're talking about *us*."

"There is no us," she said flatly, and was surprised by the twinge of pain that clutched at her heart.

"I know that and you know that, but the folks in town—"

"Forget about them," she interrupted again.

He took a long deep breath from between clenched teeth. "Easy for you to say. But as sheriff, I need to have the respect of the people I'm protecting. I don't like being the subject of gossip."

"Then tell them that. Why tell me?"

"Because if you leave, it'll stop."

She set her wineglass down before she was tempted to throw it at his rock-hard head. "I'm not leaving. And, it'll never stop, Nathan."

That statement hit him hard. She saw the proof of it flicker in his eyes. But she wasn't finished.

"Until we're ninety, people around here will be speculating and remembering...."

"Damn it, Amanda, I want you out of town."

"And I want you to stop caring what other people think," she snapped. "I guess we're both doomed to disappointment."

He set his beer bottle on the table beside her glass and moved in on her. He was so tall, he didn't have to put much effort into looming. She supposed it just came naturally to a man used to having his own way. A man accustomed to telling people what to do and having them do it.

It might have worked on her years ago, Amanda told herself, but no more. She was her own woman now. She made her own choices and decisions and lived with the consequences. She wouldn't be ordered out of town and she wouldn't be scared off by a big, gorgeous sheriff with eyes as cold as a winter wind.

"If you think you're worrying me, you're wrong."

"I don't want you worried."

"Good, because—"

"I don't want you at all."

Direct hit, she thought, as an icy fist slammed into her chest and squeezed her heart. But she wouldn't let him see it. "I don't want you, either, Nathan. I'm not that young girl anymore, dazzled because Nathan Battle noticed her. I'm not going to follow you around all doe-eyed, hoping for a smile from you. I'm—"

He grabbed her, yanked her close and kissed her with a fierce desperation that was fueled by desire and anger, all twisted up together. She could feel it in him as she felt it in herself. Past and present tangled together and memories were as thick as honey on a winter morning.

But those memories were swamped by all of the new sensations coursing through her. Amanda didn't try to pull free. Didn't pretend that she wasn't as hungry for him as he was for her. Instead, she moved into him, wrapped her arms around his neck and held on.

This is what she'd missed for so long. This man's touch. His kiss. The feel of his hard, strong body pushed up close against hers. She parted her lips for him and took him inside her. When he groaned and held her even tighter, Amanda felt bolts of heat shoot through her system like a summer lightning storm. So much electricity between them. So much heat.

Was it any wonder they had flashed and burned out too quickly?

His hands slid up and down her back, holding her, pressing her as close as he could. His mouth took hers again and again, and she met every stroke of his tongue with eager abandon. God, she'd missed him. Missed *them.* She had found nothing that could compare to what happened when they came together. No other man she'd ever met could compare to Nathan. Which meant that she was in very deep trouble.

Her mind raced even as her body lit up like a sparkler

factory. This was a huge mistake. Falling into Nathan's arms was *not* the way to get over him. But right now, all she was interested in was feeling her body come back to life as if waking up after a seven-year nap. Her skin tingled, her heartbeat crashing in her chest, and in the pit of her belly, heat settled and began to spread.

What was wrong with her, anyway?

Three

When Nathan suddenly released her and took one long step back and away, Amanda swayed unsteadily and gasped for air like a drowning woman. Her mouth burned from his kiss and her body was trembling.

"See?" he practically growled at her. "*This* is why you shouldn't have come back home."

"What?" She blinked up at him and saw that, once again, Nathan's expression seemed to be etched into stone. He looked hard, untouchable and about as passionate as a slab of granite. How did he turn it on and off like that? And could he teach her how to do it?

"I kissed you and you were all over me."

A sudden spurt of ice water flowed through her veins and put out all the lingering fires inside. Maybe he wouldn't have to teach her after all.

"Excuse me? I was all over you?" She took a step closer and stabbed her index finger at him. "Just who grabbed who, here? Who came to whose house? Who started kissing?"

His mouth worked and his lips thinned into a tight line. "Not the point."

"It's exactly the point, Nathan." Furious now, more at herself for falling so easily into old habits than at him, Amanda said, "Just like before, *you* came after *me*. You started all of this, then and now."

"And I'm going to end it."

Hurt raged inside, but was soon swallowed by a wave of fury. He decided when to start things. When to end things. And she was supposed to go quietly along. Nathan Battle, Master of the Universe.

"Big surprise. You like ending things, don't you?"

His eyes narrowed on her and his jaw muscle twitched so violently she was pretty sure he was grinding his teeth into powder. *Well, good.* She'd hate to think she was the only furious one in the room.

"I'm not the one who ended it seven years ago," he finally said, his voice a low throb of barely leashed anger.

"Not how I remember it," Amanda countered, the sting of that long-ago night still as fresh as if it had happened just yesterday. "You're the one who walked out."

"It's what you wanted." His gaze drilled into hers.

She met him glare for glare. "How would you know, Nathan? You never *asked* me what I wanted."

"This is pointless."

A long minute or two of tense silence stretched out between them. The only sound—the oven timer going off—rang out like a bell at a boxing match signaling the end of a round.

It worked to jolt both of them out of their defensive stances and a second later, Nathan was heading for her door. When he got there, he paused and turned back to look at her.

"This town chews on gossip every day, but I'm not going to be gnawed on."

"Good for you!" She picked up her wine and took a swallow she didn't really want before setting the glass down again. If he thought she was looking forward to being the topic of whispered conversations, he was nuts.

"The Battle family has a reputation in this town—"

"And the Altmans aren't in your circle, are we?" she interrupted again and felt a small swift tug of pleasure, knowing it irritated him.

"I didn't say that."

"You didn't have to." Walking toward him, Amanda glared up into his dark brown eyes. "I'm amazed you ever deigned to propose to me in the first place."

If possible, she thought his eyes actually went black for a second or two. How twisted was she that she *still* thought him the most gorgeous man on the planet?

"You were carrying my child," he told her flatly.

That statement, said with such frigid control, sliced at her like a blade and Amanda fought against the pain.

They hadn't spoken about their lost baby since the night he'd walked out on her. For him to bring it up now… "That was low."

He paused for a long minute or so, just studying her through narrowed eyes. "Yeah, it was." He scrubbed one hand across his face. "Damn it, Amanda, we've got to find a way to live in this town together."

She slid her hands up and down her arms. Funny— even with the hot, humid air of summer, she felt a chill. Maybe it was him being here, so close. Maybe it had been the loss of heat when their kiss ended. And maybe, she thought, it was because of the memories he'd brought up and waved in her face.

The memory of the child she'd carried and lost. The baby she had wanted so badly. Whatever it was, she wanted to be alone until that icy sensation was gone. She needed time to herself. To think. To regroup. And she couldn't do that until she convinced Nathan to leave.

"I'm guessing you have a plan," she said with a sigh.

"Damn straight, I do," he told her. "We go about our business. We live our lives. If we see each other, it's friendly, but distant. No more private chats. No—"

"Kissing?" she finished for him.

"Yeah. No more of that."

"Fine. Agreed." She threw both hands high. "Nathan's rules of behavior. Will you print me out a copy? I'll sign it. You want it notarized, too?"

"Funny."

"Well, blast it, Nathan, you haven't changed a bit. Still issuing orders and expecting them to be followed. Who made you the grand pooh-bah of the Western world?"

"Pooh-bah?"

She ignored that. "You come to my house. You kiss me. Then you lay down rules for me to live my life by and what? You expected me to just salute and say, 'Yes, sir'?"

"Would've been nice," he muttered.

She laughed. In spite of everything. "Yeah, well, not going to happen."

"You make me crazy," he admitted, shaking his head slowly. "You always did."

His voice was softer, deeper, and his eyes held a heat she remembered too well. So she stiffened her spine, refusing to be swayed by the urges she felt deep within her.

"Good to know," Amanda said, tipping her head back to look into his eyes. "That's some consolation, anyway."

He blew out a breath and muttered something she didn't quite catch before saying, "Fine. No rules. We go along. Stay out of each other's way."

"Fine."

"Eventually, people will stop talking or waiting for something to happen between us and—"

"You're still doing it," Amanda interrupted.

"Doing what?"

"Making rules. Setting down how things will be," she said. Tipping her head to one side, she stared up at him in complete frustration. "You can't regulate life, Nathan. It just…happens."

Like losing a baby you had loved from the moment of conception. That familiar twinge of pain, muted slightly because of time and her deliberate attempts to bury it, twisted inside her briefly.

"Unacceptable."

"You don't get to make that call, Nathan," she said softly.

"You're wrong." His eyes were hard, flinty chips of frozen chocolate. Whatever softness had been there before had completely dissipated. "My life moves just as I want it to. No exceptions." He paused. "Not anymore."

There it was, she thought. Once upon a time, *she* had been the exception to Nathan's carefully laid-out life. She'd thrown a wrench into his plans, made him scramble for a new strategy and then it had all fallen apart again. This time, though, she was older—and wiser, she hoped—and she wouldn't be sucked into Nathan's tidily arranged world. She preferred her life messy. She liked the adventure of not really knowing what to expect.

Of course, then scenes like tonight would probably rise up again to torture her, but that was a risk she'd rather take. Better than having your life plotted out on a ledger sheet, with no surprises, no jolts of pleasure or pain.

"Royal's a small town," he was saying and Amanda pushed her thoughts aside to pay attention. "But not so small that we can't comfortably ignore each other."

"That's how you want this to play out?" she asked. "We each pretend the other doesn't exist?"

"Better that way," he said.

"For who?"

He didn't answer. He just opened the door and said, "Goodbye, Amanda."

The sound of his boots on the stairs rang out like a too-fast heartbeat. A few seconds later, she heard a car engine fire up and then he was driving away.

Amanda closed her door on the world, wandered to the kitchen and retrieved the stuffed potatoes that were just a little too well-done. She idly stood there and watched steam lift off her dinner and twist in the barely moving air.

"Damn it," she whispered and stared through the window to the night beyond the glass. Her dinner was burned, her stomach was spinning and her temper was at war with her hormones.

Nathan was a force of nature. One that apparently was destined to crash in and out of her life whether she wanted him to or not. And the worst part?

"He walked away. Again."

She poured a fresh glass of wine, forced herself to eat the overdone potatoes and promised herself the next time she and Nathan were in the same room, *she* would be the one doing the walking.

* * *

The Battlelands Ranch glowed in the darkness. It
stood like a proud dowager, waiting to welcome home
its prodigal children. Practically every window shone
with lamplight. Even the outbuildings—the barn, the
foreman's house and Nathan's own place—boasted porch
lights that formed brightly lit pathways.

Just like always, Nathan felt tension slide away
as he drove down the oak-lined drive and steered his
4Runner toward the house he'd had built for himself
when he moved back to Royal. He might not be a rancher
these days, but the land was in his blood as much as it
was in his younger brother Jacob's. The Battles had been
on this land for more than a hundred and fifty years.
They'd carved out every acre. Bled for it. Wept for it,
and managed to hold on to it through all the bad times
that had come their way.

The heart of the main ranch house was the origi-
nal structure, a stately Victorian that the first Battle in
Texas had built more than a hundred and fifty years
ago to please his new bride. Over the years, that tur-
reted, gingerbread-adorned structure had been added
to, with wings spreading from each side and spilling
into the back. Most of the ranch houses in the area were
more modern, of course. Some mansions, some simple
houses, they were all interchangeable in Nathan's eyes.

This place was unique because the Battles didn't tear
something down just because it was old. They fixed it,
improved on it and kept it, always to remind them of
where they'd come from. Now that stately old Victorian
was the centerpiece of a ranch bigger and more prosper-
ous than that first Battle could ever have dreamed.

Gnarled, twisted live oaks stood like ancient soldiers
on either side of the drive and gathered in clumps along

the front and rear of the house. As Nathan parked his car and climbed out, he heard the swish of leaves in the grudgingly moving hot air.

From the main house came the sharp, clear sound of children's laughter, and Nathan smiled to himself. Lots of changes here at the Battlelands—mostly thanks to Jacob and his wife, Terri. They and their three kids were making this place come alive again as it hadn't since Nathan and Jake were kids themselves.

He glanced quickly at the wading pool and the nearby wooden swing set and climbing gym he'd helped Jacob put together for the kids. That laughter spilled from the house again and Nathan instinctively quelled the small twist of envy he felt for what his brother had. He knew Jake was happy. He had a family and the ranch he loved and Nathan didn't begrudge him any of it.

Still, it was a stunner that his younger brother had a wife and kids, but Jake had taken to life as a family man as easily as he had assumed control of the ranch years ago.

Nathan loved the place and it would always be *home* to him, but the ranch had never been at the heart of him as it had for Jake. As long as Nathan could remember, he had wanted to be a cop, while Jake wanted nothing more than to ride the range, and deal with the cattle grazing on the thousands of acres the family claimed. It had worked out well, Nathan told himself. Didn't matter that he was the eldest. It was enough for Nathan that the Battlelands was in good hands—even if those hands weren't *his*.

And, since Terri was pregnant again, Nathan knew that the family ranch was going to be in Battle hands for many more years to come. He couldn't help wondering what Jake thought of that, if his brother ever sat down and realized that his sons and daughters would be working the same land that had been handed down to him.

That twist of envy grabbed at him again and Nathan couldn't help wondering how his life might be right now if Amanda had carried their child to term. Would they still be together? Would there be more children? He tried to imagine it, but couldn't quite pull it off.

The ranch house door opened just then and a spill of light from inside poured onto the wide front porch. Grateful for the distraction, Nathan watched as his brother stepped out of the house. Talking to Jake would help him get his mind off of Amanda. Hopefully. His thoughts were crowded with her....

God, the taste of her. The scent of her. The feel of her body aligning with his and the hush of her breath on his skin—*damn it*.

Jake leaned against one of the porch posts and asked, "Late night?"

"A few things to see to," he answered vaguely and headed toward the main house.

Jake came down the steps, holding a beer in each hand. He was as tall as Nathan, but where Nathan was broad and muscled, Jake was wiry. His dark brown hair was a little too long, his jeans were worn and faded and his boots were as scarred and scuffed as Nathan's own. He was slow and steady and more at ease with himself and his world than Nathan had ever been.

Jake went his own way and managed to have a good time while he was doing it. Nathan had always admired that trait in his younger brother.

With a wide grin, Jake handed over one of the frosty bottles. Grateful, Nathan accepted it and took a long drink. When Jake wandered off, Nathan followed his brother across the yard toward the swing set. Apparently,

Jake wanted to talk—away from the house. But nothing would get Jake talking before he was good and ready, so Nathan just enjoyed the night and the returning sanity now that he was a safe distance from Amanda.

He'd thought he was well and truly over her. Nathan had deliberately put her out of his mind years ago. He'd lost himself in work and in the arms of the willing women who'd come and gone from his life without leaving so much as a trace of themselves behind. So yeah, he'd figured with Amanda back in town, he'd face her down and keep moving on.

But the hard ache in his body let him know that though his mind had let her go, the rest of him hadn't. And there she was again, he thought in disgust. Right back in his thoughts, front and center. He closed his mind to the memories and focused on the now.

There were a few dawn-to-dusk lights around the play area and he took a second or two to look it over. He and Jake had dug out the wide area beneath the playground equipment and then poured enough fine sand to sink an aircraft carrier. It had taken the two of them nearly two weeks to get everything set up and finished off for safety, but knowing his niece and nephews loved it made all the work worth the effort.

Made of sanded, polished wood—to prevent splinters in tiny hands—the climbing gym sprawled across the pristine lawn as if it had grown in that spot. Jake's five-year-old twin sons and their two-year-old sister loved climbing on it and especially enjoyed the castle-like room at the top. Gave him a good feeling, seeing the next generation of Battles clambering all over the structure, hooting and hollering at each other, just like he and Jake had done when they were kids. It also made him remember that if things had turned out differently, his own child might have been playing here as well.

He shook off that disquieting thought and buried it under another long drink of his beer.

Jake slapped one hand against the swing set and blurted, "So, how's Amanda?"

Nathan almost choked on his swallow of beer. When the coughing ended and he could breathe again, he looked at his younger brother. "How the hell did you know I went to see her?"

Jake shrugged. "Mona Greer was walking that tiny excuse for a dog of hers and saw you going into the diner apartment. She called Sarah Danvers, Sarah talked to her daughter and Amelia called Terri a while ago."

The Royal hotline was already buzzing.

"Well, hell," he muttered. So much for keeping his private life private. He hadn't seen a damn soul around the diner. Mona Greer should look into a career with the CIA or something. Even at eighty, her eyesight was damn good and she clearly had a sneaky streak.

Jake laughed. "Seriously? You thought you could slide in and out of Amanda's apartment and nobody would catch on?"

"A man can dream," Nathan mumbled.

Jake laughed even louder and Nathan told himself there was nothing more irritating sometimes than a younger brother. "Did you come out here just to bush-whack me with gossip then laugh at me?"

"Of course," his brother said with a good-natured shrug. "Not every day I get to give you grief over something."

"Glad you're enjoying yourself."

"Yeah? Well, *I'm* glad to see Amanda back. Glad to see it bugs you."

"Thanks for the support," Nathan told him and took a drink of his beer. His gaze moved over the play equipment. In the moonlight, the slide gleamed like a river of silver and the pennant flag on the castle top fluttered in the hot Texas wind.

Irritation swelled inside him. Three years he'd been sheriff. He had respect. He had the admiration of the townspeople. Now, he was just grist for the mill.

"You want support? Go back to the TCC and talk to Chance. Or Alex." Jake toasted him with his beer. "From family, you get the truth, whether you want it or not."

"I don't." Nathan leaned against one of the posts as visions of Amanda roared into his brain again. He shouldn't have gone to her. But how could he not have? They'd had to talk. But then, there hadn't only been *talking,* had there?

"I know you don't want to hear it but you're going to anyway." Jake paused, ran one hand over the heavy chain from which one of the swings hung. "So here it is. You missed your chance with Amanda back in the day."

Nathan snorted. "I didn't miss a thing. Trust me."

Shaking his head, Jake said, "You know what I mean. You let her get away."

"I didn't *let* her do a damn thing, Jake," Nathan said tightly as he pushed away from the heavy wooden post. "Her decision to walk."

Jake was unaffected by the anger in Nathan's voice. "Right. And you didn't try to talk her out of it."

"Why the hell should I have?" Stalking off a few paces, Nathan's boots slid in the sand he and his brother had laid beneath the swing set. This was his place. The home he'd grown up in. The town where he'd carved out a spot for himself. Damned if he'd let the past jump up and ruin what he'd built.

At the far end of the play equipment, Nathan turned to look at his brother. Jake looked relaxed...amused, damn him.

Well, why wouldn't he be? Jake had everything he'd ever wanted. He ran the ranch. He was married to his high school sweetheart and they had three great kids plus another on the way. Everything was riding smooth in Jake's world—not that Nathan begrudged his brother's happiness. But at the same time, you'd think Jake could manage a little sympathy.

"I'm not going to *beg* a woman to stay with me."

"Who said anything about *begging?*" Jake shot back. "You could have asked."

"No," Nathan said, shaking his head and looking away from his brother's too-sharp eyes to stare out over the moonlit lawn. "I couldn't. There were...reasons."

Reasons he'd never talked about. Never even mentioned to Jake, and Nathan was closer to his brother than to anyone else on the planet. Those reasons tried to push into his mind now and Nathan resolutely pushed them out again. He'd dealt with them all years ago. He wouldn't go back, damn it.

"You listened to the gossip. You believed the rumors instead of talking to Amanda about them."

His head snapped up and his gaze locked on his brother like a twin pair of dark brown lasers. "What do you know about the rumors?"

Jake took a sip of his beer. "Chance told me what was going on—" He held up one hand to keep his brother quiet. "And don't blame him for it. You sure as hell didn't bother to tell me. You're my brother, Nate. You could have said something."

He shook his head and squelched the burst of anger struggling to come alive inside him. "I didn't want to talk about it then—" He paused and added for emphasis, "I still don't."

He didn't like remembering those days. Remembering how he'd felt when Chance told him what people were saying. Nathan had been in the police academy in Houston, unable to get to Amanda. Hell, he hadn't even had time for a damn phone call. And when he had finally been able to go to her…

Shaking his head, Nathan mentally closed the door on the past. It was done and he wouldn't be revisiting it anytime soon.

"You always were the hardhead in the family," Jake said on a sigh.

Nathan managed a short laugh at that. "Seems to me your Terri might argue with you there."

"Probably," Jake admitted with a wince. "Nate, I don't know what happened between you two seven years ago—" he held up a hand again "—and I'm not asking. I'm just saying, she's home to stay now and you're going to have to find a way to get past whatever happened so long ago. You're going to have to deal with her. Maybe the two of you should actually try talking about what happened to break you guys up."

Nathan grimaced, took a pull at his beer and let the icy froth cool down the temper that was still simmering inside him. "Where is all this talking, share-your-feelings stuff coming from? Is Terri making you watch Dr. Phil again?"

"No." Jake looked embarrassed. "But I'm not an idiot any more than you are and I *know* you know you have to make your peace with Amanda."

Another sip of ice-cold beer slid down Nathan's throat as he thought about what his brother said. And then a fresh memory of Amanda, molding her body to his. The heat of her kiss. The scent of her filled his mind. The feel of her beneath his hands again. His body stirred and he winced at the ache that he had a feeling was going to become all too familiar.

"Jake," Nathan said softly, "you don't get it. I learned a long time ago, where Amanda's concerned, there *is* no peace."

Four

One thing Amanda had always loved about living in Royal was the big farmers' market held every weekend in the park.

Ranchers and farmers from all over the county showed up to sell fresh vegetables, fruit and preserves. There were always craft booths as well, with local artisans selling everything from jewelry to ceramics and handmade toys.

At barely 9:00 a.m., the sun was already a hot ball of misery glowering down on the town. By afternoon, the only people not huddled in an air-conditioned room would be the kids. But for right now, the park was buzzing with activity. The busiest vendors in the park were those who had claimed a spot beneath the shade of a live oak.

Amanda had the day off and she was determined to enjoy it. But, as she wandered through the market, it was clear that the Royal rumor mill was in high gear.

She felt the speculative glances thrown her way as she passed and she lifted her chin defiantly in response. No point in hiding, she told herself. Instead, she would just ignore the fact that whispered conversations would stop when she got close and pick up again as she moved off. Clearly, *someone* had seen Nathan at her place the other night and it hadn't taken long for tongues to start wagging.

Amanda stopped at a booth displaying hand-thrown pottery and idly picked up a kiln-fired, sky-blue pitcher.

The artist, a young woman with waist-length blond hair and bright green eyes, smiled at her. "I'm running a special today on the cornflower-blue pottery."

And if she'd picked up one of the earthenware jugs, Amanda thought, *that* would have been the special of the day. But she couldn't blame the woman for doing her best to make a sale. Besides, she was going to be looking for a house in town soon and she'd need to furnish it, wouldn't she? Smiling, she said, "It's lovely work. How much?"

"Only thirty-five."

"Sold," Amanda told her and set the pitcher down to reach for her wallet. She probably could have haggled, but it was beautiful and she really did want it.

Purchase made, Amanda left a satisfied artist behind her, tucked her new pitcher into the cloth shopping bag slung over her shoulder and wandered off toward the next booth.

"Amanda, hi!" Piper Kindred waved her over with a wide grin. Piper's curly red hair was drawn back into a ponytail and her green eyes were shining. "Haven't had a chance to talk to you since you moved back home."

"I know. Things have been so busy, but we have got to get together soon." Amanda had known Piper most of her life and seeing her friend now made Amanda realize again how much she'd missed being a part of Royal.

"I hear you and Nathan are getting cozy again…"

"Of course you did," Amanda said. A few days ago, Nathan had shown up at her apartment and kissed her senseless. Ever since then, she'd had dozens of customers who spent most of their time at the diner watching *her*. Including Nathan, she reminded herself. He made time to come in at least once a day. He'd order coffee, sit at the counter and watch her as she moved around the room.

Nerve-racking on all fronts.

"Anything you care to share?" Piper teased.

"Not a thing," Amanda assured her old friend, then abruptly changed the subject. "So," she asked, stepping back to read the sign strung across the front of the booth Piper was manning, "what're you selling?"

"Raffle tickets," Piper told her and used her thumb to fan a stack of them. "We're raising money to help pay for the new child-care center at the TCC."

Grinning, Amanda said, "I heard the motion passed. Beau Hacket must have been purple with fury."

"By all reports," Piper assured her. Then she sighed. "I only wish I'd seen it myself. You remember Shannon Morrison? She tells me she came within a breath of hog-tieing the old coot just for the hell of it."

Beau was possibly the last living true chauvinist in the world. He liked women fine, as long as they stayed in their "place." Amanda had never been able to figure out why a woman as nice as his wife, Barbara, had married the man in the first place. "Sorry I missed it."

"More and more women are becoming members of the TCC now that Abby Price paved the way." Piper paused. "I'm not a member or anything, but I wanted to help with this raffle. How many tickets are you going to buy?"

Shaking her head, Amanda reached for her wallet and laughed. "Give me five."

"Atta girl." Piper peeled off the tickets and waited while Amanda wrote her name and phone number on the stubs. When she was finished, Piper dropped the stubs into a steel box and said, "The draw's in a week. Who knows? You might win the grand prize."

"What is it?"

"A weekend getaway in Dallas." Piper shrugged. "Personally, I'd rather win the free dinner at Claire's."

"Hey," Amanda countered, in a mocking insulted tone, "how about you come eat at the diner instead? We've got lemon meringue pie tomorrow."

"Now you're talking," Piper said. "I'll come in around lunch. Maybe we can sit and talk over pie. You can give me the real story behind the gossip."

"You'll be disappointed. There is no story." Except for that kiss, Amanda thought. She waved a goodbye, then moved on. She was still smiling when she caught the scent of fresh-brewed coffee along with a delectable aroma of cinnamon coming from nearby. Marge Fontenot had probably brought in her homemade cinnamon rolls to sell in the coffee booth her husband ran. Amanda's stomach growled in anticipation as she headed for the vendor cart with the long line snaking in front of it.

"Doing some shopping?"

She stopped and looked at Alex Santiago as he approached her.

"I am." As the sun shone down on her, she was grateful she'd tucked her hair into a ponytail that morning. But Alex looked cool and comfortable in khaki slacks and a short-sleeved white shirt. "Living in the city, I really missed farmers' market days."

His gaze swept across the crowded park. "I admit, I

enjoy them as well. Last week I bought a new pair of boots...."

She glanced down and nodded in approval at the hand-tooled brown leather boots he wore. "Very nice."

"Thank you. And just now, I've purchased what I am told is the—" he paused to reach into a paper bag and draw out a jar long enough to read the label "—world's best huckleberry jam." He shrugged and gave her a smile that could probably melt ice at a hundred yards.

Amanda just chuckled. "If you bought that jam from Kaye Cannarozzi, I guarantee it *is* the world's best. She's won prizes for her jam every year at the state fair."

"Good to know," he said and folded up the bag again. "You can find just about anything here, I've discovered."

Amanda watched him as he looked around the park. He was dark and gorgeous and his accent made every word sound like seduction. Alex was also nice, funny and, except for his dubious taste in friends—Nathan for example—he was pretty much perfect. Too bad for Amanda that the only bell he rung for her was one of friendship.

"Hmm," Alex mused. "I'm curious as to what put a frown on your face just then. Dark thoughts?"

She forced a smile and shook her head. "Not at all. Um, I'm headed for the coffee wagon over there." She pointed and asked, "Would you like to join me?"

"I could use some coffee as well, so, yes." He fell into step beside her. "I'm looking forward to the Fourth of July celebration. I hear it's quite the event."

"Oh, it's great," Amanda told him. "Most of the town gathers right here for an all-day party. There are contests and games and the fireworks show is always amazing. If I do say so myself, we put on a terrific Fourth."

Funny how good it felt to say *we*.

"Sounds as though you've missed it."

"I really did," she admitted, glancing around the park at the people wandering from booth to booth. Kids raced away from their parents, laughing as they headed to the playground. Dogs on leashes strained against their owners' restraining hands and a hot summer wind kicked up out of nowhere.

Royal was home. There was no other place like it and she'd never really been happy anywhere else. "You know, I told myself while I was gone that I was fine. That life in the city was better, somehow. But now that I'm back, it's like I never left."

"Going home isn't always possible," he mused. "I'm glad you're finding it easier than you'd thought."

Amanda looked up at him and saw that while his stare was fixed on the distance, a slight frown was etched into his features. She didn't know Alex well, but she sensed something was bothering him. Before she could offer to help, though, he spoke again.

"I'm pleased to see that the gossip hasn't upset you."

She sighed. The downside to small-town life. She'd already had several people stop her in the park that morning, asking questions, giving her sly winks and knowing smiles. Nathan and she were the talk of the town and until something really juicy came up, that wasn't going to change.

"You've heard it, too?"

He gave her a rueful grin. "I think you would have to be on the moon to miss it."

"Know anyone who could give me a ride?"

"Sadly, no." He shrugged and added, "Though a beautiful woman shouldn't let loose talk from small minds worry her."

Amanda stopped, cocked her head and looked up at him. "You really *are* perfect, aren't you?"

His mouth quirked. "I like to think so, though I'm sure others would disagree."

"Not from where I'm standing."

"For that, I thank you. Besides, gossip isn't a static thing, Amanda," he said. "Very soon, they'll find something else to talk about."

"I suppose," she said, looking at the crowds in the park. Most of the people she'd known her whole life. Oh, there were plenty of outsiders who had come into town solely for market day. But the great majority were familiar to her. Which was probably why everyone felt free enough to talk about her.

She knew they were watching her now, too. Wondering why she was walking with Alex when it was clear she and Nathan were starting up again. A tiny twist of pain wrapped itself around her heart. "As much as I love Royal, it's not always an easy place to live."

"No place is easy," Alex said, his expression becoming thoughtful again, as if there were things chewing at him.

Somehow, she'd struck a nerve, Amanda thought. From what she knew, Alex Santiago hadn't been in town very long and she wondered if anyone really knew him well. Reaching out, she threaded her arm companionably through his. "Everything okay, Alex?"

Immediately, his handsome face brightened as he flashed her a smile. "You've a kind heart Amanda, but there's no need for concern. I'm fine."

"Am I interrupting?"

Amanda looked up when Nathan's deep voice demanded her attention. He was only a few feet away, headed right for her. The sunlight winked off the sheriff's badge pinned to his broad chest. He wore his favorite scuffed boots and a uniform shirt tucked into black jeans. The gun at his hip made him look even more formidable than usual. His gaze was fixed on hers, but still he managed to fire a brief glare at Alex.

A flash of heat shot through Amanda at Nathan's nearness and made the heat of the summer sun seem no hotter than a match-head in comparison. She wanted to fan herself, but she knew it wouldn't do any good, so she settled for sarcastic indifference instead.

"If I said 'yes you are,'" Amanda quipped, "would you go away?"

His eyes flashed. "Not until I know what you guys are talking about."

Alex grinned at his friend. "About small towns and smaller minds."

Nathan frowned and nodded. "You mean the gossip."

"Among other things," Amanda said, drawing Nathan's eyes back to her. She knew him so well she could see the tension in his face. The gossip was irritating to her. To Nathan, it had to be infuriating. "What do you want, Nathan?"

"Coffee, one of Margie's cinnamon rolls and to talk to you. Not necessarily in that order."

So, there wasn't even going to be a pretense of friendliness between them. He was acting as if the kiss they'd shared hadn't happened. As if putting it out of his mind made the whole scene disappear.

"I'm busy," she said. "Alex and I are shopping."

She should have known that men would stick together. Alex immediately said, "Actually, there are a few things I have to take care of. I've enjoyed myself, Amanda." Shifting his gaze to his friend, he nodded and said, "I'll see you later, Nathan."

"You don't have to go," Amanda told him quickly. Without Alex there, she and Nathan wouldn't have a buffer. And she suddenly wanted one really badly.

"Yeah, you do," Nathan said at the same time.

Alex only laughed. "You two are very entertaining. I'll be on my way."

Around them, conversations rose and fell. A sultry wind teased the hem of her shorts and in the distance, children played and laughed. Amanda knew that she and Nathan were now the center of attention, but she didn't care anymore. Alex had been right about one thing. Sooner or later, everyone would find a new topic of interest. Until then, her best choice was simply to ignore them all. People would talk and she couldn't stop them. So instead, she continued on toward Margie's coffee cart and wasn't surprised to have Nathan right at her side.

"Mona Greer saw me at your place when I was there a few nights ago," he told her, his voice low and deep.

"Well, that explains a few things," Amanda said wryly.

"That woman should have been a spy."

"Maybe she was. Now she's retired," Amanda mused, "and she's looking for new things to occupy her."

He snorted a short laugh. "That'd be something. Mona in the CIA."

Amanda laughed, too, then Nathan looked down at her and she caught the confusion in his eyes.

"This doesn't bother you? Being talked about?" Nathan asked.

"A little," she admitted. "Okay, a lot. But I can't stop it, so why make myself nuts?"

"Healthy attitude."

"I try," she said, and fell into line at the coffee cart.

Nathan stayed beside her and, keeping his voice low,

he said, "I still think we need to set some ground rules, Amanda."

"Like you coming around the diner to keep an eye on me?"

He frowned.

"Or are you talking about when you kissed me?"

She had the satisfaction of seeing a flash of temper spark in his eyes. Then he spoke as if she hadn't said a thing. "We agree that there's nothing between us anymore and—"

Amanda didn't have to speak. She only looked up at him, making no attempt at all to hide the smile curving her mouth. Nothing between them? Hadn't they proven just the other night that if nothing else, there was still plenty of heat between them?

He scowled, clearly understanding what she wasn't saying. Then he muttered, "That doesn't count."

"Felt like it counted to me." In fact, that one kiss had kept her awake most of the night feeling restless, edgy. Memories had crowded in on her until all she could think about was Nathan and how things used to be between them. That kiss had stirred up everything for her, making the last few days really uncomfortable. And now Nathan wanted to pretend it hadn't happened?

Nathan looked down at her and watched her meadow-green eyes narrow. She was mad. He liked that. Better than amused. Or accepting. Anger was safer. For both of them. Except for the fact that she looked so damn good when she was pissed off at him. Gave her a fire he'd never found in any other woman.

Her light brown hair was pulled into a high ponytail at the back of her head. She wore gold hoops in her ears that dangled long enough to skim her smooth shoulders, displayed nicely in a navy blue tank top. Her white shorts showed off her tan and made her legs look as if they were a mile long, and the sandals let him see she still wore the gold toe ring he'd given her on her left foot.

A breeze sent her ponytail dancing and it was all Nathan could do to keep from reaching up and twining that silky mass around his fingers. Damn it, she was in him again. As fiercely as she had been years ago. For days now, he'd been tormented by thoughts of her. By memories so thick they'd nearly choked him. He'd hardly slept for dreams of her and when he woke, it was to a body that was hard and aching for want of her.

His talk with Jake hadn't helped any. He'd meant it when he said there was no peace with Amanda. But back in the day he hadn't been looking for peace, had he? All he'd been able to think about was her. Her laugh. Her eyes. Her scent. Her taste. The feel of her hands on his body and the sweet brush of her breath when she kissed him.

Hell, no, that wasn't peaceful.

It was…consuming.

And it was happening again. Only this time, he'd come up with a plan to combat it. It had hit him in the shower just that morning—another damn cold one—that what he needed to do was get Amanda back in his bed.

Over the years, Nathan had convinced himself that he'd idealized what he and Amanda had shared. That was why he hadn't been able to find another woman to compare to her. His own mind had set him up for failure by making the memories of Amanda so amazing that what woman *could* hold a candle to her?

What was needed here was a little reality. And sex was the key. Get her in his bed, and get her out of his mind once and for all.

It was the only road to sanity.

Once he'd had her again, he could let her go. This tension between them would finally be over.

As his plan settled into his mind, he smiled to himself.

"What?" Amanda asked.

"What do you mean?"

"You're smiling," she pointed out.

"And that's bad?" He laughed a little and moved forward as the line continued to snake ahead.

"Not bad," Amanda said, still watching him warily. "Just…suspicious."

Behind them in line, someone chuckled.

Nathan frowned. Damned hard to work on seducing a woman when you had half the town watching your every move. "So when I'm angry, you're mad and when I'm not, you're worried."

She thought about it for a second, then nodded. "That's about right."

For just a moment, Nathan enjoyed the confusion in her eyes and found himself laughing briefly. "There really is no one else like you, is there?"

"Probably not," she admitted and moved a bit closer to the head of the line.

She could always drive him out of his mind, Nathan thought, letting his gaze move over her in appreciation. He'd always liked tall women—they were right in easy kissing range. Amanda, though, was like no one else. Or at least that's how he remembered it. Even in high school, when she was a freshman and he a senior, he'd been drawn to her. His friends had given him grief over it, of course—but he hadn't been able to stay away.

And then, years later, those same friends had told him about the rumors that had eventually torn him and Amanda apart.

"So tell me, Nathan," she said, shattering his thoughts and drawing him back to the moment, "are you interested in my sister?"

"What?" He goggled at her. "Where did that come from?"

She shrugged, glared at the man behind them, openly listening to their conversation, then leaned in closer to Nathan to say, "I've seen the way she watches you."

Nathan thought about that for a minute. He hadn't noticed Pam looking at him in any particular way. Okay, yes, he'd dated her a couple times a year or so ago, but it hadn't gone anywhere and they'd parted friends. Or he'd thought they had. Until now. Frowning slightly, he said, "We went out a few times a while back, but—"

Her eyes went wide. "I can't believe you dated my *sister,*" she said, cutting him off sharply.

The man behind them in line let out a long, slow whistle, but when Nathan gave him a hard look, the guy got quiet fast.

"It was a couple of dates. Dinner." He thought back. "A movie."

"It was *my sister.*" She fisted her hands at her hips. "How would you like it if I dated Jake?"

"I think his wife would mind it even more than I would."

"You know what I mean."

"Yeah, I do. But we were over, remember?" Nathan whispered and moved with the line. How long *was* this line, anyway? And were there even more people crowded around them than there had been a few minutes ago? "Besides, Pam was here and—"

"So she was *here,*" Amanda said, interrupting him again and making Nathan grind his teeth together in frustration. "Well, then. Of course I can understand that. The whole proximity factor."

The whistler behind them chuckled now and only shrugged when Nathan gave him another hard stare. This conversation was going to be all over town by suppertime, he told himself, and still he couldn't keep from saying, "At least Pam never lied to me."

She sucked in a gulp of air and her eyes shone with fury. "*Lie* to you? I never lied to you. You were the one who—"

"That's it," he muttered and grabbed hold of her arm.

He wasn't going to do this with a couple dozen people watching them with all the avid interest of a crowd at a football game.

Dragging her out of the line, he headed toward the nearest deserted spot. A shade tree close to the now-empty baseball diamond. Naturally, nothing with Amanda came easy. She tugged and pulled, trying to get out of his grip, but no way was he letting her go until they had this settled. And for this talk, they needed some damn privacy.

"Let go of me!" She kicked at him, but missed.

"In a minute," he muttered.

"I want my coffee. I do *not* want to go anywhere with you."

"That's too damn bad," Nathan told her and never slowed down. When they finally reached the shade of the oak, he let her go and she stared up at him, furious.

"I don't know who you think you are, but—"

"You know exactly who I am," he told her, voice low and filled with the temper crouched inside him. "Just like you know that I hate putting on a show for the whole damn town."

"Fine." She lifted her chin, met him glare for glare

and then said, "You want to talk, here it is. I never lied to you, Nathan."

"And I'm supposed to take your word for that?"

"Damn right, you are," she shouted, obviously not caring who was listening. "When did I *ever* give you a reason to *not* trust me, Nathan?"

She had a point, but he didn't want to admit to it. All he remembered were the rumors she hadn't been able to disprove. The sympathetic glances from his friends. The gossip that insisted on a completely different story than the one she'd told him. And his doubts had chewed on him until, ragged with temper and tension, he'd faced her down and in one night, they had lost everything.

"What was I supposed to think?" he demanded. "My best friends told me that story. Why wouldn't I believe them?"

Shaking her head, she looked at him now with more hurt than fury and that tore at him.

"Because you were supposed to *love* me. You should have taken my word for it."

Shame rippled through him and was gone an instant later. He'd done what he thought was right. Hell, he'd been half-crazed back then anyway. When he heard she had lost the baby, he was enrolled in the police academy in Dallas and hadn't been able to get to her. Hadn't even been able to call her. To figure out truth from lies.

"It was a long time ago, Amanda."

"Was it?" she asked quietly. "Doesn't feel like it right now."

No, it didn't. The past was there, in the park with them. Shadows of memories crowded together, dimming the sunlight, making the other people in the park fade away until it was just he and Amanda. He looked into her eyes and said, "All right then. Tell me now. The truth."

She sighed. "I shouldn't have to tell you again, Nathan. You know me. You knew me then. You should have believed me. I *lost* our baby."

Pain slapped at him but he pushed it away. Now that the past was here, it was time to finally settle it. If he wanted to get her out of his mind, then he was going to have to make a start right here.

"Then who the hell was it who made sure I thought you had *ended* the pregnancy on purpose?"

Five

"I don't know," Amanda said, shaking her head. She still couldn't believe anyone had spread that rumor. Couldn't believe that Nathan had thought for even a minute that she would ever do such a thing.

In a flash, Amanda was back there, on the night when everything crashed down around her. They'd been engaged for two weeks—because Nathan had insisted on a wedding the moment he found out she was pregnant. But that night, she had been the one doing the insisting.

"The wedding's off, Nathan."

"Just like that?"

"The only reason you were marrying me was because of the baby, right?" Those words cost her. She so wanted him to say that wasn't true. That he loved her. Always had. That they would be okay, they would get past this.

But he didn't.

*And she couldn't marry a man who didn't love her—
no matter how much she loved him.*

"So that's it?" he demanded. "Now that you're not
pregnant, you don't need me anymore, that it? Find
someone richer?"

Stunned, she could only look at him. She had never
cared a damn about his money. She'd loved him for as
long as she could remember. And she'd convinced herself that he cared for her, too. Even though he'd never
actually said the words. Now she could see she'd been
living in a dream world. "How can you say that?"

"Oh, I'm not done," he told her flatly. "You said you
lost the baby, but that's not the whole story, is it?"

Amanda stared up at him. She had expected him to
be supportive. To share the pain that was still tearing
through her. The loss of the baby, her hopes, her dreams
for the future. They were all gone now.

She'd needed Nathan so badly. Now that he was here,
she only wanted him gone.

"I don't know what you mean," she said finally.

"Yeah, I think you do." He stalked around the perim-
eter of her tiny Midland apartment. "Hell, you hated
the thought of marrying me so much you got rid of my
baby?"

"What?" Shock held her in place. Outrage made her
want to scream. Pain held her in such a tight grip she
could hardly breathe. "You think—"

"Thought I wouldn't find out, didn't you?" he asked,
his voice dripping with ice.

"There was nothing to find out, Nathan." Through
her pain, anger began to blossom like a black rose. She
gave it free rein. "I lost the baby. I had a miscarriage.
I told you."

He scrubbed one hand across the top of his head.

"Yeah, that's what you told me. Others told me something different."

"And you'd believe them? Believe that I could do something like that to our child?"

His eyes were hard, his expression distant, remote. "Why would anyone say that if it wasn't true?"

Good question, but that was for later. Right now, the most important question on her mind was how could he think for even a second that it was true?

"How do I know?"

"Exactly," he said. "How do I know what to believe, either?"

"I guess you have to trust me," she said, knowing he didn't. Knowing he wouldn't.

"Yeah." His eyes were as cold as the moon. Suddenly he looked like a stranger to her and Amanda knew she wouldn't be able to reach him because he didn't want to be reached.

So much lost, all in a blink of time. She swayed with the impact of what was happening.

He turned and walked to the door. There, he stopped and looked back at her. "You're right about one thing, though. The wedding's off. I was only marrying you because of the baby. With the reason gone, there's no point, is there?"

The fact that his words echoed what she had thought herself only moments before just made the pain that much deeper. Sharper. When Nathan left, the quiet click of the door shutting behind him sounded like a gunshot. It seemed to echo in the empty room long after he'd left her. Long after Amanda had curled up on the couch to cry herself to sleep.

Shaking her head as if she could somehow dislodge the painful memories, Amanda looked up at him through eyes that were no longer starry with love for a man who refused to love her back. She wasn't young and foolish anymore. If she still loved Nathan, that was her problem and she'd find a way to get over it. But he would never know that he still had so much power over her heart.

"You walked out, Nathan," she reminded him in a voice that was low and throbbing with remembered hurt.

"Yeah," he admitted, "I did. But you were the one to end things between us. Hell, I walked in the door and you handed me the ring."

"You agreed with me about calling off the wedding," she reminded him.

"Damn straight, I did. You weren't pregnant. You'd already handed me the ring—"

"You wouldn't *talk* to me," she said.

"You didn't give me a chance to say anything and even if you had, what the hell could I say?" he countered. "It was done. The baby was gone and your ring was in my fist. What do you think I should have said, for God's sake?"

"That you believed me." That was the one thing that had always stung. He had known her better than anyone else—or so she had thought. And he'd taken the word of malicious gossips over her.

How was she supposed to forget that?

He scrubbed both hands across his face as memories crowded so close he could hardly draw a breath. The rumors had driven him crazy when he couldn't get to her. At first, she was in the hospital and then when she was out, he was confined to the academy. Couldn't even talk to her. Couldn't look into her eyes and see for himself truth from lies. But by the time he finally reached her side, the crazy had taken over. The doubts. The disappointment and fury had him so tangled into knots it was all he could do to hold it together.

Hell, he prided himself on control. On being in charge of every damn thing around him. He had his own personal rules of conduct. And he'd blown them all on that long-ago night. Duty. Honor. They'd both gone out the window when anger made him blind to common sense.

Blowing out a breath, he stared up at the sky for a long minute, then lowered his gaze to hers. Doubts still gnawed at the edges of his heart, but being with her, looking into her eyes, clouded with hurt, he could see the truth that had eluded him for so long. "I do believe you."

The moment he said it, he knew it was right. Back then, he'd been young and stupid. He'd wanted her to rush into his arms looking for comfort. He'd wanted her to cry and mourn their lost child so he would *know* that she hadn't ended her pregnancy. Instead, she'd handed him the ring he'd given her and told him, more or less, to move on.

So his own self-assurance took a hit and then delivered one right back. Hurt, he'd made sure that she hurt, too. He wasn't saying he was right. He was only saying—screw it.

A sheen of tears filmed the brilliant green of her eyes, but before he could panic or kick his own ass for making her cry, she blinked them back. She took a breath, steadied herself and said, "Thanks for that, anyway. Better late than never, huh?"

"I guess," he said, but this conversation still felt unfinished.

She hitched her bag higher on her shoulder. "Now, I've got to go."

"Damn it, Amanda—don't walk away."

"What else is there to talk about, Nathan? We're over

and done, and standing here in the park together is only going to fire up the gossip train you hate."

True.

He did hate knowing that, but there didn't seem to be much he could do about it. For days now, he'd lived with everyone in town watching his every move. With having people drop by the jailhouse for a "friendly chat" when what they were really looking for was more grist for the rumor mill. They wanted exclusive news about Nathan and Amanda so *they* could be the ones to spill the next part of the story.

Hell, he was actually getting used to it.

He'd come here today, knowing the gossips were chewing on them, knowing that meeting her like this would only make things worse. But this was his plan. Talk with her, bed her, then move on and—damn it—he was going to stick to it. It was a good plan, even if it had gotten more involved than he'd originally thought it would.

Nathan hadn't meant to dig into the past. Hadn't intended to throw up that night between them like a damn battle flag. He didn't want her pissed—despite how good she looked when fire was in her eyes. He didn't want her sad. Or resigned.

He wanted her hot and ready and as eager to be with him as he was to get his hands on her. But he couldn't do that until he ended the war.

"You're off tonight, right?"

"What?" She looked as surprised as he was over his blurted question.

Taking hold of her arm again, he drew her around to the far side of the old oak, using the tree to block most people's views of them.

"Let go, Nathan."

He did, though his fingers still felt the warmth of

her skin long after he drew his hand back. Through the years, through the old pain and shared memories, the heat between them lingered. He was more convinced than ever that he was doing the right thing. Get her back into bed, feel the burn again so that he could finally let it—and her—go.

"We need some time, Amanda," he said, keeping his gaze locked with hers. "Time to talk. To find a way to be in this town together."

She was shaking her head so he talked faster, refusing to give her enough room to back away. "Come out with me tonight. We'll have dinner—and time."

"I don't know...."

Confusion etched itself onto her features. He could see her weighing her decision, so he gave her a little push. "Not afraid to be alone with me, are you?"

It worked.

Her head snapped up and she snorted. "Afraid? Please."

He grinned. "Then it's settled."

"Fine." She nodded at him. "Where do you want to meet?"

"I'll pick you up at your place about seven."

She laughed a little uneasily. "This is Saturday. Everyone for miles around will be in town. You're not worried about how many people will see us together?"

He glanced up at the crowd milling around the park before looking back to her. What was the point of hiding now? They were already the center of every conversation in town. No sense trying to fight it. "They're already talking, remember? Besides, damned if I'm going to sneak around."

She nodded. "Good point."

"All right, then. See you at seven."

* * *

Over at the diner, Pam leaned on the counter and tapped her fingernails against it in a sharp staccato. "People have been talking about them all day."

"You shouldn't be listening."

"How can I not?" She shook her head and gave a quick look around at the people sitting at the booths and counters. Peggy, the other waitress on duty, was laughing with her customers and in the kitchen behind her, Pam could hear the cooks talking while they worked. The diner was busy and that was a good thing. The fact that it was all because of Amanda made it harder to appreciate.

"She's been back home for a couple of weeks and she's taking over again."

She looked at the man sitting in front of her. JT McKenna had been her friend since school. He ran his own ranch just outside of town where he raised a small herd of cattle and his pride and joy, quarter horses.

His dark brown hair curled over the collar of his shirt and his tanned face showed a line of white across the top of his forehead where his hat normally rested. He was tall and lean and according to Pam's friends, gorgeous. She'd never really noticed because JT had always been just her friend.

Now, he cupped his hands around a cup of coffee and shook his head. "Pam, you're the one who asked her to come home."

She sighed. Hard to admit, but he was right. Pam had tried to run the diner on her own, but it just hadn't worked. She'd been overwhelmed with trying to handle the whole place on her own. But she still hated to acknowledge that Amanda had made a difference. Her younger sister had always been the golden one. Her par-

ents' favorite. Taller, smarter, prettier... Pam's fingernails sounded out like a jackhammer.

It wasn't that she didn't like her sister. But did
Amanda have to be so perfect?

"You're getting wound up over nothing, Pam," JT
said.

His brown eyes were on her and she had to sigh.
"You're probably right, but—"

"No buts," he teased and gave her a grin that lit up
his eyes. "You're so focused on Amanda and Nathan you
can't see anything else around you."

"Like what?"

JT blew out a breath and said, "Like I could use some
more coffee."

"Oh, sure." She turned to reach for the pot and told
herself she needed to calm down. But the last few days
had made that nearly impossible. Everyone was talking
about Nathan and Amanda again. Just as they had all
those years ago.

Nathan.

Her heart ached at the thought of him. Without even
trying, her little sister had even gotten the man Pam had
always wanted. All those years when Amanda was living
away from Royal, Pam had done everything she could to
capture Nathan's attention. But it was as if he was completely oblivious to her. Even the couple of times she'd
managed to get him out to dinner and to a movie, nothing had come of it.

"Still," she said thoughtfully, "according to Dora
Plant, Nathan and Amanda were arguing at the park
today."

"You're doing it again," JT told her flatly. "I can
see it in your eyes. You're thinking on how you can
get around your sister to Nathan and it's not going to

get you anywhere. You best watch your step, and move careful, Pam."

"What?"

"You and Amanda," he said gently, "you're *family*. Always will be."

"I know that—" she argued.

He cut her off. "Maybe you do, but I'm thinking you tend to forget what you don't want to think about. My point is, you should open your eyes, Pam. Nathan's not interested in you that way and probably never will be."

She flushed, but couldn't seem to stop it. Pam had hungered after Nathan for so long, it had become a way of life for her. All the time he was with her sister, that knowledge had eaten away at her like acid. But then the two of them broke up and Pam began to hope again. All right, nothing had come of their few dates, but that didn't mean she should give up.

"You don't know what it's like, JT."

He laughed shortly, shook his head and dug money out of his wallet. Laying the bills on the counter, he said, "You'd be surprised by what I know, Pam."

She watched him go, then turned back to her customers, still wondering what JT had meant.

A few hours later, Amanda was standing in front of her mirror, trying to figure out how Nathan had maneuvered her into this. She wasn't even sure why she was going along with…what was it? A date? Her stomach swirled at the thought.

"It's not a date," she said, just to hear it said out loud. She dragged a brush through her hair. "It *feels* like a date. It shouldn't, but it does. God, I haven't been on a date in—" She stopped because even if there was no one else there to hear her, admitting out loud that it had been *three years* since she'd been on a real, live, guy-picks-you-up-and-pays date was too humiliating.

No wonder she was nervous.

Music pumped from the radio in the living room and Amanda smiled at herself in the mirror. Looked more like a grimace, but she'd take it. She had no idea where Nathan was taking her, so she'd changed her outfit three times, finally settling on a pale blue skirt that hit just above her knees, a white, short-sleeved blouse that buttoned up the front and a pair of sandals with a heel that would bring her almost to eye level with Nathan.

And there was the swirl of nerves in the pit of her stomach again.

Notadate...notadate...notadate...

The chant went through her mind but couldn't seem to find anything to hold on to. Because she'd been off balance ever since she'd returned to Royal. Those first two weeks, waiting to see him again. Then that first meeting in the diner, when he'd been so cold, so remote. Only to have him show up later, right here and, after demanding she leave town, kiss her until her head was spinning.

No wonder she felt as if she were at the center of a madly spinning tornado. She had no sense of direction. Only the instinctive drive to keep her heart intact this time. To become so immune to Nathan and what he could do to her with a glance that she could finally move on. Find a nice man—one who didn't drive her to impossible highs and heartbreaking lows—and build a life. A life with the children she longed for. A life filled with the love she'd lost so long ago.

So *why* then was she putting herself through this not-a-date? Because she wasn't immune to Nathan yet and just maybe a night spent alone with him might start her on that path.

When a knock sounded at her door, she slapped one hand to her abdomen in a futile attempt to quell all the butterflies nestled in there, then told herself to get a grip. To get over Nathan, she was going to need to restrain her natural tendency to go up in flames around him. She walked across the room, deliberately casual, opened the door and nerves slid away to be replaced by something more elemental. More…hazardous, to her already iffy sense of control.

He wore black jeans, a red, button-down long-sleeve shirt open at the collar and the boots that seemed to be a part of him. He gave her a slow, thorough once-over, then an appreciative smile curved his mouth. "You look great."

Fire licked at her insides, but she squashed the flames flat before they could take hold. This wasn't a romantic thing, for heaven's sake. This was just…who knew what it was?

"Thanks." She grabbed her purse from the nearby table. God, he smelled good. "I'm ready to go."

That smile of his deepened as he turned her toward the stairs. "Always liked that about you, Amanda. None of this make-him-wait stuff." Taking her hand, he led her down the stairs and then to his car, a big, black SUV he'd left parked on the street.

Saturday night was date night in Royal for young and old alike. A lot of the local ranchers came in to treat the family to dinner out. There were shoppers hitting the stores on Main Street and pedestrians, just out watching other people. And she was sure that most of them were avidly watching her and Nathan.

Nothing could have proven to her more completely that he didn't give a damn about the gossips any more than picking her up on a Saturday night for the whole town to see.

To her left, the wide front windows of the diner shone with light and she knew that everyone in there, too, would have a perfect view of her leaving with Nathan.

As if he knew just what she was thinking, he squeezed her hand briefly and gave her a conspiratorial wink. Her heart clenched—it was almost as if the two of them were a team again. To underline that sensation, his hand around hers felt warm and strong and…right. She nearly stumbled when that thought zipped through her mind.

Thankfully, she recovered quickly, since an older woman with a crown of gray braids wrapped around her head stopped them on the sidewalk.

"Well, now, what might you two be up to on such a nice summer evening?" Hannah Poole was easily seventy-five. Her eyes—shining with glee—were razor-sharp and her nose was practically twitching with interest. If there was a gossip train in Royal, then Miss Hannah was the engineer. There wasn't a thing that went on in town that she didn't know about.

"Hello, Miss Hannah," Amanda said, tugging at Nathan's hand to stop him. "It's nice to see you."

"I'm sure it is, honey," she said as her gaze locked briefly on their joined hands. "Going somewhere, are you?"

"Yes, ma'am, we sure are," Nathan answered, then surprised Amanda by letting go of her hand only long enough to snake one arm around her waist, steering her toward the car. "And if we don't hurry we'll be late."

"Well, I wouldn't want to keep you," the woman said thoughtfully, eyes gleaming. "I've got to get on home, myself. You two young people have fun, now. Good to see the two of you back together again."

"Oh, we're not—" Amanda began.

"Thank you, Miss Hannah," Nathan said over her. "You have a good evening."

He got Amanda settled, stalked around to the driver's side and climbed in.

"Of course she had to get home," Amanda said, watching as Hannah Poole scurried down the sidewalk. Her feet, clad in sensible brown shoes, moved faster than Amanda had ever known them to go.

"What she meant was, she had to get on the phone and tell everyone who wasn't in town tonight that she saw the two of us together."

"Yep."

She turned her head to stare at him. "Doesn't that bother you?"

"Yep." He fired up the engine, checked traffic, then pulled out onto Main Street.

"That's it? Just 'yep'?" Amanda's gaze locked on him. In the old days, Nathan would have been rigidly furious to be the center of attention. This Nathan was a stranger. Mysterious. Intriguing. "Who are you and what have you done with Nathan?"

His lips quirked briefly. "What am I supposed to do? Shoot Miss Hannah? Throw her into a jail cell to keep her off the phone?" He shook his head and turned left. "Nope. No way to stop her or anyone else from talking."

"Did you have a temper transplant?"

Unexpectedly, he glanced at her and grinned. "No, but not a bad idea."

She was charmed. How could she not be? Not only was this Nathan—the man she'd been in love with since she was fourteen years old—but tonight he was…different. More relaxed. More…approachable.

Which could be risky, her mind warned. Logically,

she should pay attention to that warning. Unfortunately, her body was too busy celebrating Nathan's nearness to worry about possible future problems. And that was a whole different problem. She was supposed to be weaning herself from the allure of Nathan and now he'd made it that much more difficult.

Amanda settled back in the car seat, kept her gaze locked on the street in front of them and tried to stifle the sensations already building inside her.

It wasn't easy.

"So where are we going?"

"You still like surprises?" he asked.

"Yes…"

"Then sit back. Won't take but a minute to get there."

That narrowed down the choices. Even if he was taking her to Claire's restaurant, it was clear on the other side of town. But he wasn't headed in that direction, anyway. They'd only driven a mile or so, when Nathan pulled into a familiar parking lot.

"The TCC?" she asked.

"Problem with that?"

"No." She looked at the building that had been a part of town life since long before she was born. Built in the 1900s, it was a huge, rambling, one-story building constructed of dark stone and wood with a tall, slate roof.

She'd been inside a couple of times before—not as a guest, but as a server when her father had catered meetings. She knew the ceilings were high, the furniture and floors were dark and old-world style and the ambiance was loaded with testosterone. Sure, they were allowing female members now, but not many and not without a battle that had made the Alamo look like a playground tussle.

"I've just never—" She caught herself and shrugged. "I'm just…surprised, I guess."

"Why?" Nathan shut off the engine and looked at her. "The dining room's been open to women for years."

"True, but you never took me there before."

"Yeah," he said, "there's a lot of things I didn't do that maybe I should have."

She didn't even know what to say to that. Did he have the same kind of regrets she had for the way things had ended between them? Nathan was a master at hiding what he was feeling so unless he came right out and said so, she might never know for sure.

"Maybe that's true of both of us." She offered a truce and was pleased to see his smile in response.

"Could be you're right. But for now, let's just say I'm a changed man." He got out of the car and as he walked around the hood to come to her side, Amanda found herself hoping he hadn't changed *too* much.

Over dinner, she realized that she had forgotten just how charming Nathan could be. His gaze fixed on hers, he led their conversation to happier times. To the years before they'd split up in such a crash of emotions.

All around them, the clink of silver against china and the tinkle of crystal became no more than quiet background noise. The people, the servers, seemed to fade away. She had even stopped noticing the hunting trophies on the walls. With Nathan's full attention on her, it was impossible to be aware of anything else.

The dark paneled walls, the soft lighting and the flickering candles on the tables all made for a romantic setting that Amanda wasn't sure how to interpret. She hadn't expected romance, yet it seemed Nathan was determined to give it to her. Why?

And why couldn't she just enjoy it while it lasted?

They talked about old times, without touching on the painful parts. They talked about what each of them had been doing over the last seven years and slowly, began to work into…what? A friendship? No. That was too pale a word for the connection that hummed between them, whether they were acknowledging it or not.

Of course, because they were in a small town where they knew everyone, their dinner wasn't completely private. Several people paused at their table to say hello and Amanda watched as Nathan became what he was: the sheriff. A man respected and trusted by everyone in town, he answered questions patiently and promised a couple of people to look into their problems. He carried power easily and she realized that the last several years had made a difference. He wasn't the young, arrogant man she'd known back then. Oh, he was still cocky, that came across just fine, but there was an underlying thread of patience that the old Nathan had lacked.

It wasn't just him that had changed. The years had left their mark on both of them. They weren't the same people they had been seven years before. And maybe, if faced with the same situation today, they'd each react differently.

Not that it would change anything now, but she couldn't help wondering how things might have been if only they had trusted each other more. *Talked* to each other, rather than reacting to the pain of the moment.

When they finished their meal, Amanda took a moment to glance around at the elegant dining room, filled with TCC members and their guests. No doubt every one of them would be spreading the word about this dinner she and Nathan had shared—but at the moment, she just didn't care.

Seated across the linen-draped table from him drinking a cup of coffee, Amanda said, "Thank you. For... bringing me here. I had a great time."

"Good." He glanced at their bill, tucked money inside, then set the black leather folder at the edge of the table. Lifting his own coffee cup, he toasted her and said, "So did I, but the night's not over yet."

"Really? What could possibly top that fabulous dinner?"

"Dessert."

She had to laugh. "Nathan, we both passed on dessert, remember?"

"You won't pass on the one I've got in mind," he assured her.

Amanda looked into his eyes and in the dancing candlelight, she read *desire* in those depths. Tingles of something expectant, something amazing, went off like sparklers in the pit of her belly and even lower.

A deep, throbbing ache pounded out inside her to the rhythm of her own heartbeat and the longer she held his gaze, the faster that rhythm became. Here was the danger, she told herself sternly. And if she had a single ounce of common sense, she'd ask him to take her home. Now.

But she knew she wasn't going to do that.

It had been seven long years since she and Nathan had been alone together. Seven years since she'd felt this sizzle of bone-deep attraction. Years since she'd been able to look into those chocolate-brown eyes and see the need she saw now.

No. No matter what happened next, she wouldn't be leaving him. Not yet.

"Well, now I'm intrigued," she managed to say.

"Then let's get going." He stood up and held one hand out to her.

She only hesitated a moment before laying her hand in his and allowing him to draw her to her feet. Their gazes met and in the quiet elegance of the room, it felt as if explosions were going off all around them but only *they* could feel them. If interested gazes followed them as they left, Amanda was oblivious to them.

Nathan led her out of the club, into the warm, moist air of a Texas summer's evening. Wherever they were headed next, she knew there was nowhere else she'd rather be.

Six

As they drove through town and took a turn in the direction of the Battlelands, Amanda looked at Nathan's profile. There was a slight smile on his face, but that told her nothing other than that he was pleased with himself. *Hmm.*

"Are we going to the ranch house?"

He glanced at her and smiled. "You'll see."

Why was he being so secretive? What was he up to?

She could play along, so she said, "It'd be nice to see Jake and Terri again. Been a long time since I've seen their kids."

"Uh-huh. You will eventually."

So, probably not going there right now. Okay, fine. She could be patient. To a point.

"How're you and Pam getting along these days?"

The question caught her off guard and made her a little uncomfortable at the same time.

"About the same," she said. "She's glad I'm there in the diner, but I think she'd rather if I could phone in the work from somewhere else."

He frowned. "She's got some issues with you."

"There's a news flash," she murmured. She had a couple of issues with Pam, too, now that she knew her sister had dated Nathan. Probably shouldn't matter since she and Nathan were *so* done when it had happened. But it *did* matter, darn it. She didn't like her big sister making a move on her ex. And one of these days, she and Pam were going to have to talk about that. But for now, she changed the subject. "Speaking of families, how're Jake and Terri doing?"

Now he gave her a *real* smile. "They're great. I know you've kept up with what's going on here in Royal, so I'm guessing you know they have twin boys and a little girl?"

"Yeah," she said, smiling wistfully. "Last time I came home to visit my dad before he—well, I made sure you were nowhere around and I met Terri and the kids in town."

Nodding, he said only, "The twins are in kindergarten now and Emily's talking all the time."

A small ache settled in her chest, thinking about Nathan's nephews and niece. Children always did that to her, though—made her remember that she'd been cheated out of her child. Amanda had been playing what-if for more than seven years—wondering how her life might be different if only she hadn't lost Nathan's child. They'd have married, of course—Nathan wouldn't have had it any other way. But would they be happy? Or would he have always felt trapped by circumstances? Would she always wonder if he really loved her or had married her solely out of duty? Questions she would never have the answers to.

She tried to shake them off. "Emily's almost two now, isn't she?"

"Yeah, and a beauty. Has Jake wrapped around her tiny fingers, too." He chuckled and shook his head. "Hard to believe sometimes that Jake's a father, but he's damn good at it."

So would you have been, she couldn't help thinking. And maybe his thoughts were mirroring hers because his features slid into more somber lines.

A few miles of silence filled the big black car before Nathan took a turn she recognized.

"So we're not going to the ranch house at all."

"Nope."

"We're going to the river."

"That's the plan."

Nerves jittered and Amanda told herself not to build anything out of this. After all, Nathan had grown up on this land. He and Jake had spent most of their childhoods at the river, fishing, swimming, avoiding chores. For him, this place was just a part of his life. There was no reason to believe that Nathan felt the same…affection for this spot that she did. For Amanda, this river was magical. This one slice of his family's ranch would always be special to her.

Cutting right through the heart of the Battlelands, the fast-moving river was shaded on either bank by ancient live oaks. It was cool and green and lush. As they approached, she couldn't help remembering—and didn't try too hard to stop—that she and Nathan had been in this private place when they made love for the first time so long ago.

Her heartbeat quickened as the memories inside her mind played out like a movie. She could see them both so easily. Young, eager, and for her at least, so much in love she was drowning in the overflow of emotions. Nerves had been thick, but desire was more prominent. It was as if in this one place, time had stopped. The world had dropped away and she became a part of the one man she had always wanted.

Was he remembering? Did he think about that night and all the nights that had followed? Did he have the same regrets she did? Or had he really moved on from their shared past—and if he had, why were they here together now?

The sun was so low now, that only the barest hint of color remained in the sky. Amanda turned her head to the side, looking away from Nathan. What was she supposed to think about this? What was he expecting? Was he deliberately trying to recreate that night? Did he really think that after all these years, all it would take is this one romantic setting and time would roll back?

Oh, God. What if he was right?

The Texas landscape stretched out for miles beneath a faintly rose-colored sky. Grasses waved in a sultry wind on either side of the lonely road and Amanda drew an uneasy breath. Years without Nathan and now, in a single day, he was wiping away the emptiness and drawing her back into a net designed to reawaken emotions she'd thought long buried. How could he take her from fury to desire so easily? And how could she defend her heart against him when all she really wanted was what they'd once had?

"Look familiar?" he asked, voice deep enough to rumble along her spine like tentative fingertips.

"Really does," she said, steeling herself before she turned to look at his profile in the growing darkness. She couldn't read on his face what he was thinking. As always, he had tucked his emotions away, offering the world no peek at what he was feeling. "Why are we here, Nathan?"

He glanced at her, then shifted his gaze back to the road. "We need to talk and I couldn't think of a more private place."

Oh, it was private all right, Amanda thought as another slow swirl of anticipation spread through her. This could be dangerous, she warned herself, but at the same time, she wasn't that young, desperately-in-love girl anymore. She'd grown and changed and lived through a heartbreak she had thought at the time would kill her. She was strong enough now to withstand the churning emotions inside. Strong enough to hold her own against a man who was an overwhelming presence in her life.

At least, she hoped she was.

Otherwise, history would repeat itself tonight—and she honestly couldn't have said which she was hoping for.

He pulled the car off the road and steered it toward a stand of oaks. She took a breath and let it out slowly, determined to keep what she was feeling to herself. Shouldn't be hard since her feelings right now were so jumbled even she was confused.

He parked the truck beside the trees, then gave her a look she couldn't interpret. "Everything should be ready. Let's go."

She had no idea what he was talking about but there was only one way to answer her questions. Besides, Amanda wasn't about to let him know that being here made her feel as if she were off balance on a high wire. She opened the door and stepped out into the warm embrace of the summer air. Tipping her head back, she glanced up at the sky. The first stars were just blinking in and out of existence as clouds scudded past. The wind was soft, like a warm caress, as she walked around the front of the car to join Nathan. "What're you up to?"

He smiled. "Come with me and see."

He held out one hand toward her and Amanda hesitated only a moment before laying her palm against his. She was in this far, she told herself, no point in trying to back out now. Besides, she was curious.

Why had he brought her here? What was *ready?* And who was this man, anyway? Less than a week ago, he'd told her flat out that he wanted her to leave town. Tonight, he was being Prince Charming. Tall, dark, gorgeous and using his smile like a well-honed weapon.

She was completely unsteady and she thought that was exactly the way he wanted her.

Nathan gave her hand a gentle squeeze, then led her through the trees to the river. The whisper of leaves sounded overly loud, like hushed conversations you couldn't quite make out, and the muted roar of the river grew louder as they walked closer. Wind plucked at her hair, her heels wobbled on the sunbaked ground. Nathan lifted branches out of their way as they passed and she felt herself slipping further and further into the past as memories became as thick as the shadows.

They stepped free of the trees and Amanda stopped dead, pulling her hand free of Nathan's to stare at what lay in front of her. A blue-and-white quilt was spread out on the grass. A hurricane lamp was lit, the flame flickering in the soft breeze. A cooler sat at one side of the blanket and two place settings of china and crystal were laid out, just waiting for them.

It had been different in the past, she thought, mind racing as the years rolled back and suddenly she was a shy, nervous high school senior again. Nathan was home from college and he'd brought her here, to "their spot."

He had talked about school, what he was doing, who he was meeting, and all she could do was look at him, storing up image after image in her mind so that when he left again, she wouldn't feel so alone.

They'd had a picnic, right here. Nathan had positioned his car so that the headlights shone down on them and the car radio had provided music. They'd talked and laughed and made plans for a misty future neither of them could fully imagine.

And then they'd made love, right here, beneath the stars, for the first time. Everything had changed for them that night. She could still remember his face, as he rose over her, as she took him inside her. The surge of love, of need, filled her now as it had then and had her turning to look at the man beside her.

"What are you doing, Nathan?"

"Remembering," he said, his gaze fixed on the scene laid out in front of them. Then he turned those eyes on her. "Since you've been back I've been doing a lot of that."

"Me, too."

"And you remember what happened here?"

"Not likely to forget," she said with a lightness she didn't feel.

"Good," he said and took her hand again, drawing her toward the scene so meticulously laid out.

It really didn't matter, but she heard herself ask, "Who did all of this?"

"Louisa," he told her just before he eased down to the quilt and drew her down beside him. "She probably had Henry drive her out here and help, but she packed the cooler and set everything up."

Louisa Diaz, the housekeeper at Battlelands. She'd been running that ranch house for twenty years. Of course Nathan would go to her for help. "Wasn't she curious about why you wanted this set up?"

"If she was, she'd never admit it," he said, opening the cooler to draw out a bottle of chilled white wine. He poured two glasses and handed her one. "We've got strawberries and whipped cream and some of Louisa's famous pecan cookies, too."

She stared at the golden liquid in her glass. She was still off-kilter. He'd gone to so much trouble, setting all of this up, it made her wonder what was behind it all. Just memories? Or was there something more? "It seems you've thought of everything."

"I think so."

"The question remains," she said. "Why?"

He sighed heavily, impatiently. And suddenly he seemed more like the Nathan she'd been dealing with since returning to Royal rather than the younger man she'd given her heart to.

"Does there have to be a reason? Can't we just enjoy it?"

Enjoy it. Reliving a memory that was so cherished it still haunted her dreams? Remember a time when she'd had the world at her fingertips—only to lose it a year later? Pain floated just beneath the surface and Amanda had to fight it back. If she knew what he wanted, expected, maybe this would be easier. But because she couldn't read him, she was left to stumble around in the dark. She took a sip of wine, letting the dry, icy flavor ease the tightness in her throat.

Silence blossomed between them and seemed to grow unchecked for what felt like an eternity before Nathan spoke, shattering the stillness.

"There's no great plan here, Amanda." His voice was deep, and each word seemed to rumble along her spine.

"I just wanted to bring you to a place where we could talk."

"And you chose *here*."

A flicker of a smile touched his mouth then faded almost instantly. "You're not the only one who remembers, you know. This was a good spot for us, once."

"Yes," she agreed, her own voice sounding strained and rough. "It was. But Nathan—"

He shook his head. "But nothing. We're here. We'll talk. Have dessert. Relax, Amanda."

Relax?

This from the most tightly wound man she'd ever known?

She looked into his brown eyes and tried to see beyond what he was showing her. But he'd clearly gotten more adept over the years at hiding what he was thinking, feeling, and Amanda was left to take him at his word. Dangerous? Maybe.

But she couldn't ask him to take her home now. She'd look as though she were afraid to be here alone with him and she wouldn't give him that much power. Besides, she could consider this a test of her own resolve. If she and Nathan were going to live here in Royal together, then she had to get past the desire that swept through her every time he was near. She could hardly live her life in a constant state of expectation.

"Okay," she said at last, taking another sip of her wine. "We'll talk."

He gave her a quick, disarming grin that jolted her heartbeat into a thundering gallop and she knew that for her, at least, there wouldn't be any *relaxing* happening tonight.

"I came better prepared this time, too," he said and reached behind the cooler for a small, battery-operated radio. He turned it on and a woman's voice soared into the shadows, singing of love. "Remember the battery on my old truck died that night? Left the radio playing too long and we had to use the ranch walkie-talkie to get Henry to come out and give us a jump?"

She remembered. She also remembered the knowing look Henry had given the two of them. But the ranch foreman hadn't said a word. He'd only gotten Nathan's truck running again and then left.

"That was embarrassing," she said with a sad smile.

"It was," he agreed, then gave her another quick grin. "But it was worth it."

Her hand tightened on the slender base of the crystal wineglass. Nathan was pushing past all of her defenses, one smile at a time.

She turned away from him and looked out over the river. At its widest point, it was no more than six feet across, but it was a wild river, fed from the distant mountains and left unchecked. The water frothed on the surface, slapping against the banks and over rocks worn smooth over time. While she watched, a trout jumped from the water only to splash back down. Wind sighed through the trees, rattling the leaves.

It was perfect.

A summer night, with the stars overhead. Soft music playing accompaniment to the roar of the river and the man who had been the great love of her life at her side. How many times had she wished for just this over the years?

She looked at Nathan as he reached into the cooler and pulled out two cookies. Handing one to her, he smiled and said, "You always did like Louisa's pecan cookies."

Her heart fisted in her chest. He looked so damn… harmless. And he so wasn't.

"You're evil," she said, nipping the cookie from his fingers and taking a bite.

He nodded. "You used to like that about me."

"There are a lot of things I used to like."

"But not anymore." The words were clipped. Cool.

"I didn't say that."

"Didn't have to," he told her and then shrugged as he took a bite of his cookie. "I feel the same way."

"Good to know," she muttered, as her foolishly hopeful heart sunk a little in her chest.

"Things've changed," he said.

"If that's what you brought me out here to tell me," Amanda said, "you wasted your time. I already knew that."

"But the thing is," he said, as if she hadn't spoken at all, "*some* things don't change."

He reached out and stroked the tip of his fingers down the back of her hand and along her arm. Amanda shivered.

"Not fair." She pulled her hand free of him and dropped the cookie to the quilt before she stood up and moved to the edge of the river.

Music continued to sail into the deepening night. The river rushed on and, above her, the stars were glittering against the dark sky.

She heard him stand, then walk up behind her. When his hands dropped onto her shoulders, she was already braced for the heat that poured from his body into hers.

"Why the hell should I play fair?" he demanded and turned her around to face him.

"Why are you playing at all?" she countered and waited, watching his features in the indistinct light.

"Because I can't get you out of my head," he admitted, his voice harsh and deep, as if it were crawling up from the center of him.

If he could admit at least that much, then she could, too. "I feel the same way."

He slid his hands up and down her upper arms as if chasing away a chill she didn't have. In fact, she was so hot at the moment, she couldn't imagine *ever* being cold again.

Amanda took a breath, tipped her head back to look up at him and said, "Wine. Cookies. Music." She waved one hand at the frothy river beside them. "This place. What is it you want, Nathan? Truth."

"Truth." He tasted the word as if trying to decide if he liked the idea of it or not. Finally, though, he nodded and said, "Truth is, Amanda, there's a lot of history between us and until we get it sorted out, life in Royal's going to be harder than it has to be for both of us."

Disappointment flashed through her before she could stop it. Of course that's why he'd done all this. To soften her up. To make her malleable enough to agree to however he wanted to handle things. So much for change, she thought glumly.

"We've already had our 'talk,' Nathan."

"Yeah, we did," he agreed. "But it wasn't enough."

She pulled away from him and walked even closer to the river's edge, where spray reached up from the water's surface to kiss her skin. She turned her face up to the sky and fixed her gaze on one star in particular. It was a focus point, to center her thoughts, to gather her frazzled nerves.

She didn't want to talk about the past anymore. It only brought pain. Still watching that star, she asked, "What more is there to say, Nathan?"

She heard him move to stand behind her again. She

felt the heat of his body reaching out for hers. Felt the frisson of something incredible that she *always* felt when close to Nathan.

Once again, his hands came down on her shoulders and a whip of electricity snaked through her in an instant. She closed her eyes and took a breath to steady herself—an idea that went to hell the moment he started speaking. "Can we leave the past where it is, Amanda? Live here in town without going back there?"

"I want to," she said and it was the truth. The past was pain and she'd had enough of that to last a lifetime.

"Then we make a pact. We deal with the present. Starting fresh."

"Just like that?" Was it even possible? she asked herself.

"Won't be easy," he admitted, "but it's easier than hauling the past around with us wherever we go."

It sounded good, but she wasn't as sure as he was that it could be done. But, talking with him, being with him, without the hurtful memories, was worth taking the chance.

"A pact," she agreed and held out one hand.

He looked at it, smiled, then took her hand in his, smoothing his fingers over her knuckles. His voice was soft, low and as mesmerizing as the rush of the river below.

"You're still in my blood, Amanda."

Her heart jumped into high gear and she swayed on her feet. But his hands only tightened on her shoulders. He bent his head until his mouth was beside her ear. His voice came again and his warm breath dusted her skin.

"I think about you. Dream about you. *Want* you."

"Nathan…" Her blood felt as if it were bubbling in her veins.

He spun her around, pulled her close and took her right hand in his left. Confused, Amanda only stared at him, until he said, "Dance with me."

He didn't give her a chance to answer. To decide yes or no. Instead, he began to sway to the music and she let herself move with him. He held her tightly, her body pressed along the length of his and she felt…everything, just as he'd wanted her to.

Her body lit up inside as desire pulsed like a beacon deep within her. He must have sensed it. Must have felt her body's surrender because he dipped his head to steal a hard, fast kiss that left her reeling.

"Tell me you don't the feel the same damn thing," he demanded.

Amanda knew that if she looked into his eyes again, the very foundation of what little self-control she'd managed to cling to would be shaken. But she couldn't resist. Couldn't deprive herself of the chance to see those dark brown eyes flashing with need again.

The moment she did, she felt herself falling into a whirlwind of emotion. Long-buried feelings resurfaced with a vengeance and were tangled up with something new. Something still fragile, but so much deeper than anything she'd known before.

Their dance ended abruptly. He shifted his grip on her, sliding his hands up to cup her face. His thumbs traced the edges of her cheekbones and his gaze moved over her features hungrily. She felt every nerve in her body leap to attention. Every square inch of her wanted him so desperately she trembled with the need.

It would be so easy to give in, she thought wildly as she lost herself in the dark chocolate of his eyes. To surrender to her body's demands. To push away the past and think only of the now. But where would that put them? Where would they go from here?

"Nathan, this is crazy...."

"Nothing wrong with crazy," he murmured and leaned in to leave a light-as-a-feather kiss on her forehead.

She swallowed hard. "But if we do this—it will only make living in this town together harder."

He snorted a laugh. "I can't get much harder."

"Oh, God." Her breath caught in her lungs as he pulled her in close to him. Close enough to discover that he was right. Much harder and he'd turn to stone.

A burn started low and deep within her, spreading with a swiftness that made her feel as if she had a sudden fever. A fever only Nathan could assuage.

Shaking her head both at her own thoughts and at him, she pulled free and took a staggering step backward just for an extra measure of safety. Not that she was afraid of Nathan. No, she was more afraid that her good intentions would be blown out of the water by her own need.

"Damn it, Amanda," he said roughly. "You want this, too. I can feel it."

"Yes," she admitted when she could talk around the knot lodged in her throat. "I do. But I'm not going to do it."

"Why the hell not?"

"Because it wouldn't solve anything, Nathan."

He threw both hands high and wide then let them fall to his sides again. "Why the hell does it have to *solve* anything? We're not kids anymore. Can't it just be what it is and leave it at that?"

"Not between us," she said, a little steadier now that he wasn't touching her. "It's never simple between us, Nathan, and you know it."

He shoved both hands into his jeans pockets and let

his head fall back briefly as if looking for patience in the wide Texas sky above them. When he looked at her again, he said, "You can't let go of the past, can you?"

Bristling a little, she countered, "Can you?"

Shaking his head, he pulled one hand free of his pocket and ran it over his face. "Not entirely, no."

"Then how can us sleeping together help?"

"How can it hurt?" he argued.

"Nathan, sex doesn't solve a problem, it only creates *new* problems."

"Maybe that's enough for now," he said tightly.

"Not for me," she answered.

"What the hell do you want, then?"

A thousand disjointed thoughts swept through her mind in one confusing instant. What did she want? *Him,* mostly. She'd tried to fool herself into believing that she just wanted to move on. To find a new man and build a life with him.

But there were no other men for Amanda. There was only Nathan, now and always. She wanted what they hadn't had before. Trust. Love. A future. And she knew Nathan wasn't interested in anything like that.

So that left her exactly where?

Alone, she thought. She'd be alone.

He closed the gap between them in one long stride and grabbed her up close again. Here was the danger, she thought. Feeling him pressed close to her, knowing that he wanted her as much as she wanted him. But want wasn't enough, as they'd already discovered.

"Don't make this harder," she whispered.

"Why should I make it easy?" he asked.

She looked up at him and when he kissed her, Amanda lost herself in him. His mouth covered hers with a fierce tenderness that quickly became a dance of desperation.

Their tongues met again and again, stroking, caressing, tasting. Hunger built and spread, wrapping them both in a wash of heat that was inescapable. His hands swept up and down her back and finally came to rest on her behind. He held her tightly to him and ground his hips into hers. She gasped and lifted one leg instinctively, wrapping it around his thigh, trying, but failing to bring him even closer.

His mouth continued to overwhelm her and all of Amanda's good intentions were swept away on a tide of passion too staggering to fight. Her mind splintered under the onslaught of too many sensations. It had been so long, was her only coherent thought. So long since she'd felt his hands on her body, his breath on her face. How could she not have him? What did it matter what happened tomorrow, if tonight, she could have *this?*

One of his strong hands held her thigh up along his hip, his fingers digging into her flesh. With his free hand, he lifted the hem of her skirt, then slipped his hand beneath the hem of her panties and down to the trembling, heated core of her.

At the first brush of his fingers, Amanda gasped, and tore her mouth from his. Reeling, she tipped her head back and stared into his eyes as he stroked her hot, damp center. His brown eyes were flashing with fire and need. His breath came as fast and sharp as hers. Her fingers clutched at his shoulders, as she fought for balance and for the orgasm that was rushing toward her.

He dipped one finger and then two into her depths, stroking both inside and out as he plunged and withdrew in a rapid rhythm that tortured as it pleasured. Amanda's hips rocked into his hand as she struggled to find the release that he was promising her. Her mind was shutting down. Who needed to think when he was offering her so much to *feel?*

Again and again, she whimpered and twisted against his touch. His thumb rolled over one sensitive spot and she cried out his name in a broken voice torn from a throat nearly too tight to allow breath.

"Come for me," he whispered, kissing her mouth, her eyes, her nose. "Come now, Amanda, and let me see you shatter."

Stars shone overhead. A Texas wind caressed her bare skin. Her lover's eyes held hers. And Amanda surrendered to the inevitable with a groan of release and a whispered sigh that was his name.

Seven

She was limp in his grasp and Nathan had never felt more alive. His body hard and aching, his pulse scrambling, he continued to stroke her intimately, loving the feel of her slick flesh beneath his fingers. Her breath hitched and she jerked in his arms as her still-sensitive body reacted to his touch.

No woman in the world affected him like this one did. With just a sigh, she could inflame him or bring him to his knees. Which is why he was here, he reminded himself. This was the plan. To have sex with her again so that he could walk away. He looked down into her face and saw a soft, satisfied smile. Saw her meadow-green eyes glazed with passion. Saw the rapid pulse beat at the base of her throat and he wasn't thinking about walking away. He was thinking only of burying himself inside her. Feeling her body close around his again.

"Nathan…that was…"

"Foreplay," he groaned past the hard knot of need lodged in his throat and waited for her reaction. He touched her again and she trembled. In his arms, she felt vulnerable, soft, and every protective instinct he had roared to life. In that moment, he wanted to stand between her and the rest of the world. He wanted to always see her like this, looking up at him with stars in her eyes and a breathless plea on her lips.

Seconds ticked past as she looked into his eyes. He held perfectly still. He wouldn't touch her again until she said yes. Until she admitted that sex was the *one* thing they both could agree on. That they both needed. He hoped to hell she'd say it. If she still said no, it just might kill him.

She lifted one hand to cup his cheek and stroked her thumb along his cheekbone. "I'm tired of being sensible," she said. "I don't want to think about tomorrow. I only want tonight. With you."

He waited a beat or two, letting her words sink in. Then, for his own sanity, he demanded, "You're sure?"

She smiled and linked her arms behind his neck. "About this, yes."

"Thank God," he muttered and spun her around in a quick circle before lowering her to the quilt spread beneath the gnarled, twisted arms of the oaks surrounding them.

Quickly, they worked to clear the quilt, setting the wine aside and shifting the cooler off into the thick grass. The radio played on, music shifting now to a low, throbbing beat that seemed to echo what each of them was feeling.

They turned to each other, tearing at clothing, needing to touch only skin. Needing to feel the heat that flesh against flesh created. The summer wind slid over them as hands and mouths rediscovered the magic that pulsed between them.

Nathan couldn't seem to touch her enough. The feel of her soft, smooth skin beneath his fingers fed the fire inside that was engulfing him. His brain hazed out, his vision narrowed until all he saw was *her*. The woman who had haunted him for years. The woman he'd lost and never forgotten.

He eased back, taking a moment to just look at her, enjoy this moment when she was his again. Her hair spilled across the quilt beneath her. Her long, tanned limbs were lean and smooth and her breasts were high and full. His hands itched to cup them, to tease those pebbled nipples until she was moaning and arching into his touch.

Shaking his head, he murmured, "Been thinking about this since that first day I saw you in the diner."

She laughed a little and the sound rose over the roar of the river to become part of the music of the night. "You mean when you walked in all fiery-eyed, wanting me to leave town?"

"Yeah, only I didn't want you out of town as much as I just *wanted* you," Nathan told her, dipping his head to taste first one dark nipple and then the other.

She gasped, then sighed, a slow exhalation of breath that seemed to slide right into the heart of him. When he lifted his head again, she looked up into his eyes and said, "You hid it really well, being all crabby."

He gave her a quick grin. "Couldn't let the town gossips know what I was thinking. Hell, I didn't want *you* to know what I was thinking."

"Oh, me neither," she admitted, holding his head to her breast. Her fingers threaded through his short hair, her nails dragging across his scalp.

He was on fire. His whole damn body felt as if it were lit up from the flames about to swallow him. "Shoulda done this days ago."

"Oh, yeah," she whispered and arched into him as he moved down her body, trailing damp kisses along her skin…down her chest, along the line of her stomach and across her abdomen. She tasted of summer and smelled like a spring meadow. He was surrounded by her taste, scent, touch. And still it wasn't enough. His body ached like a bad tooth. He needed her and damned if he wanted to *need*. Being sucked into a maelstrom of emotions hadn't been the plan. The plan was simply to bed her, so he could get her out of his system once and for all.

The plan. He fought to hold on to it. To remember why it was important. Nathan Battle didn't do anything without a damn plan and once it was made, it was golden.

And yet…his brain shied away from thinking at all. Nathan wanted to concentrate solely on this moment, not what had led to it or what might come after. All he wanted right now was to revel in finally having her here, beneath his hands again.

Her body was long and slim with just the right amount of curves to tempt a man. In the starlight, her skin seemed like warm honey. He dragged the tips of his fingers across her flat belly and smiled to himself when she sucked in a gulp of air. He traced the tan lines that striped over her breasts and then along the narrow strip of paler skin that lay across the triangle of light brown curls at the juncture of her thighs.

"You wear a tiny bikini," he murmured and wished he'd seen her in it.

She smiled. "No point in wearing a big one, is there?"

"Nope, guess not," he agreed, sliding one hand down to cup her heat. "What color is it?"

She gasped and rocked her hips into his hand. "What? Color? What?"

"Your bikini, Amanda," he whispered, "what color is it?"

He dipped a finger into her heat and she hissed a breath. "Is that really important right now?"

"Humor me," he told her and swirled the tip of his finger around an already sensitive spot.

"Okay, okay, just don't stop," she ordered, then swallowed hard. "It's white. With red…" She broke off and shuddered, as he continued to stroke her with slow deliberation.

"Red what?"

"Huh? Red? Right." She nodded, licked her lips and wiggled her hips into his touch. "Red, um, dots. Polka dots."

"Sounds nice."

"Uh-huh," she whispered. "I'll be sure to show you sometime. But for right now could we…"

"You want more?" he asked, knowing she did, drawing out the suspense, the waiting, the wanting, for both of them.

"I want it all." Her eyes snapped open and she met his gaze squarely. "Honestly, Nathan, if you don't get inside me within the next minute or so…"

"You'll what?" He grinned at her, enjoying the frustration in her eyes, in her voice. "Leave?"

She blew out a breath and scowled at him. "Funny. No, I'm not leaving, but Nathan—"

He rose up over her, looked down into her eyes and whispered, "You're still so beautiful."

"I'm glad you think so." She sighed and reached for him, but he pulled back, grabbed the jeans he'd tossed aside a few minutes before and rummaged in the pockets until he came up with a foil square.

"Pretty sure of yourself, weren't you?" she asked wryly.

"Pretty sure of *us*," he told her as he ripped the foil open, then took another moment to sheathe himself.

Her expression was carefully blank as his gaze met hers and she asked, "Is there an us, Nathan?"

That was a good question, he thought, his eyes locked on hers. And he didn't have an answer. Yesterday, he might have flatly said no. Tomorrow, he might do the same. But now… "There is tonight."

A flicker of sorrow danced across her eyes and was gone again so quickly he could almost convince himself he hadn't noticed it at all. He didn't want to hurt her, but damned if he'd pretend something that wasn't so. Besides, he didn't want to think beyond the moment. *Us?* No, there was no us. But there was *now*.

"No more thinking," he murmured and ended any further conversation by taking her mouth in a kiss that left them both breathless. His brain went blank and his body took over. Her hands slid up and down his back, her neat nails scraping across his skin, letting him know that the hunger that crouched inside him lived within her, too.

The past dropped away as they found each other again in the most elemental way. Every touch was a reaffirmation of what they'd once been. Every kiss and gasped breath was a celebration of what they were discovering now. In the warm summer air, they gave and took from each other until passion was a living, breathing entity, wrapping them so tightly together they might never completely be apart again.

They rolled across the quilt, arms and legs wrapped around each other as the river rushed on and the music continued to pump into the night air. Wind whispered through the trees and their strained breathing added to the symphony.

His hands moved over her body and every touch was achingly familiar while, at the same time, it all felt new, electrifying. As if this were their first time coming together.

He pushed her over onto her back and went up on one elbow to look down at her. She looked like a summer goddess, stretched out on that blue-and-white quilt, with starlight dancing on her skin. His breath caught when she licked her lips and smiled up at him. Her eyes were glazed with a burning desire that reached out to engulf him in the same flames. The fire felt good after so many years in the cold, he thought wildly. But he wasn't about to wait another damn minute before claiming her and all she was.

He shifted, kneeling between her legs and when she parted her thighs and lifted her arms to him in welcome, he groaned in satisfaction. He pushed himself home in one long, smooth stroke and hissed out a breath at the sensation of her hot, tight body gripping his.

She gasped, lifted her legs and locked them around his hips, pulling him deeper, tighter. She arched, her hips rising to meet his, drawing him as close as she could. Then she trembled as pleasure whipped through her—a bright, white-hot thing that glittered in her eyes. He felt her pleasure with her every sigh. Felt the tension coiling in her body just from the way she moved with him.

As if they were somehow connected on a deeper level than just physically, he felt what she did, knew when he looked into her eyes how close she was to climax. He knew her as he'd known no other woman. Her body was as familiar to him as his own. Her passion as important as his own.

Her hands clutched at his back, his shoulders, his arms. Every strangled breath and sigh fed the fires inside him. His hips pistoned into hers as he withdrew from her body only to plunge deep inside her heat again.

Her gasps and sighs filled him, pushing him harder, faster, as he quickened the rhythm between them and she rushed to meet him. He took her mouth, his kiss demanding, hungry. She had demands, too. Silent, desperate demands that he met eagerly.

"Nathan. Nathan." His name became a chant that was caught up by the wind and tossed into the night sky. She whispered and pleaded, moving her body into his, fighting for the release that waited for her.

And when the first tremor hit, she clung to him, riding out wave after wave of pleasure tearing through her. Nathan felt her body fist on his as her completion took her. Only then did he give himself up to the coiled tension inside, finally releasing his stranglehold on control, surrendering to what only Amanda could do to him.

His body exploded, his mind shattered and when he collapsed against her, Amanda's arms came around him in the darkness.

Amanda's heartbeat was racing. With Nathan's heavy weight covering her, she felt, for the first time in years, *complete.* Ridiculous to admit, even to herself, but without him in her life she'd always felt as though something was missing. Something vital.

Now, here it was.

But she didn't know how long this could last.

He'd already told her that as far as he was concerned they weren't together. This was just sex. *Stupendous* sex, but just sex. If she made more of it than that, she would be setting herself up for pain and disappointment.

He shifted and rolled to one side of her, drawing her with him until she was nestled against his chest. Amanda listened to the sound of his rapid heartbeat and knew that he was as affected as she was. Some consolation in that, she supposed.

The silence between them stretched on for what seemed forever until she simply couldn't stand it anymore. Best, she told herself, to be the one to speak first. To set a tone that would let him know that she wasn't going to swoon into his arms or cry and beg him to stay.

Not that she didn't want to, but he didn't have to know that, did he?

"Nathan, that was—"

"Yeah," he agreed. "It was."

"So," she said, lifting her head to look at him, "come here often?"

He grinned, fast and sharp and her breath caught.

"Haven't been here in years," he said. "Not since—"

He stopped, but now she knew that he hadn't brought another woman to what was most definitely "their" place. Funny how much comfort that brought her. Oh, he was no monk and during the time they were apart—there had no doubt been *dozens* of women in his life. She winced at that thought. But at least he hadn't brought them here.

"It's beautiful here," she told him, glancing at the moonlight on the water.

"Yeah, it is. Look, Amanda…"

Oh, that sounded like the beginnings of a we-have-to-talk speech. Which she really didn't want to hear at the moment. She preferred the teasing, tempting Nathan who had just shattered her so completely. She didn't want to talk to the dutiful and honorable Nathan. Not now.

So she just wouldn't give him the opportunity to turn this moment into a regret-filled this-will-never-happen-again speech. Abruptly, she sat up and reached for her shirt. Dragging it on over her head, she flipped her hair back over her shoulder and asked, "How about some of that wine?"

He studied her for a long minute, then sat up and reached for his own clothes. "Sure, that'd be good."

"And cookies," she reminded him, determined to keep a cheerful, nonchalant attitude. Standing up, she stepped into her panties and then her skirt, smoothing the material before sitting down on the quilt again. "I think we need more cookies."

Once he was dressed, he sat down opposite her on the quilt and watched her warily, as if she were a time bomb with a faulty fuse and could go off any second. "Cookies."

"Why not?" she asked. "Don't you remember? Sex always gives me an appetite."

Unexpectedly, he smiled as he poured them each a fresh glass of wine. "I do remember all of the picnics we had in bed."

Stillness washed over her as memories slammed into her mind. So many nights they'd spent in bed, laughing, loving and then feeding each other whatever they'd been able to find in the refrigerator. "We had a lot of good times, Nathan."

He handed her a full glass, then clinked his to hers. "Yeah, we did. But, Amanda…"

She cut him off and saw his jaw tighten at being interrupted. "Let's just leave it there, okay? We had good times back then and we had a good time tonight. Isn't that what you said earlier? We have tonight?"

"Yeah, I did."

"So, let's enjoy it."

"You are the most confusing woman I've ever known."

Amanda laughed. "I think I'm flattered."

"You would be," he said wryly. "You always knew how to twist me around until I didn't know which end was up."

He sounded almost wistful and Amanda's heart lurched in her chest. Memories were swimming in the air between them, rising and falling as swiftly as the frothy waves on the nearby river. Amanda took a sip of her wine to ease the knot in her throat before she trusted herself to speak. "You used to like that about me."

"Yeah," he admitted. "I did."

Her gaze caught with his. "I've missed you, Nathan."

"I've missed you, too."

And maybe, Amanda told herself, for tonight, that was enough.

"You had sex."

"Piper!" Amanda jolted and looked around the diner guiltily, making sure no one was within earshot. Thankfully, most of the lunch crowd was long gone and she and her friend had the back of the diner practically to themselves. Amanda grabbed her cup of coffee for a sip, then asked, "Could you say that any louder?"

"Probably," Piper said. "Want me to try?"

"No!" Amanda shook her head and tried for a little dignity. What? Was the truth stenciled on her forehead? *I had sex with Nathan last night.* Who else had noticed? Oh, God.

"I don't know what you're talking about," Amanda told her, deciding to plead ignorance and let it go at that.

"Sure," her old friend said with a smirk. "I'll buy that. And any bridges you might have lying around."

Amanda frowned and leaned back into the rush of cool air pouring down on her from the overhead air-conditioning vent. Irritating to be read so easily—and by someone she hadn't even seen in years. Well, clearly there was no point in pretending with Piper. "Fine. Yes. You're right, Ms. Mind Reader."

Piper laughed and took a bite of the lemon meringue pie Amanda had promised her the day before. "Honey, I don't need to read your mind. It's in your eyes—not to mention the whisker burn on your neck."

She slapped one hand to the right side of her throat. A quick tingle whipped through her as she recalled how it had felt, having Nathan's whiskery cheeks buried in the curve of her neck. Of course that didn't mean she wanted the world noticing what she'd been up to. Amanda had been so sure she'd managed a makeup miracle. Now she didn't know why she had bothered.

"Honestly, I don't know how they can call that foundation 'full coverage,'" she muttered. "I should send them an email, complaining."

"You do that," Piper said with a chuckle. "So, how is Nathan?"

"He's…*good.*" Better than good. Fabulous, really. A smile curved her mouth as she remembered the night before.

By the time Amanda had gotten home, she was more tired and more energized than she'd been in years. Every cell in her body had felt as if it had just come to life after long years of sleep. She'd felt almost like Sleeping Beauty, except that Nathan wasn't exactly Prince Charming and she was no damsel in distress waiting to be rescued.

No, last night hadn't been the beginning of anything. She wouldn't fool herself into hoping for more when she was pretty sure that Nathan was considering what had happened at the river to be just a good time.

But it had been more. For her, at least. Despite what she had said to Nathan, Amanda wasn't a sex-is-just-sex kind of girl. If sex didn't mean anything, what was the point to it all? No. The only reason she had slept with Nathan was because she still had feelings for him.

"And so," Piper persisted, "this means you're back together?"

"No," Amanda said, shaking her head. "I'm not kidding myself about that. Last night was just...last night." She wasn't going to invent dreams and let them soar only to come crashing back to earth again. She'd already lived through that pain once and really had no desire to do it one more time. "Nathan and I didn't work out before, remember?"

Piper winced. "I know, but you're both different now."

"Are we?" she wondered aloud. Amanda had been doing a lot of thinking about this since the night before. Sure, they were older, hopefully wiser, but was it enough to make a new relationship possible? Did Nathan even want a new relationship with her?

She was getting a headache.

"I don't know," she said finally. "Nathan will always be important to me. But—"

"No buts," Piper insisted. "There don't have to be any buts."

Amanda chuckled. "In a perfect world..."

A loud noise from across the room caught her attention and Amanda glanced at her sister, who was slamming the coffeepot back onto the warming burner. It was a wonder the pot hadn't shattered. Amanda frowned when Pam turned her head long enough to fire a glare at her.

"Wow, Pam's in a good mood today."

"Yeah," Amanda said. "She's been like this all morning."

"Not surprising," Piper told her. "She's been after Nathan for years and she's probably guessed by now that she's never going to get him."

"What?"

"You probably know that she and Nathan went out a couple times while you were gone." When Amanda nodded, Piper continued. "Well, it didn't go anywhere. Nathan wasn't interested. And let's just say if I could notice the whisker burn on your neck, then Pam noticed, too."

"Perfect." So not only was her life in turmoil over Nathan, but she also had to worry about her sister's anger, too.

Piper shot a quick glance at Pam over her shoulder before turning back to Amanda. She leaned in closer to say, "Everybody knows Pam's been crazy about Nathan since school. Just like everyone knows that she's jealous of you."

"Everyone but me," Amanda said and picked up her coffee for a sip. Yes, she knew Pam had had a crush on Nathan when they were in school. What girl *hadn't* back then? But jealous? "Why should she be jealous of me?"

"Hmm…" Piper pretended to ponder the question. "Let's see. You're younger, prettier, you've got a college degree she never bothered to go after and most importantly—you have Nathan."

"Had."

Piper's eyebrows lifted. "You sure about the past tense, there?"

The old-fashioned jukebox was playing in the corner, some classic rock and roll song streaming through the one large speaker. A couple of people sat at the counter having a late lunch and two elderly women occupied a booth and shared tea and cake. Most people around here stayed home on Sunday and had family meals together so it was a slow day for the diner, which was both a burden and a blessing.

Since Amanda hadn't gotten much sleep the night before, she was grateful to not be so busy. But not being busy meant that Pam had the time to make Amanda's life miserable. Which, she had to say, her sister was getting really good at.

But the worst part about a slow day at the diner? It gave Amanda too much time to think. Too much time to wonder about what had happened the night before between her and Nathan. And no matter how much thought she put into the situation, she was no closer to understanding it.

She knew that the two of them together were magical. But she also knew that didn't guarantee a happy ending.

"Whatever you're thinking," Piper said quietly, "you should stop it. Doesn't look like it's making you happy."

"It's not." Amanda took a bite of her pie and let the dense lemon flavoring explode on her tongue. When she'd swallowed, she said, "I don't know that last night meant a darn thing, Piper."

"If you want it to mean something, it will."

She laughed shortly. "Not that simple. What if I want it and Nathan doesn't?"

"*Make* him want it," Piper suggested with a shrug.

"Oh, well, that should be easy," she mused.

"No, it won't," Piper told her. "Nothing worth having comes easy. The question is, do you want him?"

"Wish that was the only question," she murmured and finished off her pie.

<u>Eight</u>

A few days later, Amanda realized she had forgotten just how much she enjoyed small-town Fourth of July celebrations.

All of Royal seemed to be gathered at the park. The sun glared down from a brassy sky and promised to get even hotter as the day wore on. Nobody seemed to mind much. Texans were a tough bunch and no matter how miserable the heat and humidity, they didn't let it get in the way of a good time.

There was a community baseball game in full swing on the diamond. Picnic blankets dotted the grass and families settled in for a long day that wouldn't end until after the big fireworks show. Kids raced through the park, laughing and shouting, oblivious to the heat that was already beginning to wilt their parents.

Dozens of game booths were scattered around the park, each of them offering chances to win everything from goldfish to teddy bears. And at the far end of the parking lot, a small carnival had set up shop and the taped calliope music was fiercely cheerful.

Amanda grinned at the little boy in front of the booth she was manning. He was about six, with a missing front tooth, hair that was too long and a T-shirt already stained with what looked like mustard. At the moment, he was biting his lip and considering the last softball he held. He had already gone through most of his pocket money, buying chances to knock over bowling pins with the softball to win a prize.

"It sure is harder than it looks, ma'am," he said with a shake of his head.

"It is, isn't it?" Amanda was trying to figure out a way she could "help" the boy win, when Nathan walked up.

A now familiar flash of excitement zipped through her at just the sight of him. He wore a beige uniform shirt, with the sheriff star on his chest glittering in the sunlight. His jeans were faded, his boots were scuffed and his hat was pulled low enough on his forehead to throw his eyes into shadow.

It had been a few days since their night by the river and since then, things had been…different between them. Well, of course—they'd had sex. Things would be *different,* not that they'd slept together since. But there was less tension between them. And, she thought wistfully, more confusion.

"Afternoon, Amanda," he said, then shifted his gaze to the boy. "Carter, how you doing?"

"Not so good, Sheriff," the boy answered and scowled at the one softball he had left to throw. "I figured I'd win one of those teddy bears for my baby sister." He shrugged. "Girls like that sort of thing, but like I told Miss Amanda, it's a lot harder than it looks."

"What're you doin' running around on your own? Where're your folks?"

Carter pointed over one shoulder at a young family sitting on a blanket under a tree. "They're all right there."

"That's good." Nathan dropped one hand on the boy's narrow shoulder, then ruffled his hair. "Maybe we can try together, what do you think?"

The boy looked up at him as if Nathan were wearing a cape and had just swooped in to the rescue.

Amanda watched Nathan with the child and swallowed a sigh. If she hadn't lost their baby, it would now be about this boy's age. Boy? Or girl? It had been too early to know at the time, but that hadn't stopped her from wondering. From picturing what her child with Nathan might have been like. And in this boy, with the light brown hair and brown eyes, she saw...what might have been. And the tiny ache that settled in the corner of her heart felt like an old friend.

"How about I give you a hand?" Nathan asked, then flashed a smile at Amanda. "That is, if Miss Amanda doesn't mind."

"That'd be great, Sheriff," Carter answered, then turned to Amanda and asked, "Is it okay?"

"Well, you know, back when the sheriff was in high school, he was the star pitcher."

Nathan smiled at her as if pleased she remembered. How could she forget? She'd spent hours in the bleachers at Royal high school, watching Nathan play ball. And every time he went up to bat, he'd look at her first, as if he were checking she was still there, still watching.

"Really?" Carter brightened up even further.

"No pressure," Nathan muttered with a shake of his head.

"C'mon, Sheriff," she said and stood back as Nathan

took the ball from Carter and tossed it in the air a couple times to get its weight. "Show us what you've got."

He nodded at the boy then winked at Amanda. "Well, now, let's see what we can do."

He wound up, threw the ball and sent three bowling pins clattering to the floor. Carter whooped with delight and even Amanda had to applaud.

"You won, Sheriff!" Carter clapped, too. "Nice throw!"

Amanda picked up one of the teddy bears lining the prize shelf and handed it to Nathan, who gave it to Carter.

"My baby sister's gonna like this a lot. Thanks, Sheriff!" Clutching the bear, the boy took off and was swallowed by the crowd moments later.

Amanda looked up at Nathan and smiled in approval. "That was nice of you."

"Carter's a good kid." Nathan shrugged and leaned one hip against the edge of the booth. His gaze swept up and down her body thoroughly until she felt a heat that had nothing to do with a hot Texas day.

"So," he said, "how'd you come to be running the PTA booth?"

"Patti Delfino had to take care of the baby so I offered to help."

"Falling right back into life in Royal, huh?"

"It wasn't that hard," she said. Although being around him *was*. She didn't know where they stood. Didn't know what was going to happen next. They'd had that one incredible night together and since then…nothing. Well, except for him stopping in at the diner a few times a day. But they hadn't been alone again and she was hungering for him. Did he feel the same? Or had he considered that night a one-time thing? A sort of goodbye to the past?

The questions running through her mind were driving her crazy.

A little girl ran up and patted Nathan's thigh to get his attention. When he looked down at her, the girl's big blue eyes fixed on him. "I wanna teddy bear, too."

"You do, huh?" He grinned and looked at Amanda. "Apparently Carter's bragging how he got hold of his bear."

"And what are you going to do about it, Sheriff?" Amanda teased.

He dug in his wallet and slapped down a twenty-dollar bill. "Guess I'll be throwing softballs."

The little girl clapped and bounced up and down in excitement. Amanda handed him three softballs to get him started and then stood back and watched as he mowed through the prize shelf. Over and over again, he threw the balls at the bowling pins and soon he had a crowd of kids surrounding him, each of them waiting to be handed one of the stuffed bears.

Amanda watched him, saw his eyes shining with pleasure, heard him laughing with the children and a part of her wept for what they might have had together. He was so good with kids. He would have been a wonderful father if only...

By the time it was over, the bears were all gone and the last of the children had wandered off, clutching their prizes. When it was just Nathan and Amanda again, he said, "Looks like you're out of business. What do you say we find Patti and hand over the cash box, then you and I go join Jake and Terri for some lunch?"

"Aren't you on duty?"

"I can keep an eye on things—and you—at the same time."

Pleasure whipped through her as she grabbed up the metal cash box and swung her legs over the side of the booth. "I think I'll let you."

He took her hand in his and as they walked through the mob of people, Amanda felt that sense of rightness again. Did he feel it, too?

The rest of the day went by in a sort of blur. It had been so long since Amanda had really enjoyed a Fourth of July. When she was away, she would sit on the balcony of her apartment and watch distant fireworks alone. She could have gone out with friends, but her heart hadn't been in it. Instead, she had wished to be back here. At home in Royal.

And the town wasn't disappointing her.

After lunch with Jake and Terri and the kids, Nathan and Amanda spent the rest of the day with them. Nathan was called away a few times to settle disputes ranging from an argument over the umpire's call on the baseball field to a broken windshield in the parking lot. He always came back, though, and Amanda saw that with his family, Nathan was more relaxed. More ready to enjoy himself than she remembered him ever being before.

Back in the day, he'd been too driven, too determined to carve out the life he wanted to take the time to slow down with family. Maybe, she thought, they'd both changed enough over the years that they could find a way back to each other.

With the fireworks about to start, Jake and Nathan walked the kids over to get some Sno-Kones, while Amanda and Terri settled on the quilt and waited for the show.

"I'm so glad you're home," Terri said abruptly.

"Oh, me, too. Believe me." Amanda looked around the park at all the familiar faces and smiled to herself. Older couples sat in lawn chairs, holding hands, gazes locked on the sky. Young marrieds herded small children and the older kids raced through the park waving sparklers, flashes of light trailing behind them like high-tech bread crumbs.

Whatever happened between her and Nathan, Amanda was home to stay. "I really did miss this place."

"Hmm," Terri mused. "You missed Royal? Or Nathan?"

"Sadly, both." Terri knew her too well to believe a lie, so why not admit the truth? "But that doesn't mean anything, Terri."

"Sure it does," she said, biting into one of the last pecan cookies with relish. "It means you guys belong together. Everybody knows that."

"Everybody but Nathan," Amanda muttered, glancing at her friend. Terri was tiny, trim and summer cute in a hot pink sundress with spaghetti straps. Her long, dark brown hair was in a single braid that hung down the middle of her back.

As Amanda watched her, Terri licked a crumb from her bottom lip and popped the rest of the cookie into her mouth. As she chewed, she said, "Nathan's been on edge since you got back."

"Great. On edge."

Terri just stared at her for a second, then shook her head. "Seriously? Do you know nothing about men? On edge is just where you want them. That way they're never sure which way to turn."

"And that's a good thing?" Amanda asked with a laugh.

"Absolutely." Terri grabbed a bottle of water and took a long drink. "Why would you want Nathan all relaxed and complacent about you?"

She hadn't thought about it that way, but now she was. Maybe Terri had a point. Kicking off her sandals, Amanda folded her legs under her. Bracing her elbows on her knees, she cupped her chin in her hands and looked at her friend. "So, you keep Jake guessing, do you?"

"All the time, sweetie," Terri assured her with a laugh. "Why do you think he adores me so?"

"Because he's smart enough to know how good he's got it?"

"Well, that, too." Terri laughed. "But mostly because I keep him on his toes. He's never sure what I'll do next."

As she reached for another cookie, Amanda shook her head. "How do you stay so thin when you eat like this?"

"Won't be thin for long," Terri said with a smile and a gentle pat on her belly. "I'm pregnant again."

Instantly, Amanda felt a quick slice of envy poke at her. Terri had three wonderful kids and a husband who really did adore her. While Amanda was happy for her friend, it was hard not to wish that her own life was as full.

"I saw that," Terri said and reached out to pat Amanda's hand. "Sweetie, I'm sorry. I didn't mean to make you feel badly."

"Don't be silly." Amanda squeezed her hand and shook her head. "I'm happy for you. Really. I just..." She looked out over the park again, toward the booth where Jake and Nathan shepherded twin five-year-old boys and a darling two-year-old girl. As she watched, Nathan scooped up little Emily and cradled her in one arm. The girl laid her head on Nathan's chest and snuggled in. Smiling sadly, she looked at Terri and admitted, "Sometimes I just wish things were different."

Terri sighed. "Sweetie, maybe it's time to stop wishing and start *making* things different."

Amanda looked back at Nathan in time to see him laugh at something one of the twins said. A jolt of longing hit her hard. That smile of his would always turn her to butter.

Maybe Terri was right, she thought. Maybe it was time to take a stand. To fight for what she wanted. And what she wanted was Nathan.

When the fireworks started, Nathan settled down beside her and Amanda leaned her head back against his broad chest. They stared up at the sky, which was exploding with sound and color. He wrapped one arm around her and held her close and, despite the fact that they were surrounded by people, Amanda felt as if they were the only two people in the world.

The next morning, Amanda woke up to Nathan's kiss at the back of her neck. She smiled lazily, remembering the long night before. After the fireworks, they'd come back to her apartment over the diner and created a few fireworks of their own.

"Good morning."

"Mmm," he murmured, dragging one hand down her side, following the dip of her waist and the curve of her hip. "It's looking pretty good right now."

She smiled, then sighed as his hand moved to slide across her behind. Somehow, they'd crossed a bridge yesterday. Maybe it was the hours spent with his family. Maybe it was just that enough time had passed for them both to realize that they wanted to be together. Whatever the reason, Nathan had stayed here with her last night, not caring that the town gossips would surely notice his car parked in front of her place all night.

When he shifted his hand to cup her breast, Amanda hissed in a breath and rolled onto her back so she could look up at him. She didn't think she'd ever tire of that. His dark eyes could flash with temper, shine with kindness or, like right now, glitter with desire. She lifted one hand to his cheek and scrubbed at his whiskers with her thumb.

Smiling, she whispered, "I'm glad you stayed last night."

"Me, too," he told her and gave her a long, slow, deep kiss that quickened the still-burning embers inside her. "And I'd really like to stay now, but I've gotta get to work."

She glanced at the window, where the soft, early-morning light was sifting through the curtains. "Me, too."

He kissed her again and tenderness welled up between them, stinging Amanda's eyes and tearing at her heart. This is what she wanted. Nathan, all of Nathan. Not just the fire that quickened her blood and made her heart race—but the warmth that touched her soul and made her yearn.

When he lifted his head and looked down into her eyes, he whispered, "Maybe I don't have to leave right this minute."

She nodded and cupped his face in her hands. "I think I could spare some time, too."

And this time when he kissed her, she forgot about everything else and let herself slide into a sensual haze that only he could create.

"Did you hear that?" Pam stopped in front of JT and automatically refilled his coffee cup.

"Hear what?"

"Hannah Poole was telling Bebe Stryker about Nathan's car being out front of the diner all night."

JT sighed, shook his head and took a sip of coffee. "What do you care about that?"

She looked at him as if he'd just grown another head. "The whole town's talking about Nathan and Amanda. If it gets bad enough, he'll leave again."

"Not a chance," JT muttered but Pam hardly heard him.

"I can't believe Amanda's starting up with him again." Huffing out a breath, she added, "I can't believe Nathan would *want* her again. After what she did…"

JT's eyes narrowed. "Thought you didn't like gossip."

She flushed. "I don't."

"Then maybe you should give your sister the benefit of the doubt on all that old stuff." Frowning, he added, "I never believed it for a second."

"You, too?" she demanded in a harsh whisper. "You're going to be on Amanda's side?"

"Not taking sides," he said, pausing for a sip of coffee. "I'm just saying, you're her sister. You should know her better than anyone else and I'm thinking you didn't believe any of that nonsense people were talking about years ago, either."

She flushed again and wasn't happy about JT making her feel guilty. "It's always Amanda," she said bitterly. "Nathan's never looked at me the way he looks at her. How can *anyone* be so blind?"

"Was wondering the same thing myself," JT answered and stood up. He dropped money on the counter and said, "I'll see you tomorrow, Pam."

She watched him go and felt a twinge of regret for fighting with her best friend, but honestly. Since he *was* her best friend, shouldn't he understand how she felt about all of this? Shouldn't he be on *her* side?

The more she thought about it, the angrier she became, and watching Hannah Poole scurry to yet another table to spread the word about Nathan and Amanda was all the impetus she needed to go and face down her sister.

"What is wrong with you?"

Amanda's sister stormed into the office at the back of the diner a couple of hours later. Morning sunshine streamed through the window and the scent of coffee and fresh cinnamon rolls flavored the air-conditioned air. Amanda sighed and dropped her pen to the desk as the last, lingering effects of early-morning lovemaking disappeared with one look at the woman facing her. Pam's eyes were narrowed, a flush stained her cheeks and her mouth was set in a tight, grim line.

Amanda set aside the paperwork she was laboring over and thought she'd even take a fight with Pam over filling out the supply list for the coming week. She *hated* paperwork and Pam knew it. So, naturally, her sister had completely abdicated that task the minute Amanda came back to town.

She had really hoped that Pam calling and asking for her help meant that her older sister was going to welcome her home. But, if anything, Pam's antagonism seemed fiercer than ever.

Her conversation with Piper ran through Amanda's mind as she looked at Pam, quietly fuming. *Jealousy?* Was it possible? If so, Amanda didn't know how she would fix what was wrong between her and her sister. Because she wasn't about to give up Nathan to make Pam feel better.

"What're you talking about?"

Pam stepped into the office and closed the door quietly behind her with a soft click. Then she leaned against that door, hands behind her back. "You know exactly what I mean, Amanda. The whole town is talking about you. And Nathan."

Her stomach jittered a little, but she'd known going in that she was going to be the hot topic of conversation in Royal. Ever since their dinner out at the TCC, people had been whispering. And Nathan leaving his car parked outside her place all night had pretty much put the capper on the whole situation.

"I know," she said with a helpless shrug, "but there's nothing I can do about it."

"Well, you could stop chasing after him, that might be a start," Pam snapped, pushing away from the door to stalk to the window overlooking the parking lot behind the diner.

Okay, she was willing to talk. To try to smooth things over with Pam. But she wasn't going to sit there and be attacked without defending herself, either.

"Chasing him?" Amanda stood up. "I'm not chasing Nathan. I've *never* chased him."

Pam whirled around and glared at her, eyes flashing. "Oh, you *love* being able to say that, don't you?"

"What, the truth?"

Pam laughed harshly, walked toward the desk and leaned on the back of the visitor's chair, positioned directly opposite Amanda. Shaking her short hair back from her face, she stared at her sister and blew out a breath before saying, "That just makes it better for you, doesn't it? It's the truth. Nathan chased after you all those years ago and now he's doing it again."

Just for a second, Amanda saw a sheen of tears in her sister's eyes and she felt terrible. Then Pam spoke again and all sympathy went out the window.

"Hannah Poole is sitting out there right now," Pam said, stabbing one finger toward the diner, "telling *ev-*

eryone how she saw Nathan's car parked outside your place *all night*."

Amanda winced a little. Well, they'd both known it would happen. They'd just have to ride out the gossip and wait for the first wave to dissipate.

"And this is *my* fault?" Amanda demanded.

"Oh, please." Pam pushed off the chair, making the wooden legs clatter against the linoleum. "Like you don't do everything you can to make sure he notices you. Big eyes. Soft voice."

Amanda laughed shortly. This was getting weird. And how come she had never noticed before just how jealous of her Pam really was? "What are you talking about?"

"When you guys broke up before, it nearly ruined him," Pam told her flatly. She took a deep breath and blew it out again before adding, "He stayed away from Royal for three years. He only saw his brother when Jake went to Dallas to visit him."

They'd both lost a lot, Amanda thought. They had been so young that neither of them had reacted the way they should have to the tragedy that had torn them apart. They'd cut themselves off from not only each other, but also from their friends, their families. It was time they'd never get back, but hopefully, they'd learned something from all of that, too.

But even as she thought it, she wondered if she'd ever really be able to trust Nathan again. He hadn't believed her. Hadn't *loved* her when she had needed him most. Those dark days came back in a rush, swamping her mind with painful shadows until all she could do was whisper, "I stayed away, too, remember?"

Pam waved that off as if Amanda's pain meant nothing. "This was Nathan's home and he didn't come back because he didn't want to deal with having the town gossips tearing him apart. Over *you*."

And just like that, old pain gave way to fresh anger. Pam was her sister and she was taking Nathan's side in this? *"And?"*

"And now they're doing it again." Pam folded her arms over her chest and tapped the toe of one shoe against the floor. "And just like before, it's all because of you."

In a blink, Amanda's temper ratcheted up to match her sister's. Funny, when they were kids, Amanda had always looked up to Pam. And in an argument, Amanda had always backed down, both intimidated by her sister and unwilling to risk alienating Pam entirely. Well, she thought, those days were long gone. They were both adults now and Pam had been on her case for weeks already. Fine. They had problems—they'd either work them out or not. But damned if Pam was going to wedge herself between Amanda and Nathan.

"This isn't any of your business, Pam. So back off."

Pam drew her head back in surprise. But her stunned silence only lasted a second or two. "I'm not backing off. I'm the one who's been here, Amanda. I'm the one who saw what you did to Nathan before. And I'm the one telling you to stop ruining his life."

"Ruining his life? A little dramatic, don't you think?"

"Hah. If the gossips chew on him for too long he'll leave again."

"Has it occurred to you that they're gossiping about *me,* too?" She tipped her head to one side, mirrored Pam's stance and waited. She didn't have to wait long.

"That's your own fault," Pam scoffed. "For God's sake, you lured him up to your bed and then were too stupid to tell him to move his car. You *wanted* the whole damn town to see."

"I didn't *trick* him into bed, Pam."

"You didn't have to." Pam blinked frantically to clear away the fresh sheen of tears in her eyes. "All you have to do is be there and he can't see anything else."

Amanda steeled herself against feeling sympathy for her sister. Of course she was sorry to see Pam in pain, but not sorry enough to back away from Nathan so her sister could try to get him. Again. "I still don't see how that's my fault *or* your business."

"Of course you don't," Pam said with an exasperated huff. "It's my business because I care about Nathan. When he came home, I was the one who helped him settle in. He was unhappy for a long time. And, Amanda—" she paused and took a breath "—I just don't want to see him like that again."

That much, Amanda could understand. She didn't want that, either. Because it would mean that whatever was between them had shattered again. Just the thought of that had a cold ball of ice settling in the pit of her stomach. Oh, God, she was never going to get over Nathan. How could she, when she was still in love with him?

Staggered by the sudden acknowledgment of what she was really feeling and worried about what it meant to her present—let alone her future—Amanda plopped down into her desk chair. Love? She hadn't counted on that at all. She'd hoped to make her peace with her memories—not build new ones.

She was in deep trouble. Nausea rolled through her stomach in a thick wave that had her swallowing spasmodically.

"Hey…" Pam's tone changed from banked anger to concern. "Are you okay?"

"No," Amanda told her, and cupped her face in her

hands. Oh, God, she was still in love with Nathan. A man she wasn't sure she could trust. She didn't even know how he felt about her! Seven years ago, Nathan had never told her that he loved her. Had left her the moment the reason for marrying her was gone.

Okay, yes, she was the one who had called off the marriage. But he hadn't fought her. He'd simply walked away. As if losing her and their baby meant nothing to him.

Today, there was still no mention of the *L*-word and that hadn't stopped her from once more falling for the only man she would ever love. She'd just tossed her heart into the air not knowing if it was going to crash and burn or find a safe home. "I really don't think I'm okay at all."

"This isn't just a cheap ploy to end the argument, is it?"

On a sardonic laugh, Amanda looked up and met her sister's eyes. "Trust me when I say, I really wish this was a ploy."

Nine

Summer was rolling along like a runaway freight train. Temperatures were high, tempers were even hotter and Nathan spent most of his time stepping in between arguing parties. Nothing unusual about any of it but for the fact that his head just wasn't in the game.

Hadn't been since that night with Amanda by the river.

Scowling, Nathan was alone in his office, thinking about that morning with Amanda. Waking up in her bed, her body wrapped around his, had eased a sore spot inside him he hadn't even realized was there. Making slow, languid love to her had carried that feeling further, until he was so caught up in her, he'd had to force himself to crawl out of that bed and go to work.

"So much for the plan," he muttered, taking a sip of his coffee.

He guessed it was safe to say his plan was shot. Not

only had he not gotten her out of his system, but she was also all he could think about anymore.

It had all seemed so simple. Get Amanda back into his bed and finally get over her. Let go of the past and move the hell on. Instead, she was deeper into his gut than she had been before. Not quite sure how that had happened, Nathan was even less sure about how to reverse the damage already done. Especially when all he wanted to do was make love to her again.

Hell, he was walking around town with a body so hard and tight, it was all he could do to keep from groaning in public. He needed…hell. He just *needed*.

Worse, he didn't want to need Amanda. He wanted to be free of her. Didn't he? Nathan scrubbed one hand across his face and tried to wipe away all of the thoughts clashing together in his mind.

To distract himself, he stared around the inside of his office, letting his gaze sweep across the familiar symbols of the life he'd built for himself in Royal. But none of it brought him the pleasure he usually found in just being there. Until Amanda came back to town, he'd been content. Now, contentment just wasn't enough. He wanted more. Wanted *her*.

The problem was…how to get her.

Oh, sex was great, but that was easy. What he wanted would be more difficult. Hell, he could admit, at least to himself, that he wanted it all. Not just Amanda, but the life they could make together. House. Family. A damn white picket fence.

But he knew the past still loomed between them, a big ugly wall they'd both ignored rather than dealt with.

He leaned back in his chair, kicked his feet to the corner of his desk and crossed them at the ankle. Staring up at the ceiling, he told himself that maybe the past should stay right where it was. Maybe they didn't have to dissect it. Maybe all they had to do was learn from it and let it go.

Trust would be an issue between them for a while, of course, but he could *show* Amanda that he had her back now. Over time, she'd eventually come to believe it.

Nodding to himself, he could see the future play out in his mind. He and Amanda, living in his house on the ranch. Having kids that would play with Jake and Terri's bunch. Long nights and lazy mornings in his bed, wrapped in each other's arms. It was what they should have had years ago.

And what they would have now.

When the door opened, Nathan looked over at the doorway, a scowl on his face.

"Nice welcome," Chance said.

"Sorry. I was doing some thinking." Nathan's feet dropped to the floor, then he stood up and held out a hand to his friend. "What's going on?"

Chance's blond hair looked as though he'd been stabbing nervous fingers through it for hours. His green eyes were troubled and he didn't meet Nathan's gaze directly. Not a good sign.

"Everything okay, Chance?"

"Not really," his friend muttered and rubbed one hand across the back of his neck.

He was backlit by the bright afternoon sunlight and when he turned to close the door, Nathan noticed he locked it, too.

"Okay, what's this about?"

"Nathan, I wouldn't be here if I didn't think you should know about what people are saying."

Instantly, Nathan's back went up and he shook his head. Seven years ago, Chance had been the one to tell

Nathan about the rumors spreading. The rumor that Amanda had deliberately ended her pregnancy. Back then, Nathan had been young enough to listen and stupid enough not to question.

Today was different.

"Don't want to hear it," he said and turned his back on Chance to walk to a file cabinet on the far wall.

"Don't you think I know that?" Chance's voice was reluctant but firm. Clearly, he wouldn't be leaving until he'd had his say.

Nathan spun around and said, "I don't give a good damn what people are saying, Chance."

The moment the words left his mouth, he realized they were completely true. Somehow, he just didn't care about being the center of gossip. And damned if he was going to listen to anything people had to say against Amanda. He might make mistakes, but hell if he'd make the *same* ones.

"Well, you'd better listen." Chance glared back at him. "The word is you're not the only guy she's sleeping with. People are saying she's slipping out of town, meeting some other guy. So if she turns up pregnant this time, who's to say you're the father?"

He felt like he'd been punched dead-center in the chest. And for one miserable moment, he let those words slam into his head and heart, too. But they didn't stay because they weren't true and he knew it. Knew it down to his bones. Amanda wasn't a cheat and she wasn't a liar.

His hands curled into fists at his sides and he took one long step toward one of his best friends.

Chance held up both hands and took a step back. "Hey, I didn't say I believed any of the talk."

"Then why the hell are you telling me this?"

He pushed a hand through his hair. "I didn't want to,

but if you want a life with Amanda, then you'd better find out who's spreading the poison and get it stopped."

Chance was right. Years ago, someone had spread lies about Amanda aborting their baby. And yeah, now he could see the lies for what they were. Amanda never would have done that. Back then, he'd been too young and stupid to think past his own fury.

Now things were different.

"On that, we totally agree," Nathan muttered darkly. "I'll find whoever it is and when I do..."

A couple of days later, the diner was packed and Amanda was still reeling from the realization that she was in love. On top of that, her stress level was sky-high just from keeping what she was feeling from Nathan. Then there was the situation with Pam.

She shot a covert look at her sister, ringing up a customer at the cash register. Things were still strained there, but at least they hadn't argued again.

"Everything okay?"

Amanda turned and forced a smile for Alex Santiago. She refilled his coffee cup, then set the pot down onto the counter.

"Everything's fine," she lied.

He studied her for a moment or two then nodded. "Yeah, I can see that."

"What about you, Alex?" Now that she was looking at him, she noticed that he wasn't giving her one of his million-dollar smiles. His eyes looked shadowed, as if he hadn't been getting much sleep. "Are you all right?"

"I'm fine. Just..." He shrugged and tried, but didn't quite manage to smile at her. "You know how it is. Sometimes, you've got too much to think about."

"That, I understand completely." Whispered conversations from off to her left caught her eye, but Amanda ignored them. If people were going to talk about her, she couldn't stop them.

"I think you do," he said, then took a sip of coffee. "Don't worry about me, Amanda. Everything will be fine."

She might have said something else, tried to draw him out a little if only to erase some of the worry in his eyes, but a shout sounded out.

"Amanda, honey, how long till that burger of mine is ready?" John Davis slapped one meaty hand to his broad chest and gave a groan. "I'm a starvin' man, darlin'."

Alex laughed a little. "Go. Feed the man before he dies of hunger."

She rolled her eyes and patted Alex's hand. "I will. But if you need anything, all you have to do is ask."

He covered her hand with his briefly and said, "You've a kind heart."

Amanda went to pick up John's lunch, then delivered it, all the while wondering about Alex. But by the time she got back to the counter, he was gone. His coffee was still steaming and there was a five-dollar bill next to the saucer. She frowned and looked through the front window in time to see Alex hurry down the street.

A few days later, Nathan answered the phone at the sheriff's office and smiled. "Alex. What's up?"

"Nothing much," his friend said, then asked, "Are you going to be at the TCC meeting tonight?"

"I'll be there," Nathan said on a tired sigh. "With Beau Hacket still making waves over the child-care center, figured I should attend just to keep him in line."

"That's good," Alex said. "After the meeting, I'd like to talk to you. Privately."

Nathan frowned and straightened up in his desk chair.
There was just something about the tone of his friend's
voice that set off small alarm bells in Nathan's mind.
"Everything all right?"

"Yes," Alex told him quickly. "Absolutely. I'd just
like to talk to you."

"Okay, sure." Still frowning, Nathan suggested, "We
could grab a late dinner."

"That would be good," Alex said and now relief colored his words. "I'll see you later, then."

"Right." Nathan hung up, but his mind raced with
questions.

That night at the meeting, Nathan wished he could
just leave. His heart just wasn't in being there. He'd have
much rather been with Amanda.

What had he come to? He laughed at himself. Who
would have guessed a few weeks ago that he'd be feeling
downright...domesticated? He wasn't sure what it was
they had going between them, but he was damn sure he
didn't want it to end. Was this love? Hell if he knew. He'd
imagined himself in love with her seven years ago, but
what he felt now was different. Bigger.

He glanced around the meeting room, but didn't make
eye contact with any of the people. They were all busy,
talking, visiting, but Nathan wasn't in the mood. Hell,
he wasn't in the mood for much here lately. Not until
he found out who was behind the rumors designed to
hurt Amanda.

And, now there was the question of what was bothering Alex, as well. He glanced at the empty chair behind
him and wondered again where his friend was. Alex
hadn't shown up for the meeting and though Nathan
kept telling himself the man would appear at any mo-

ment, the meeting was almost over and there was still no sign of him. For the moment, though, he let thoughts of Alex slide away as Amanda's situation took precedence.

From the corners of his eyes, Nathan looked at the familiar faces around him and wondered if it could be one of them. One of his "friends" who had deliberately sabotaged his relationship with Amanda so long ago and was now trying to do the same. But what the hell did anyone have to gain by spreading lies? Not like anyone was going to stop eating at the diner. Or talking to Amanda, for that matter.

So what was the point?

Well now, he thought, he'd know that as soon as he found the bastard.

Raised voices caught his attention and Nathan dragged his thoughts back to the present. Just like every other weekly meeting, there were the same people gathered, having the same arguments. Beau and his bunch were still bitching about the new child-care center and Abby Price looked downright pleased to be able to tell them all to shove off. Couldn't blame her, Nathan thought. She'd fought hard to become a member here at the club. It had to be satisfying to now be able to ensure that not only more women were welcome here, but their kids as well.

Shaking his head, Nathan wondered why Beau couldn't let it go. It was a done deal. Move on.

He caught Chance's eye across the table and the two of them shared a smile.

"I tell you, it's disgraceful," Beau was sputtering. "Putting a babysitting club in the billiards room? Our founding fathers are probably spinning in their graves."

A few raised voices shouted in unison with Beau and the little man seemed to get bigger every time someone sided with him. So before he got out of line entirely, Nathan spoke up.

"No one even *plays* billiards anymore, Beau." The older man was nearly purple in frustrated rage, but Nathan wasn't impressed. He knew Beau was mostly talk. "Hell, when was the last time *you* played the game?"

"Not the point, Nathan Battle, and your own pa would be sore disappointed to hear you taking up on the side of these females." The man wagged a finger at Nathan as if he were a ten-year-old boy.

Chance smothered a laugh and Nathan felt all eyes on him as he said, "That's the thing, Beau. My dad would have been the first one to take a hammer to that moth-eaten old billiards table. And he'd have shamed *you* into giving us a hand remodeling that room for the kids, too."

Beau's color got even worse. His jaw worked and his lips pursed as if there were legions of words trapped inside trying to fight their way out. But he managed to hold on to them and Nathan thought that was probably for the best.

"Now, why don't we end this meeting so we can get on home?" Nathan looked over at Gil Addison, who gave him a wink and a nod before slamming his gavel down with a hard crash.

"Meeting is concluded," Gil announced a second later. "See y'all next week."

Chair legs scraped against the wood floor. Glasses were set onto the table with sharp clicks. Beau was the first one to storm out of the room and once he was gone, conversation picked up as people meandered toward the exit.

"Nice speech," Abby called out as she waved to Nathan.

He smiled and nodded and then turned to Chance when he walked up.

"You shut down Beau pretty well," Chance said.

"Not hard," Nathan answered. "The man's from the Stone Age. Don't know how his wife, Barbara, puts up with him."

"Must have his good points."

"I suppose," Nathan mused, his gaze scanning the TCC members as they filed out, still looking for Alex to come rushing in late. But he didn't show. A trickle of unease rolled along Nathan's spine. He was getting a bad feeling about this—and he'd learned to listen to those bad feelings.

Wasn't like Alex to miss an appointment. In the short time he'd been in Royal, the man had shown himself to be a fiend for schedules. So if he'd wanted to meet with Nathan, where the hell was he?

"Have you seen Alex?" Nathan asked suddenly.

"Not since a day or two ago. Saw him at the diner, talking to Amanda."

People got busy, Nate told himself. Maybe something had come up. But he'd made a point of setting up a private meeting with Nathan. So if he wasn't going to show, why wouldn't he have called to cancel? That bad feeling was getting stronger. He didn't have a concrete reason for it, he supposed, but he couldn't shake that niggling sensation chewing at the back of his mind. Nathan frowned to himself, because he knew a cop had to trust his instincts before anything else. "It's not like him to miss the meeting."

"You know," Chance said, as he also looked around the quickly emptying room, "now that you mention it, I had wondered where he was tonight."

"That's what I'm saying."

Chance shrugged. "Maybe he's on a date or something. Or maybe he just wasn't in the mood to deal with Beau tonight. God knows I wasn't."

"Yeah, but you came anyway," Nathan said firmly. "So would Alex." Especially since he'd wanted to speak privately with Nathan.

"Then where is he?"

"That's the question," Nathan said. "Isn't it? I'll go by his place see what I can find out."

"I've got another question for you." Chance shoved his hands into the pockets of his slacks and started for the door, Nathan walking alongside him. "Discover anything about our gossip starter?"

"No. Not yet." He'd been asking discreet questions all over town, too. Trying to wheedle information out of folks without letting them know that's what he was doing. Most he spoke to were embarrassed to talk to him about the rumors, but they all denied knowing who had started them. It was always, "I heard it from so and so who got it from what's her name." Didn't seem to be a starting point.

But there was one.

And Nathan was going to find it.

"A whole lot of weird going on all of a sudden," Nathan muttered the next morning. "Alex has dropped off the radar and now this at the diner. Doesn't feel like they're connected, but it's damn odd."

"Tell me about it." Amanda's stomach twisted with nerves and knots. "When I got home from your place I went up the back stairs to my apartment and took a shower. I came down after to open up the diner and found this. Then I went to your office to get you."

"Just the right thing," Nathan said as he eased past

her in the doorway. "You stay out here, I'll go in and check things out."

"I don't think so," she said and walked into the diner right behind him. "This is my place, Nathan. I'm not waiting outside."

Grimly, he looked at her, mumbled something she didn't quite catch, then said, "Fine. At least stay behind me and don't touch anything."

They walked through the back door directly into the diner kitchen. Amanda looked around the room and still couldn't believe what she was seeing.

The grill was smashed, as if it had been beaten with a hammer. Flour was strewn across everything, making it look like there'd been a snowstorm in the kitchen. Jars of spices lay shattered on the floor, their contents spilled across the flour in festive patterns. Plates were smashed, drawers yanked out and dumped. In essence, the kitchen was a disaster.

"Somebody did a number on this place," Nathan murmured more to himself than to her.

"If I'd been upstairs last night, I would have heard them, damn it." Anger was burning through her nerves.

"Yeah," he said thoughtfully, "you would have. Funny, isn't it, that whoever did this waited until you were spending the night with me on the ranch to do this damage?"

That clicked in immediately. Why hadn't she thought of that? "So who knew I went to the ranch yesterday?" As soon as she asked the question, she sighed in disgust. "Half the town, probably. Everyone saw me leave with you last night."

"Yeah," he said, tipping her chin up so he could look into her eyes. "But not many of them knew you'd be *staying*."

She thought about that for a minute, realized he was right, then tried to make a mental list of who actually knew she'd be gone overnight. "There's Pam, of course. And Piper. I told her. And Terri." She shook her head, disgusted. "They could have told people, I suppose, but I just can't think of anyone who would do this."

"We'll figure it out." He glanced back at the mess. "I'll have the kitchen fingerprinted, but there are so many people in and out of this diner every day I don't know that we'll find anything."

"No," she grumbled, crossing her arms over her chest. "Probably not. When I first walked in and saw this, I was scared. Now, though, I'm just mad." She kicked at some flour and watched it puff into the air before settling. "This will shut us down for days."

"Might not be too bad," he said. "But you're gonna need a new grill."

She sighed, then tried to look on the bright side. "Well, that grill is older than I am, so maybe we needed a new one anyway. So, once you do your fingerprint thing, I'll call Pam and we'll get this mess cleaned up."

Nathan smiled, shook his head, then grabbed her and pulled her in close for a hug. "You're really something, Amanda Altman."

"Thanks, Sheriff," she said with a smile then sobered. "This is pretty ugly, but I know how concerned you are about Alex. Finding him is important, too."

"Not even really sure why I'm worried," he admitted. "The man could be off taking care of business none of us knew about."

"True," she said, staring up into his eyes. "But you said yourself that he wanted to talk to you about something. Wouldn't he have called to let you know he couldn't make it?"

"Yeah." Frowning, he said, "He would have. You haven't thought of anything else? What he talked about when he was at the diner the other day?"

"No," she said softly. "Ever since you asked me that last night, I've been thinking about it and there's just nothing." Shrugging, she added, "He seemed distracted. Worried about something maybe. But he didn't say anything specific."

He huffed out a breath and shook his head. "Damned strange. All of it."

"I know." She hugged him tightly then let him go. "I've got a lot of work to do here, Sheriff. So I'll get to it and you go find Alex and catch me a bad guy."

Ten

Nathan spent a couple of frustrating days trying to track down answers to his questions. He couldn't find Alex Santiago and he had no clue who had vandalized the diner kitchen. Frustration chewed at him. That bad feeling about Alex was intensifying, and as for Amanda…

This was damn personal. Someone was out there trying to hurt her and damned if he'd let them. Amanda was *his* and nobody was going to mess with her and get away with it.

Of course, he mused ruefully, he hadn't told Amanda yet how it was going to be between them. Now that he'd decided that they were going to be together, he wanted to take his time. Keep seducing her with sex, get her used to the idea of having him back in her life before he actually told her it was time to get married. He wasn't an idiot, after all. The last time he'd asked her to marry him it was because of the baby and none of it had ended well.

It shamed him to remember it now, but it was best to go into any tricky situation with your thoughts and goals straight. Looking back, Nathan was willing to admit he'd handled that situation badly long ago.

This time would be different.

Amanda was a hell of a woman, but she had a spine and was likely to fight him on this whole marriage thing if he didn't work it just right.

Not that it mattered if she fought him. He would have her, in the end. It would just be easier all the way around if he could just keep reminding himself to be patient.

But he wouldn't be patient in finding whoever was behind this mess at the diner. Because he knew, whoever it was, would also turn out to be the source of the rumors. Highly unlikely that two different people would both be harassing Amanda at the same time.

When the phone rang, he snatched it. "Sheriff's office."

"Hey."

"Chance." Nathan straightened, grabbed a pen and slid a pad of paper in front of him just in case he needed to take notes. "You hear anything?"

"Nada." Chance sounded disgusted. "I've talked to everybody I can think of and nobody's seen Alex."

"Damn." He sat back in his chair and tossed the pen to the desktop. "I talked to Mia Hughes yesterday—Alex's housekeeper. She hasn't seen him in days. Says he hasn't been home at all."

"Well, where the hell is he, then?"

"I don't know, Chance." Nathan shook his head and stared off into space. "It's like he dropped off the face of the earth."

"I don't mind admitting that I'm getting worried, Nate," Chance said. "This isn't like Alex."

Nathan was worried, too. It just didn't seem reasonable that *nobody* in Royal had heard from or seen Alex. And why the hell would he leave town without at least telling Mia? Something was definitely wrong here and Nathan didn't like it.

Usually, in a town like Royal, the "crimes" he dealt with were kids getting into trouble or the occasional battle between neighbors. Now he had a missing man and a break-in.

"Any news on what happened at the diner?" Chance asked.

"No." One word. Disgusted. Nathan had never felt helpless before and he didn't care for it. He couldn't find his friend and he hadn't been able to discover who was behind the vandalism to Amanda's place.

Though he did at least have a half-baked suspicion on that one. Didn't make much sense to him, but he'd check it out. And if he were right…it would help prove to Amanda that she could trust him—in spite of the mistakes in their past.

"What is *with* Royal this summer, man?"

"Wish to hell I knew," Nathan answered.

The upside of having her diner demolished, Amanda thought, was that she had more time with Nathan.

He hadn't wanted her staying alone in the apartment over the diner until he found whoever had done the damage. So, she'd been staying here, at the house he'd had built for himself on the Battlelands. Normally, she might have fought him over his bossy, take-charge attitude, but she hadn't wanted to stay there, either. As much as she liked the little apartment, it would never really feel safe to her again.

Nathan's place, as great as it was, was temporary

and she knew it. The only answer was to find a place of her own.

"Guess it's time to look for that house," she said aloud.

"You have a house," Terri told her firmly. "Right here."

"This is Nathan's," Amanda said, shaking her head as she took a sip of her tea. "Being here with him is wonderful, but it isn't permanent."

"Honestly, I don't know which of you has the harder head." As if accepting that she wouldn't change Amanda's mind, Terri sighed and went to a new subject. "How's the diner coming along, anyway?"

"We'll be able to open again on Monday. We've got a new grill and Pam's been helping me clean up and restock the kitchen."

"There's a miracle," Terri murmured. "Pam doesn't exactly strike me as the helpful type."

Amanda had to chuckle. She'd been surprised by her sister's assistance, too. "That's one good thing that came out of all of this. Pam did such a turnaround this last week—she's been so nice it's almost eerie."

"And all it took was the destruction of the diner."

"Whatever caused the change, I'm happy about it." Amanda had never wanted to be at war with her sister. Over the last week, they'd worked together in the kitchen, straightening up, restoring order. Not that she and Pam were joined at the hip or suddenly becoming best buddies...but it was a start. If this new relationship with her sister continued, then the vandalism would have been worth it.

Terri set a paper sack on the kitchen table and pushed it toward Amanda. "I got what you asked for at the store."

Amanda's stomach flip-flopped as she reached for the bag. She took a deep breath then blew it out again.

"Thanks, Terri. If I had gone into a store anywhere near here to buy it myself, everyone in town would have known by the end of the day."

"Amanda…"

She cut her friend off. "Remember, you promised. Not a word. Not even to Jake."

Terri made a quick cross over her heart and held her hand up. "I swear. But you're crazy, you know that, right? You should tell Nathan."

"I will," Amanda said. "If there's anything to tell."

"Stubborn," Terri said. "Okay, fine. Do it your way."

"Wow, thanks for that, too," Amanda said with a smile.

"Okay, I'm going. But if you need me, just call. It'll take me a whole ten seconds to walk over here from the main house."

"I'm fine, Terri. But thanks. I appreciate it."

"You're welcome. And I really hope you get this straightened out already. It'd be nice to have you here on the ranch permanently."

When the kitchen door closed behind her friend, Amanda picked up her tea and the small paper bag and wandered out of the room. Her gaze slipped over Nathan's place and in her mind, she instinctively added pillows, splashes of color, vases filled with summer flowers.

Terri was right about one thing. Amanda didn't want to buy another house. She wanted to live here. With Nathan. But she couldn't do that without love.

Nerves skittered through her already uneasy stomach and Amanda swallowed hard to settle everything down. She'd been here in this house with Nathan for nearly a week and it was becoming too comfortable. Being here with him, having breakfast and dinner together, waking up in his arms—it all felt just right. As it was supposed to have been seven years ago.

But no promises had been made. No talk of a future. No mention of love.

Amanda's heart twisted a little as she reminded herself of that. She couldn't let herself slide into a relationship with Nathan that had no chance of succeeding. And the longer she stayed here with him, the harder it was going to be to leave.

Especially now.

She stopped at a window overlooking the front yard of the main ranch house. Jake and Terri's kids were clambering over the jungle gym Nathan and Jake had built for them. Their shouts and laughter pealed through the morning air and Amanda smiled wistfully as she listened to them.

If things had been different, her child would have been out there with them. *Her child.*

Taking a breath, she turned around and headed for the stairs. She carried her tea up to the master bedroom, sliding her hand along the polished oak banister as she went. Nathan was in town at the sheriff's office. He'd be there for hours.

So, she told herself, there was no better time for her to find out the answer to a question that had been nagging at her for a week.

Pam looked horrible.

It was the first thing Nathan noticed when she opened the front door of her house to him. And that gave Nathan the answer he was looking for. In between his regular town duties and the unofficial search for Alex, Nathan had been working on the vandalism at the diner.

He'd spent hours thinking about this, looking for witnesses, anything to help him figure out who was behind Amanda's troubles. And the one name that kept coming back to him was Pam.

No one else in town had any real issues with Amanda. But her sister hadn't exactly made a secret of the fact that she resented Amanda's presence even though her return to Royal had been at Pam's request. So he was playing a hunch. Trusting his instincts. He'd come to Pam's house to talk to her about this, maybe get her to confess. Now, looking into her eyes, he knew he was right about it all.

"Nathan."

"We need to talk." Nathan walked past her into the darkened house. Drapes were drawn, shutting out the sunlight, as if she were in hiding.

He marched through the small, familiar house and stopped in the living room. Then he snatched off his hat and turned to face the woman following him.

Abruptly, tears filled her eyes and spilled over to run unchecked down her cheeks. "Nathan—"

"You're sitting here in the dark," he pointed out. "Looking mighty miserable and I think there's a reason for that. See, I came here on a hunch," he said, his voice clipped and hard. "The only person in town who has a problem with Amanda is *you,* Pam. No one else would have had access to the diner without breaking a window or something to get in." That fact had bothered him from the jump. The lock on the door hadn't been jimmied, so either he was looking for a skillful vandal with terrific lock-picking talents, or… "But you had a key. You went there in the middle of the night, let yourself in and tore that kitchen apart, didn't you?"

"I swear I didn't go there intending to wreck the place," she murmured, wrapping her arms around herself as if searching for comfort. "I went to get a bottle of wine from the fridge. Then I was there, alone and started thinking about you. And Amanda. And the more I thought, the angrier I got and before I knew it..."

His stance didn't soften, his voice didn't warm when he said, "Why? Why would you do that to your sister? To your own damn business?"

She unfolded her arms and wiped tears away with both hands before taking a long breath and saying, "I've been so angry for so long."

"Angry about what?" he demanded, his gaze locked on her as if seeing her clearly for the first time. She looked miserable, eyes gleaming with tears, her teeth biting into her lower lip and her shoulders hunched as if she were somehow trying to disappear inside herself.

"You," she admitted finally, staring up at him.

"What the hell are you talking about?"

She laughed harshly. "God, I'm an idiot. Look at you. You have no idea."

"Pam," Nathan growled, "my patience is stretched as thin as it can get. I've had a bad week and I'm not much in the mood for guessing games with you, so whatever's stuck in your craw, spit it out."

"Fine. Why not finish the humiliation?" She threw her hands high and let them slap down against her sides. Shaking her head, she blurted, "I was always crazy about you, Nathan, but you never looked at me. Never *saw* me."

"Pam—" Nathan said her name and watched her flinch.

She shook her head and held up one hand to keep him quiet. "Please don't say anything. Bad enough I have to say this. Bad enough that I wasted *years* pining after you when I never had a chance." She huffed out a strangled breath. "It was always Amanda for you, wasn't it?"

"Yeah, it was." He didn't feel sorry for her. She'd

caused a lot of trouble. He did feel badly that he'd never noticed that her fondness for him had become an obsession. That much was his fault. If he'd been paying attention, he could have spared everyone a lot of misery. As it was, he played another hunch. "What about the rumors attacking Amanda? The ones seven years ago and now? Was that you, too?"

She inhaled sharply and winced as if she were in pain. "Yeah. That was me." She turned away from him as if she couldn't bear to face him. "God, this is like a nightmare. Even I can't believe what I've done."

"Pam—" He broke off and shook his head. Hard to believe this one woman had caused so much damage. All of it stemming from jealousy. "You spread those lies about Amanda, suggesting she got rid of our baby. And you thought that would make me care for you?"

Her voice dropped to a whisper but in the stillness Nathan heard every word. "I never thought you'd find out."

"And the diner kitchen? What was that about?"

"God. I was in the diner alone." Her strained whisper sounded as if she were having to *push* every word through her throat. "Amanda was spending the night at the ranch. With you. I swear I didn't consciously mean to do all of that. But I picked up an iron skillet and just started beating the grill. I was so angry, so—it doesn't matter," she said brokenly. "It was like I lost my mind for a few minutes. I was so furious with her, for coming home." She looked around at him. "For taking you from me. I just lost it."

He wasn't moved by her confession. If anything, his jaw clenched tighter and his eyes narrowed more. All Nathan could think was that because of Pam, he and Amanda had lost seven years together. "She couldn't take me from you because I was never *with* you."

She dropped into a chair, wrapped her arms around her middle and rocked. "I know. And I'm sorry. I really am. For everything. I wasted so much time. But, Nathan—"

"No, there's no excuse for any of this, Pam," he told her flatly. "And if Amanda wants to press charges against you, I'll throw you into a cell so fast, the world will be a blur."

Her stomach sank. "You're going to tell her?"

"No," he said. "You are."

"Oh, God."

"Yeah," Nathan went on. "See, Amanda's going to marry me as soon as I get around to telling her how things are going to be. And I'm not going to be the one to break the news that her only family betrayed her."

Pam winced at that, but Nathan didn't give a good damn if her feelings were hurt. "Fine," she said. "I'll tell her."

"Do it fast." He stalked out of the house and slammed the door behind him.

Seven years wasted. But it wasn't all Pam's fault and he knew it. As much as he'd like to forget, Nathan had to acknowledge that if he'd had more faith in Amanda and more damn spine, he never would have believed a word of those rumors. Instead, he'd been young enough and stupid enough to let lies throw his life off track.

Well, no more.

Nathan was still fighting off the anger Pam had churned up in him when he parked outside his house. In no mood to talk to Jake, he was glad it was late enough that his brother and his family were already at dinner.

He got out of his car, slammed the door and took a minute to calm himself before going inside to see

Amanda. Like he told Pam, he didn't want to be the one to tell her that her own sister had been behind the harassment aimed at her. And if he went in there furious, she'd worm the information out of him whether he wanted to tell her or not.

Still, hard to believe that Pam was the vandal. And the one who'd started all the vicious rumors. But hell, at least he'd solved *one* mystery. Alex's disappearance was still chewing on Nathan. He was making calls, talking to people and, so far, he had nothing. As Alex's friend, Nathan was worried. As a cop, he was frustrated.

Shaking his head, he stared at his house and in spite of everything, the tension inside him easing. Lights were on, and it struck him suddenly that he really liked coming home to this. Always before, he'd leave work and drive up to an empty house, dark windows and a silence that grew thicker with every passing moment. But for the last week, Amanda had been here and she'd etched herself into every damn corner of that house—as well as his heart.

If she left him today—an option that would not be allowed to happen—he still would see her all over his house. He would hear her laugh, catch her scent on every stray breeze, reach for her across his bed.

Even after the rough day he'd had, Nathan smiled as he noted the pots of bright yellow and blue flowers Amanda had set on the porch yesterday. His chest tightened as he recalled her walking along the wraparound porch, muttering to herself about rockers and matching chairs and tables and how nice it would be to sit out on a summer night and watch the moon crawl across the sky.

He wanted that. With her. Wanted to come home to a well-lit house holding the woman he loved. All right, yes, he loved her. He hadn't told her, of course, because their past was still between them and he knew that though she might not admit it, she didn't completely trust him again yet. He couldn't blame her—hell, thinking back about what had happened between them years ago, how they'd ended, made him want to kick his own ass.

But he'd give her everything else. His name. His home. His children. And one day, he'd confess his love and she'd believe him. She'd trust him to not hurt her again as he had before.

He had to have her. Hell, he couldn't draw a breath inside that house without taking the essence of her into his soul. It had always been that way between them. Seven years ago, he'd just been too young to appreciate what he had when he had it. Now he was going to set things right.

Clutching his hat in one fist, he started for the porch. Time to get this done. He'd walk right in there and tell her they were getting married. Amanda was a logical sort of woman. She'd see it was the best plan right off. They'd have a small wedding, here on the ranch. Nathan took the front steps two at a time, a smile on his face.

The front door flew open just as he approached it and Amanda was standing there, staring at him through wide, wonder-filled eyes.

"Amanda?" He stopped dead. "Are you okay?"

"I'm pregnant."

Eleven

Okay, Amanda thought, she'd had that planned a lot better in her mind. She hadn't meant to just blurt it out like that, but on the other hand, even if she had taken ten or fifteen minutes to tell him, the result would've be the same.

She looked up at him and waited what felt like forever for his reaction. Would he be as happy as she was? Would he be upset? *Say something!*

He scrubbed one hand across his face. "You're what?"

"Pregnant." It felt so good to say. What felt like champagne bubbles were swimming through her system, making her nearly giddy.

"You're sure?"

"Positive." She laughed a little as she'd been doing all afternoon since taking that wonderful little test that Terri had picked up for her. "At least, that's what the test said. Positive."

He shook his head. "How?"

"Really?"

He laughed. "That's not what I meant. We used condoms."

"They don't always work, you know." She paused and added, "They didn't work seven years ago, either."

"I remember." He reached out and skimmed his fingers along her cheek.

Memories swirled around them, thickening the air with the haunting ghosts of shattered dreams and broken promises. They'd made an agreement to leave the past behind, but could it ever really be forgotten? Weren't you supposed to not dismiss your past, but learn from it?

Well, Amanda had. She'd lived through the pain, built a life, grown and changed. But the dreams of her heart were still there. Nathan. A family. She caught his hand in hers and held tight. Amanda had had a couple of hours to get used to this news and she figured it would take Nathan at least a few minutes to do the same. She wanted him to be happy about it, but the honest truth was, even if he didn't want the baby, *she* did.

Seven years ago, she'd been young and scared and too unsure about her own future to feel capable of raising a child on her own. But she was different now.

She had a home. A job. A place in this town. And if she had to, she would gladly raise this baby as a single mom. It was as if she'd been given a second chance to have all of the dreams she'd been denied so many years ago.

"This is…" He drew her into the house and closed the door. Tossing his hat onto the nearest chair, he laughed again. "This is *great.*"

Relief and joy swept through Amanda on a tide so

high and wide, she could barely breathe through the richness of it. "You're happy about the baby?"

"Happy?" Nathan laughed, reached out, grabbed her and swung her in a circle before finally setting her on her feet and pulling her in close. "Amanda, it's like we've got a second chance, here."

"That's just what I was thinking," she agreed, wrapping her arms around his waist and holding on. She leaned her head on his chest and listened to his galloping heartbeat.

"We can get married here at the ranch," he said. "Actually, I was planning for us to be married, anyway."

She went still, then drew her head back and looked up at him. "I'm sorry. You were planning for us to be married?"

"Yeah. I was going to tell you about it tonight." He grinned at her. "But your news kind of threw my plan off."

"Your plan." A trickle of cold began to seep through the happy glow she'd been carrying inside.

He gave her a hard hug. "I figured we could get married here at the ranch."

"Did you?" The cold went a bit deeper now, but she steeled herself against it.

The past seemed suddenly so much closer. She was reliving it all. His announcement that they would be married. The baby she carried. Would she also relive the shattered dreams?

Nathan frowned a little. "We don't have to hold the ceremony at the ranch, but I thought it'd be easier. Terri will help you set everything up. I'll help when I can, but I'm still looking for Alex and—"

He had it all worked out. And with every word he spoke, her heart sank a little bit more. The buzz of excitement and joy she'd felt earlier was quickly being swamped by feelings of disappointment and, okay, yes, irritation. She couldn't believe this. Although, it was so typical of Nathan, she really should have expected it. Seven years ago, he'd done the same and she'd allowed it because she had wanted him badly enough to hope that one day he might tell her he loved her. Now, though, she wouldn't settle. Slipping out of his arms, she took a step away from him, folded her arms over her chest and stared at the man who had held her heart since she was a kid.

How could she be so dispirited and so in love with him at the same time? Had to be a sort of cosmic joke on her that the one man who could drive her to distraction was the only man she'd ever wanted.

"So you've got everything figured out, have you?" Amanda asked, her voice soft and cool.

"Not completely," he admitted. "But between the two of us it shouldn't take long."

"You're right about that," Amanda said, shaking her head as she looked up at him. "Won't take long at all, since I'm not going to marry you."

"Of course we're getting married."

"Nothing's changed, has it?" she asked, not really expecting a response. "Seven years ago, you decided we'd get married and I went along." He opened his mouth to speak, but she continued quickly. "But I'm not a kid anymore, Nathan. I make my own choices. My own decisions. I won't let you push me into a marriage you don't really want."

"What're you talking about?" He looked as astonished as he sounded.

"What I'm saying is, this is just like before. You're offering marriage because I'm pregnant. Because it's the *right* thing to do." She turned abruptly and walked away from him, into the living room. He was right behind her.

The huge room boasted views of the ranch from every window. Across the drive, the main ranch house was brilliantly lit and Amanda knew that inside, Terri and her family were cozy and happy. Envy curled inside her and twisted around her heart like tangled ribbons. She'd like that for herself. For her child. But she wasn't going to make the same mistakes she'd made seven years ago. She wouldn't be a duty. She wouldn't be a problem that Nathan felt honor bound to clean up.

"It's the right thing to do because we belong together," Nathan argued.

"Do we?" She didn't know anymore. She'd always believed it, but she'd been shot down before and now, if she went along with Nathan's plan she'd only be setting herself up for a possible repeat of history.

"I think we should talk this through," he said.

She shook her head, never taking her gaze from the scene sprawling outside the window. She would miss it here, but it was definitely time to leave. Glancing over her shoulder at him, she said, "I don't think so, Nathan."

He was looking at her as if she'd sprouted another head. She could almost smile about that. Nathan was so used to being obeyed, he didn't know what to do when someone simply said no.

So she took a breath and tried to explain. "Nathan, I know this is just instinct to you. To do the right thing. The honorable thing."

"And that's *bad?*"

"Of course it's not bad," she countered, and gave him a sad smile. "But it's no reason to get married. I went along with your demands last time because, frankly, I was too scared to have a baby on my own. But I've changed, Nathan. And I'm not going to be just another duty to a man with too much honor. I want to be loved Nathan, or I'm not going to get married at all."

He threw up his hands. "But I *do* love you."

Pain sliced at her. If he'd led with that, maybe things would be different right now. But he hadn't mentioned anything about love until he absolutely *had* to, so how could she trust it? How could she believe anything but that Nathan would use whatever he had to to win.

"I wish I could believe that," she said after a long moment. "I really do."

"Why the hell can't you?" he argued. "Is it so impossible to believe?"

"Yeah, it is," she said and moved farther away. God, she couldn't stay here. Couldn't be this close to him, knowing that she couldn't have him. She needed to be home. Back in the tiny, hot box of an apartment over the diner. She needed to think.

"Amanda," he said, stepping closer, keeping his gaze locked with hers. "You can believe me. I do love you."

"No, you don't," she said, shaking her head as she backed up toward the chair where she'd dropped her purse earlier. "You just want me to fall in line and you know this is the way to manage it. No. It's just a little too convenient, don't you think? I say I won't get married without love and boom. Suddenly you love me? I don't think so."

"It's not suddenly," he argued. "I've loved you most of my life."

That stopped her for a second as his words ricocheted around inside her, tearing at her heart. She wanted to believe, she really did, for both her own sake *and* the baby's. But how could she? And if she took a chance—

trusted him with her heart—and was wrong…then it wasn't only she who would pay the price. She had her child to think about now.

"Why is it, then, that you've never mentioned it before now, Nathan?" she asked quietly, sadly.

"I don't know," he muttered, shoving one hand through his hair.

She picked up her purse and rummaged one hand inside for her car keys. When she found them, she curled her fingers around them and said, "Until you know the answer to that, Nathan, there's nothing else to talk about. Now, I'm going home."

"You are home, Amanda."

That little arrow scored a direct hit on her heart. She had hoped this would be home. Had imagined it. But she couldn't have what she wanted—without first having what she needed. Amanda needed to be loved by the very man standing there giving her all the right words without the meaning.

"No, I'm really not." She shook her head and walked past him. He stopped her with a hand on her arm.

"Don't go."

She looked down at his hand then shifted her gaze to his eyes. "I have to."

He released her then and Amanda felt the loss of his touch all the way to her bones. It took everything she had to walk out the door and down the front steps. Before she reached her car, she looked back over her shoulder and Nathan was standing there, in the open doorway, watching her.

"This isn't over," he said, his deep voice carrying on the warm summer air.

Amanda knew that all too well. What she felt for Nathan would *never* be over.

* * *

"Anyway," Pam said later that evening. "What I'm trying to say is, I'm sorry."

What a day this had been, Amanda thought, staring at her sister in dumbfounded shock. A surprise pregnancy, a surprise proposal and now…a sister who had hated her enough to try and ruin her life. Her heart hurt at the realization that Pam had been behind the rumors that had torn Amanda and Nathan apart so long ago. But a voice in her mind whispered that Nathan shouldn't have believed those rumors. He should have loved her enough to know they weren't true.

And he hadn't.

"You're sorry." Amanda whispered the words and watched Pam flinch. "For all the rumors or for the diner?"

"Both." Pam dropped into a chair beside the sofa where Amanda was curled up.

The diner apartment was too warm, the air conditioner wasn't working again. Amanda reached for her glass of iced tea and took a long drink as she studied her sister. Pam looked awful. Her eyes were red and puffy from crying. Her hair was in a tangle as if she'd forgotten to brush it and misery pumped off of her in waves.

Right now, Amanda told herself, she should be furious. Should be raging at her sister for all the damage Pam had done over the years. But the bottom line was, Amanda's heart was already too broken to break again. And fury seemed to require more effort than she had the energy for at the moment.

"God," Pam said softly, "I was always so jealous of you."

"Why?" Amanda shook her head and stared at her. "You're my big sister, Pam. I always looked up to you."

Pam winced. "And I resented you. You were always the favorite. With Mom and Dad, with our teachers at school. With Nathan."

"I don't even know what I'm supposed to say to that," Amanda said quietly. "Mom and Dad loved us both and you know it."

"Of course they did, and I'm an idiot for clinging to all that junk from when we were kids and letting it chew on me until I lost it."

"Pam…"

"There's nothing you have to say. It was all me, Mandy," Pam whispered, unconsciously using the name Amanda hadn't heard since she was a little girl. "I got so twisted up inside, I couldn't see anything but my jealousy of you. And even if you don't believe me, I am really sorry."

"I do believe you." Funny. She could accept Pam's apology but she couldn't trust Nathan's proclamation of love. A very weird day.

Pam looked at her from where she was sprawled in the overstuffed, faded chair. "You do?"

"Yeah." She shook her head tiredly. "Not that it's okay with me, what you did. And we're going to have to talk about this more, figure out where we go from here, but you're still my sister…." Heck, Amanda understood better than anyone what it was to be so crazy about Nathan that you could lose yourself in the emotional pool. And, there was the fact that Amanda was going to need her sister in the coming months. She could raise a child alone, but she wanted her baby to have a family. An aunt to love him or her.

Pam drew a deep breath and let it out on a relieved sigh. Her lips curved in a tired smile that looked quivery at the edges. "I didn't expect you to forgive me so easily."

Amanda tried to find a return smile, but couldn't. "I didn't say it would be easy. You're paying for the damage to the diner."

"Agreed," Pam said.

"And," Amanda continued, since she had her sister at a disadvantage at the moment, "you're taking over the paperwork again."

Pam nodded. "I only dumped it on you because you hate it. I actually sort of like it. I was always good with numbers."

"I know, I used to envy that," Amanda mused, realizing that for the first time in years, she and her sister were having a real conversation. "Maybe you should think about going back to school. Getting an accounting degree."

Pam thought about that for a second and then smiled. "Maybe I will." She pushed her hair back behind her ears. "Gotta say, Amanda, you've been a lot nicer to me about this than I deserve."

"You know," Amanda said thoughtfully, "you're lucky you picked today to dump all of this on me."

"Why?"

Amanda frowned and tapped her fingernails against the glass she held. "Because I'm too tired from dealing with Nathan at the moment to work up any real rage for you."

"I'm so sorry, Amanda," Pam said again. "I know you and Nathan were having a hard time and I didn't make it any easier. But he made it clear today that you two were getting married and—"

Amanda went still as stone. "He what?"

Pam shrugged. "He said you would be marrying him as soon as he told you his plan and—"

"He told you he was going to marry me even before he bothered to mention it to *me?*"

"Yeah, apparently."

There was a part of Amanda that was excited to hear it. After all, he'd seen Pam *before* he knew about the baby. So he had planned to propose anyway—that was something. It didn't change the fact that he'd mentioned nothing about love, though, until he was forced to by the situation.

"Well," she murmured, "it doesn't change anything. I already told him I'm not going to marry him just because he decrees it to be so."

"You said no?" Incredulous, Pam's voice went high.

"Of course I said no. I'm not going to agree to marry him just because I'm pregnant again."

"You're pregnant?"

Amanda wrapped her arms around her middle as if giving her unborn child a comforting hug. "I am, and I can raise *my* baby all by myself. The baby will have a mom and an aunt, right?"

Smiling, Pam said, "Absolutely. Aunt Pam."

Amanda nodded. "I can do this and I can do it without Nathan Battle if I have to."

"If he lets you," Pam muttered.

"Lets me?" Amanda repeated, staring at her sister. "Did you just say if he *lets* me?"

Pam lifted both hands. "You know Nathan. He doesn't usually hear the word 'no.'"

"Well, he'll have to hear it this time. I'm going to live my life my way. I'm not going to be told what to do and where to go and who to love." She walked over to the window and stared down at Royal. It was dark and streetlights created puddles of gold up and down the street.

Overhead, the moon hung like a lopsided teeter-totter and the stars winked down on the world.

And over on the Battlelands, the man she loved was alone with his *plans*. She hoped he was as lonely as she was.

"Sure am glad the diner's back open."

It was a couple of days later when Hank Bristow lifted a cup of coffee and took a long, leisurely sip. He sighed in pure pleasure before picking up his coffee and heading for a group of his friends at a far table. "Didn't know what to do with myself when you girls were closed."

"We're glad to be open again, too, Hank," Amanda assured him as he walked away.

She glanced at her sister. Pam was like a different person. The old bitterness was gone and she and Amanda had spent the last couple of days building a shaky bridge between them. Someday, Amanda hoped the two of them would be close. It wouldn't happen overnight, of course, but at least now there was a chance that the Altman girls were finally going to have a good relationship.

"Earth to Amanda…"

She jolted a little and, laughing, turned to look at Piper, sitting on a stool at the counter. "Sorry. Mind wandering."

"It's okay, but since I'm starving, how about a doughnut to go with this excellent coffee?"

"You bet." It was good to have friends, Amanda thought as she opened the door to the glass display case and set a doughnut on a plate. Piper had been the one Amanda went to after Nathan's abrupt proposal. And Piper was the one who had insisted that Nathan *did* love Amanda, that he was just being male and sometimes that had to be overlooked.

Amanda wasn't so sure. She'd missed Nathan desperately the last couple of days. He hadn't called. Hadn't come to her. Was he waiting for *her* to go to *him?* How could she?

She set the doughnut in front of Piper and whispered, "Thanks again for everything."

"No problem," Piper told her and took a sip of coffee. "I'm guessing you still haven't heard from him."

"No." Amanda planted both hands on the counter. "I don't think I will, either. Nathan's a proud man—maybe *too* proud. And I turned him down and walked away."

"Then maybe you should go to him," Piper said matter-of-factly.

"How can I?" Amanda shook her head.

"Give him a chance, Amanda. Heck, everyone in town knows Nathan's crazy about you. Why can't *you* believe it?"

She wanted to. More than anything.

Walking along the length of the counter, Pam refilled coffee cups, chatted with customers and stopped when she reached JT in his usual spot. "More coffee?"

"Thanks." He watched her in silence for a second, then said, "Looks like you and Amanda got things sorted out."

She set the coffeepot down and glanced at her sister. "We're getting there. I guess you could say I finally grew up."

All around them, the diner was buzzing with morning conversations, so JT's words were almost lost in the sound when he said, "It's about time."

Pam smiled. "True enough. JT, why are you always so nice to me?"

In answer, he stood up and came around the end of the counter. When he was close enough, he grabbed hold of Pam, pulled her in tight, then bent her over in a dip as he kissed her, long and slow. Finally, he swung her back onto her feet and let her go.

"*That's* why," he said, grinning at her. "Any other questions?"

The whole diner was silent as everyone in the place focused on the drama playing out right in front of them. A second ticked past, then two. Pam lifted one hand and rubbed her fingertips across her lips, then grinned widely. "Only one question, JT McKenna. What in hell took you so long?"

Applause burst into the room as Pam leapt into JT's arms and kissed him back.

The rest of the day passed quickly as people came and went, and life in Royal marched on. Amanda did her work, smiled and talked with her customers all while trying to breathe past the knot in her throat. Thoughts of Nathan crowded her mind and the emptiness she felt without him left an ache in the center of her chest.

JT had taken up permanent roost at the end of the counter and Pam took every chance she could to stop for a kiss as she passed him. A patient man, JT had waited years for Pam to finally realize that *he* was the man for her.

Nathan wasn't patient, Amanda told herself. He didn't wait. He pushed. He nudged. He ordered and when that didn't work, just went ahead and did whatever he thought was the right thing to do.

As those thoughts wandered through her mind, Amanda realized that she'd always known that about Nathan. And she loved him for who he was, irritations and all. So how could she blame him for doing everything he could now to make sure she married him?

Sighing, she glanced out the front window toward Main Street and her breath caught when she saw Nathan headed for the diner. Just one look at him and her heartbeat jumped into a gallop. He had his hat pulled down low against the brilliant summer sunshine and his steps were long and determined. She could almost feel the intensity preceding him as he stalked ever closer, people instinctively moving out of his way.

Amanda fought for calm and didn't find it. Her heartbeat continued to race and her stomach swirled with expectation.

He stepped into the diner and his gaze swept the place in seconds, finally landing on her as if drawn to her by some immutable force. She felt the power of his stare from across the room and couldn't look away from those dark brown eyes that were filled with heat and charged with emotion.

The crowd in the diner took a collective breath and held it. Excitement fluttered through the room as people shifted positions to get a good view of whatever was coming next. Amanda didn't care. She wasn't thinking about anything but Nathan and why he'd come. If he was just here for more of the same, she'd have to tell him no and send him away again, though the thought of that tore at her.

Yes, he was arrogant and pushy and bossy and proud and she loved him desperately.

"Amanda," he announced, loud enough for everyone to hear, "I've got a few things to say to you."

"Here?" she asked. "In front of half the town?"

"Right here, right now," he told her, and his gaze bored into hers. "We've been trying to outrun or hide from gossip and rumor for so long... I think it's time we just took a stand." He moved a bit closer to her and his voice dropped a notch or two. "I don't care what they think. What they say. Let 'em look, Amanda. We're done hiding."

A flush of heat swamped her, but she found herself nodding in agreement. He was right. They had worried over rumors. They'd allowed vicious lies to split them up seven years ago. Maybe it was time to just be themselves without worrying over what the rest of the town had to say about it.

"You're right," she said. "No more hiding."

One corner of his mouth lifted into a brief half smile and she saw pride glittering in his eyes. For a second or two, the terrible tension in her chest eased and Amanda felt as if she and Nathan were a team. The two of them against the gossips.

Close enough to touch her now, he started talking. "I thought a lot about what we talked about the other night."

His voice was low and deep and seemed to reverberate up and down her spine. His eyes were locked on hers and she couldn't have looked away if she'd tried.

Reaching out, he stroked his fingertips along her cheek and Amanda shivered, closing her eyes briefly to revel in the sensation of his touch. When she opened her eyes again, he was still watching her.

"You were right, Amanda," he said. "The night you told me about the baby, I said the words you needed to hear to help convince you to marry me."

It felt as if all the air slid from her lungs at once. The tightness in her chest was painful and tears pooled at the backs of her eyes.

"But—" He cupped her face in his palms, and held her, forcing her to keep looking into his eyes. "That doesn't mean they weren't true."

"Nathan—" She shook her head and tried to look away. He wouldn't allow it.

"I do love you. I always have." He bent and kissed her gently on the lips and the taste of him lingered on her mouth. "Maybe telling you when I did was bad timing."

"Maybe?" she managed to ask.

He gave her a nod and a rueful smile. "You threw me that night, Amanda, but I *do* love you, with everything in me. If I hadn't been too young and too arrogant to say the words seven years ago…maybe things would have been different for us."

Amanda knew the whole diner was listening in and found she didn't care. The only person she was interested in now was Nathan. "I want to believe you," she said. "I really do."

"You *can*," he told her, moving into her, until every breath she took drew the clean, fresh scent of him deep into her lungs. "We're meant to be together, and I think you know it."

He reached into his pocket and pulled out a small, red velvet jeweler's box. Her gaze landed on it even as her heart took another tumble in her chest. When she looked up at him again, he smiled.

"This is for you, Amanda."

She shook her head even as he opened the lid to display a brilliant topaz stone surrounded by diamonds and set in a wide, gold band.

"This stone is sort of the color of your eyes," he whispered, "at least, *I* think so. Every time I look in your eyes, I fall in love again. You're the woman for me, Amanda. The *only* woman. So I'm asking you now. The right way. Amanda Altman, will you marry me?"

She shook her head and blinked to clear away the tears blurring her vision. He was offering her everything she'd ever wanted. Love. The promise of a future together. All she had to do was trust her heart and take a leap of faith.

She looked away from the ring and into his eyes and nearly cried again when she read in his eyes the truth she'd needed so much to see. Warmth, passion, *love*.

Before she could say anything, Nathan continued. "When you left the other night, you took my heart with you," he said, gaze moving over her face like a caress. "I couldn't breathe. Couldn't sleep. Couldn't do anything but try to think of a way to bring you back home where you belong."

"Oh, Nathan." The diner, their audience, the whole world fell away and all that was left was the two of them. She and Nathan, together as she'd always dreamed they would be.

"I let you go once," he said tightly. "I don't know how I lived these years without you, but I *know* I can't live the rest of my life without you."

Her tears overflowed and tracked along her cheeks unheeded. Gently, he used his thumb to wipe the tears away and gave her a sad smile.

"I was young and stupid seven years ago," Nathan said, "but I've changed as much as you have. I know you could raise our child on your own—but I hope you won't." He took the ring from the box and slowly, carefully, slid it onto her ring finger, then kissed it as if to seal the ring in place. When he looked into her eyes again, he said, "I want to be with you, Amanda. Always. I need you. And our baby. And the family we'll build together. The family we should have started all those years ago."

She couldn't look away from his eyes and, in truth, she didn't want to. The ring felt warm on her hand and her heart felt even warmer. Amanda took a breath and slowly let it out, enjoying this moment, wanting to treasure the memory of this one small slice of time forever.

This was everything she'd ever wanted. He was saying the words that were so important to her. Offering her the life she craved. And she believed him. Nathan's eyes were filled with love as he looked at her and she knew that she would never doubt him again.

All around her, she sensed people's attention, knew they were all listening in and found she simply didn't care.

"I love you, too, Nathan," she said and smiled when he grinned down at her. "I just needed to believe."

"And now you do?" he asked, wrapping one arm around her waist to hold her to him.

"Now I do," she said and realized she'd never been more sure of anything than she was of what she and Nathan shared. For a while, she had allowed doubts and fears from the past to cast dark shadows over the present and the future. But she was through looking backward.

"I swear, you'll never be sorry." He swept her up tightly to him and kissed her so deeply, Amanda would never again have any doubts about his feelings.

And while the people in the diner broke into applause, Amanda knew that she finally had everything she had ever wanted.

The man she loved, loved her back, and there was nothing in the world more beautiful than that.

Epilogue

The wedding wasn't as small as Nathan wanted and not as large as Amanda had feared.

There was family—Jake, Terri and the kids. Pam and JT, practically joined at the hip. Amanda had the distinct feeling it wouldn't be too long before there was another wedding in Royal.

And there were friends. Piper and Chance and Abby and so many others gathered together to wish them well.

Nathan had surprised her by outfitting the wrap-around porch of their home with all of the rockers and gliders and chairs that she'd talked about once. She could see them in the years to come, sitting on that porch, surrounded by family, and it filled her heart to the point of bursting.

To avoid the steaming heat of a Texas summer, on the last day of July, the wedding was held in the evening. Lanterns were strewn across the yard, lending a soft glow that was matched only by the early starlight. Flowers in vases, wreaths and vines trailed from every available surface and sweetened the air with a perfume that flavored every breath.

Tables groaned with food and music played from the stereo situated on Jake's front porch. Children clambered all over the swing set Jake and Nathan had built while their parents chatted with friends. There was laughter and there was *love*.

Amazing how love, when it finally arrived, made the whole world shinier, brighter, more filled with promise.

"A bride as beautiful as you are shouldn't be standing here alone," Nathan said as he came up behind her and wrapped his arms around her waist.

She leaned back into him and smiled, loving the feel of him pressed close, knowing, *trusting* now, that he always would be. "I was just thinking how perfect today was."

"Agreed," he said and dipped his head to kiss her cheek. "The only way it could have been better was if Alex were here, too."

Amanda turned in his arms and looked up at him. She knew his friend's disappearance was haunting Nathan. It had been nearly a month now and there were just no clues to follow. "You'll find him, Nathan. And everything will be okay."

He nodded, glanced out over the crowd gathered at the Battlelands, then turned his gaze back to hers. "I'm going to have to officially declare him missing."

A twinge of worry caught her, but she let it go again because of her faith in Nathan. He would find a way to make this right. "You'll find him."

"I will," he said, then smiled. "But that's for tomorrow. Today is for dancing in the moonlight with the woman I love."

"I'm never going to get tired of hearing that, you know."

He led her onto the makeshift dance floor installed on the front yard specifically for the wedding. And as they moved to the music and their friends and family applauded, Nathan promised, "I'm never going to stop saying it."

Amanda gave herself up to the moment, to the magic, to the man who would always be the very beat of her heart.

* * * * *

THE SECRET IN HIS HEART

CAROLINE ANDERSON

Caroline Anderson has the mind of a butterfly. She's been a nurse, a secretary, a teacher, run her own soft furnishing business, and now she's settled on writing. She says, 'I was looking for that elusive something. I finally realised it was variety, and now I have it in abundance. Every book brings new horizons and new friends, and in between books I have learned to be a juggler. My teacher husband John and I have two beautiful and talented daughters, Sarah and Hannah, umpteen pets, and several acres of Suffolk that nature tries to reclaim every time we turn our backs!' Caroline also writes for the Mills & Boon® Medical Romance™ series.

CHAPTER ONE

SILENCE.

No bleeps, no clipped instructions or clattering instruments, no hasty footsteps. Just a blissful, short-lived hush.

James stretched out his shoulders and felt the tension drain away. The relief was incredible. He savoured it for a moment before breaking the silence.

'Great teamwork, guys. Thank you. You did a good job.'

Someone chuckled. 'Would you accept anything less?'

He grinned. Fair cop, but it worked. Their critically injured patient was stabilised and on her way to Theatre, and for what seemed like the first time that day the red phone was quiet. Time to grab a break.

He glanced up at the clock. Ten to four? No wonder he was feeling light-headed. And his phone was jiggling again in his pocket.

'Right, this time I'm *really* going for lunch,' he said drily. 'Anything less than a MAJAX, you're on your own.'

There was a ripple of laughter as he tore off the thin plastic apron, dropped it in the bin with his gloves and walked out of Resus, leaving the rest of the team to clear up the chaos and restock ready for the next emergency. One of the perks of being clinical lead, he thought wryly as the door dropped shut behind him. God knows there were few enough.

He took the shortcut to the coffee shop, bought a coffee and a soft wholegrain roll stuffed with ham and salad, added a chocolate bar to boost his blood sugar and headed outside, drawing the fresh summer air deep into his lungs.

One of the best things about Yoxburgh Park Hospital was its setting. Behind the elaborate facade of the old Victorian building a modern general hospital had been created, providing the community not only with much needed medical facilities, but also a beautiful recreational area. It was green and quiet and peaceful, and he took his breaks out here whenever he could.

Not nearly often enough.

He found an empty bench under the trees and settled down to eat his lunch, pulling his phone out simultaneously to check for messages. It had jiggled in his pocket more than once in the last hour, but there were no messages, just two missed calls.

From Connie?

He frowned slightly. He hadn't heard from her in ages, and now two missed calls in the space of an hour? He felt his heart rate pick up and he called her back, drumming his fingers impatiently as he waited for the phone to connect.

She answered almost instantly, and to his relief she sounded fine.

'James, hi. Sorry, I didn't mean to disturb you. Are you at work?'

'Yeah—doesn't matter, I'm on a break now. How are you, Connie? You've been very quiet recently.' Well, not even that recently. Apart from the odd email saying nothing significant and a couple of ridiculously brief phone calls, she hadn't really contacted him since she'd got back from Afghanistan after Christmas. It wasn't just her fault. He hadn't contacted her, either, and now he felt a flicker of guilt.

She laughed, the soft musical sound making him ache a little inside. There'd been a time not so long ago when she'd never laughed…

'What, you mean I've left you in peace, Slater?'

'Something like that,' he said mildly. 'So, how are you?'

'Fine. Good. Great, really. Ready to move on.' The silence stretched out for a heartbeat, and then she said, 'Actually, I need to talk to you about that.'

She sounded oddly hesitant, and his radar started beeping.

'Fire away.'

That troubling silence again. 'I don't think it's something we can do over the phone,' she said eventually. 'I'd thought you might be off today as it's Sunday, and I thought maybe we could get together, it's been a while, but obviously not if you're working. Have you got any days off coming up?'

'Tomorrow? I'm off then for a couple of days. I don't get many weekends at the moment—crazy staffing issues—but I can always come over and see you tomorrow evening after you've finished work if it's urgent.'

'No, don't do that, I'll come to you. I'm not working at the moment so I've got plenty of time. And it isn't really urgent, I just—I wanted to talk to you. Can I pop over in the morning?'

Pop? From a hundred and thirty odd miles away? And why wasn't she working? 'Sure. Why don't you

stay over till Tuesday, if you're free? We can catch up.'
And I can find out what the hell's going on that's so
'not urgent' that you have to come tomorrow morning.

'Are you sure? It would be lovely but I've got the dog,
don't forget. Can you cope with that? She's very good
now—housetrained and all that, but I can't put her in
kennels at such short notice.'

Had she mentioned a dog? Possibly, but it didn't matter. He had a secure garden. She'd be fine. The dog was
the least of his worries.

'I'm sure we'll cope,' he said. 'Come. It'll be lovely
to see you.'

'Thanks. When do you want me?'

Always...

He crushed the inappropriate thought. 'Whenever
you're ready,' he said. 'Give me a call when you're an
hour away, so I can be sure I'm at home. I'll see you
tomorrow some time.'

'Great. Thanks, James.'

'No worries. Drive carefully.'

Ending the call, he ate the soft, squishy roll, drank
his coffee and tasted neither. All he could think about
was Connie and her non-urgent topic of conversation.
He ripped the wrapper off the chocolate bar and bit
into it absently.

What the hell did she want to talk to him about? He
had no idea, but he was beginning to regret his invitation. He must have been crazy. His place was a mess,
he had a zillion and one things to do, and catching up
with Connie just wasn't on his agenda—especially not
like this. The prospect of being alone with her for thirty-
six hours was going to test him to the limit. Not that he
wasn't looking forward to seeing her. Not at all.

Just—maybe a little too much...

Crushing the cup in his hand, he headed off back to the department, his thoughts and emotions tumbling.

Connie. His old friend, his ex-colleague, and his best friend's wife.

No. His best friend's *widow*. The woman he'd promised to take care of.

'*When it happens, James—*'

'*If it happens—*'

'*When it happens—promise me you'll take care of her.*'

'*Of course I will, you daft bastard. It won't happen. It's your last tour. You'll be fine.*'

Famous last words.

The ache of loss, still raw after two years, put everything back in perspective and gave him a timely reminder of his duties and responsibilities. It didn't matter what else he'd had planned, whatever his personal feelings for her, his duty to Connie came first and right now she needed him.

But apparently not urgently. Tomorrow would do.

Sheesh.

Savagely tossing the crushed cup into a bin, he strode through the door and headed back to work.

'Well. We're going to see James. What do you think of that, Saffy? Do you think he'll understand?'

Saffy thumped her tail once, head on Connie's foot, eyes alert as she peered up at her. Connie reached down a hand and stroked her gently, and Saffy groaned and rolled over, one leg lifted to reveal the vulnerable underside she was offering for a tickle.

'Hussy,' she crooned, rubbing the scarred tummy, and the dog's tail wagged again. She licked Connie's ankle, the contact of her warm, moist tongue cement-

ing the already close bond between them. Almost as if
she understood. No, of course she didn't, Connie told
herself. How could she, even though Connie had told
her everything there was to tell about it all in excruci-
ating detail.

'Sorry, sweetheart,' she murmured, straightening up
and getting to her feet. 'No time for cuddles, I've got
too much to do.'

If she was going to see James tomorrow, she needed
to pull herself together and get ready. Do some washing
so she had something other than jeans and a ratty old
T shirt to wear. Pack. Make sure the house was clean
and tidy before they left.

Not that it was dirty or untidy, but now the decision
was made and she was going to see him, to ask him the
most monumental and massive favour, she needed to
do something to keep herself busy or she'd go crazy.

She'd rehearsed her speech over and over again, gone
through what she was going to say until she'd worn it
out. There was nothing left to do but clean the house,
so she cleaned it until it squeaked, and then she fell into
bed and slept restlessly until dawn.

God, the place was a tip.

He'd been going to tackle it last night, but as usual
he'd been held up by admin and hadn't got home until
ten, so he'd left it till this morning. Now, looking round
it, he realised that had probably been a massive mistake.

He blitzed the worst of it, made up a bed for her and
went back downstairs.

Better. Slightly. If he ever had any regular time off
he might stand a chance, but right now that was just a
distant dream. He glanced at his watch. Ten to ten. Supermarket now, or later, after she'd arrived? She was

an early riser but the journey would take her a good two hours.

Now, he decided, if he was quick, and ten minutes later he was standing there in the aisles and trying to remember what she liked. Was she a vegetarian?

No, of course she wasn't. He recalled watching her eating a bun crammed with roast pork and apple sauce at the Suffolk Show, the memory still vivid. It must have been the first year he'd been in Yoxburgh, and Joe had been on leave.

And he'd been watching her eat, his body throbbing with need as she'd flicked out her tongue and scooped up a dribble of apple sauce on her chin. He'd dragged his eyes away and found Joe staring at him, an odd expression on his face.

'Food envy,' he'd explained hastily, and Joe had laughed and bought him another roll from the hog roast stand.

He'd had to force himself to eat it, because he hadn't had food envy at all, just plain old envy. He was jealous of Joe, jealous of his best friend for being so ridiculously happy with his lovely wife. How sick was that? How lonely and empty and barren— Whatever. She wasn't vegetarian, so he picked up a nice piece of fillet steak from the butchery counter, threw some other stuff into the trolley and headed home, wondering for the hundredth time what she wanted to say to him. She'd said she was ready to move on, and now it was in his head a disturbing possibility wouldn't go away.

Was there someone new in her life?

Why not? It was perfectly plausible. She was a beautiful woman, she was alone, she was free to do whatever she liked—but even the thought of her replacing the best friend a man could wish for, the kindest and most courageous man he'd ever known, made him feel sick.

Dismissing the pointless speculation, he drove down Ferry Road towards the little community grouped around the harbour mouth, turned onto the gravel track that led past a little string of houses to his cottage and pulled up on the drive next to a four-wheel drive he'd never seen before, just as his phone pinged.

Damn. He'd meant to be here, but she hadn't rung—or had she, while he'd been vacuuming the house?

Yup. There was a missed call from her, and a voice-mail.

'I've arrived. Couldn't get you on the phone earlier, but I'm here now so I'm walking the dog. Call me when you get home.'

He dialled her number as he carried the bags into the kitchen and dumped them on the worktop, and she answered on the second ring, sounding breathless.

'Hi—did you get my message?'

'Yeah. Sorry I wasn't here, I went food shopping. I'm back now. Where are you?'

'On the sea wall. I'll be two ticks, I can see the cottage from here,' she told him, so he opened the front door and stood on the porch step scanning the path, and there she was, blonde hair flying in the breeze, a huge sandy-coloured dog loping by her side as she ran towards him, her long limbs moving smoothly as she covered the ground with an effortless stride.

God, she was lovely.

Lovelier than ever, and that took some doing. His heart lurched, and he dredged up what he hoped was a civilised smile as he went to meet her.

She looked amazing, fit and well and bursting with energy. Her pale gold hair was gleaming, her blue eyes bright, her cheeks flushed with the sea breeze and the exertion as she ran up, her smile as wide as her arms, and threw herself at him. Her body slammed into his and knocked the breath from him in every way, and he nearly staggered at the impact.

'Hey, Slater!'

'Hey yourself, Princess,' he said on a slight laugh as his arms wrapped round her and caught her tight against him. 'Good to see you.'

'You, too.'

She hugged him hard, her body warm and firm against his for the brief duration of the embrace, and he hugged her back, ridiculously pleased to see her, because he'd missed her, this woman of Joe's. Missed her warmth and her humour, missed the laughter she carried with her everywhere she went. Or had, until she'd lost Joe.

Don't tell me you're getting married again—please, don't tell me that...

Swearing silently, he dropped his arms and stepped back, looking down at the great rangy hound standing panting at Connie's side, tongue lolling as it watched him alertly.

'So—I take it this is your rescued dog? I'd pictured some little terrier or spaniel.'

Connie winced ruefully. 'Sorry. Teensy bit bigger. This is Saffy—Safiya. It means best friend. Joe sort of adopted her in Afghanistan on his last tour. He was going to bring her home, but—well, he didn't make it, so I brought her back.'

Typical Joe, he thought with a lump in his throat. Big tough guy, soft as lights. And he'd just bet she'd been his best friend, in the harsh and desolate desert, thousands of miles from home. A touch of humanity in the inhumanity of war.

He held out his hand for Saffy to sniff. She did more than sniff it. She licked it. Gently, tentatively, coming closer to press her head against his shoulder as he crouched down to her level and stroked her long, floppy ears. A gentle giant of a dog. No wonder Joe had fallen for her.

He laughed softly, a little taken aback by the trusting gesture, and straightened up again. 'She's a sweetie,' he said, his voice slightly choked, and Connie nodded.

'She is. I had to bring her home.'

Of course she'd had to, because Saffy was her last link to Joe. If Joe had been soft, Connie was softer, but there was a core of steel in there, too. He'd seen plenty of evidence of that in the past few years.

He'd seen her holding herself together when Joe was deployed to Afghanistan for what was meant to be his final tour, and then again, just months later, when he came home for the last time in a flag-draped coffin—

'So, this is the new house, then,' she said, yanking him back to the present as he opened the gate and ushered her and Saffy through it.

He hauled in a breath and put the memories away. 'Hardly new. I've been here over two years. I'd forgotten you hadn't seen it.'

'No, well, things got in the way. I can't believe it's that long,' she said. She looked slightly bemused, as if the time had somehow passed and she'd been suspended in an emotional void. He supposed she might well have been. He had, for years. Still was in many ways, and it was a lonely place.

Take care of Connie.

Guilt ate at him. He should have been there more for

her, should have looked out for her, emailed her more often, rung her. It had been months, and he'd just let it drift by. Too busy, as usual, for the things that really mattered.

There didn't seem to be anything else to say, so he took her into the house, looking at it with the critical eyes of a stranger and finding it wanting. Not the house, but his treatment of it. The house was lovely and deserved better than a quick once-over as and when.

'Sorry, it's a bit of a mess. I haven't done a great deal to it, but the people I bought it from left it in great condition so I just moved in and got on with other things. I've been so busy I haven't even unpacked the books yet.'

She looked around and smiled. 'I can see that. You haven't put any pictures up, either.'

'I've got the sea. I don't need pictures,' he said simply, and she turned and looked out of the window, feeling the calming effect of the breakers rolling slowly in, the quiet suck of the surf on the shingle curiously soothing.

'No, I suppose you don't,' she said. She glanced around again. The living space was all open, the seating area at the front of the house facing the sea, the full-width dining and kitchen area at the back overlooking the marshes and the meandering river beyond. There was an unspoilt beauty about the area, and she could absolutely see why he'd bought the cottage.

'It's lovely, James. Really gorgeous. I was expecting something tiny from the name.'

'Thrift Cottage? There's a plant called sea thrift— *Armeria maritima*. The garden's full of it. I don't know which came first but I imagine that's the connection. It was certainly nothing to do with the price,' he said drily. 'Coffee?'

She chuckled. 'Love one. I haven't had my caffeine fix yet today.'

'Espresso, cappuccino, latte, Americano?'

She blinked. 'Wow, you must have a fancy coffee machine.'

He grinned. 'Some things have to be taken seriously.'

'So do me a flat white,' she challenged, her eyes sparkling with laughter.

Typical Connie, he thought. Never take the easy route or expect anyone else to. He rolled his eyes, took the milk out of the carrier bag he'd just brought home and started work while she and the dog watched his every move, Connie from the other side of the room, Saffy from her position on the floor just close enough to reach anything he might drop. Hope personified, he thought with a smile.

'You do know I was a *barista* while I was at uni?' he offered over his shoulder, the mischievous grin dimpling his lean cheek again and making her mouth tug in response.

'I didn't, but it doesn't surprise me.'

She watched him as he stuck a cup under the spout of the coffee machine, his broad shoulders and wide stance reminding her of Joe, and yet not. Joe had been shorter, stockier, his hair a lighter brown, and his eyes had been a muted green, unlike James's, which were a striking, brilliant ice-blue rimmed with navy. She noticed the touch of grey at his temples and frowned slightly. That was new. Or had she just not noticed before?

'So how long did the drive take you?' he asked, turning to look at her with those piercing eyes.

'Just over two hours—about two fifteen? I had a good run but I had to stop to let Saffy out for a minute.'

She stepped over the dog and perched on a high stool

beside him, and the light drift of her perfume teased his nostrils. He could feel her eyes on him as he foamed the milk, tapping the jug, swirling the espresso round the warmed cup before he poured the milk into it in a carefully controlled stream, wiggling the jug to create a perfect rosetta of microfoamed milk on top of the crema.

'Here,' he said, sliding the cup towards her with a flourish, pleased to see he hadn't lost his touch despite the audience.

'Latte art? Show-off,' she said, but she looked impressed and he couldn't resist a slightly smug chuckle.

He tore open a packet of freshly baked cookies from the supermarket, the really wicked ones oozing with calories. He wouldn't normally have bought them, but he knew Connie was a sucker for gooey cookies. He slid them towards her as Saffy watched hopefully.

'Here. Don't eat them all.'

'Whatever gave you that idea?' she said innocently, her smile teasing, and he felt his heart lurch dangerously.

'I've never yet met a woman who could resist triple choc chip cookies still warm from the oven.'

Her eyes lit up. 'Are they still warm?' she said, diving in, and he watched in fascination as she closed her eyes and sank her teeth into one.

He nearly groaned out loud. How could eating a cookie be so sexy?

'Murgh,' she said, eyes still closed, and he gave a strained chuckle and trashed his own rosetta as his hand jerked.

'That good?' he asked, his voice sounding rusty, and she nodded.

'Oh, yes,' she said, a little more intelligibly, and he laughed again, set his own coffee down on the breakfast bar and joined her on the other stool, shifting it away from her a little after he'd taken a cookie from the bag.

Her eyes were open again, and she was pulling another one apart, dissecting it slowly and savouring every bit, and he almost whimpered.

He *did* whimper. Did he? *Really?*

'Saffy, don't beg,' she said through a mouthful of cookie, and he realised it was the dog. He heaved a quiet sigh of relief and grabbed the last cookie, as much as anything so he wouldn't have to watch her eat it.

And then, just because they had to talk about something and anyway, the suspense was killing him, he asked, 'So, what did you want to talk to me about?'

Connie felt her heart thump.

This was it, her chance to ask him, and yet now she was here she had no idea—*no* idea—how to do it. Her carefully rehearsed speech had deserted her, and her mind flailed. *Start at the beginning*, she told herself, and took a deep breath.

'Um—did you realise Joe and I were having problems?' she asked tentatively.

'Problems?'

James stared at her, stunned by that. Problems were the last thing he would have associated with them. They'd always seemed really happy together, and Joe, certainly, had loved Connie to bits. Had it not been mutual? No, Joe would have said—wouldn't he? Maybe not.

'What sort of problems?' he asked warily, not at all sure he wanted to know.

'Only one—well, two, if you count the fact that I spent our entire marriage waiting for the doorbell to ring and someone in uniform to tell me he was dead.'

'I'd count that,' he said gruffly. He'd felt it himself, every time Joe had been deployed on active service— and it didn't get much more active than being a bomb disposal officer. But still, he'd never really expected it to happen. Maybe Connie had been more realistic.

'And the other problem?'

She looked away, her expression suddenly bleak. 'We couldn't have children.'

He frowned, speechless for a second as it sank in. He set his cup down carefully and closed his eyes. When he opened them she was watching him again, her bottom lip caught between her teeth, waiting for him to say the right thing.

Whatever the hell that was. He let out a long, slow sigh and shook his head.

'Ah, Connie. I'm so sorry. I didn't realise there was anything wrong. I always thought it was by choice, something you'd get round to when he'd finished that last tour.'

...except he never had...

'It was.' She smiled a little unsteadily, and looked away again. 'Actually, he was going to come and see you about it when he got home.'

'Me?' he asked, puzzled by that. 'I don't know anything about infertility. You're a doctor, you probably know as much about it as I do, if not more. You needed to see a specialist.'

'We had. It wasn't for that. We'd had the tests, and he was the one with the problem. Firing blanks, as he put it.' She grimaced a little awkwardly, uncomfortable revealing what Joe had considered a weakness, a failure, something to be ashamed of. 'I wanted him to tell you, but he wouldn't, not for ages. He was psyching himself up to do it when he got home, but it was so hard for him, even though you were so close.'

'We were, but—guys don't talk about that kind of thing, Connie, especially when they're like Joe.'

'I know. It's stupid, I feel so disloyal telling you because he just wouldn't talk about it. I would have told you ages ago, but he couldn't, and so nor could I because it wasn't my secret to tell.'

He sighed and reached out a hand, laying it over her arm and squeezing gently. 'Don't feel disloyal. I loved him, too, remember. You can tell me anything you need to, and you know it won't go any further.'

She nodded. 'I know. I just wish he'd felt he could tell you.'

'Me, too.' He sighed again and withdrew his hand. 'I'm really sorry, Connie. That must have been so tough to deal with.'

She looked down at her coffee, poking at the foam with the teaspoon, drawing little trails absently through the rosetta, and he noticed her cheeks had coloured a little.

She sucked in a slightly shaky breath. 'He was going to tell you, as soon as he got back. He wanted to ask you...' *Oh, just spit it out, woman! He can only say no!*

She sat up straighter and made herself look him in the eye, her heart pounding. 'He was going to ask you if you'd consider being a sperm donor for us.'

He stared at her blankly, the shock robbing him of his breath for a moment. He hauled it back in and frowned.

'Me?'

They'd wanted him to give them a child?

'Why me?' he asked, his voice sounding strangely distant. *Of all the people in the world, why me?*

She shrugged. 'Why not? I would have thought it

was obvious. He doesn't have a brother, you were his best friend, he loved and respected you. Plus you're not exactly ugly or stupid. Who better?' She paused for a second, fiddled with her spoon, then met his eyes again, her own a little wary. 'Would you have said yes?'

He shook his head to clear it, still reeling a little from the shock.

'Hell, I don't know, Connie. I have no idea.'

'But—possibly?'

He shrugged. 'Maybe.'

A baby? Maybe not. Most likely not.

'Definitely maybe? Like, probably?'

Would he? He tried to think, but he was still trying to come to terms with it and thinking seemed too hard right then.

'I don't know. I really don't know. I might have considered it, I suppose, but it's irrelevant now, so it's hard to know how I would have reacted. But you would have been brilliant parents. I'm just so sorry you never had the chance. That really sucks.'

She'd shifted her attention to the cookie crumbs on the breakfast bar, pushing them around with her fingertip, and he saw her swallow. Then she lifted her head and met his eyes. Her whole body seemed to go still, as if every cell was holding its breath. And then she spoke.

'What if it wasn't irrelevant now?'

CHAPTER TWO

WAS THIS WHY she'd wanted to see him? To ask him *this*?

He searched her eyes, and they didn't waver.

'What are you saying, Connie?' he asked quietly, but he knew already, could feel the cold reality of it curling around him like freezing fog.

He saw her swallow again. 'I wondered—I don't know how you'll feel about it, and I know Joe's not here now, but—James, I still really want a baby.'

He stared at her, saw the pleading in her eyes, and he felt suddenly drenched with icy sweat. She meant it. She really, really meant it—

He shoved the stool back abruptly and stood up, taking a step away on legs that felt like rubber. 'No. I'm sorry, Connie. I can't do it.'

He walked away, going out onto the veranda and curling his fingers round the rail, his hands gripping it so hard his knuckles were bleached white while the memories poured through him.

Cathy, coming into their bedroom, her eyes bright with joy in her pale face, a little white wand in her hand.

'I might've worked out why I've been feeling rough...'

He heard Connie's footsteps on the boards behind him, could feel her just inches away, feel her warmth, hear the soft sigh of her breath. Her voice, when she spoke, was hesitant.

'James? I'm sorry. I know it's a bit weird, coming out of the blue like that, but please don't just say no without considering it—'

Her voice cracked slightly, and she broke off. Her hand was light on his shoulder, tentative, trembling slightly. It burned him all the way through to his soul.

'James? Talk to me?'

'There's nothing to talk about,' he said, his voice hollow. 'Joe's dead, Connie. He's gone.' *They're all gone...*

Her breath sucked in softly. 'Do you think I don't know that? Do you really think that in the last two years I haven't noticed? But I'm still here, and I'm alive, and I'm trying to move on with my life, to rescue something from the wreckage. And you could help me do that. Give me something to live for. Please. At least think about it.'

He turned his head slightly and stared at her, then looked away again. 'Hell, Connie, you know how to push a guy's buttons.' His voice was raw now, rasping, and he swallowed hard, shaking his head again to clear it, but it didn't work this time any more than it had the last.

'I'm sorry. I know it's a bit sudden and unexpected, but—you said you would have considered it.'

'No, I said I *might* have considered it, for you and Joe. Not just for you! I can't do that, Connie! I can't just hand you a little pot of my genetic material and walk away and leave you on your own. What kind of person would that make me?'

'Generous? I'd still be the mother, still be the primary carer, whatever. What's the difference?'

'The difference? The *difference* is that you're on your

own, and children need two parents. There's no way I could be responsible for a child coming into the world that I wasn't involved with on a daily basis—'

'So—what? You want to be involved? You can be involved—'

'What? No! Connie, no. Absolutely not. I don't want to be a father! It's not anywhere, anyhow, on my agenda.'

Not any more.

'Joe said you might say that. I mean, if you'd wanted kids you would have got married again, wouldn't you? But he said you'd always said you wouldn't, and he thought that might be the very reason you'd agree, because you might see it as the only way you'd ever have a child…'

She trailed off, as if she knew she'd gone too far, and he stared down at his stark white knuckles, his fingers burning with the tension. One by one he made them relax so that he could let go of the rail and walk away. Away from Connie, away from the memories that were breaking through his carefully erected defences and flaying him to shreds.

Cathy's face, her eyes alight with joy. The first scan, that amazing picture of their baby. And then, just weeks later…

'No, Connie. I'm sorry, but—no. You don't know what you're asking. I can't. I just can't…'

The last finger peeled away from the railing and he spun on his heel and walked off, down the steps, across the garden, out of the gate.

She watched him go, her eyes filling, her last hope of having the child she and Joe had longed for so desperately fading with every step he took, and she put her hand over her mouth to hold in the sob and went back to the kitchen to a scene of utter chaos.

'Oh, Saffy, no!' she wailed as the dog shot past her, a slab of meat dangling from her jaws.

It was the last straw. Sinking down on the floor next to the ravaged shopping bags, Connie pulled up her knees, rested her head on them and sobbed her heart out as all the hopes and dreams she and Joe had cherished crumbled into dust.

It took him a while to realise the dog was at his side.

He was sitting on the sea wall, hugging one knee and staring blindly out over the water. He couldn't see anything but Connie.

Not the boats, not the sea—not even the face of the wife he'd loved and lost. He struggled to pull up the image, but he couldn't, not now, when he wanted to. All he could see was Connie's face, the hope and pleading in her eyes as she'd asked him the impossible, the agonising disappointment when he'd turned her down, and it was tearing him apart.

Finally aware of Saffy's presence, he turned his head and met her eyes. She was sitting beside him, the tip of her tail flickering tentatively, and he lifted his hand and stroked her.

'I can't do it, Saffy,' he said, his voice scraping like the shingle on the beach. 'I want to help her, I promised to look after her, but I can't do that, I just can't. She doesn't know what she's asking, and I can't tell her. I can't explain. I can't say it out loud.'

Saffy shifted slightly, leaning on him, and he put his arm over her back and rested his hand on her chest, rubbing it gently; after a moment she sank down to the ground with a soft grunt and laid her head on her paws, her weight against him somehow comforting and reassuring.

How many times had Joe sat like this with her, in the heat and dust and horror of Helmand? He stroked her side, and she shifted again, so that his hand fell naturally onto the soft, unguarded belly, offered with such trust.

He ran his fingers over it and stilled, feeling the ridges of scars under his fingertips. It shocked him out of his grief.

'Oh, Saffy, what happened to you, sweetheart?' he murmured. He turned his head to study the scars, and saw feet.

Two feet, long and slim, slightly dusty, clad in sandals, the nails painted fire-engine-red. He hadn't heard her approaching over the sound of the sea, but there she was, and he couldn't help staring at those nails. They seemed so cheerful and jolly, so totally out of kilter with his despair.

He glanced up at her and saw that she'd been crying, her eyes red-rimmed and bloodshot, her cheeks smudged with tears. His throat closed a little, but he said nothing, and after a second she sat down on the other side of the dog, her legs dangling over the wall as she stared out to sea.

'She was injured when he found her,' she said softly, answering his question. 'They did a controlled explosion of an IED, and Saffy must have got caught in the blast. She had wounds all over her. He should have shot her, really, but he was racked with guilt and felt responsible, and the wounds were only superficial, so he fed her and put antiseptic on them, and bit by bit she got better, and she adored him. I've got photos of them together with his arm round her in the compound. His

commanding officer would have flayed the skin off
him if he'd known, especially as Joe was the officer in
charge of the little outpost, but he couldn't have done
anything else. He broke all the rules for her, and nobody ever said a word.'

'And you brought her home for him.'

She tried to smile. 'I had to. I owed it to her, and anyway, he'd already arranged it. There's a charity run by
an ex-serviceman to help soldiers bring home the dogs
that they've adopted over there, and it was all set up,
but when Joe died the arrangements ground to a halt.
Then a year later, just before I went out to Afghanistan,
someone from the charity contacted me and said the
dog was still hanging around the compound and did I
still want to go ahead.'

'And of course you did.' He smiled at her, his eyes
creasing with a gentle understanding that brought a
lump to her throat. She swallowed.

'Yeah. Well. Anyway, they were so helpful. The
money wasn't the issue because Joe had already paid
them, it was the red tape, and they knew just how to
cut through it, and she was flown home a month later,
just after I left for Afghanistan. She was waiting for me
in the quarantine kennels when I got home at the end
of December, and she's been with me ever since, but it
hasn't been easy.'

'No, I'm sure it hasn't. Poor Saffy,' he said, his hand
gentle on her side, and Connie reached out and put her
hand over his, stilling it.

'James, I'm really sorry. I didn't mean to upset you. I
just—it was the last piece of the puzzle, really, the last
thing we'd planned apart from bringing Saffy home.
We'd talked about it for so long, and he was so excited
about the idea that maybe at last we could have a baby.

He didn't know what you'd say, which way you'd go, but he was hoping he could talk you into it.'

And maybe he could have done, she thought, if James had meant what he'd said about considering it. But now, because Joe was dead, James had flatly refused to help her because she'd be alone and that was different, apparently.

'You know,' she said softly, going on because she couldn't just give up on this at the first hurdle, 'if you'd said yes to him and then he'd been killed in some accident, for instance, I would still have had to bring the baby up alone. What would you have done then, if I'd already had a child?'

'I would have looked after you both,' he said instantly, 'but you haven't had a child, and Joe's gone, and I don't want that responsibility.'

'There is no responsibility.'

He stared at her. 'Of course there is, Connie. I can't just give you a child and let you walk off into the sunset with it and forget about it. Get real. This is my flesh and blood you're talking about. My child. I could never forget my child.'

Ever...

'But you would have done it for us?'

He shook his head slowly. 'I don't know. Maybe, maybe not, but Joe's not here any more, and a stable, happily married couple who desperately want a baby isn't the same as a grieving widow clinging to the remnants of a dream.'

'But that's not what I'm doing, not what this is about.'

'Are you sure? Have you really analysed your motives, Connie? I don't think so. And what if you meet someone?' he asked her, that nagging fear suddenly rising again unbidden and sickening him. 'What if, a couple of years down the line, another man comes into your life? What then? Would you expect me to sit back and watch a total stranger bringing up my child, with no say in how they do it?'

She shook her head vehemently. 'That won't happen—and anyway, I'm getting older. I'm thirty-six now. Time's ebbing away. I don't know if I'll ever be truly over Joe, and by the time I am, and I've met someone and trust him enough to fall in love, it'll be too late for me and I really, really want this. It's now or never, James.'

It was. He could see that, knew that her fertility was declining with every year that passed, but that wasn't his problem. Nothing about this was his problem. Until she spoke again.

'I don't want to put pressure on you, and I respect your decision. I just—I would much rather it was someone Joe had loved and respected, someone I loved and respected, than an anonymous donor.'

'Anonymous donor?' he said, his voice sounding rough and gritty to his ears.

'Well, what else? If it can't be you, I don't know who else it would be. There's nobody else I could ask, but if I go for a donor how do I know what they're like? How do I know if they've got a sense of humour, or any brains or integrity—I might as well go and pull someone in a nightclub and have a random—'

'Connie, for God's sake!'

She gave a wry, twisted little smile.

'Don't worry, James. It's OK. I'm not *that* crazy. I won't do anything stupid.'

'Good,' he said tautly. 'And for the record, I don't like emotional blackmail.'

'It wasn't!' she protested, her eyes filling with tears.

'Really, James, it wasn't, I wouldn't do that to you. I wasn't serious. I'm really not that nuts.'

He wasn't sure. Not nuts, maybe, but—desperate?

'When it happens—promise me you'll take care of her.'

'Of course I will, you daft bastard. It won't happen. It's your last tour. You'll be fine.'

But he hadn't been fine, and now Connie was here, making hideous jokes about doing something utterly repugnant, and he felt the weight of responsibility crush him.

'Promise me you won't do anything stupid,' he said gruffly.

'I won't.'

'Nothing. Don't do anything. Not yet.'

She tilted her head and searched his eyes, her brows pleating together thoughtfully. 'Not yet?'

Not ever, because I can't bear the thought of you giving your body to a total stranger in some random, drunken encounter, and because if anybody's going to give you a baby, it's me—

The thought shocked him rigid. He jack-knifed to his feet and strode back to the house, his heart pounding, and after a few moments he heard the crunch of gravel behind him on the path.

Saffy was already there at his side, glued to his leg, and as he walked into the kitchen and stared at the wreckage of his shopping bags, she wagged her tail sheepishly, guilt written all over her.

A shadow fell across the room.

'Ah. Sorry. I was coming to tell you—she stole the steak.'

He gave a soft, slightly unsteady laugh and shook his head. 'Oh, Saffy. You are such a bad dog,' he murmured, with so much affection in his voice it brought a lump to her throat. He seemed to be doing that a lot today.

'She was starving when Joe found her. She steals because it's all she knows, the only way she could survive. And it really is her only vice. I'll replace the steak—'

'To hell with the steak,' he said gruffly. 'She's welcome to it. We'll just have to go to the pub tonight.'

Better that way than sitting alone together in his house trying to have a civilised conversation over dinner and picking their way through this minefield. Perhaps Saffy had inadvertently done them both a favour.

'Well, I could have handled that better, couldn't I, Saff?'

Saffy just wagged her tail lazily and stretched. James had gone shopping again because it turned out it was more than just the steak that needed replacing, so Connie was sitting on a bench in the garden basking in the lovely warm June sunshine and contemplating the mess she'd made of all this.

He'd refused her offer of company, saying the dog had spent long enough in the car, and to be honest she was glad he'd gone without her because it had all become really awkward and uncomfortable, and if it hadn't mattered so much she would have packed up the dog and her luggage and left.

But then he'd said 'yet'.

Don't do anything yet.

She dropped her head back against the wall of the cabin behind her and closed her eyes and wondered what he'd really meant by 'yet'.

She had no idea.

None that she dared to contemplate, anyway, in case a ray of hope sneaked back in and she had to face having it dashed all over again, but he'd had a strange look about him, and then he'd stalked off.

Run away?

'No! Stop it! Stop thinking about it. He didn't mean anything, it was just a turn of phrase.'

Maybe…

She opened her eyes and looked up at the house, trying to distract herself. It was set up slightly above the level of the garden, possibly because of the threat of flooding before the sea wall had been built, but the result was that even from the ground floor there were lovely views out to sea across the mouth of the estuary and across the marshes behind, and from the bedrooms the views would be even better.

She wondered where she'd be sleeping. He hadn't shown her to her room yet, but it wasn't a big house so she wouldn't be far away from him, and she felt suddenly, ridiculously uneasy about being alone in the house with him for the night.

Crazy. There was nothing to feel uneasy about. He'd stayed with them loads of times, and he'd stayed the night after Joe's funeral, too, refusing to leave her until he was sure she was all right.

And anyway, what was he going to do, jump her bones? Hardly, James just wasn't like that. He'd never so much as looked at her sideways, never mind made her feel uncomfortable like some of Joe's other friends had.

If he had, there was no way she would have broached the sperm donor subject. Way too intimate. It had been hard enough as it was, and maybe that was why she felt uneasy. The whole subject was necessarily very personal and intimate, and she'd gone wading in there without any warning and shocked his socks off.

It dawned on her belatedly that she hadn't even asked

if there was anyone else who might have been a consideration in this, but that was so stupid. He was a fit, healthy and presumably sexual active man who was entitled to have a relationship with anyone he chose. She'd just assumed he wasn't in a relationship, assumed that just because he'd never mentioned anyone, there wasn't anyone.

OK, so he probably wasn't getting married to her, whoever she might be, but that didn't stop him having a lover. Several, if he chose. Did he bring them back here?

She realised she was staring up at the house and wondering which was his bedroom, wondering where in the house he made love to the *femme du jour*, and it stopped her in her tracks.

What was she *doing*, even *thinking* about his private life? Why the hell was she here at all? How had she had the nerve to ask him to do this?

But he'd said 'yet'…

She sighed and stopped staring up at the house. Thinking about James and sex in the same breath was *so* not the way forward, not if she wanted to keep this clinical and uninvolved. And she did. She had to, because it was complicated enough. She looked around her instead, her eye drawn again to the cabin behind her. It was painted in a lovely muted grey-green, set up slightly on stilts so it was raised above the level of the garden like the house, with steps up to the doors.

She wondered what he used it for. It might be a store room, but it seemed far too good to use as a glory-hole. That would be such a waste.

Home gym? Possibly, although he didn't have the sort of muscles that came from working out. He looked like more of a runner, or maybe a tennis player. Not that

she'd studied his body, she thought, frowning at herself.
Why would she? But she'd noticed, of course she had.

She dragged herself back to the subject. Hobbies
room? She wasn't aware that he had any. James had
never mentioned it, and she realised that for all she'd
known him for years, she hardly *knew* him. Not really.
Not deep down. She'd met him nine years ago, worked
with him for a year as his SHO, seen him umpteen times
since then while she'd been with Joe, but he didn't give
a lot away, at least not to her. Never had.

Maybe that was how she'd felt able to come down
here and ask him this? Although if she'd known more
about how he ticked she could have engineered her argument to target his weak spot. Or had she inadvertently
done that? His reaction had been instant and unmistakeable. He'd recoiled from the idea as if it was unthinkable, but then he'd begun to relent—hadn't he?

She wasn't sure. It would have helped if Joe had
paved the way, but he hadn't, and so she'd had to go in
cold and blunder about in what was obviously a very
sensitive area. Pushing his buttons, as he'd put it. And
he'd said no, so she'd upset him for nothing.

Except he hadn't given her a flat-out no in the end,
had he? He'd said don't do anything *yet*. Whatever yet
meant.

She sighed. Back to that again.

He didn't really need another trip to the supermarket.
They could have managed. He'd just needed space to
think, to work out what, if anything, he could do to stop
Connie from making the biggest mistake of her life.

Or his.

He swore softly under his breath, swung the car into
a parking space and did a quick raid of the bacon and

sausage aisle to replace all the breakfast ingredients Saffy had pinched, then he drove back home, lecturing himself every inch of the way on how his responsibility to Connie did *not* mean he had to do this.

He just had to stop her doing something utterly crazy. The very thought of her with a total stranger made him gag, but he wasn't much more thrilled by the idea of her conceiving a child from a nameless donor courtesy of a turkey baster.

Hell, it could be anybody! They could have some inherited disease, some genetic disorder that would be passed on to a child—a predisposition to cancer, heart disease, all manner of things. Rationally, of course, he knew that no reputable clinic would use unscreened donors, and the checks were rigorous. Very rigorous. He *knew* that, but even so...

What would Joe have thought about it? If he'd refused, what would Joe and Connie have done next? Asked another friend? Gone to a clinic?

It was irrelevant, he told himself again. That was then, this was now, this was Connie on her own, fulfilling a lost dream. God knows what her motives were, but he was pretty sure she hadn't examined them in enough detail or thought through the ramifications. Somehow or other he had to talk her out of it, or at the very least try. He owed it to Joe. He'd promised to take care of her, and he would, because he kept his promises, and he'd keep this one if it killed him.

Assuming she'd let him, because her biological clock was obviously ticking so loud it was deafening her to reason. And as for his crazy reaction, that absurd urge to give her his baby—and without the benefit of any damn turkey baster—

Swearing viciously under his breath, he pulled up in

a slew of gravel, and immediately he could hear Saffy yipping and scrabbling at the gate.

'Do you reckon she can smell the shopping?' Connie asked, smiling tentatively at him over the top, and he laughed briefly and turned his attention to the shopping bags, wondering yet again how on earth he was in this position. Why she hadn't warned him over the phone, said something, anything, some little hint so he hadn't been quite so unprepared when she'd just come out with it, though quite how she would have warned him—

'Probably,' he said drily. 'I think I'd better put this lot away in the fridge pronto. I take it she can't open the fridge?'

'She hasn't ever done it yet.'

'Don't start now,' he said, giving the dog a level stare immediately cancelled out by a head-rub that had her shadowing him into the kitchen.

Connie followed him, too, hesitating on the threshold. 'James, I'm really sorry. I didn't mean to put you in a difficult position.'

He paused, his hand on the fridge door, and looked at her over his shoulder. 'You didn't,' he said honestly. 'Joe did. It was his idea. You were just following up on it.'

'I could have let it go.'

'So why didn't you?'

Her smile was wry and touched with sadness. 'Because I couldn't,' she answered softly, 'not while there was any hope,' and he straightened up and shut the fridge and hugged her, because she just looked so damned unhappy and there was nothing he could do to make it better.

No amount of taking care of her was going to sort this out, short of doing what she'd asked, and he wasn't sure he would ever be able to do that, despite that visceral urge which had caught him off guard. Or because of it? Just the thought of her pregnant with his child...

He let her go, easing her gently away with his hands on her shoulders and creating some much-needed distance between them, because his thoughts were suddenly wildly inappropriate, and the graphic images shocked him.

'Why don't you stick the kettle on and we'll have a cup of tea, and then we can take Saffy for a walk and go to the pub for supper.'

'Are we still going? I thought you'd just been shopping.'

He shrugged. 'I didn't bother to get anything for tonight. The pub seemed like a good idea—unless—is Saffy all right to leave here while we eat?'

She stared at him for a second, as if she was regrouping.

'Yes, she's fine. I've got a big wire travelling crate I use for her—it's a sort of retreat. I leave the door open all day so she can go in there to sleep or get away from it all, and I put her in there at night.'

'Because you don't trust her?'

'Not entirely,' she said drily. 'Still early days, and she did pinch the steak and the sausages.'

'The crate it is, then.' He smiled wryly, then glanced at his watch. 'Why don't we bring your luggage in and put it in your room while the kettle boils? I would have done it before but things ran away with us a little.'

Didn't they just? she thought.

He carried the dog's crate, she carried her overnight bag and the bag of stuff for Saffy—food, toys, blanket. Well, not a blanket, really, just an old jumper of Joe's she'd been unable to part with, and then when Saffy had come home she'd found a justification for her sentimental idiocy.

'Can we leave the crate down here?' she asked. 'She'll be fine in the kitchen, she's used to it.'

'Sure. Come on up, I'll give you a guided tour. It'll take about ten seconds. The house isn't exactly enormous.'

It wasn't, but it was lovely. There were doors from the entrance hall into the ground floor living space, essentially one big L-shaped room, with a cloakroom off the hallway under the stairs, and the landing above led into three bedrooms, two doubles and a single, and a small but well-equipped and surprisingly luxurious bathroom.

He showed her into the large bedroom at the front, simply furnished with a double bed, wardrobe and chest of drawers. There was a pale blue and white rug on the bare boards between the bed and the window, and on the edge of it was a comfy armchair, just right for reading in. And the bed, made up in crisp white linen, sat squarely opposite the window—perfect for lying there drinking early morning tea and gazing out to sea.

She crossed to the window and looked left, over the river mouth, the current rippling the water. The window was open and she could hear the suck of the sea on the shingle, the keening of the gulls overhead, and if she breathed in she could smell the salt in the air.

'Oh, James, it's lovely,' she sighed.

'Everyone likes this room.' He put her bag down and took a step towards the door. 'I'll leave you to settle in.'

'No need. I travel light. It'll take me three seconds to unpack.'

She followed him back out onto the landing and noticed another flight of stairs leading up.

'So what's up there?' she asked.

'My room.'

He didn't volunteer anything else, didn't offer to show it to her, and she didn't ask. She didn't want to enter his personal space. Not under the circumstances. Not after her earlier speculation about his love life. The last thing she needed was to see the bed he slept in. So she didn't ask, just followed him downstairs, got her walking boots out of the car and put them on.

'In your own time, Slater,' she said lightly, and he gave her one of those wry smiles of his and got off the steps and led her and Saffy out of the gate.

CHAPTER THREE

SHE PUT SAFFY on a lead because she didn't really want to spend half the evening looking for her if she ran off, but the dog attached herself to James like glue and trotted by his side, the lead hanging rather pointlessly across the gap between her and Connie.

Faithless hound.

'So, where are we going?' she asked, falling in beside them.

'I thought we could go along by the river, then cut inland on the other side of the marshes and pick up the lane. It'll bring us out on the sea wall from the other direction. It's about three miles. Is that OK?'

'Sounds good.'

The path narrowed on top of the river wall, and she dropped back behind him, Saffy still glued to his heels, and in the end she gave him the lead.

'You seem to have a new friend,' she said drily, and he glanced down at the dog and threw her a grin over his shoulder.

'Looks like it. Is that a problem?'

'No, of course not,' she said promptly. 'I'm glad she likes you. She does seem to like men, I expect because she's been used to them looking after her out in Helmand, but she'll have to get over it when we go home tomorrow. I hope it won't unsettle her.'

'Do you think it might?'

'I don't know. I hope not. She's doing so well.'

'Apart from the thieving,' he said drily, and she gave a guilty chuckle.

'Yeah, well. Apart from that.'

They walked in silence for a while by the muddy shallows at the edge of the river, and then as they turned inland and headed uphill, he dropped back beside her and said, 'So, how was Afghanistan? You haven't really told me anything about it.'

'No. It was a bit strange really. A bit surreal, but I'm glad I went. The facilities at Camp Bastion are fantastic. The things they do, what they achieve—for a field hospital it's unbelievable. Did you know it's got the busiest trauma unit in the world?'

'I'm not surprised. Most of them aren't in an area that has conflict.'

'No. No, they aren't. And I found that aspect really difficult.'

'Because of Joe?'

She nodded. 'Sort of. Because of all of them, really. I had second thoughts about going, after he died. I didn't know how I'd feel facing the stark reality of it, but I realised when the first wave of grief receded that I still wanted to go. There was so much I wanted to try and understand, such as why it was necessary, why he'd gone in the first place, what he'd been trying to achieve.'

'And did you?'

'No. No, I still don't understand, not really. I don't think I ever will and I'm not sure I want to. People killing each other, maiming each other—it all seems so pointless and destructive. There must be a better way than all this senseless violence.'

'It must have been really hard for you, Connie,' he said, his voice gentle. 'Very close to home.'

She nodded slowly, remembering the shock of seeing the first casualties come in, the realisation that this was it, this was what really happened out there. 'It was. I'd seen videos, had training, but I hadn't really understood what it was like for him until then. Seeing the injured lads there, though, fighting so hard to save them—it brought it all home to me, what he'd gone through, the threat he'd faced every day, never knowing when or if it might happen to him. That was tough.'

'I'm sure. He mentioned you were talking about going. I got the feeling he didn't like it much.'

'No, he didn't. I don't think he wanted to be worrying about me while he was trying to do his job, and he'd tried to put me off when I joined the Territorial Army as a volunteer doctor four years ago, but I thought, if Joe can do it, so can I. Not in the same way, but to do something, to do some good—and I'm glad I did, even though it was tough, because it's an incredible experience as a doctor.'

They fell silent for a while, then she went on, 'It's amazing what they can do there, you know, saving people that in civilian medicine we simply couldn't save because we just don't get to them fast enough or treat them aggressively enough when we do.'

He followed her lead and switched the conversation to practical medical aspects. 'So what would you change about the way we do things here?'

'Speed. Blood loss. That's the real killer out there, so stopping that fast is key, and transfusions. Massive transfusions. We gave one guy a hundred and fifty units of whole blood, plasma, platelets—you name it. No mucking about with saline and colloids, it's straight in with the blood products. And total body scans, the second they're stable enough to go, so they can see exactly what's wrong and treat it. We should really be doing that with multiple trauma, because it's so easy to miss something when there's loads going on.'

He nodded. 'If only we could, but we just don't have the resources. And as for the time issue—we lose people so often because they just get to us too slowly.'

'Oh, they do. We have the golden hour. They have the platinum ten minutes—they fly out a consultant-led team, scoop them up and bring them back and they're treating them aggressively before the helicopter's even airborne. Every soldier carries a tourniquet and is trained to use it in an emergency, and it's made so much difference. They save ninety per cent of multiple trauma patients, where in the rest of the world we save about twenty per cent. And I realised that if Joe died despite everything they were able to throw at him, it was because he was unsaveable. That was quite cathartic.'

He nodded slowly. 'I can imagine it would be. So, will you go again?'

'No,' she said softly. 'I'm glad I went, because it helped me let go of Joe, but I've done it now, and I've said goodbye and I've left the TA. I need to move on. I have other goals now.'

A baby, for one.

He went quiet for a while, then turned his head and looked at her searchingly.

'So how come you aren't working at the moment?'

She gave him a fleeting smile and looked away again. 'I wondered if you'd ask that. I could blame it on Saffy, say she'd taken a lot of time, a lot of training, and in a way it's true, but really she's just an excuse. I guess I was—I don't know... Taking time out to regroup, maybe? I worked solidly for the first year after he died, and I didn't give myself time to think, and then I went off to Afghanistan and put even more pressure on myself. That was a mistake, and by the time I got back after Christmas I was wiped. I needed time just to breathe a bit and work out where I go from here. A bit of a gap year, in a way. So I took it—or a few months, anyway. Just to try and make some sense of it.'

She made herself meet his eyes again, and found a gentle understanding in them.'Yeah. I did that after Cathy died. Took a gap year and grabbed the world by the throat, trying to make sense of it.'

'Did it help?'

He thought back to the aching emptiness, the people he'd met who'd scarcely registered in the haze of grief that had surrounded him. 'No. I don't know. Maybe. Maybe not. It took me away from it, but when I came back it was still there, lurking in wait. The grief, the loneliness.'

It was the closest he'd ever got to talking about Cathy, so she pushed a little more, to see if he'd open up further.

'She had cancer, didn't she?'

The shadows in his eyes darkened. 'Yes. One minute she was fine, the next she was dying.'

Connie felt her heart ache for him. 'Oh, James. It must have been dreadful watching that.'

He could see her now, the image crystal clear, pale as a ghost against the crisp white sheets, trying to smile at him, the small, neat curve of her doomed pregnancy so prominent in that thin frame.

'It was,' he said simply.

They reached the lane then, and he led the way, walking in single file for a while, facing the oncoming traffic.

Convenient, she thought, since it meant they couldn't talk. Far from opening up, he'd shut down again, so she left him alone, just following on behind until they reached the sea wall again and turned left towards the harbour and the little community clustered around the river mouth.

As they drew nearer they passed a house, a sprawling, ultra-modern house clad in cedar that had faded to silver. It was set in a wonderful garden on the end of the little string of properties, and there were children playing outside on the lawn, running in and out of a sprinkler and shrieking happily, and a woman with a baby on her hip waved to him.

He waved back, and turned to Connie as they walked on. 'That's Molly. She and her husband used to own my house. They outgrew it.'

'I should think they did. There were a lot of children there.'

'Oh, they're not all hers,' he said with a fleeting smile. 'The baby's theirs and she's got a son of about twelve, I think, and they've got another little one. The others will be her sister-in-law's. They didn't want to move away from here, but with two children and room for her painting they were struggling for space, as you can imagine, and then that house came on the market and David pounced on it.'

'It's an amazing house. They must have had a stash of cash somewhere or a lottery win.'

He chuckled, the sombre mood seeming to slip away. 'Oh, it didn't look like that when they bought it, but I don't think they're exactly strapped. David's a property developer and he part-owns a chain of boutique hotels in Australia. His father's a local building contractor, and they extended the house massively. She's got a great studio space and gallery there, and they've done a lovely job of it. They're nice people. Good neighbours.'

She wondered what it must be like to live in one place long enough to get to know your neighbours. She'd moved so much with Joe, shifting from one base to another, never putting down roots, and it hadn't been much better in her childhood. She envied James the stability of his life, even if he was alone. Not that she knew that for sure, she reminded herself.

He cut down off the sea wall to his garden gate and held it for her. 'Right, I need a shower, and then shall we go over to the pub? I haven't had anything but those cookies since breakfast and I'm starving.'

'Me, too, but I need to feed the dog. You take the bathroom first.'

'No need. I've got my own upstairs.'

She felt the tension she'd been unaware of leave her. So, no sharing a bathroom, no awkward moments of him tapping on the door or her being caught in the hall with dripping hair.

Heavens, what was wrong with her? This was *James*!

'Half an hour?' he suggested.

'That's fine. I'll feed Saffy first.'

He disappeared up the stairs, and she fed the dog and put her in the crate, not taking any chances while she was getting ready to go out. This would *not* be the diplomatic time to find out that Saffy could, indeed, open the door of the fridge.

She put her hair up in a knot and showered quickly, then contemplated her clothes. She hadn't really brought anything for going out, it hadn't occurred to her, but it was only the pub and she'd got a pretty top that would do. She put it on over her cropped jeans, let her hair down and then put on some makeup. Not much, just a touch of neutral eyeshadow, a swipe of mascara and a clear, shimmery lipgloss. Just enough to hide behind.

'Stupid woman,' she muttered. They were going to the local pub for a quick meal to make up for the fact that Saffy had stolen the steak. It wasn't an interview, and it sure as hell wasn't a date.

Not even remotely!

So why did she feel so nervous?

She looked gorgeous.

She wasn't dressed up, but she'd put on a little bit of makeup and a fine, soft jersey top that draped enticingly over her subtle curves.

She wasn't over-endowed, but she was in proportion, and when she leant forward to pick up her drink the low neckline fell away slightly, just enough to give him a tantalising glimpse of the firm swell of her breasts cradled in lace.

Fine, delicate lace, the colour of ripe raspberries.

He hauled his eyes away from her underwear and sat back, propping an ankle on the other knee to give his unruly body a little privacy. God, what was *wrong* with him?

'So, what are you going to eat?' he asked, studying the menu even though he knew it by heart.

'I don't know. What's good?'

'All of it. I eat here fairly often, and there's always something new on. The specials are worth a punt, but if you don't fancy anything on the board there's a good menu.'

She swivelled round to look at the board, arching

backwards so she could get a better view, and the top pulled tight over those lace-clad breasts.

Raspberry lace, the fruit inside them ripe and soft and full, he thought, and almost groaned out loud.

'Do they do good puds?'

An image of her eating the cookies with such relish popped into his head, and gave a slightly strangled chuckle. 'Yes,' he said, feeling doomed. 'They do brilliant puds. Save room.'

'Just what I was thinking.'

'Yeah. It wasn't hard to read your mind. I can hear it from here.'

She turned back, the top sliding back into place and settling down, and he breathed a tiny sigh of relief.

Regret?

Hell, Slater, pull yourself together!

'I think I'll have the shell-on prawns.'

He might have known. Now he'd have to spend the whole meal watching her sucking her fingers while the juice ran down her chin. He was beginning to think the steak at home might have been easier...

'That was amazing. Thank you. I wish you'd let me pay.'

'Why? I invited you to stay.'

'And you bought steak,' she pointed out, still feeling guilty, 'and my dog ate it.'

He gave a wry smile. 'And I should have put it in the fridge.'

'OK, I give up, have it your way, I'll pay next time,' she said with a laugh, and they headed up the gravel track away from the pub, cut across to the sea wall and went back along the top. She paused for a moment, looking out over the estuary, absorbing the scene. It felt oddly romantic, standing there with him as the evening sun slanted across the marshes behind them and turned everything to gold. Absurdly romantic. Crazy. This was James—

'Slack water. The tide's just on the turn. Look—the boats are swinging at anchor.'

He pointed back upriver, and she nodded, watching the fishing boats and little cabin cruisers trying to make up their minds which way to point. 'It's so peaceful. Joe said it was lovely here. No wonder you bought the cottage.'

'It was just lucky it came up when I was looking. Properties down here are pretty rarely on the market, and they have a ridiculous premium, but I fell in love with it.'

'I'm sure. I can see why. Was the cabin there?'

'Oh, yes. I wouldn't have added it, I simply don't need it. Molly used to use it for paying guests. That was how she met David, apparently, and then after they were married she used it as her studio. I just sling the garden furniture in it for the winter, which seems a wicked waste. I put a bed in there in case I ever needed to use it, and there's even a small shower room, but I'm hardly short of guest rooms,' he said drily, 'and anyway, I don't seem to have time for entertaining these days. Life is more than a tad hectic at work.'

'So what's this staffing problem?' she asked.

'Oh, one of the ED consultants had a brain tumour last autumn and he's been off for months. He's only recently come back part time, and he's decided he wants to keep it like that, which would be bad enough without him going off on paternity leave any minute now, but that's just the usual ongoing nightmare. Finding someone to cover the other half of his rota permanently is much more of a problem. Decent well-qualified trauma specialists are hard to find; they aren't usually kicking about without a job, and even if they are, they don't want to work part time, and we're on a bit of limb here out in the back end of Suffolk.'

'Really?' she said, surprised. 'But it's gorgeous here, and anyway, you wanted to do it so why not other people?'

'It was a golden opportunity for me. I'd had a consultancy, it was a chance at a clinical lead job in a small department, a brilliant rung on the ladder—it was perfect for me, so perfect I might just stay here forever.'

And she guessed he didn't care where he lived because he had no ties. Fewer, even, than her, because she at least had a dog now. James had nothing.

They got back to the cottage and she took Saffy out for a little walk along the sea wall to stretch her legs, then settled down with the dog on the veranda, soaking up the last rays of the evening sun while James made the coffee.

He came out, slid the tray onto the table as he sat down and eyed her thoughtfully. 'You OK?'

'Mmm. Just basking in the sun. It's lovely here. I could stay forever just chilling out.'

'Well, if you haven't got any ties, why don't you stay on for a bit, have a break? God knows I've got the space.'

'A break from what? I'm not doing anything. Anyway, I can't. I've got to go back to my friend's house and pack it up because she's home in a couple of weeks and I need to find myself a job and another house to live in. It's time to get back to reality and frankly I'm running out of money.'

He eyed her thoughtfully. He'd already told her that people of her calibre were hard to find, especially ones who would work part time. Would she consider it? Locum for him part time, and chill out the rest?

'Are you sure you're ready to work?'

'Yes. Absolutely.'

I am, she realised suddenly, and she felt as if a weight had been lifted off her. *I'm ready now, more than ready. Ready to move on, to start my life again in every way.*

'In which case, do you want the locum job?'

She sat bolt upright and turned to stare at him. 'What?'

'The locum job—the other half of Andy's job. Just for a while, to ease yourself back in. You could stay here, in the cabin if you wanted, if I give it a bit of a scrub. It would be perfect for you and Saffy, and when you felt ready or we got someone else, you could move on. It would give you time to work out what you're going to do, to look for a job properly without any haste, no strings, no rent, no notice period. Well, a week or two might be nice, but not if it compromised an opportunity, and you could have the cabin for as long as you want.'

She searched his face for clues, but there were none. 'Why are you doing this?' she asked, perplexed.

He laughed. 'Why? *Why?* Haven't you been listening? I can't get a locum for love or money. Andy's about to go off on paternity leave, and I'm already pretty much covering half his workload already. I can't do the other half. I need you, Connie, I genuinely need you. This isn't charity, we're desperate, and if you're really ready to start again, you'd be saving my life.'

She thought about it, considering it carefully. It would be so easy—too easy?

'Decent pay?'

'Yes, absolutely. It's a consultant's post. This is a

straightforward offer, Connie, I'm not just being nice to you. There is just one condition, though.'

She searched his eyes, and they were serious, not a hint of a smile.

'Which is?'

He looked away. 'I can't do the baby thing,' he said, his voice oddly expressionless. 'I would help you if I could, but I can't, so please don't ask me again.'

She nodded slowly. No. She'd realised that. Just not why.

'Can you tell me why?' she asked softly. 'Just so I can understand? Because plenty of women have babies on their own and manage fine, so that just doesn't make sense to me that that's the reason.'

'It does to me,' he said firmly.

'Why? I would have been bringing up the baby mostly anyway, even if Joe was still alive. Is it because you don't trust *me*?'

'Oh, Connie, of course I trust you, but you couldn't just hand your baby over to me and let me get on with it, could you? So how can you expect me to do it for you?'

'Because you don't want a baby,' she said, as if it was obvious. 'You've said that. You said you don't want a child, that it's never going to be on your agenda. You don't want to be involved, but that's fine, because it would be *my* baby! All you'd have to do is—well, you know what you'd have to do,' she said, blushing furiously and looking away. 'I'd be the one to carry it, to give birth to it, to bring it up—'

'No. It would be *our* baby, my son or daughter,' he told her, the words twisting his insides. 'I would insist on being involved right from the beginning, whether I wanted to or not, and I can't do that. Please, Connie, try and understand. It's not that I don't trust you, I just don't want the emotional involvement and the logistics of it are a nightmare. We'd have to live near each other, which probably means I couldn't stay here, and I like it here. I'm settled. It's taken me a long time to reach this point, and I don't want that to change. I just want peace.'

She nodded slowly, her eyes filling. 'No—no, I can see that. I'm sorry. It's a lot to ask, to be that involved with me, I see that.'

He sighed. 'It isn't that. And anyway, there's still the possibility that another man will come along and snap you up. Look at you, Connie—you're gorgeous. You'll find someone, someday, and I don't know how I'd feel about another man being involved with bringing up my child if you got married again.'

'We've had this conversation. I won't get married again.'

'You don't know that.'

She gave him a keen look that seemed to slash right to the heart of him. 'You seem to.'

He looked away. 'That's different.'

'Is it? You don't seem to have moved on in the nine years I've known you, James. You're still single, still shut down, still alone, and it's not because you're hideous or a lousy catch. You're not. Women must be throwing themselves at you. Don't tell me you don't notice. Or is there someone? A woman in your life? I didn't even think of that before, but is that why? Because there's some woman lurking in the wings who might not like it?'

'There's no woman in my life, Connie,' he said quietly, feeling curiously sad about it all of a sudden. 'I don't do relationships. They get demanding. People have expectations, they want more than I'm prepared to give, and I can't and won't meet them. So, no, there's nobody who's got any right to have an opinion. It's entirely my decision and that's the way it's staying. I'm not interested in dating.'

'Why?'

Because they're not you.

He closed his eyes briefly. 'This is irrelevant. The point is, there's more to bringing up children than I've got time to commit to, and I don't want to go there. I don't know if we'll feel the same way about things, and we have to be able to compromise when we disagree, trust each other's judgement. We have to like each other, even when the chips are down and the gloves are off, and I don't know if we can do that.'

That shocked her. 'You don't like me?' she asked, feeling gutted, because it was the one thing that had never occurred to her, but he shook his head instantly.

'Connie, don't be ridiculous, of course I like you. I've always liked you. It's just such a significant thing, so monumental, and I just don't think I can do it. And I don't want you building your hopes up, allowing yourself to imagine that this is all going to work out in the end, because it's not. So, there you have it. You wanted to know why I can't help you. That's why.'

She lifted her shoulders slightly. 'So that's it, then. I go down the anonymous donor route,' she told him simply.

He held her eyes for a moment, then looked away, hating the idea, unwilling to confront the reality of her doing what she'd said. Watching another man's child grow inside her, knowing it could have been his.

No. That was never going to happen. The immediate future was bad enough, though, the prospect of being close to Connie for weeks or maybe even months with this ridiculous longing for her, this burning need occupying his every waking thought. Could he do it without losing his mind?

'Fair enough. It's your decision. So, will you still take the job?'

He could feel her eyes on him, and he turned his head and searched them.

'Yes. Yes, I will. Why not? I need a job and somewhere to live. You need a locum, I'm certainly qualified enough, and the cabin would be brilliant. It would be great for Saffy, and it would give us both privacy and enough space to retreat if we get on top of each other. It would be perfect.'

He didn't want to think about them getting on top of each other; the images it brought to mind were enough to blow his mind. But she was right, it would be perfect for her and the dog, and it would solve his staffing crisis. And despite him telling her he wouldn't talk about it and couldn't do it, it would give him a chance to get to know her, to understand her motivations for wanting a baby.

So he could give her the child she so desperately wanted?

Panic clawed at him. Hell, what on earth was he getting himself into? The very thought of his child growing in her body made his chest tighten with long-buried emotions that he really didn't want to analyse or confront. But…

'So?' she prompted. 'Do we have a deal?'

He met her eyes, and she saw the tension in his face, the reluctance, the hesitation, and something else she didn't really understand, some powerful emotion that scared her slightly because it was the closest she'd ever come to seeing inside his soul. It was so raw, so elemental, and she was about to tell him to forget it when he nodded his head.

Just once, slowly.

'OK. Do the locum thing, but I don't want to hear another word about this baby idea. OK?'

'OK. So—can I look at this cabin?'

He gave a short huff of laughter. 'Um—yeah, but it's not exactly pristine. I haven't even opened the door for months.'

'Well, no time like the present,' she said cheerfully, putting her mug down. 'Come on. Where's the key?'

'Right here.'

He unhooked it from the back of the kitchen door and went down the steps and across the lawn, put it in the lock and swung the door open, flicking on the light to dispel the gathering dusk.

'Wow.'

He looked around and winced. Maybe he should have left the light off. 'I'll clear it out and give it a good clean. It's a tip.'

'No, it's fine. OK, it's a bit dusty, but it's lovely! Oh, James, it'll be perfect!'

He studied it, trying to see it through her eyes, but all he could see was the garden furniture stacked up against the wall and the amount of work he'd have to do to clean it up.

'I don't know about perfect, but you're right, it would be ideal for you and the dog. We could easily rig up a small kitchen area, a kettle and toaster, something like that. I can get you a small fridge, too.'

'Are you sure?'

Was he? Probably not, but he'd said he'd do it now so how could he change his mind and let her down? The enthusiasm in her eyes was enough to cripple him.

'Yes, I'm sure,' he said gruffly. 'When do you want to start?'

* * *

Well, she wasn't getting what she'd come for, but he'd taken a lot of the stress and worry out of the next few weeks at a stroke, and she supposed she should be thankful for that.

And she'd be working with James again, after all this time. She'd never thought she'd do that again, and the prospect was oddly exciting.

She'd loved working with him nine years ago. He'd been a brilliant doctor and a skilful and patient mentor and she couldn't wait to work with him again. And she was looking forward to getting back to normality, to real life. Not the strange and somehow dislocated life of an army wife trying to keep her career going despite the constant moves, or the empty and fruitless life of a woman widowed far too young and unfulfilled, but real life where she could make her own decisions.

She'd thought about it all night, lying awake in that beautiful bedroom listening to the sound of the sea sucking on the shingle, the rhythm curiously soothing. She'd had to go down and let Saffy out in the middle of the night, and once she'd settled her she'd curled up in the chair in the bedroom window staring out over the moonlit sea and hoping she wouldn't let him down.

Not that there was any reason why she should, of course. She was a good doctor, too, and she had confidence in herself. And if he didn't want to give her a child, felt he couldn't do it—well, he had the right to do that. It was a shame, though, because he was perfect for the job. Intelligent, good looking, funny, kind to animals, he could make amazing coffee...

He'd make someone a perfect husband, if only he wasn't so set against it. What a waste. But that was his business, his decision, his choice to make. And when it came to the baby thing, there were other ways, other avenues to explore.

Except maybe, of course, if she was working along-side him, he might change his mind—

She'd stopped that train of thought right there, gone back to bed and tried to sleep, but it had been pointless and she'd got dressed and come downstairs shortly be-fore six, let Saffy out again and made herself a cup of tea, taking it out onto the veranda and huddling up on the bench waiting for James to wake up.

She'd agreed to come back down to Yoxburgh in two weeks, when Andy was due off on paternity leave, and all she had to do was go back to Angie's house and pack her things and come back. She didn't have much to pack. Most of her stuff was in store, flung there in haste after Joe died when she'd had to move out of the married quarters; she still had to go through it prop-erly, but that task would keep until she had somewhere permanent.

Somewhere for her and a baby?

She pressed a hand to her chest and sucked in a breath, and Saffy got to her feet and came and put her nose against her arm, nuzzling her.

'Oh, Saffy. I wonder where we'll end up?' she mur-mured, and then she heard sounds behind her and James appeared in a pair of jeans and bare feet, looking tou-sled and sleepy and more sexy than a man of forty-two had any right to look.

Sheesh. She yanked her eyes away from his bare chest and swallowed hard.

'Morning,' she managed, and he grunted.

'Coffee?'

'Please. Just a straight, normal coffee.'

'That's all you get at this time of day. It's too early for party tricks.'

He walked off again, going back into the house and leaving her on the veranda, and she let out the breath she'd been holding and stared up at the sky. Wow. How had she never *noticed* before?

Because you were in love with Joe. Why would you notice another man? You had a husband who was more than man enough for you!

But—James was every bit as much a man as Joe had been, in his own way, and anyway, she had noticed him, all those years ago when she'd first met him. She'd asked about him hopefully, and been told about Cathy. Not that anyone knew very much, just that his wife had died and he didn't talk about it.

Didn't talk about anything except work, really, and didn't date as far as anyone knew, but then one weekend she'd been out with friends and bumped into him in a bar, and he'd introduced her to Joe.

And that was that. Joe with his wicked smile and irrepressible sense of humour had swept her off her feet, and she'd fallen hook, line and sinker. Now she was back to square one, noticing a man who still wasn't interested, who was still shut down, closed off from life and love and anything apart from his work.

A man she'd tried to talk into agreeing to something that he was obviously deeply reluctant about—

'Hey, what's up?'

He set the coffee down on the table in front of her and she looked up at him, searching his eyes for the reticence that had been there last night, but there was none, just gentle concern, so she smiled at him and reached for her coffee, telling herself she was relieved that he'd pulled a shirt on.

'Nothing,' she lied. 'I'm fine—just a bit tired. I didn't sleep very well—it was too quiet and all I could hear was the sound of the sea.'

'I can't sleep without it now,' he said wryly, dropping down beside her on the bench and fondling Saffy's ears. 'So, how was your night, Saffy? Find anything naughty to do in the cage?'

'She was fine. I came down at three and let her out because I could hear her whining, but I think she just wanted reassurance.'

'I heard you get up.'

So he hadn't slept, either. Wondering what he'd let himself in for?

Nothing, she reminded herself. They were just going to work together, and the baby conversation—well, it was as if it had never happened. They'd just opened the door on the subject, that was all, and he'd shut it again.

Only, maybe, it would never be the same again. Whatever happened now, that door had been opened, and she sensed that it would have changed something in the dynamic of their relationship.

'Connie? I'm sorry I can't help you.'

How did he know what she was thinking? Could he read her mind? Or perhaps, like her, it was the only thing *on* his mind?

She nodded, and he reached out a hand—a large, square hand with strong, blunt fingers—and laid it gently over her wrist.

'Whatever happens, whatever you decide to do, I'll always be here for you,' he said quietly. 'I promised Joe I'd take care of you if anything happened to him, and I will, and if you decide to take the clinic route and have a baby, I'll still be here, I'll still support you in your decision even if I don't agree with it. You won't ever be alone. Just—please, don't be hasty.'

'Oh, James…'

Her eyes filled with tears, and she put her coffee down and sucked in a shaky breath.

He stared at her in dismay. Hell. Now he'd made her cry.

'Hush, Connie, hush,' he murmured, gathering her against his chest. 'It's OK. I didn't mean to make you cry. Come on, now. It's all right. It'll be OK.'

'Why are you so damn nice?' she said unsteadily, swiping tears out of her eyes and wondering why his chest felt so good to rest her head against. She could stay there all day in his arms, resting her face against the soft cotton of his shirt, inhaling the scent of his body and listening to the steady thud of his heart while he held her. It had been such a long time since anyone had held her, and it had been him then, too, after Joe's funeral.

He'd held her for ages, letting her cry, crying with her, and nobody had held her since. Not really. She'd had the odd hug but nothing like this, this silent support that meant more than any words.

But she couldn't stay there all day, no matter how tempting, so she pulled herself together, swiped the tears away again and sat up.

'So what about this breakfast then?' she asked, her voice uneven, and he gave a soft laugh and leant back, his arm along the bench behind her.

'Drink your coffee and let me have mine. I can't function this early, I need a minute. And don't talk. Just sit and relax and stop worrying. I can hear your mind from here.'

Sound advice. She didn't think it had a hope in hell of working, but she was wrong. The distant sound of the shingle sighing on the beach, the drone of bees in the honeysuckle, the whisper of the wind in the tall grass beyond the garden—all of it soothed her, taking away the tension and leaving her calm and relaxed.

Or was that the touch of his hand on her back, the slow, gentle circling sweep of his thumb back and forth over her shoulder blade? She closed her eyes and rested her head back against the wall of the house, and felt something that had been coiled tight inside her for so long slowly give way.

CHAPTER FOUR

HE WATCHED HER sleep, his arm trapped behind her, unable to move in case he disturbed her.

And he didn't want to disturb her, because as long as she was sleeping he could watch her.

Watch the slight fluttering of her eyelashes against her faintly flushed cheeks, still streaked with the dried remnants of her tears. Watch the soft rise and fall of her chest with every breath, and hear the gentle sigh of air as she exhaled through parted lips that were pink and moist and so damn kissable it was killing him.

He looked away, unable to watch her any longer, unable to sit there with his arm around Joe's wife and lust after her when she'd been entrusted to his care.

And he'd actually agreed to let her come and live with him and locum in the department? He must have been mad. He'd have to sort the rota so that they worked opposing shifts—not that that would help much, but at least she was living in the cabin rather than the house. And that was essential because if he didn't keep his distance, he wasn't sure he could keep these deeply inappropriate feelings under wraps.

And he needed to start now.

He shifted his hand a fraction, turning his thumb out

to take it off her shoulder blade, and she rolled her head towards him, those smoky blue eyes clear and unglazed.

She hadn't been asleep at all, apparently, just resting her eyes, but now they were open and she smiled at him.

'Can I speak yet?' she asked cheekily, her mouth twitching, and he laughed and pulled his arm out from behind her, shifting slightly away to give himself some much-needed space.

'If you can manage not to say anything contentious.'

'I don't know what you mean.'

That taunting smile playing around her mouth, she sat up straighter, moving away from him a little more, and he had to remind himself that that was good.

'I was going to say, if I'm going to be working with you here, it might be an idea if I knew what I was signing up for.'

He nodded, knowing exactly what kind of exquisite torture *he* was signing up for, but the exit door on that had slammed firmly shut already so analysing why he'd done it was purely academic. He was already committed to the emotional chaos and physical torment that was bound to come his way with having her underfoot day in, day out. He must have been mad to suggest it.

'Sure. Want a guided tour of the hospital?'

'That would be good. Can we have breakfast first? I'm starving.'

He gave a soft huff of laughter and stood up, taking the empty coffee cup from her and walking back inside, and she watched him go and let out an almost silent groan.

How could she be so *aware* of him? OK, it had been a while, but—James? Really? Not that there was anything wrong with him, far from it, but there was more than good looks and raw sex appeal in this. There was

his relationship with Joe—*her* relationship with Joe—
and she knew for him that would be a massive issue.

And Joe had made him promise to take care of her?
Trust him. Trust Joe to pile that kind of responsibility
on his friend, but she reckoned he would have become
her self-appointed guardian anyway regardless of what
Joe might have said, because he was just like that, so
she'd just have to learn to live with it and make very,
very sure he got no hint of her feelings.

Not that she knew what they were, exactly.

A flicker of interest?

OK, more than a flicker, then, a lot more, but of
what? Lust?

No. More than that. More than a flicker, of more
than lust. And that was deeply scary. This situation
was complicated enough without this crazy magnetic
attraction rearing its head.

She got to her feet and stuck her head round the
kitchen door. 'Want a hand?'

'No, I'm fine.'

'Right. I'll take Saffy for a quick run. Ten minutes?'

'Barely. Don't be longer.'

'I won't.'

She shoved her feet into her abandoned trainers,
put Saffy's lead on and escaped from the confines of
James's garden. She ran along the river wall this time,
retracing their footsteps of the day before beside the
remains of the old rotting hulks, their ribs sticking up
like skeletons out of the mud of the little natural inlets
in the marshy river bank.

The smell was amazing—salt and mud and fish, all
mingled together in that incredible mix that reminded
her of holidays in Cornish fishing villages and sailing
in the Solent in her childhood.

Wonderful, evocative smells that brought back so many happy memories. And the sounds—amazing sounds. The clink of halliards, the slap of wavelets on the undersides of the moored boats, the squeak of oars in rowlocks, the putter of an outboard engine.

And the gulls. Always the gulls, wheeling overhead, keening their sad, mournful cry.

The sunlight was dancing on the water, and the tide had just turned, the boats swinging round so they faced downriver as the water began surging up the estuary with the rising tide. She stood and watched for a moment as the last of the boats swung round and settled on their moorings.

Just twelve hours, she thought, since they'd watched this happen together. Twelve hours ago, she'd had no idea of what her future held, just a flat no to her request for a baby and a massive question mark hanging over her next job, next home, all of it. Yet in the past twelve hours all that had become clearer, her immediate future settled and secure if not in the way she'd hoped.

Unless he changed his mind? Unlikely, but just in case, she'd make sure she kept a lid on her feelings and kept them to herself, and then maybe…

She glanced at her watch, and yelped. She was going to be late for breakfast, and he'd told her not to be longer than ten minutes. She had three to get back, and she made it with seconds to spare.

He was propped up in the doorway, arms folded, legs crossed at the ankle, and his lips twitched.

'Close,' he said, glancing at his watch, and she smiled, hands propped on her knees, her breath sawing in and out.

'Sorry. I was watching the tide turn. I could watch it all day.'

'Well, four times, anyway. Scrambled or fried?'

She straightened up, chest heaving, and grinned, oblivious of the effect she was having on him. 'Scrambled.'

Like his brains, he thought desperately, watching her chest rise and fall, the wild tangle of blonde hair spilling over her shoulders, the faint sheen of moisture gilding her glowing skin—

'Can I do anything?'

'Yes,' he said blandly. 'Get the dog out of the kitchen. She's eyeing up the sausages.'

They left, and he braced his hands on the worktop, breathed in and counted to ten, then let the air out of his lungs on a whoosh and turned his attention to the eggs.

Working with her, all day, every day, and having her here at home? For months?

It was going to kill him.

'This is such an amazing building.'

'Isn't it? It's all a front, of course, all this beauty, and it hid a hideous truth. Apparently it used to be the pauper lunatic asylum.'

'How frightfully politically correct.'

He grinned wryly. 'Not my words. That's the Victorians for you. Actually it was a workhouse taking advantage of the inmates, and I'd like to be able to say it's moved on, but in the last few months I've wondered.'

'Ah, poor baby. That'll teach you to be clinical lead.'

He rolled his eyes and punched her arm lightly. 'Do you want this job or not?'

'Is this a formal interview?'

He laughed. 'Hardly. Any qualified doctor with a pulse would get my vote at the moment. The fact that you've got all the necessary and appropriate qualifications and outstanding experience to back them up is just the cherry on top. Trust me, the job's yours.'

'I'm not sure I'm flattered.'

'Be flattered. I'm fussy who I work with. That's why there isn't anyone. We're round here in the new wing.'

He drove round the corner of the old building and pulled up in a marked parking bay close to the ED, and her eyes widened.

'Wow. That's a bit sharper. I did wonder if we'd be working by gas light.'

'Hardly,' he said with a chuckle. 'We're very proud of it—of the whole hospital. It was necessary. People living on the coast were having to travel long distances for emergency treatment, and they were dying—back to your platinum ten minutes, I guess. We can treat them much quicker here, and if we have to we can then refer them on once they're stable. That said we can do most stuff here, but it's not like Camp Bastion.'

'Hopefully it doesn't need to be,' she said quietly, and he glanced down and saw a flicker of something wounded and vulnerable in her eyes and could have kicked himself.

'Sorry. I didn't mean to drag it all up.'

'It's OK, it's never far away.' She gave him a too bright and very fleeting smile. 'So, talk me round your department, Mr Clinic Lead Slater.'

He took her in via Reception so she could see the triage area where the walking wounded were graded according to severity, and then went through into the back, to the row of cubicles where the ambulance cases were brought directly.

'We've got four high dependency beds where we can keep people under constant observation, and we can accommodate three patients in Resus at any time. It's not often idle.'

They stood at the doors of Resus and watched a team working on a patient. It looked calm and measured. A man looked up and smiled at James through the glass, waggling his fingers, and he waved back and turned to her. 'That's Andy. He's been damn lucky. He had an awake craniotomy and had to talk through it to make sure his speech centre wasn't damaged when they removed the meningioma, but the post-op swelling gave him aphasia. He lost his speech—nothing else. He could understand everything, all the words were on the tip of his tongue, he just couldn't find them, but of course he couldn't work until he got his speech back, and he was tearing his hair out for weeks.' He grinned wryly. 'So was I, because there was no guarantee he ever would recover completely.'

'You still are, aren't you? Tearing your hair out, trying to replace half of him?'

He shrugged. 'Pretty much. It's a bit frustrating trying to get anyone decent all the way out here, but he's brilliant and getting anyone as good as him is just not possible on a part-time contract. And no,' he said with a smile, holding a finger up to silence her, 'before you say it, that's not a criticism of you, because I know you've got bigger fish to fry and you aren't here for the long haul. I wish to God you were. You'd solve all my problems at a stroke.'

Well, not quite all. Not the one of having enough distance between them so that he wasn't being constantly reminded of just how damned lovely she was and how very, very inaccessible.

Not to mention asking the impossible of him...

The door to Resus opened and Andy came out, his smile a little strained. 'Hi. Did you get my text?'

'Your text?' he said, getting a bad feeling.

'Yes. Lucy rang. She says she's in labour and she doesn't hang about. I'm just about to bail, I'm afraid.'

He swore silently, closed his eyes for a moment and then opened them to find Connie smiling knowingly.

'Yes,' she said.

He let out something halfway between a laugh and a sigh and introduced them. 'Connie, this is Andy Gallagher. Andy, this is Connie Murray. I worked with her several years ago, and she was obviously so inspired by me she became a trauma specialist.'

Andy eyed her hopefully. 'Tell me she's our new locum.'

'She is, indeed, as of—well, virtually now. Say hello to her very, very nicely. She wasn't due to start for a fortnight.'

'Oh, Connie—I'm so pleased to meet you,' Andy said fervently, his shoulders dropping as a smile lit up his face. 'I thought I was about to dump a whole world of stuff on James, so to know you're here is such a relief. Thank you. From the bottom of my heart. And his,' he added with a grin. 'Probably especially his.'

This time James gave a genuine laugh. 'Too right. You'll be out of here in ten seconds, if you've got any sense, and utterly oblivious to the chaos you're leaving in your wake, which is exactly how it should be. Go. Shoo. And let us know the minute it's born!'

'I will!' Andy yelled over his shoulder, heading out of the department at a run.

James let his breath out on a low whistle and pushed open the door of Resus. 'You guys OK in here, or do you need me?'

'No, we're all done. He's on his way to ICU. They're just coming down for him.'

'OK, Andy's gone but I'm around, page me if you need me. Pete's on later, and I'll be in tomorrow morning first thing. Oh, and this is Connie Murray. She's our new locum, starting tomorrow. Be really, really nice to her.'

They all grinned. 'You bet, Boss,' one of them said, and they all laughed.

He let the door shut, turned to Connie and searched her eyes, still not quite able to believe his luck.

'Are you really OK with this?'

'I'm fine,' she said, mentally running through the logistics and counting on her fingers. 'Look, it's eleven o'clock. I can get home, grab my stuff and be back here by eight tonight at the latest. That'll give me three hours to pack and clean the house, and it won't take that long.' She hoped. 'Can you cope with Saffy if I leave her? I can't get her and all my stuff in the car.'

'Sure. She can help me scrub out the cabin.'

'Yeah, right. Just don't let her run off,' she warned as they walked briskly back to the car.

'I won't. Don't worry, Connie, the dog's the least of my problems. You saw that cabin.'

She ignored him. 'Put her in the crate if you have to go back to the hospital,' she said as she put on her seat belt. 'She's used to it. And she has a scoop of the dry food twice a day, morning and evening, so you might need to feed her if I'm held up in traffic—'

He stopped her, his hand over her mouth, his eyes laughing. 'Connie, I can manage the dog. If all else fails, I'll bribe her with fillet steak.'

She left almost immediately when they got back to the cottage, and as she was getting in the car he gave in to impulse and pulled her into his arms and hugged her.

'Thank you, Connie. Thank you so much. I'm so, so grateful.'

'I'll remind you of that when I'm driving you crazy,' she said with a cheeky grin, and slamming the door, she dropped the clutch, spraying gravel in all directions. 'See you later!'

'Drive carefully,' he called after her, but she was gone, and he watched her car until she'd turned out onto the road and headed away, the imprint of her body still burned onto his.

'Well, Saffy,' he said softly as he went back into the garden and shut the gate firmly. 'It's just you and me, old thing, so no running off. Shall we go and have a look at this cabin?'

It was worse than he'd thought.

Dirtier, dustier, mustier. Oh, well, he could do with a bit of hard physical graft. It might settle his raging libido down a bit after that innocent hug.

He snorted. Apparently there was no such thing as far as his body was concerned.

He threw open all the windows and the doors, took everything including the bed outside and blitzed it. He vacuumed the curtains, washed the windows, mopped the walls and floors, slung the rug over the veranda rail and bashed it with a broom to knock the dust out before he vacuumed it and returned it to the now dry floor, and finally he reassembled it all, stripped the bedding off the bed upstairs and brought it all down and made up the bed.

And through it all Saffy lay there and watched him as if butter wouldn't melt in her mouth. He trusted her about as far as he could throw her, but she seemed content to be with him, and once it was all tidy and ready for Connie's return, he took her out for a walk, picking up his phone on the way.

And he had a message, a text with a picture of a new baby. Very new, a mere two hours old, the caption reading, 'Daniel, eight pounds three ounces, both well'.

He felt something twist inside him.

'Congratulations!' he texted back, and put the phone in his pocket. Saffy was watching him closely, head cocked on one side, eyes like molten amber searching his face.

'It's OK, Saffy,' he said, rubbing her head, but he wasn't sure it was. Over the years countless colleagues had had babies, and he'd been happy for them. For some reason this baby, this time, felt different. Because the possibility was being dangled in front of his nose, tantalising him?

The possibility of being a father, something he'd thought for the past eleven years that he'd never be? He'd said no to Connie, and he'd meant it, but what if he'd said yes? What if he'd agreed to give her a child?

A well of emotion came up and lodged in his chest, making it hard to breathe, and he hauled in a lungful of sea air and set off, Saffy trotting happily at his side as he broke into a jog.

He ran for miles, round the walk he'd taken Connie on yesterday, but with a detour to make it longer, and Saffy loped easily along at his side. He guessed she ran with Connie—another thing they had in common, apart from medicine? Maybe.

He wondered what else he'd find. Art? Music? Food he knew they agreed on, but these were irrelevancies. If he'd agreed to her suggestion, then she'd be bringing up his child, so he would have needed to be more concerned with her politics, her attitude to education, her ability to compromise. It didn't matter a damn if they both liked the same pictures or the same songs. It mattered if she thought kids could be taken out of school in the term time to go on holiday, something he thought was out of the question. How could you be sure they wouldn't miss some vital building block that could affect their entire future?

And what on *earth* was he doing worrying about that? He'd said no, and he'd meant it! He had! And anyway, there were bigger things to worry about. Things like his ability to deal with the emotional minefield that he'd find himself in the moment her pregnancy started to manifest itself—

'What pregnancy?' he growled, startling Saffy so that she missed her stride, and he ruffled her head and picked up the pace, driving on harder to banish the images that flooded his mind.

Not images of Cathy, for once, but of Connie, radiant, glowing, her body blooming with health and vitality, the proud swell of her pregnancy—

He closed his eyes and stumbled. Idiot.

He stopped running, standing with one hand on a fence post, chest heaving with emotion as much as exertion. This was madness. It was hypothetical. He'd said no, and she was going to a clinic if she did anything, so nothing was going to happen to her that involved him.

Ever.

But that just left him feeling empty and frustrated, and he turned for home, jogging slowly now, cooling down, dropping back to a walk as they hit the sea wall and the row of houses. And then there was Molly, out in the garden again with David and their children, and he waved to them and Molly straightened up with a handful of weeds and walked over.

'So who's your friend?' she asked, openly curious as well she might be, because he hardly ever had anyone to stay, and certainly never anyone single, female and as blatantly gorgeous as Connie.

'Connie Murray. She's a doctor. I've known her for years, she was married to a friend of mine.'

'The one who died? Joe?'

He nodded. 'She's going to be here for a while—she's taking the locum job I've been trying to fill, and she'll be living in the cabin.' He got that one in quick, before Molly got any matchmaking ideas, because frankly there was enough going on without that.

But it didn't stop the little hint of speculation in her eyes.

'I'm glad you've got someone. I know you've been working crazy hours, we hardly ever see you these days.' She dropped the weeds in a bucket and looked up at him again. 'You should bring her to my private view on Friday.'

'That would be nice, thanks,' he said, fully intending to be busy. 'I'll have to check the rota, though.'

'Do that. And change it if necessary. No excuses. You've had plenty of warning. We told you weeks ago.'

He gave a quiet mental sigh and smiled. 'So you did.'

She laughed and waved him away. 'Go on, go away. We'll see you on Friday at seven. Tell her to wear something pretty.'

He nodded and turned away, walked the short distance to his house while he contemplated that sentence, and let Saffy off the lead in the garden.

She found her water bowl on the veranda while he was doing some stretches, drank noisily for a moment and then flopped down in the shade under the bench and went to sleep, so while she was happy he ran upstairs and showered, then on the way down he gathered up Connie's things from her bedroom, Molly's words still echoing in his head.

Tell her to wear something pretty.

Like the top she'd worn last night which was lying on the chair, together with the raspberry red lace bra and matching lace shorts that sent his blood pressure into orbit? Or then there were her pyjamas. Thin cotton trousers and a little jersey vest trimmed with lace. They were pretty, but nothing like substantial enough to call pyjamas, he thought, and bundling them up with the other things, he grabbed her wash bag out of the bathroom and took them all down to the cabin.

Saffy was still snoozing innocently, so he topped up her water bowl, filled a glass for himself and drained it, then put the kettle on to make tea and sat down with the paper and chilled out.

Or tried to, but it seemed he couldn't.

Connie would be back in a very few hours, and from then on his space would be invaded. He wasn't used to sharing it, and having her around was altogether too disturbing. That lace underwear, for example. And the pyjamas. If he had to see them every morning—

He got up, prowling round the garden restlessly, and then he saw the roses and remembered he'd been going to put flowers in her room yesterday, but he'd run out of time.

So he cut a handful and put them in a vase on the chest of drawers and went back to reading the paper, but it didn't hold his attention. The only thing that seemed to be able to do that was Connie.

And going to Molly's private view with her just sounded altogether too cosy. And dangerous. He wondered what pretty actually meant, and how Connie would interpret it. He was rather afraid to find out.

But how the hell could he get out of it?

It didn't take long to pack up her things.

Much less than the three hours she'd allowed, and because she'd cleaned the house so thoroughly on Sunday there was nothing much to do, so she was back on the road by three-thirty and back in Yoxburgh before six.

She wondered if James would be around, but he was there, sitting on the veranda in a pair of long cargo shorts with Saffy at his feet, reading a newspaper in the early evening sun.

He folded it and came down to the gate, leaning on it and smiling as she clambered out of the car and stretched.

'You must drive like a lunatic.'

She laughed softly and shook her head. 'That was Joe. I'm not an adrenaline junkie. There was practically nothing to do.'

And not that much in the way of possessions, he thought, looking at the back of her small SUV. Sure, it was packed, but only vaguely. She handed him a cool box out of the front footwell. 'Here, find room for that lot in the fridge,' she said, locking the car and coming through the gate to give Saffy a hug. 'Hello, gorgeous. Have you been a good girl?'

Saffy wagged her tail and leaned against her.

'She's been fine. We went for a run.'

'Oh, she will have enjoyed that! Thank you. She loves it when we run.'

'She seemed to know the drill.'

'What, don't stop in front of you to sniff something so you fall over her? Yeah. We both learned that one the hard way.'

He laughed and carried the cool box up to the kitchen, shocked at the lightness in his heart now she was back, with her lovely smile and sassy sense of humour.

'So how did you get on with the cabin?' she asked, following him up the steps to the kitchen.

'OK, I suppose. It's clean now, but I'm sure you'll want to do something to it to make it home.'

He turned his head as he said that, catching a flicker of something slightly lost and puzzled in her expression, and could have kicked himself.

Home? Who was he kidding? She hadn't had a proper home for ages now, not since she'd met Joe. They'd moved around constantly from one base to another, and she'd had to move out of the married quarters pretty smartly after he'd died. By all accounts she'd been on the move ever since, living in hospital accommodation in the year after Joe died, then out in Afghanistan, then staying with a friend. It was only one step up from sofa-surfing, and the thought of her being so lost and unsettled gutted him.

But the look was gone now, banished by a smile. 'Can I put my stuff straight in there?'

'Sure. I'll put Saffy in her crate, so she doesn't run off while the gate's open. The door's not locked.'

Connie opened the cabin door, and blinked. The dust was gone, as was the stack of garden furniture, and it was immaculate. He'd made the bed up with the linen she'd had last night, and her pyjamas were folded neatly on the pillow, her overnight bag on the bed. She stuck her head round the bathroom door and found her wash things on the side, and when she came back out she noticed the flowers on the chest of drawers.

Roses from the garden, she realised, and a lump formed in her throat. He hadn't needed to cut the roses, but he had, to make her welcome, and the room was filled with the scent of them.

It was the attention to detail that got to her. The careful way he'd folded her pyjamas. The fact that he'd brought her things down at all when it would have been so easy to leave them there.

'I hope you don't mind, I moved your stuff in case you were really late back, so you didn't have to bother.'

'Mind? Why should I mind?'

And then she remembered she'd left yesterday's clothes on the chair—her top, her underwear. Yikes. The red lace.

Don't be silly. He knows what underwear looks like.

But she felt the heat crawl up her neck anyway. 'It looks lovely,' she said, turning away so he wouldn't see. 'You've even put flowers in here.'

'I always put flowers in a guest room,' he lied, kicking himself for doing it in case she misinterpreted the gesture. Or, rather, rumbled him? 'I would have done it yesterday but I ran out of time. Give me your car keys, I'll bring your stuff in.'

She handed them over without argument, grateful for a moment alone to draw breath, because suddenly, with him standing there beside her and the spectre of her underwear floating in the air between them, the cabin had seemed suddenly airless.

How on earth was she going to deal with this? Thank God they'd be busy at work, because there was no way she could be trusted around him without him guessing where her feelings were going, and there was no way she was going to act on them. He was a friend, and his friendship was too important to her to compromise for something as fleeting and trivial as lust.

'So where do you want this lot?'

He was standing in the doorway, his arms full, and she groped for common sense.

'Just put everything down on the floor, I'll sort it out later.'

She walked past him, her arm brushing his as he turned, and she felt a streak of heat race through her like lightning.

Really? *Really?*

This was beginning to look like a thoroughly bad idea...

CHAPTER FIVE

'SUPPER AT the pub?'

She straightened up from one of the boxes and tried to read his eyes, but they were just looking at her normally. Odd, because for a second there—

'That would be great. Just give me a moment to sort out some work clothes for tomorrow and I'll be with you.'

'Do you want the iron?'

She laughed. 'What, so I make a good impression on the boss?'

He propped himself up on the doorframe and grinned mischievously. 'Doesn't hurt.'

'I think I'll pass. I'll just hang them up for now and do it when we've eaten—if I really have to. Have you fed Saffy?'

'Yes, just before you got back. She seemed to think it was appropriate.'

'I'll bet,' she said with a chuckle, and pulling out a pair of trousers and a top that didn't cling or gape or otherwise reveal too much, she draped them over the bed and gave up. 'Right, that'll do for tomorrow. Let's go. I'm starving, it's a long time since breakfast.'

'You haven't eaten since breakfast? You're mad.'

'I just sort of forgot.'

'You emptied the fridge. There was food in your hands. How could you forget?'

Because she'd been utterly distracted by the thought of what she was doing? Because all she could think about was that she was coming back here to James, taking the first step towards the rest of her life?

'Just call me dozy,' she said, and slinging a cardi round her shoulders in case it got cold, she headed for the door.

They took Saffy with them and sat outside in the pub garden, with the lead firmly anchored to the leg of the picnic bench in case a cat strolled past, and he went in to order and came back with drinks.

'So, what time are we starting tomorrow?' she asked, to distract herself from the sight of those muscular, hairy legs sticking out of the bottom of his shorts. Definitely a runner—

'Eight, technically, but I'd like to be in by seven. You can bring your car and come later if you like. I'll sort you out a parking permit.'

'I can do seven,' she said. 'I'll have to walk Saffy first, and I'll need to come back at lunchtime to let her out and give her a bit of a run so I'll need my car anyway, if you can sort a permit for me that soon. Will that be all right?'

'That's fine. I don't expect you to work full time, Connie. I know you've got the dog, I know you haven't worked since you got her and I know you can't leave her indefinitely. I expect HR will want to check all sorts of stuff with you before they let you loose on a patient anyway, so there's no point in being too early. I take it you've brought the necessary paperwork?'

'Oh, sure. I've got everything I need to show them. So, did you hear from Andy? Is there any news?'

'Ah. Yes. He sent me a text.'

'And?'

'It's a boy,' he said, the words somehow sticking in his throat and choking him. 'Daniel. Eight pounds three ounces. Mother and baby both doing well.'

'Did he send a picture?'

'Of course.' And she would want to see it, wouldn't she? He pulled his phone out of his pocket and found the text, then slid it across to her. 'There.'

'Oh—oh, James, he's gorgeous. What are the others?'

'Girls. Three girls. Emily, Megan and Lottie.'

'And now they've got their boy. Oh, that's amazing. They must be so thrilled.'

'Yeah.' He couldn't bring himself to speculate on their delight, or debate the merits of boys or girls. It was all too close to home, too close to the reason she was here—and the very reason he didn't want her here at all.

No, that was a lie. He did want her here. Just—not like this. Not for why she'd come, and not feeling the way he did, so that he had to be so damn guarded all the time in case he gave away how he felt about her. And if he could work *that* one out for himself he'd be doing well, because frankly at the moment it was as clear as mud.

'So, tell me about this friend you've been staying with,' he said, changing the subject without any pretence at subtlety, and after a second of startled silence, she cleared her throat.

'Um. Yeah. Angie. Long-time friend. We worked together a couple of times. She's been in Spain for a few months visiting family but she's back in a week or so—I really ought to write to her and thank her for lending me the house. It's been a lifesaver. Getting a rented place with a dog is really hard, especially a dog like Saffy.'

She pricked up her ears at her name, and James reached down and rubbed her head. She shifted it, putting her chin on his foot and sighing, and he gave a wry chuckle.

'I can imagine. I thought you and Joe had bought somewhere?'

'We had. It's rented out, on a long lease. The tenant's great and it pays the mortgage.'

'So why not live there?'

She shrugged. 'It was where we were going when he came out of the army. It was going to be our family home, where we brought up our children.'

And just like that, the subject reared its head again. James opened his mouth, shut it again and exhaled softly.

'Don't say it, James. I know we aren't talking about it, I was just stating a fact.'

'I wasn't going to.'

'Weren't you?'

He shrugged. The truth was he hadn't known what to say, so he'd said nothing.

'Two sea bass?'

He sat back, smiled at the waitress and sighed with relief.

'Saved by the bass,' Connie said drily, and picking up her knife and fork, she attacked her supper and let the subject drop.

HR wanted all manner of forms filled in, and it was driving her mad.

She was itching to get to work now, if only to settle her nerves. She'd been away from it too long, she told herself, that was all. She'd be fine once she started. And then finally the forms were done.

'Right, that's it. Thank you, Connie. Welcome to Yoxburgh Park Hospital. I hope you enjoy your time with us.'

'Thanks.'

She picked up her bag and legged it, almost but not quite running, and made her way to the ED. She found James up to his eyes in Resus, and he glanced up.

'Cleared for takeoff?' he asked, and she nodded.

'Good. We've got an RTC coming in, nineteen year old male pedestrian versus van, query head, chest and pelvic injuries and I haven't got anyone I can spare. Do you feel ready to take it?'

She nodded, used to being flung in at the deep end as a locum. 'Sure. Where will you be, just in case I need to check protocol?'

'Right here. Don't worry, Connie, I won't abandon you. I won't be much longer here.'

She nodded again, and he pointed her in the direction of the ambulance bay. She met the ambulance, took the history and handover from the paramedics, and by the time they were in Resus she was right back in the swing of it.

'Hi, there, Steve,' she said to the patient, holding her face above his so he could see her without moving. 'I'm Connie Murray, and I'm the doctor who's going to be looking after you. Can you tell me where you are?'

'Hospital,' he said, but his voice was slurred—from the head injury, or the morphine the paramedics had given him? She wasn't sure, but at this stage it was irrelevant because until she was sure he wasn't going to bleed out in the next few minutes the head injury was secondary.

'OK. Can you tell me where it hurts?'

'Everywhere,' he mumbled. 'Legs, back—everything.'

'OK. We'll soon have you more comfortable. Can we have an orthopaedic consultant down here, please? This pelvic fracture needs stabilising, and can we do a FAST scan, please? We need a full trauma series—do we have a radiographer available? And a total body CT scan. I need to know what's going on here.'

She delegated rapidly, and the team working with her slipped smoothly into action, but throughout she was conscious of James at the other end of the room keeping an ear open in case she needed backup.

The X-rays showed multiple fractures in his pelvis, and the FAST scan had shown free fluid in his abdomen.

She glanced up and he raised an eyebrow.

'Do we have access to a catheter lab? I think he's got significant vascular damage to the pelvic vessels and I don't want to wait for CT.'

'Yes, if you think it's necessary. What are his stats like?'

'Awful. He's hypotensive and shocky and the ultrasound is showing free fluids in the abdomen. He's had two units of packed cells and his systolic's eighty-five and falling. We need to stop this bleed.'

'OK. Order whatever you need. I won't be a tick.'

He wasn't. Moments later, he was standing opposite her across the bed, quietly taking his cues from her and nodding to confirm her decisions.

And when they'd got him stable and shipped him off to the catheter lab for urgent vascular surgery prior to a CT scan to check for other injuries, he just smiled at her and nodded. 'You've learned a lot since I last saw you in action.'

'I'd hope so. It's been more than eight years.' Years in which she met, married and lost his best friend.

'I always said you had promise. It's nice to see you fulfilling your potential.'

Crazy that his praise should make her feel ten feet tall. She knew she was good. She'd worked with some of the best trauma surgeons in the world, she didn't need James to tell her.

And yet somehow, those few words meant everything to her.

'Want me to talk to the relatives?' he asked, but she shook her head.

'No, I'm fine with it. Come with me, though. I might need to direct them to where they can wait.'

'OK.'

They spoke to the relatives together; she explained the situation, and James filled in the details she'd missed—the name of the orthopaedic surgeon, where the ward was, how long it might take, what would happen next—and then as they left the room he looked up at the clock and grinned.

'Coffee?'

'I've only just started work!'

'You can still have coffee. I'm the boss, remember? Anyway, it's quiet now and it won't last. Come on. I reckon we've got ten seconds before the red phone rings.'

'How far can we get?'

'Out of earshot,' he said with a chuckle, and all but dragged her out of the department.

They ended up outside in the park, sitting on a bench under a tree, and she leant back and peeled the lid off her cappuccino and sighed. 'Bliss. I'm going to like working here.'

He snorted rudely. 'Don't run away with the idea that it's always like this. Usually we don't have time to stop.'

'The gods must be smiling on us.'

James laughed and stretched out his legs in front of him, ankles crossed. 'Don't push your luck. How did you get on with HR?'

'I've got writer's cramp.'

He laughed again and took a long pull on his coffee. 'That good, eh?'

'At least. I hate paperwork.'

'So don't ever, ever find yourself winding up as clinical lead,' he said drily, just as his pager bleeped. He glanced at it, sighed and drained his cup. 'Duty calls.'

'Really?' She sighed, took a swallow of her coffee and burnt her tongue.

'That's why I never have a cappuccino at work,' he said, getting to his feet. 'It takes too long to cool down. Bring it with you. I can hear a siren.'

And just to punctuate that, his bleep went off again.

She followed him, coffee in hand, and she almost—almost—got to finish it by the time it all kicked off again.

He sent her home at one to let Saffy out, and she walked back in to the news that the pedestrian had died of his head injury.

'You're kidding me,' she said, the colour draining from her face. 'Oh, damn it. Damn it.'

And she walked off, back rigid, her face like stone. He couldn't follow her. He was up to his eyes, about to see a relative, but as soon as he was free he went to look for her.

He found her under the tree where they'd had their coffee, staring blindly out across the grass with the drying tracks of tears down her cheeks.

'Why did he have to die?' she asked angrily. 'My first patient. Why? What did I do wrong, James?'

He sat down next to her and took her hand in his. It was rigid, her body vibrating with tension.

'You didn't do anything wrong. You know that.'

'Do I?' she said bitterly. 'I'm not so sure.'

'Yes, you are. We can't save everyone.'

'But he died of a head injury. All I was worried about was stopping him bleeding out, and all the time it was his head I should have been thinking about.'

'No. His pelvic injury was horrific. If you'd sent him for CT before he was stable, he would have bled out and died anyway. You did what you had to do, in the order you had to do it, and he didn't make it. It was a no-win situation. Not your fault. I wouldn't have done anything different, and neither would Andy.'

'But he was nineteen,' she said, her voice cracking. 'Only nineteen, James! All that wasted potential—all the effort and time put into bringing him up, turning him into a young man, wiped out like that by some idiot—'

'He had headphones in his ears. He wasn't listening to the traffic. It wasn't the van driver's fault, and he's distraught that he hit him. He's been hanging around waiting for news, apparently, and he's devastated.'

Connie turned her head and searched his eyes. 'It was Steve's fault? Are you sure?'

'Apparently so, according to the police. And it certainly wasn't your fault he died.'

She looked away again, but not before he saw the

bleakness in her eyes. 'It feels like it. It feels like I let him down.'

'You didn't, Connie. You did your best with what you were given, that's all any of us can do.' He pressed her hand between his, stroked the back of it with his thumb. 'Are you OK to go back in there, or do you need some time?'

'No. I'm fine,' she said, even though she wasn't, and tugging her hand back she got to her feet and walked away.

He followed slowly, letting out his breath on a long sigh, and found her picking up a case in cubicles. He said nothing, just laid a hand on her shoulder briefly and left her to it, and at five he found her and told her to go home.

'James, I'm fine.'

'I don't doubt it, but you're supposed to be part-time and Saffy's been in the cage long enough. Go home, Connie,' he said gently. 'I'll be back at seven.'

She went, reluctantly, because she didn't want to be alone, didn't want to go back to the empty house and think about the boy she'd allowed to die.

Instead she worried about Saffy, because the cabin was in full sun and she should have thought of that. Another layer of guilt. What if the dog was too hot? What if she'd collapsed and died?

She hadn't. She let her out of the crate the moment she got home, and Saffy went out to the garden, sniffed around for a few minutes, had a drink and flopped down under a tree in the shade.

Connie poured herself a drink and joined her, fondling her ears and thinking about her day.

She was still angry with herself for losing Steve, but she knew James was right. She'd done everything she could, and you couldn't save everyone. She knew that, too. She'd had plenty of evidence.

She went into the cabin and changed into shorts and a sleeveless vest, slid her feet into her trainers and took Saffy for a run. Anything to get away from the inside of her head.

She went the other way this time, up the sea wall, along the lane and back along the river, and as she reached the beginning of the river wall she saw another runner up ahead of her.

It stopped her in her tracks for a moment, because he'd lost one leg below the knee and was running on a blade. Ex-military? Possibly. Probably. So many of them ended up injured in that way.

Or worse. She'd spoken to the surgeon who'd gone out to Joe in the helicopter, and he'd told her about his injuries. And she'd been glad, then, for Joe, that he'd died. He would have hated it.

The man veered off at the end of the path, and she carried on at a slower pace, cooling down, then dropped to a steady jog, then down to a walk as they reached the end of the path.

Molly was there with the children, the baby in a buggy, a little girl of three or four running giggling round the grass chasing a leggy boy of twelve or so. Happy families, Connie thought as Molly smiled at her.

'Hi there. You're Connie, aren't you? It's nice to meet you properly. So, are you coming on Friday to my private view?'

She stared blankly, and Molly rolled her eyes.

'He hasn't mentioned it, has he?' Connie shook her head, and she tutted and smiled. 'Men. He probably hasn't even told you I'm an artist. Seven o'clock, Friday night, our house. We'd love to see you.'

'Thanks. I'd love to come. I love art exhibitions, even though I can hardly hold a pencil. I haven't seen the rota yet, but if I'm not on, it would be great. Thank you.'

'I told James to change the rota. He'd better have done it. And I also told him to tell you to wear something pretty.'

She blinked. 'Pretty? How pretty?'

'As pretty as you like,' Molly said, deadpan, but there was a subtext there Connie could read a mile away, and she wondered if Molly was matchmaking. She could have saved her the trouble. James wasn't interested in her. He wasn't interested in anything except work. He certainly wasn't interested in babies.

'I'll see what I've got,' she said, and towed Saffy away from the little girl who'd given up chasing her brother and was pulling Saffy's ears gently and giggling when she licked her. 'I'd better get back, I need to feed the dog, but I'll see you on Friday and I'll make sure James changes the rota.'

'Brilliant. We'll see you then.'

She walked away, glancing back in time to see the runner with the blade join them. David? Really? He swept the little girl up in his arms and plonked her on his shoulders, and her giggle followed Connie up the path, causing an ache in her heart.

They looked so happy together, all of them, but it obviously hadn't been all plain sailing. Was it ever? And would she find that happiness, or a version of it, before it was too late?

Maybe not, unless James changed his mind, and frankly she couldn't really see that happening. She trudged up the steps to the veranda and took Saffy in to feed her.

* * *

'So how was the cabin last night?' he asked as she plonked the salad bowl down on the newly evicted garden table. 'You haven't mentioned it so I imagine it wasn't too dreadful. Unless it was so awful you can't talk about it?'

'No, not at all, it was fine. Very nice, actually. It's good to have direct access to the garden for Saffy, although I have to admit she slept on the bed last night. I'm sorry about that.'

'I should think so. Shocking,' he said, his eyes crinkling with amusement.

Connie frowned. 'She's not supposed to,' she said sternly. 'She's supposed to have manners.'

The crinkles turned to laughter as he helped himself to the salad. 'Yeah. I'm sure she is. She's not supposed to steal, either, but I wouldn't beat yourself up over it. The family dog slept on my bed his entire life, and then his successor took over.'

'Well, I don't want Saffy doing that. She's too big and she hogs the bed.'

'She can't be worse than Joe. I remember sharing a tent with him in our teens. Nightmare.' And then he looked at her, rammed a hand through his hair and sighed sharply. 'Sorry. That was tactless.'

'True, though. He did hog the bed. At least the dog doesn't snore.' She twiddled her spaghetti for a moment, then glanced up at him. 'James, about earlier. I know it wasn't my fault Steve died. I was just raw. It was just—so wrong.'

'It's always wrong. Stuff happens, Connie. You know that.'

She held his gaze for a long time, then turned slowly away. 'I know. I'm sorry I got all wet on you.'

'Don't be. You can always talk to me.'

'You can talk to me, too,' she pointed out, and he looked up from his plate and met her eyes. His smile was rueful.

'I'm not good at talking.'

'I know. You weren't nine years ago, and you haven't got better.'

'I have. Just not at the talking.'

'I rest my case.'

'Physician, heal thyself?'

She held his eyes. 'Maybe we can heal each other.'

His gaze remained steady for an age, and then he smiled sadly.

'I wish.'

'Will you tell me about her?' she asked gently. 'About how she died?'

Could he? Could he find the words to tell her? Maybe. And maybe it was time he talked about it. Told someone, at least, what had happened.

But not yet. He wasn't ready yet.

'Maybe one day,' he said gruffly, then he got up and cleared the table, and she watched him go.

Would he tell her? Could he trust her enough to share something so painful with her?

It was a nice idea. Something from cloud cuckoo land, probably. There was no way James would have let anyone in in the past, and she wasn't sure he'd changed that much.

He stuck his head back out of the kitchen door.

'Coffee?'

'Lovely. I'll have a flat white, since you're offering.'

She heard the snort as his head disappeared back into the kitchen, and she smiled sadly. She could hear him working, hear the tap of the jug, the sound of the frother, the sound of Saffy's bowl skidding round the floor as he fed her something. Probably the leftover spaghetti. She'd like that. She'd be his slave for life if she got the chance.

The light was fading, and he paused on the veranda, mugs in hand. 'Why don't you put Saffy on a lead and we'll take our coffee up on the sea wall? It's lovely up there at night.'

It was. The seagulls were silent at last, and all they could hear was the gentle wash of the waves on the shingle. The sea was almost flat calm, and the air was still.

Saffy lay down beside him, her nose over the edge of the wall, and they sat there side by side in the gathering dusk drinking their coffee and listening to the sound of the sea and just being quiet.

Inevitably her mind went back over the events of the day, and sadness came to the fore again.

'How are Steve's parents going to feel, James?' she asked softly. 'How will they get over it?'

'They won't. You don't ever get over the loss of a child. You just learn to live with it.'

It was too dark to read his expression but his voice sounded bleak, and she frowned.

He'd never had a child. She knew that. And yet—he sounded as if he understood—really understood, in the way you only could if you'd been through it. Or perhaps he knew someone who had.

And maybe he was just empathetic and she was being ridiculous.

She was about to change the subject and tell him she'd seen David and Molly when he started to speak again.

'It's probably time I told you about Cathy.'

She sucked in a quiet breath. 'Only if you want to.'

He made a sound that could have been a laugh if it hadn't been so close to despair, but he didn't speak again, just sat there for so long that she really thought he'd changed his mind, but then he started to talk, his voice low, hesitant as he dug out the words from deep inside.

'She wasn't well. She felt sick, tired, her breasts were tender—classic symptoms of early pregnancy, so she did a test and it was positive.'

'She was pregnant?' she whispered, and felt sick with horror. 'Joe never told me that—!'

'He didn't know. He was away at the time and I didn't tell anyone. Anyway, there wasn't really time. She was nearly twelve weeks by the time she realised she was pregnant, and she was delighted, we both were, but she felt dreadful. By sixteen weeks I thought she ought to be feeling better. She'd been to see the doctor, seen the midwife, been checked for all the normal pregnancy things, but she was getting worse, if anything. So she went back to the doctor, and he referred her to the hospital for tests, and they discovered she'd got cancer. They never found the primary, but she was riddled with it, and over the next six weeks I watched her fade away. She was twenty-two weeks pregnant when she died.'

Too soon for the baby to be viable. She closed her eyes, unable to look at him, but she could hear the pain in his voice, in every word he spoke, as raw as the day it had happened, and the tears cascaded down her cheeks.

His voice was so bleak, and she could have kicked herself. He'd lost a child, albeit an unborn one, and she felt sure he still grieved for it. No wonder he hadn't wanted to help her have a baby. How must he have felt when she'd blundered in and asked him to help her?

Awful.

He must have been plunged straight back there into that dreadful time. Not that it was ever far away, she knew from experience, but even so.

She shook her head, fresh tears scalding her eyes. 'I'm sorry,' she said softly, 'so, so sorry. I should never have asked you about the baby thing. If I'd known about Cathy, if I'd had the slightest idea that she was pregnant, I would never have asked you—never—'

His hand reached out in the darkness, wiping the tears from her cheeks, and he pulled her into his arms and held her.

'It's OK. You weren't to know, and I'm used to it, Connie. I live in a world filled with children. I can't avoid the subject, try as I might.'

'No. I guess not, but I'm still sorry I hurt you so much by bringing it up.'

'But you did bring it up, and because of that you're here, and maybe you're right, even if I can't make that dream come true for you, maybe we can help each other heal.'

'Do you think so?' she asked sadly, wondering if anything could take away a pain that great.

'Well, I'm talking to you now. That's a first. I didn't tell anyone. I didn't want their pity. I didn't want anything. I lost everything on that day. My wife, my child, my future—all at once, everything was gone and I wanted to die, too. There was no way I could talk about it, no way I could stay there. I had nothing to live for, but I was alive, and so I packed up the house, sold it, gave everything away and went travelling, but it didn't really help. It just passed the time, gave me a bit of distance from it geographically and emotionally, and I worked and partied my way around the world. And all the time

I felt nothing. A bit of me's still numb, I think. I guess you can understand that.'

She nodded. 'Oh, yes. Yes, I can understand that. It's how I felt after Joe died—just—nothing. Empty. Just a huge void. But at least you had the chance to say goodbye. That must have been a comfort.'

'No. Not really,' he said softly, surprising her. 'I didn't even have the chance to say hello to our baby, never mind goodbye, and with Cathy—well, you can't ever really say goodbye I don't think, not in any meaningful way, because even though you know it's happening, you still hope they might be wrong, that there's been a mistake, that there'll be a miracle cure. You just have to say the things you need to say over and over, until they can't understand any more because the drugs have stolen them from you, and then you wait until someone comes and tells you they've gone, and even then you don't believe it, even though you were sitting there watching it happen and you knew it was coming.'

She nodded. 'I did that with Joe,' she told him softly. 'I didn't watch him die, but from the moment I met him I waited for it, knowing it was coming, unable to say goodbye because I kept hoping it wouldn't be necessary, that it wouldn't happen, and in the end it took almost seven years. I always knew I'd lose him, just not when, so I never did say goodbye.'

He sighed and took her hands with his free one, folding them in his, warming them as they lay in her lap. 'I should never have introduced you. You could have been happily married to someone else, have half a dozen kids by now, not be here like this trying to convince me to give you the child you wanted with Joe.'

'I won't ask you again. I feel dreadful—'

'Shh.' He pressed a finger to her lips, then took it

away and kissed her, just lightly, the slightest brush of his lips on hers. 'It's OK, Connie. Truly. I'd rather you'd come to me like that than call me one day and tell me you'd been to a clinic and you were pregnant. At least this way I'm forewarned that it's on the cards.'

'I'm sorry you don't approve.'

'It's not that I don't approve, Connie. I just don't want you to make a mistake, to rush into it.'

'It's hardly a rush. We started trying four years ago. That's a lot of time to think about it.'

'I wish I'd known.'

'I wish you'd known. I wish we'd known about Cathy. Maybe we could have helped you.'

'We'll have to look after each other, then, won't we?'

Could they? Maybe. She sucked in a breath and let it go, letting it take some of the pain away.

'Sounds like a plan. I saw Molly's husband today, by the way, out on a run,' she went on, after a long and pensive silence. 'I didn't know he'd lost his leg. Is he ex-army?'

'No. He got in a muddle with a propeller in Australia.'

'Ouch. Some muddle.'

'Evidently. He doesn't let it hold him up much, though. I run with him sometimes and believe me, he's pretty fit. Oh, and incidentally, Molly's having a private view on Friday. She wants us to go.'

'Yes, she mentioned it. She said she'd told you to tell me.'

'Sorry. Slipped my mind,' he said, but she had a feeling he was lying.

'So, how's the rota looking for Friday?' she asked lightly.

He turned his head, the moon coming out from behind the clouds just long enough for her to see the wry grin. 'Don't worry, I'll be there and so will you. And Molly said wear something pretty, by the way.'

She grinned back at him, feeling the sombre mood slip gently from her shoulders, taking the shadows of the past with it. 'Is that you or me?' she teased.

He chuckled, his laugh warm, wrapping round her in the darkness of the night just like the arm that was still draped round her shoulders, holding her close. 'Oh, I think you do pretty rather better than me,' he said softly, and she joined in the laughter, but something in his voice made her laugh slightly breathless.

She looked up at him, their eyes meeting in the pale light of the moon, and for an endless moment she thought he was going to kiss her again, but then he turned away and she forced herself to breathe again.

Of course he hadn't been going to kiss her! Not like that. Why on earth would he do that? He didn't have anything to do with women, he'd told her that, and certainly not her.

'I'll try not to let you down,' she said, her voice unsteady, and his wry chuckle teased her senses.

'Oh, you won't let me down, Connie,' he said softly, and she swallowed hard.

Was he flirting with her? Was she with him? Surely not. Or were they? Both of them?

She gave up talking after that in case it got her into any more trouble, just closed her eyes and listened to the sea, her fingers still linked with his, his other arm still round her, taking the moment at face value.

One day at a time. One hour at a time.

Or even just a stolen ten minutes on a dark, romantic night with an old friend. Maybe more than an old friend.

Right now, tonight, she'd settle for that.

CHAPTER SIX

HE FELT SLIGHTLY shell-shocked.

He'd come home that evening uncertain of what he'd find after the rough start she'd had, and he'd walked into a warm welcome, food ready for the table, and company.

Good company. Utterly gorgeous company, if he was honest. She'd been for a run, she said, and she'd obviously showered because she smelled amazing. Her hair had drifted against him at one point, and he'd caught the scent of apples. Such a simple thing, but it made his gut tighten inexplicably.

It had been so long since anyone other than his mother or the wife of a friend had cooked for him—except, of course, that Connie *was* the wife of a friend.

Only this evening it hadn't felt like it, not really. It had felt more like two old friends who were oddly drawn to each other, sharing a companionable evening that had touched in turn on trivia and tragedy and somehow, at points, on—romance? Innuendo? A little light flirtation?

The food had been simple but really tasty, and they'd sat there over it and talked about all sorts of things. Friendship, and Joe's sleeping habits and the dog's, and how he ought to talk more. How they could help each other heal.

He still wasn't sure about the possibility of that. Some wounds, surely, never truly healed. Acceptance, he'd discovered after a while, was the new happy, and that had seemed enough—until now. And suddenly, because of Connie, he was wondering if there might be more out there for him than just this endless void.

With her?

No. That was just fantasy. Wasn't it? He didn't know, but he'd felt comfortable with her in a way he hadn't felt comfortable with anyone for years, possibly ever, and it wasn't because the subjects were comfortable, because they weren't.

They'd talked about Steve and how his parents would be feeling, and then somehow he'd found himself able to tell her about Cathy and the baby. He still couldn't quite believe that, couldn't believe he'd let her in, shared it so easily.

And it had been easy, in a way. Easier than he'd thought, although it had made her feel guilty. Still, at least now perhaps she'd understand his reluctance to discuss the baby thing, the emotional minefield that it meant for him, and it would help her understand his refusal.

Then they'd talked about Molly's private view, and her looking pretty, and he'd flirted with her. What had he been thinking about? He must have been mad, and he'd come so close to kissing her. Not the light brush of his lips on hers. That didn't count, although it had nearly killed him to pull away. But properly.

He let his breath out on a short sigh and closed his eyes. Too close. Thankfully it had been dark, just a sliver of moonlight, so maybe he'd got away with it, but Friday was going to be a trial, with her all dressed up.

He was actually looking forward to it—not to the

art, he'd meant what he'd said about not needing pictures, but to seeing Connie wearing whatever she'd decided was 'pretty'.

Hell, she'd look pretty in a bin bag. She couldn't help it. The anticipation kept him on edge all night, humming away in the background like a tune stuck in his head, and when he slept, she haunted his dreams, floating through them in some gauzy confection that left nothing to the imagination.

He got up at six, had a cold shower to dowse his raging hormones and met her in the kitchen. In her pyjamas, if you could call them that, which totally negated the effects of the shower.

'You're up early,' he said, noticing the kettle was already on.

'I've been up for ages. I couldn't sleep.'

'Worrying about work?'

'No. Saffy snoring on the bed. I take back what I said about Joe, she's much worse. She really has no manners.'

He laughed then, glancing down at Saffy who was lying on the floor and watching him hopefully. Better than studying Connie in her pyjamas. It was going to kill him, having this encounter every morning.

'I haven't done anything about getting you a kettle and toaster,' he said, changing the subject abruptly. 'I'll order them today.'

'Don't do that, I've got both of them in storage. I've got all sorts of things in storage, I just haven't dealt with them. They don't give you long to move out of married quarters, and I just packed everything up and got it out of the way.'

He eyed her thoughtfully. 'Maybe you need to deal with it.'

She nodded. 'Probably. I would, if I had anywhere to put the stuff.'

'You could bring it here. Put it in a spare room. I have three, after all. You're welcome to at least two.'

'Are you sure?'

'Why not?'

'I don't know. It just seems an imposition.'

'It's no imposition. How much is there? Is it furniture as well?'

'Oh, no, I put the decent stuff into our own house and gave the rest away. It's just personal stuff, really.' She looked troubled, and he wondered whose stuff. Joe's?

'Think about it,' he said, reaching for a pair of mugs and sticking them in front of the kettle. 'Tea or coffee?'

'Oh—tea. It's way too early for coffee. Are you going to work already?'

'Might as well. Why don't you come in at nine? There's always a rush then in Minors. I could do with someone reliable in there if you wouldn't mind.'

She gave him a wry smile. 'Is this because you feel you can't use me on the front line after Steve?'

He rolled his eyes. 'Connie, I *know* I can use you on the front line, but I need someone I can trust in Minors. And I can call you if I need to. And I will, believe me.'

'Promise?'

He met her eyes, saw the challenge in them and smiled. 'Promise.'

'Thank you. Have you made that tea yet?'

She thought she'd be bored, but actually working in Minors was busy, varied and interesting, and she found herself enjoying it.

And then he rang her, just when she was beginning to think he'd lied.

'We've got an RTC, two vehicles, mother and child in a car, and a van driver, all trapped. They need a team on site and we need to leave now. I'm in the ambulance bay.'

Her heart skipped. 'I'm on my way.'

She passed the fracture case she was dealing with to the SHO and met James in the ambulance bay. He handed her a coat that said 'DOCTOR' on the back in big letters, and they ran for the door.

'So what do we know?' she asked as the rapid response car pulled away, sirens blaring.

'Not a lot. Three casualties, one's a small child. It's not far away.'

It wasn't, ten minutes, tops, but it was a white knuckle ride and she was glad when they got there. The police were already in attendance, and an officer came over as they pulled up and got out.

'The woman in the car might have chest injuries, she's complaining of shortness of breath and pain, and we can't get to the child but it's screaming so it's alive. The car's rolled a couple of times but it's on its wheels. She swerved to avoid a cyclist and hit the van and it flipped her over into a field.'

'And the van driver?' James asked briskly. She could see him eyeing the scene and weighing up their priorities, and they could hear the child crying already.

'He's conscious, breathing, trapped by one leg but not complaining. She was clearly on the wrong side of the road and going too fast. Oh, and she's pregnant.'

Connie saw the blood drain from his face.

'Right. Connie, come with me,' he said tautly. 'The van driver'll keep till the ambulance gets here. Let's look at the mother and child. Can we get in the car?'

'Not yet. The fire crew's on its way.'

'Right.'

He wasn't impressed by what they found. It was a mess. All the windows were shattered, and the roof was bent and twisted. It wasn't going to be quick or easy to open the doors, but they could probably get in if they had to.

He crouched down and peered through the shattered glass of the driver's door, and his heart rate kicked up another notch.

The woman was pale, very distressed and covered in blood from superficial glass injuries, and he reached a hand in and touched her shoulder, smiling reassuringly—he hoped—as she turned back to face him.

'Hi there. I'm James Slater, I'm a doctor. Can you tell me your name?'

'Judith. Judith Meyers.'

'OK, Judith. Can you tell me how you're feeling? Any pain, shortness of breath, numbness, tingling?'

'Can't breathe. Banged my knee. Please, look after my little boy. Get him out—please, get him out!' She pressed her hand to her chest and gave a little wail of distress, and then tried to open the door.

'I can't get out,' she sobbed, her breath catching, and there was a blue tinge to her lips.

Damn. He straightened up and tugged the door. Nothing.

'Right, I need this door open now. Where the hell is the fire crew?' he growled.

'I can see them, they'll be here in seconds,' the police officer told him.

'Good.' He tried the handle again, tugged the door harder but it wouldn't give, and he glanced across the dented roof and saw Connie leaning in the back window.

'How does it look your end?' he called, and she pulled her head back out and shrugged.

'He's still restrained by the car seat, seems OK, moving well but I can't really assess him without getting in there. He's yelling well, though.'

He smiled thinly. 'I can hear that. Just hang on, the fire crew'll be here in a tick. Do what you can. OK, Judith, we're going to get the door open soon so we can get a better look at you, and we'll get your baby out as soon as we can, but yelling's good. What's his name?'

'Zak,' she said unevenly, her breathing worsening, and he frowned and checked her air entry again.

'OK, Connie, we've got a— Connie? What are you doing?' he asked, pointlessly, because he could see exactly what she was doing. She'd crawled into the car through the broken window and she was running her hands over Zak's limbs, oblivious to the broken glass and shattered debris on the back seat. She was going to be cut to ribbons.

'Checking the baby. He seems fine. Hey, Zak, you're all right, Mummy's just there.'

'Can you get him out?'

'Yes. He's moving well, no obvious signs of injury. Frankly I think he just needs a cuddle more than anything at the moment. He's fighting to get out but I'll need someone to take him from me. How's mum?'

'Reduced air entry on the left. Query pneumothorax. I need to fit a chest drain. Can you help me from there?'

'Not easily. Can you do it on your own?'

'I can if you can hold stuff.'

'Sure. I can do that. I'm going deaf but hey.'

By that time the fire crew was there and managed to wrench the driver's door open so he had better access, and Connie was leaning through the gap between the seats to help him when someone yelled.

'Clear the vehicle, Doc,' the fire officer in charge said quietly in his ear. 'Fuel leak.'

His heart rate went into hyperdrive, and he felt sick. He turned his head so Judith couldn't lipread. 'I can't move her yet. I need to secure her airway, get a spinal board on her and lift her out.'

'Not before we've made it safe.'

He ducked out of the car for a second. 'I can't leave her, she'll die. They'll both die, her and her unborn baby, and the baby'll die in the next few minutes if I can't secure that airway,' he said bluntly. 'Just do what you have to do and leave me to do the same.'

He stuck his head back in and met Connie's challenging eyes. 'Out,' he said, but she just shook her head.

'I'll get Zak out. Here, someone, take the baby carefully, please!' she said, and freeing little Zak, she lifted him up to the window and handed him over, then with a wriggle she was next to him on the passenger seat, sitting on another load of broken glass and debris.

'Right, what can I do?'

'You need to get out—'

'Shut up, Slater. You're wasting time. Where's the cannula?'

He was going to kill her.

Right after he'd hugged her for staying to help him save Judith's baby. He hoped.

They'd got Judith out in the nick of time, and just moments after they'd loaded her into the ambulance the car had gone up. If it had happened sooner—

'Hey, Slater, why the long face?'

He just stared at her expressionlessly. 'Your cuts need attention.'

'Later. I'm not finished with Judith. How's Zak?'

'He's fine. Check her over, make sure the baby's all right and get an X-ray of those ribs if you can.'

'James, I can manage,' she said firmly, and turned her attention to Judith as they wheeled her into Resus.

'Hi, Judith, remember me? Connie? I'm taking you over now from James Slater, the clinical lead, because he's looking after Zak, OK? You don't need to worry about him, he seems fine but James just wants to check him out.'

'I want to see him!' she sobbed hysterically. 'Please, let me see Zak. I need to know he's all right.'

'He's all right,' James said from behind her. 'Don't worry, Judith, I'll just look at him and do a few tests and then I'll bring him over to you. You just lie still and let Connie check you over.'

Fat chance. She stopped fighting the restraints, but moved on to another worry that was obviously eating holes in her, her hand grabbing at Connie and hanging on for dear life. 'How's the baby?' she asked, her eyes fixed on Connie's. 'Tell me it's all right, please. It has to be all right.'

'I'm going to do an ultrasound now. Cold gel coming.' She swept the head of the ultrasound over Judith's bump, and the sound of the baby's strong, steady heartbeat filled Resus.

Judith sobbed with relief, and behind her Connie heard James let out a ragged sigh.

'There you are,' Connie said with more confidence than she felt, her legs suddenly like jelly. 'Good and solid. Let me just get a look at the placenta—it's fine, no obvious signs of bleeding. How many weeks are you?'

'Thirty-one tomorrow.'

'So even if you did go into labour the baby's viable now. We just need to make sure that you don't if possible, so I want you to lie here and relax as much as you can, and I'll get an obstetrician to come down and look at you.'

She checked her thoroughly, did a full set of neuro

obs, and the neck X-rays came back clear and so did
the ribs.

'Any back ache? Leg pain?'

'No. Only from lying flat, and no leg pain.'

'We'll log-roll her to check and then she can come
off the spinal board,' James said, appearing at her side
with the little boy in his arms. 'Here, Judith, have a
cuddle with your little man for a moment. He's fine.'

'Mumum,' he said, reaching out to her, and James
laid him carefully down in his mother's arms.

Then he glanced up and met Connie's eyes, and she
smiled at him, searching his face.

'OK?' she said softly, and his mouth twisted in a
cynical smile.

'Apart from being ready to kill you,' he said, so softly
that only she could hear, but it didn't faze her, it was
exactly how Joe would have reacted.

She held his eyes for a moment, just long enough to
say she understood, and he frowned and looked down
at the mother and child snuggled up together.

'I don't want to break up the party, but could I have
Zak, Judith? We need to take you off the board and
check your back.'

'Oh—yes, of course. Sorry, I'm being so pathetic but
I just can't believe we're all all right.'

'Don't worry, I'd expect you to be concerned. I'd
worry much more if you weren't.'

Her back was fine, and apart from a few cuts and
bruises and the pneumothorax, so was the rest of her.
More or less.

'There's a bruise on her temple,' Connie told James,
and he knew instantly that she was thinking of Steve
and his head injury.

* * *

'I think we'll keep her here under observation overnight, check her head injury, keep an eye on the baby, unless you want to do it in Maternity?'

He glanced past her with a smile, and she looked up as a man in scrubs approached.

'Do what in Maternity?'

'Observe a pregnant patient overnight. Minor head injury, pneumothorax from seat belt injury, a few cuts and bruises, thirty-one weeks tomorrow, rolled the car. We've just got back from freeing her.'

'Yikes. OK. Shall I take a look at her?'

'Please. Connie, this is Ben Walker. Ben, Connie. Want to talk him through it?'

She shook his hand, introduced him to Judith and filled him in on her findings. He was gentle, reassuring and happy to have her for the night.

'Just to be on the safe side,' he said with a smile. 'I'll make sure we've got an antenatal bed for you when they're ready to transfer you.'

He turned back to James with a grin. 'So, met little Daniel Gallagher yet?'

James ignored the odd sensation in his chest. 'No. How is he?'

'Fine. Gorgeous. Lovely healthy baby. Fighting fit. They're still here—he was a little bit jaundiced so we've kept them in till this afternoon. You ought to pop up and say hello.'

He could feel that his smile was strained, but there was nothing he could do about it. 'I think we're probably a bit busy. I'm sure I'll see him soon enough. We'll send Judith up as soon as we're done with her.'

'Do that. Cheers. Nice to meet you, Connie.'

'You, too.'

Connie watched him go out of the corner of her eye, most of her attention on James. Wall to wall babies today, or so it seemed, and he wasn't enjoying it one bit. It was right what he'd said last night, he couldn't avoid it, he was surrounded by children in one way or another, and so was she. They just had to deal with it, but it didn't make it easy.

She did the paperwork for Judith's transfer, handed little Zak over to the woman's harassed husband when he arrived and then went over to James.

'Anything else I can do?'

He shook his head. 'Just get your cuts seen to,' he said tightly.

'You're welcome.'

He sighed. 'Thank you, Connie. Really, thank you. Now, please, get your cuts seen to.'

She did. They were worse than she'd realised, little nicks all over her legs and bottom from the car seats, but she wasn't worried about herself. She'd seen his face in the car, seen the tension in his shoulders in Resus until they'd heard the baby's heartbeat. He wasn't alone, everyone in there had been worried for them, and if she hadn't known about Cathy she probably wouldn't have thought anything of it, but there was just something else, another element to his concern that underlined his lingering grief.

And Andy's baby. He'd definitely not wanted to go up and see it. OK, so they probably were busy, but even if they hadn't been he wouldn't have gone. Because it hurt too much?

She changed into scrubs, because her trousers were ruined, and went back to work to carry on with her fractures and squashed fingers and foreign bodies up the noses of small children, but he was at the back of her mind for the rest of the day.

'How are the cuts?'

'I'll live.'

He snorted. 'Not for want of trying, you crazy woman. You should have got out when I told you.'

'What, and leave a pregnant woman stuck in a car that was about to blow? Not to mention you. No way was I going anywhere without both of you, so save your breath, Slater.'

'Damn you, Connie,' he growled, and with a ragged sigh he hauled her into his arms and hugged her hard. 'Don't ever do that to me again.'

'What, stand up to you?'

'Put your life in danger.'

'Don't get carried away, I didn't do it for you,' she said, leaning on him because it felt so good and she'd been worried sick about him underneath the calm.

'I know that.'

He rested his head against hers and let out a long, slow sigh. 'Thanks for staying. You were good with her. She was pretty hysterical.'

'She was scared. All I did was reassure her and try and keep her calm.'

'And you did it well. You were really good. Calm, methodical, systematic—and you didn't waste any time.'

'Well, I wonder who I got that from?' she teased, and he gave a soft huff of laughter. 'It's true,' she protested. 'I modelled myself on you. I always loved watching you work. You're funny, warm, gentle, cool as a cucumber—and terrifyingly efficient.'

He lifted his head and stared down into her eyes. 'Terrifyingly?'

'Absolutely. You were a brilliant role model, though.'

'You were a pretty good student.'

'Then I guess we're both pretty marvellous.'

He laughed softly, then the laughter died and he stared down at her mouth.

It was the lightest kiss. Fleeting. Tender, like the kiss of the night before.

The kiss of a friend?

Probably not, but it was over so soon she couldn't really assess it. She just knew it was too short.

He stepped back, dropping his arms and moving away from her, and she swayed slightly without his support.

He frowned at her. 'Have you eaten?'

'Um—no. I wasn't really hungry. I had some chocolate.'

'Nice balanced diet. Good one, Connie.'

'What about you? It's late, James. Surely you've eaten something at work?'

He shook his head. 'I'll have some cheese on toast. Want some?'

'Yeah. Just a slice.'

She followed him into the kitchen, Saffy following hopefully at her heels, and perched on the stool and watched him as he made bubbly cheese on toast, and then afterwards he found some ice cream and dished it up, and they all ate it in silence.

Too tired to talk? Or was the kiss troubling him as much as it was troubling her?

'Is there any more of that ice cream left?'

'A scraping.' He opened the freezer and handed her the plastic container. 'Here. Be my guest. Coffee?'

'Mmm. Can we take it on the wall?'

He made coffee, she scraped the ice cream off the sides of the container, licked the spoon one last time and put it in the dishwasher, and they headed to the sea wall with Saffy in tow.

'So what are you wearing tomorrow night?' he asked, trying not to think too hard about the flimsy thing in his dream and failing dismally. That kiss had been such a bad idea.

She slurped the froth off her coffee and licked her lips. 'Dunno. Define pretty in this part of the world. What do your dates wear?'

He laughed at that. 'I have no idea, Connie. You're asking the wrong person. I thought I'd told you that. I don't date, I never go out except for dinner with friends occasionally. I have absolutely no idea what women wear these days.'

She turned and studied him curiously. 'You don't date at all?' Not even for sex, she nearly asked, but shut her mouth in the nick of time.

'Not any more. After Cathy died I went a bit crazy, sort of tried to lay her ghost, but I just ended up feeling dirty and disappointed and even more unhappy, so I gave up. So, no, I don't date. Not even for that, before you ask. I was just scratching an itch, and frankly I can do that myself and it's a lot less hassle.'

Wow. She thought about that. Thought about his candid statement, and felt herself colouring slightly. It wasn't the fact, it was his frankness that had—well, not shocked her, exactly, but taken her by surprise. Which was silly, because Joe had never been coy and she'd never blushed before. Maybe it was because it was James and his sex life they were suddenly and inexplicably talking about. She changed the subject hastily.

'So—dress? Long linen skirt and top? Jeans and a

pretty top? Or I've got a floaty little dress that's rather lovely, but it might be too dressy.'

Gauze. Pale, oyster pink gauze, almost the colour of your skin, with dusky highlights over the nipples and a darker shadow—

He cleared his throat. 'I don't know. It's an art exhibition. Something arty, maybe? Molly will probably wear some vintage creation.'

Please don't wear gauze.

'So who will be there?'

'Oh, all sorts of people. David's family and the people he works with, his old friends, some of the doctors. They asked me to spread the word and gave me some invitations to hand out, but how many of them will come I don't know. Andy and Lucy Gallagher probably won't, with a three day old baby, but they might because they were seriously interested, and Ben and Daisy wanted to come because they've done up their house and they're looking for artwork for it. Otherwise I'm not sure. The movers and shakers of Yoxburgh society, I imagine.'

She gave a little splutter of laughter. 'Does Yoxburgh society have movers and shakers?' she asked, slightly incredulously.

'Oh, yeah. David's probably one of them. His family own that hotel and spa on the way in, near the hospital site. The big one with the Victorian facade.'

'Wow. That's pretty smart.'

'It is. Ben and Daisy got married there and it was lovely.'

'Is that the Ben I met today?'

'Yes. Daisy's an obstetrician, too, but I think she's pretty much on permanent maternity leave and she's loving every minute of it, apparently. They've got two little ones and Ben's got an older daughter.'

Another happy family twisting the knife. Yet it was interesting, she thought, that all of his friends seemed to be family-orientated. To replace his own family? He had no one. Like her, he was an only child, and he'd lost both his parents in his twenties, and then he'd lost Cathy and the baby. And if that wasn't enough, he'd lost Joe, his closest friend. He must be so *lonely*, she thought. She knew she was. It was why she'd brought Saffy home, and part of the reason she wanted a baby, to have someone of her own to love.

'Why are you frowning? You look as if you disapprove.'

'No. Not at all. I was thinking about my clothes,' she lied glibly.

But Saffy was lying propped against him, her head on his lap, and he was fondling her ears absently as he sipped his coffee and stared out over the darkening sea. Maybe she should give Saffy to him? She seemed to adore him. At least that way he wouldn't be alone. Or she could stay with him, and they could live together and have a family and all live happily ever after.

And she was in fantasy land again.

'I could sit here all night,' she said to fill the silence, and he gave a slightly hollow laugh.

'Sometimes I do. You know, on those nights when you can't sleep and things keep going round and round your head? I don't know what it is—the sound of the sea, maybe. It just seems to empty out all the irrelevancies, like when you clean up your computer and get rid of all the temporary files and other clutter, the cookies and all that rubbish, and everything seems to run faster then, more efficiently. Only the stuff that really matters is left.'

She wondered what that was, the stuff that was left, the stuff that really mattered to him now.

'Interesting theory. I might have to try it.'

'Do. Be my guest.'

She laughed softly. 'Nice idea, but I'll take a rain check. If I'm going to look pretty tomorrow night, I need my beauty sleep or I'll look like a hag and frighten off all the potential buyers. Molly wouldn't like that.'

He chuckled and stood up, shifting Saffy out of the way, and the dog shambled to her feet and stretched, yawning and wagging her tail and looking lovingly up at him.

'No way,' he said firmly. 'I'm not sharing my bed with a dog. I've done enough of that in my time.'

'Are you sure? I'm happy to lend her to you.'

Her voice was wry and made him chuckle. 'No, thanks. Although I did wonder about her being shut in the crate all day.'

'It's not all day. And I don't like it, either, but what else can I do?'

'I could build her a kennel outside, and a run,' he suggested. 'She'd have access to water, then, and she wouldn't have to cross her legs till you get home.'

'She might bark.'

'But she doesn't, does she? I've never heard her bark.'

'No, but I can't guarantee it, and I wouldn't want to annoy your neighbours,' she said, but she was seriously tempted to take him up on it. 'I could buy a kennel if you didn't mind making her some kind of run. It would have to be pretty strong.'

'I know that. Leave it with me. I'll think about it.'

They paused at the foot of the veranda steps and he stared down at her, his eyes in shadow. 'Are your cuts really all right?'

'Why, are you offering to dress them?'

Why on earth had she said that?

He frowned. 'Do they need it?'

'No. Really, James, I'm all right. They're just little nicks. Tracy had a look for me.'

He nodded, looking relieved. 'OK. Well, keep an eye on them. I'll see you tomorrow. Come in at nine again. It seems to work.'

'OK. Thanks.'

'You're welcome.'

His face was still in shadow, so she couldn't read his expression, but she could feel his eyes on her, and for a moment she wondered if he was going to kiss her again. Apparently not.

'Goodnight, Connie,' he said eventually, his voice soft and a little gravelly. 'Sleep tight.'

'And you. 'Night, James.'

She took Saffy into the cabin. By the time she'd finished in the bathroom, Saffy was ensconced on the bed, so she turned out the light and stood at the window for a minute, watching the house through a gap in the curtains.

He was in the kitchen. Every now and then he walked past the window and she could see him. Then the light went off, and she watched the progress of the lights—the landing, then a thin sliver of light across the roof from his bathroom. Then that went off, leaving a soft glow—from his bedroom?

After a few minutes that, too, went off, plunging the house into darkness. She pressed her fingers to her lips and softly blew him a kiss.

'Goodnight, James,' she whispered. 'Sleep tight.'

And pushing Saffy out of the way she crawled into bed, curled on her side and tried to sleep.

It was a long time coming.

CHAPTER SEVEN

HE SPENT HALF the night wondering why the hell he'd kissed her again and the other half dreaming about her flitting around in the garden in that scrap of gauze he couldn't get out of his mind.

He really, really wasn't thrilled when the alarm went off, but by the time he'd washed and dressed and gone down to the kitchen, Saffy was waiting for him on the veranda, tail wagging, and there was a little plume of steam coming from the kettle.

He stuck his head out of the door and found Connie with her feet up on the veranda rail, dressed in another pair of those crazy pyjamas, her nose buried in a mug.

'More tea?' he asked, and she shook her head, so he made himself a lethal coffee and took it out and sat himself on the bench beside her. Her feet were in sun, the bright clear sun of an early summer's morning, slanting across the corner of the house and bathing them in gold.

Her toenails had changed colour. They were greeny-blue today, and pearly, the colour changing according to the angle of the light, and the sun made them sparkle dazzlingly bright.

'Interesting nail varnish.'

'Mmm. I thought I'd go arty, for tonight,' she said, grinning at her toes. 'Cool, aren't they?'

'I don't think they'd suit me.'

'Well, we've already established I do pretty better than you.'

Their eyes locked for a moment, something—an invitation?—glimmering in hers for the briefest instant. Surely not. Really, he needed more sleep. He grunted and stretched his legs out, turning his attention to his coffee as a potential means of keeping his sanity. 'So, about this dog run.'

'Really? It's a lot of effort, and where would you put it?'

'I've been thinking about that. There's a little store room under here. I could divide it off so there was a kennel one side and a store the other, and build a run off it against the fence. What do you think?'

'Are you sure? Because I do worry about her and that would be amazing. I'd pay for all the materials.'

'OK. It shouldn't take much. We'll have a look at it after work.'

'No we won't, because we're going out. You hadn't forgotten, had you?'

Fat chance. How could he forget, with 'pretty' haunting his every waking moment and tantalising him in his sleep? Never mind those kisses he couldn't seem to stop giving her.

'Of course I haven't forgotten.' He downed his coffee and went back into the kitchen, grabbed a banana, slung his jacket on and headed out of the door.

'I'll see you later,' he muttered, running down the steps, and she dropped her feet to the veranda floor and wriggled them back into her flip-flops as she watched him go. He looked hunted, for some reason. Because of the private view?

She had no idea, but it was the last thing they'd talked about and he'd taken off like a scalded cat.

'Fancy a run, Saffy?' she asked, and Saffy leapt to her feet, tail lashing. 'That's a yes, then,' she said, and pulled her clothes on, locked up the cabin and the house and headed off.

She went on the sea wall for a change, and ran along to the end of the sea defences, then up a long set of steps to the top of the cliff and back down towards the harbour through the quiet residential streets.

She'd never been along them before, but it was obviously where the movers and shakers lived, she thought with a smile, and she wondered how many of them would be coming tonight.

She felt a tingle of anticipation, and realised she was actually looking forward to it. It was ages since she'd been out, ages since she'd had an occasion to dress up for, and she was determined to enjoy herself. And if she had anything to do with it, James would enjoy himself, too.

He felt ridiculously nervous.

He didn't know what to wear, so in the end he wore a lightweight suit with a silk shirt. No tie, because that would be overdoing it, but a decent silk shirt, open at the neck because it was a warm night.

Maybe not as warm as he felt it was, though. That was probably because he was waiting for Connie to come out of her cabin, and he was on edge.

She'd left him out something to eat, and he hadn't seen her since he'd got home. Saffy was in the garden, though, so he sat on the veranda and watched the cabin door and waited.

* * *

Was it all right?

She'd settled on a knee-length dress with a flirty hem in a range of sea colours from palest turquoise to deep, deep green, and it was soft and floaty and fitted like a dream. She'd bought it last year for a friend's wedding and she'd thought it would be perfect for tonight, but now she wasn't sure.

What if she'd overdone it? There was no long mirror in the cabin, so she'd had to make do with peering at the one in the shower room and trying to angle her head to see herself, but she couldn't. Not adequately.

And it was five to seven, and James was on the veranda, watching her door and tapping his fingers on the bench.

She took a steadying breath, slipped her feet into her favourite strappy sandals with killer heels, because, damn it, why not, and opened the door.

'Does this count as pretty?'

He felt his jaw drop.

He'd seen her looking beautiful before, lots of times, when she'd been with Joe. At their engagement party. On her wedding day. At a ball they'd all attended. Hell, sitting on the deck in her pyjamas this morning she'd nearly pushed him over the edge.

But this…

'I think you'll do,' he said, his voice sounding strangled.

Her face fell. 'Do?'

He got up and went to the top of the steps, looking down at her as she walked towards him and climbed the steps on incredibly sexy, utterly ridiculous heels that showed off her legs to perfection, and stopped just beneath him.

'Connie, you look—' He closed his eyes, then opened them again and tried to smile. 'You look beautiful,' he said, and his voice had handfuls of gravel in it.

'Oh.' She laughed, and her whole body relaxed as the laugh went through her. 'I thought, for a minute—you looked so—I don't know. Shocked.'

'Shocked?'

Try stunned. Try captivated. Try completely, utterly blown away.

'I'm not shocked,' he said. 'I just—'

He didn't like it. Damn. He was just being nice. 'Look, I can go and change. There isn't a mirror in there, but it's probably a bit much. A bit too dressy. I just don't have a lot to choose from, and—well, Molly did make a point—'

'Connie, you look fine,' he said firmly. 'Utterly gorgeous. Believe me. There's nothing wrong with the way you look. You're lovely. Very, very lovely.'

'Really?'

Her eyes were soft and wide, and he so badly wanted to kiss her again. 'Really,' he said, even more firmly. 'Let me just put Saffy away and then we'd better go.'

He called the dog, put her in her crate in the cabin and breathed in the scent of Connie. It had been diluted in the garden, drifting away on the light sea breeze, but in the confined space of the cabin the perfume nearly blew his mind.

'Good girl, Saff,' he said, closing the door on her. She whined, and he promised her he'd make her a run, then closed the cabin door and braced himself for an evening in Connie's company.

Torture had never smelt so sweet.

* * *

It was already buzzing by the time they got there.

She'd heard lots of cars going past on the gravel road, and so she wasn't surprised. And she wasn't over-dressed, either, she realised with relief. All the women were in their designer best, diamonds sparkling on their fingers, and the men wore expensive, well cut suits.

None of them looked as good as him, though, and she felt a shiver of something she hadn't felt for years.

'Connie, James, welcome!' David said, pressing glasses of champagne into their hands. 'Just mingle and enjoy—the pictures are all over the place, and there's a pile of catalogues lying around somewhere on a table. Just help yourselves. And there are some canapés coming round.'

'Wow,' she said softly as he moved away, and James raised an eyebrow.

'Indeed. The movers and shakers,' he murmured.

She suppressed a giggle, the bubbles of the champagne already tickling her nose. 'I ran past some pretty smart houses this morning up on the clifftop. I guess they're here.'

'Undoubtedly. His friends are pretty well connected. Ah—Andy and Lucy *are* here. Come and say hello.'

Not only were they there, she realised as he made the introductions, they had the baby with them, snug in the crook of Andy's arm, and her heart turned over.

James leant over and kissed Lucy's cheek, his smile looking entirely genuine if you ignored the tiny tic in his cheek. 'Congratulations. How are you? I didn't really expect to see you here so soon.'

'Oh, I'm fine,' Lucy said, positively glowing. 'My parents are here helping us out for a few days, and we really wanted to come, so we thought we'd sneak out while the going was good. And I'm really glad, because I get to meet Connie and say thank you for stepping in like that so I can have Andy at home.'

'Oh, you're welcome,' Connie said with a laugh, liking Lucy instantly. 'It's nice to be back at work. I've had a sabbatical and I was beginning to feel a bit redundant.'

'Oh, well, glad to be of service,' Lucy said with a chuckle. 'And this is Daniel, the cause of all the trouble.'

'Oh, he's so beautiful,' she whispered, and she felt her eyes fill with tears. 'Sorry. Babies always do that to me,' she said with a light laugh, but she could feel James watching her.

'Oh, good,' Andy said. 'You can hold him while I dig out my chequebook. Lucy's found a picture and I need to pay for it. Here.'

And he reached over and gave her little Daniel. Just like that, her arms were full of new baby, closing round him automatically and cradling him close, and she felt the threatening tears well again. 'Hello, little guy,' she crooned softly, breathing that wonderful new baby smell and welling up again. It just felt so *right*. 'Aren't you gorgeous?'

James felt his heart squeeze just looking at them together. *She should be a mother,* he thought suddenly. *She's born for it. It could be my child, but if I stop her, it'll be someone else's, and how will that feel?*

'So how do you two know each other?' Lucy asked, and James dragged his eyes off Connie and the baby before he went crazy.

'We worked together nine years ago, and we've kept in touch.'

He noticed Lucy's eyes flick to Connie's wedding ring, and winced inwardly, but he didn't say any more, and neither did Connie. She was absorbed by the baby, utterly focused, and she just looked so damned *right* holding him that he could hardly think straight, never mind make small talk or fend off gossip. Not that Lucy was a gossip, but he didn't feel it was up to him to broadcast Connie's personal circumstances.

'All done.'

Connie looked up at Andy and smiled ruefully. 'Does that mean you want him back?'

'Afraid so, having gone to all that trouble to get him.'

So she handed him back, releasing him reluctantly, her arms feeling suddenly desperately empty and un-fulfilled.

And then she glanced at James and saw a muscle clench in his jaw, and she thought, *I'm not alone. He feels it, too. The ache. The need. The emptiness. Only how much worse is it for him?*

'So what do you think of the exhibition?' Lucy asked.

James shrugged. 'I don't know, we've only just ar-rived.'

'Well, you'd better go and look, the red dots are going on faster than a measles epidemic,' Andy said with a grin.

'Oh, I don't do pictures. It would require finding a hammer and a nail to put it on the wall, and that would mean unpacking the boxes.'

Andy laughed, and James was still smiling, but it was lingering there in his eyes, she thought. The emptiness.

He still wants a child, she realised with sudden clar-ity. *He wants one, but he doesn't know how to move on.* But maybe, once he'd got to know her—maybe she'd be able to do something about that…

'Well, hi.'

'Ben! Nice to see you. How's our patient?'

'Fine. Doing well.'

'Are you two going to talk shop?' Lucy asked pointedly, but Connie just grinned.

'No, we three are. Sorry. So how is she? How's the head injury?'

'A nice shade of purple, and so's her knee, but she's fine. This is Daisy, by the way.'

She was scintillating.

She mingled with everyone with the confidence of someone totally at ease with herself, smiling and laughing and waving her hands all over the place to illustrate what she was saying. Which was great, because it meant he didn't need to stand right next to her all night, breathing in that intoxicating perfume and threatening to disgrace himself.

'So, what do you think?'

He turned round to Molly. 'Great exhibition. Really good.'

'I meant of Connie.'

'Connie?'

'Oh, James, come on, you haven't taken your eyes off her. Doesn't she look beautiful?'

Well, he could lie, or make some excuse, or drop his drink.

Or he could just be honest.

'Yes. She does. It's the first time I've seen her look happy in ages. Thanks for inviting her. She's really enjoyed dressing up, I think. She's even got crazy matching nail varnish on her toes.'

Molly chuckled. 'Not that you noticed, of course.'

'Of course not. Why would I? I'd better go and rescue her, that guy's getting a bit pushy.'

'He's harmless, James. I'm sure she can cope,' Molly murmured, but *he* couldn't. Couldn't cope at all with the good-looking bastard oozing charm all over her like some kind of vile slime, and the words she'd said to him less than a week ago were echoing in his head. Words about pulling some random stranger in a club. Or at an art exhibition?

Fighting off the red mist, he made his way over to her, smiling grimly.

'There you are,' he said, slipping his hand through her arm, and he stuck his hand out. 'James Slater.'

The man blinked, introduced himself as Tony and made himself scarce. Excellent.

Connie turned slowly and looked up at him. Not that far up, not now, because she was teetering on those sky-scrapers that messed with his head and they brought her up almost to eye level with him.

'So what was that all about?' she asked, laughter dancing in her eyes.

'He was flirting outrageously.'

'Yes. He was. And I was perfectly happy letting him make a fool of himself. It was quite fun, actually.'

At which point James began to wonder if he was making a fool of his own self. Very probably. He tried not to grind his teeth. 'I thought he might be annoying you.'

'In which case I would have told him where to go. James, I've lived on an army base for years,' she said patiently, her eyes laughing at him. 'Several of them. And in every one there was someone like that. I can deal with it.'

He nodded. Of course she could. He'd seen her doing it years ago, for God's sake, handling the drunks on a Friday night in the ED. Tony whoever was nothing. 'Sorry. I didn't mean to come over all heavy, I just...'

He shrugged, and she shook her head slowly and smiled at him.

'You're crazy. Come with me. There's a picture I want to show you.'

She tucked a hand in his arm and led him through to another room. It was quieter in there, and she pulled him to one side and then turned him.

And there, on the wall opposite them, was a blur of vibrant colour. It radiated energy, and for a second he couldn't work out what it was. And then the mist seemed to clear and he could make out the figure of a runner, smudged with speed, the power almost palpable, and at the bottom was a fine, curved line.

'It's called Blade Runner,' she said softly. 'Isn't it amazing? As if she's tapped into his soul.'

'Amazing,' he echoed. 'It's incredible. It must be David.'

'I would think so. It's not for sale.' Connie let him stand there for a minute, then she tugged his arm. 'Come on. There are others. Have you looked at them?'

He shook his head. 'No. No, not really.' *Because he'd been watching her. Picturing her with a baby in her arms. Picturing her pregnant. Fantasising about getting her that way—*

'You should. Your walls are crying out for colour, for movement. And these are fantastic.'

He stopped thinking about Connie then and started to look at them, really look at them, and he was blown away.

'Wow. I love this one,' Connie said, pausing in front of a very familiar scene. At least he thought it was familiar, but Molly's work was blurred and suggestive rather than figurative, and he wasn't entirely sure.

'It looks like the marshes from my veranda.'

'Gosh, yes. I think you're right—what does it say?'

'"Mist over the ferry marshes",' he told her. 'I'm sure it is. I recognise the pattern of the landscape.'

'It's the view out the back here, she paints it all the time. She loves it,' David said in passing, and gave him another drink. He took it without thinking. So did Connie, and by the time they'd worked their way round the exhibition again, they'd had another two. At least.

Realising he'd lost count, he took a closer look at Connie and sighed inwardly. She was tiddly. Not drunk, certainly not that, but gently, mildly inebriated. At the moment. And frankly, so was he.

'I think it's time to go home,' he murmured.

'Really?'

'Really.' The crowd was thinning out, Andy and Lucy with their tiny baby were long gone, and he figured that he just about had time to get Connie home before the last glass entered her system and pushed her over the edge.

'Fabulous exhibition. I love every single one,' she told Molly fervently. 'I want them all, but I haven't got any money, and more importantly I haven't got any walls or I might have to start saving.'

Molly laughed. 'Thank you. I'm glad you like them. And you'll have walls one day.'

'I've got walls right now that need pictures,' James said, surprised to realise that he meant it. 'Can I come and see you tomorrow?'

'Sure. We're opening the door at ten. Come before then. Both of you, come for coffee.'

'That'll be lovely. Thanks.' He kissed her cheek, shook David's hand and ushered Connie out of the door.

'Can we walk by the sea?' she asked, so he led her up onto the sea wall, her hand firmly anchored in his.

'Oooh. That's a bit steep. When did that happen?' she asked, eyes rounded, and giggled.

'When you had all that champagne,' he told her wryly, and she laughed and tucked her arm in his and they walked arm in arm along the sea wall until they reached his house. Then she looked down at the bank.

'Hmm. We walked along the road before, didn't we?'

'We did.'

'Oh.'

If it was anybody else, he would have thought it was staged, but Connie wasn't that artful. He shook his head and hoisted her up into his arms, and she gave a little shriek and wrapped her arms around his neck.

'What are you doing?'

'Carrying you down the bank so you don't break your ankle in those crazy shoes.'

'Don't you like my shoes?' she asked, lifting one foot up and examining it thoughtfully, and he turned his head and looked at her leg and groaned softly.

'Your shoes are fine,' he said a little abruptly, and put her down. She slid down his front, ending up toe to toe with him, their bodies in contact from chest to knee.

Dear God.

'James?' she whispered.

She was so close her breath teased his cheek, and it would take only the tiniest movement of his head to bring their lips into contact.

He moved, brushed his mouth against hers. Pulled back, then went in again for more, his hands tunnelling into her hair, his tongue tracing her lips, feeling them part for him. He delved, and she delved back, duelling with him, driving him crazy.

She whimpered softly, and he pulled away, resting

his head on hers and breathing hard, stopping now while he still could.

'More,' she said, and he shook his head.

'Connie, no. This is a bad, bad idea.'

'Is it?'

'Uh-huh.'

'What a shame.' She hiccupped, and looked up at him, her eyes wide in the moonlight. 'Do you think we might be just a teeny, tiny bit drunk?' she asked, and then giggled.

He closed his eyes, the imprint of her body against his burning like flames, the touch of her lips branding him forever. 'Just a teeny, tiny bit,' he agreed. 'Come on, Connie, it's time you went to bed.'

And he turned her and pointed her in the direction of the cabin, unlocked the door and pushed her in.

Quickly, before he did something that couldn't be undone, something he'd regret for the rest of his life.

Something like cup that beautiful, laughing face in his hands once more and bend his head and kiss her again, only this time, he knew, he wouldn't stop...

How ironic. And what a brilliant way to find out that he was ready to move on.

With his best friend's widow.

Great move, Slater, he told himself in disgust. He picked up a pebble off the sea wall and hurled it into the water. Or tried to. The tide was too far out, and he missed by miles.

That was champagne for you.

Or the distracting realisation that you were about to make a real idiot of yourself.

Even more disgusted, he threw another one, and this time he was angry enough that it made its mark.

Better.

So he did it again.

She was woken by Saffy scratching at the door.

'Saff, no, it's too early, come and lie down,' she pleaded, her head thrashing, but Saffy wanted out, and she wasn't giving up. She whined, then gave a soft bark, and Connie stumbled out of bed and opened the door.

James was on the veranda, sitting there in the pre-dawn light, a mug cradled in his hands.

'Is that tea?' she asked, her throat parched and her head pounding.

'You need water,' he told her, and dropped his feet to the deck and stood up. 'Gallons of it.'

She walked barefoot across the dewy grass and climbed the steps gingerly. 'I want tea.'

'Water first,' he insisted, handing her a glass.

'I wasn't that bad,' she protested, but a sceptical eyebrow flickered and she scowled at him. 'I wasn't!'

'No. To quote you, you were only a teeny, tiny bit drunk.'

'Oh, God,' she moaned, and slumped down onto the bench and put her head in her hands. 'Did I disgrace myself?'

'No. You were lovely,' he said, his internal editor clearly on holiday, and she dropped her hands from her face and straightened up, turning slowly to look at him.

'I was?'

'Well, of course you were.'

She smiled and leant back, picking up the glass. 'Phew. For a moment there I thought I might have made a fool of myself.'

He chuckled. 'You didn't, but probably only because I got you out of there in time.'

'You didn't *have* to carry me home,' she pointed out, which answered the question of how much she remembered. More than he'd expected, probably. The kiss?

'I didn't. I just carried you down the bank.'

'Yeah. Crazy shoes. I bought them after Joe died. He was only three inches taller than me, and they're five inch heels. And I love them soooo much.'

'I don't know how the hell you walk in them.'

'Carefully,' she said with a little laugh. 'So—I've drunk the water. Can I please have tea now? Because I do have a teensy little headache.'

'I'll just bet you do,' he grumbled, getting to his feet again. 'What did your last servant die of?'

And then he stopped in his tracks, swore viciously and turned back to her. Her eyes were wide with shock, all laughter gone, and he could have kicked himself.

'Ah, hell, Connie, I'm sorry—I didn't mean—' He swore again, and dropped his head against the doorframe, banging it gently. OK, maybe not so gently. 'I'm really sorry. That was inexcusable. I can't believe I said it.'

'Hey. It's all right,' she said softly. 'It was just a silly remark. We all do it. And it's exactly the sort of thing Joe used to say to me. I'll forgive you if you get me tea and stop making wisecracks about my hangover. Done?'

'Done,' he said, sending her a wry, apologetic smile. 'Do you want anything to eat?'

'It's a bit early.'

'Not if you've been up all night.'

'Survivors' breakfast?' she said, and there it was again, the spectre of Joe between them, and this time it was her fault.

I can't do this, he thought. *I can't just be with her feeling like this with Joe hanging over us. And I'm not*

*sure I can cope with the idea of giving her a baby. Ever.
I can't even cope with thinking about it because I want
it so much. How did I get myself in this mess?*

Easy. He'd been forced into a corner by the staffing
crisis, and he'd been so desperate for help that Connie had seemed like the answer to his prayers, so he
hadn't let himself think about it too hard. The trouble
was, she was hoping he'd be the answer to hers, or at
least give her the answer to her prayers in the form of
a baby, and he really wasn't sure he could. Not in the
way she wanted, anyway, just a clinical donation of his
DNA. Not when the real alternative was growing more
and more compelling by the second—

'Something like that,' he said mildly. 'Bacon sandwich?'

'Oh, amazing! That would be so good.'

'Coming up.'

And he retreated to the kitchen, dragging the task
out far longer than necessary while he tried to work out
if she'd remembered the kiss or if she was just avoiding
the subject like him.

'Are you growing that tea?' she asked, appearing
in the doorway in those inadequate pyjamas, and he
slid the mug towards her, fished the bacon out of the
pan and dropped it on the bread and hesitated, sauce
bottle in hand.

'Ketchup or brown sauce?'

'Neither. As it comes. Unless you've got fresh tomato?'

He gave an exaggerated sigh, got a tomato out of
the fridge and sliced it, and handed her the sandwich.
'Right. I'm going for a run,' he said, and left the kitchen
before his body gave him away. He was going to cut
those pyjamas up, he vowed, plodding up the stairs

and turned the corner into his bedroom, to come to a dead halt.

'Connie! Your dog's up here, in my bed, and she's eating my trainers!'

Saffy was in disgrace.

They'd been his favourite running trainers, he said, and she felt racked with guilt.

'I'm really sorry—I'll buy you a new pair,' she promised, but of course that didn't help him, he wanted to go for a run there and then, and so he wore his old ones and came back with blisters. He had, however, taken Saffy with him, and she came back panting, as if the run had been further and harder than she was used to.

'Poor Saffy. Did he wear you out, darling?' she crooned, and he laughed.

'Poor Saffy?' he said with studied sarcasm. 'She's had a great time. She chased the seagulls, and played on the beach with a Labrador, and she's had brilliant fun.'

'You let her off the lead?' she squawked.

'Don't sound so horrified, she was fine.'

But she was horrified, because the only time she'd tried it, it had taken her all day to find the wretch. But that was her, and this was James, and Saffy worshipped him. Even to the point of wanting to eat his smelly old trainers.

'I'm going to shower. Try and make sure she doesn't eat anything else while I'm gone,' he said drily, and so just to be on the safe side she took Saffy back into the cabin with her and put her in the crate while she had a shower herself.

'So, jeans and a T, or my blue dress, Saffy?' She looked at the options, debated for a second and then grinned at Saffy. 'Blue dress. Excellent choice. It's going to be a hotty.'

She pulled on the sundress, found some flip-flops and slid her feet into them, and went out to find James with his head in the store under the veranda. The kennel?

Oops, she thought. Poor old Saffy really was in trouble!

'Is this a work party? Because if so I probably ought to change, only I thought we were going up to Molly and David's this morning.'

He pulled his head back out of the doorway and thumped it on the head of the frame. 'Ouch. No, it's not a work party,' he said, and then looked at her stupidly for a moment.

She looked—well, she'd been beautiful last night, elegant and sophisticated and downright stunning. Now, she just looked plain lovely, the dress that barely brushed the top of her knees leaving those gorgeous legs exposed to taunt him again, and he wanted to walk over to her, scoop her up in his arms and carry her up to bed.

Which was *so* not going to happen!

'I thought I'd investigate the possibilities before she eats anything else of mine,' he said, trying not to sniff the air to see if she'd used that same shampoo. She didn't have the perfume on, he was sure of that, because even in the garden he would have been able to smell it.

'And?'

And? And what? 'Um—yes, it'll work,' he said hastily, retuning. 'We'll do it later. So, are you ready to go?'

CHAPTER EIGHT

THE PICTURES WERE every bit as good in the cold, sober light of day as they had been last night with the clever lighting, but there was nothing there that just said, Buy me.

'There are some others,' David said. 'We ran out of wall space. Come and have a look.'

He took him through into Molly's studio, and immediately he was captivated by a canvas propped up on the easel.

'Oh, wow.'

It was a view across the harbour mouth, painted from the vantage point of the sea wall, he thought, looking out. The sea was a flat, oily calm, the skies threatening, and it was called 'Eye of the Storm'.

He loved it. Loved everything about it. The menace. The barely leashed power. The colours in the lowering sky.

'She got drenched doing the sketches for that,' David said with a chuckle.

'It was worth it.'

'What was worth what?'

He turned and smiled at Connie. 'Getting drenched.'

'Wow. I can see why. That sky looks pretty full.'

'It was a lot emptier a few minutes later,' Molly said

drily. 'I had to retreat to the bedroom to carry on. I painted it standing at the window in the attic bedroom at your house, James, and I never finished it because I couldn't seem to get the sea right. I got it out again the other day and it sort of fell into place. Do you want another coffee?'

'No, thanks. I think I want to buy this picture. Kind of poetic, taking it home. I might even hang it in the bedroom, since my sitting room is still a work in progress. I know it's not in the exhibition, but is it for sale?'

He found the hammer and some picture hooks, buried in the back of the tool shed under the veranda, and he took Connie inside to help him hang it.

'So, where?'

'Sitting room?'

He looked around, but there wasn't anywhere obviously right for it. The books were still in boxes and he wasn't sure if the furniture worked where it was, and just then sorting it out and unpacking the books and getting to grips with it seemed too big a task.

'No. Bedroom. Come and help me place it.'

So not a good idea, he thought the moment they were in there. The walls seem to close in, the air was sucked out of the room and the bed grew until it filled all the available space.

'So—' He cleared his throat and looked around a trifle desperately. 'Whereabouts would you put it?'

'I don't know. You want to be able to see it from the bed, don't you?'

'Probably.'

And before he could breathe she was there, sitting cross-legged at the top of the bed, bossing him about.

'Try there.'

Try what where? The only thing he wanted to do was crawl onto the bed beside her and kiss her. Drag her into his arms and slide that blue dress off over her head and kiss her from top to toe—

Focus!

'Here?'

'No. Angle's wrong. Try that side—that's better. Down a bit. Perfect.'

And she scrambled off the bed and took the picture from him. 'You look at it. Go and lie on the bed and look at it.'

Really? Right there, where she'd just been? Where he'd been fantasising about kissing her?

'Is it really necessary—? OK, OK,' he grumbled, defeated by that challenging stare, and he threw himself down on the bed, propped himself up on the pillows and was immediately swamped by the scent of her. Had she *bathed* in the perfume? Sprayed it on her legs? Sheesh!

'Well? My arms are aching.'

'Um—yeah, that's really good.' He swung his legs off the side, found a pencil and went over to mark the top of the picture so he could put a hook in the wall, but she was just there, so close, and the urge to lean into her, to take the picture from her and put it down and kiss her nearly—so nearly—overwhelmed him.

He reached past her and marked the wall before he lost it completely. 'OK,' he said, and she stepped back so he could put the hook in, then she settled the picture on it.

'Great,' she said. 'One down, however many more to go.'

'What?'

Connie turned to look back at him; she was already heading down the stairs to get away from the image of him lying sprawled on his bed where she'd imagined him so many times. She simply hadn't done him justice.

'The rest of the house,' she explained. 'The sitting room needs at least three pictures—unless you have one huge one.'

'I can't afford a huge one. This one was bad enough.'

'I'm sure she'd do a bulk discount. There was that fabulous one of the marshes. It would go really well in there.'

She left him standing there staring at her, and ran down the stairs and out onto the veranda. She needed fresh air. The window had been open in his room but—well, clearly on a hot day the heat rose to the top of the house. There couldn't be any other explanation, or not one she wanted to consider.

Not James! she told herself. *You can't fall for James! You'll just break your heart. You can't just have a trivial affair with him, and you know he doesn't want more than that! Hell, he doesn't even want that, and especially not with you. If he did, he wouldn't have stopped after that kiss. So, keep out of his bedroom, keep out of his way, just—keep out of his life! It's not safe, not at all. He's not in the market for anything permanent, and if you mess this up he won't even be your friend. Don't do it!*

'Coffee?'

'Mmm. Flat white, if you've got the milk, please. And good and strong.'

'Coming up.'

She spent the next few minutes lecturing herself along the same lines, until James appeared on the veranda again with her coffee. Interesting, she thought as he put it down in front of her a few moments later. The rosetta was a mess.

'Losing your touch?' she teased, trying to introduce a light note, but he avoided her eyes.

'I knocked my hand on the kettle,' he said, but he sounded evasive and she just—wondered...

He was a man, after all, and she knew she wasn't exactly ugly, and she'd been sitting on his bed. And he'd already admitted that he didn't have a woman in his life and hadn't for ages. And he'd kissed her.

Was it mutual, this insane and crazy attraction?

Surely not. It wasn't her. Probably any half-decent woman with a pulse would make him think twice if she was sitting on his bed. It hadn't even occurred to her, and it probably should have, but it wasn't happening again. No, no, no, no, no!

She drank her coffee without a murmur and got out of his hair the moment it was done.

'Wow. What are you doing?'

'Making the kennel—what does it look like?'

Like he'd emptied the shed out all over the garden, was what, but she had the sense not to say so. 'Want a hand?'

He hesitated, then nodded. 'It might be useful. Steadying things, you know.'

'I'll put Saffy in her crate out here so she can watch us. I don't think she needs to get involved with this lot.'

'Probably not. Do you want a cold drink before we start?'

'That would be good. I wouldn't mind a sandwich, either. Have you eaten?'

'No. I've got some ham and salad, and a few cartons of soup in the fridge. Want to make us something?'

'Sure.'

She changed into her scruffiest clothes, because there

was no way this was going to be anything other than a hot, dirty, sweaty job, and then threw together some lunch before they started.

'In your own time, Slater,' she said, carrying it all out to the table in the garden next to Saffy, and he washed his hands and joined her.

'Looks good. It's a long time since we had breakfast.'

'Yeah. Bacon and tomato sandwich, ham salad sandwich with tomato soup—do you see a pattern emerging? Maybe I need to go shopping later this afternoon and stock up the fridge.'

'Only when this run's made. I'm not having anything else chewed up. I loved those trainers.'

'Oh, Saffy,' she said slowly. 'Are we in trouble?'

'Too right.' He swiped the tail end of his sandwich around his empty soup bowl and sat back with a sigh. 'That was good. Thanks.'

'Tea?'

'If you insist.'

'I do. You need liquids.'

'Says she, the queen of dehydration.'

'I was not dehydrated.'

He snorted softly and got up. 'Call me when it's made. I want to see if I've got enough wood to make a doorframe.'

It took them ages. Far longer than he'd anticipated, and he'd had to go shopping twice for materials, but finally Saffy had a kennel with a run, and his possessions were safe.

The only downside was that he'd had to spend the afternoon with Connie, and every second of it had been exquisite torture. She might have changed, but she was still wearing that perfume, and working in the confined space of the kennel had been enough to push him over the brink.

He'd kept bumping into her, her firm-yet-soft body close enough to him that he could feel the warmth coming off it, and then every now and then he'd shift or she'd reach up and they'd bump. Just gently. Just enough to keep his hormones simmering on the brink of meltdown.

He banged in the last nail and threw the hammer down. 'Right, that's it, I'm calling it a day. If that's not good enough, I give up.'

'What are you talking about? It's fantastic. Brilliant. Saffy, come on, come and have a look at what James has made you.'

She was wary, but with a little coaxing she went inside and had a sniff around. 'She might feel happier if her crate was in there, with the door open,' Connie suggested, so he wrestled it through the narrow doorway and set it down at the back, and Saffy went straight in it and lay down, wagging her tail.

'Excellent. Job done,' Connie said, and gave him a high five. She was laughing, her whole face lit up, and he felt a huge ache in the centre of his chest.

'Great. Let's clear up the tools and have a drink.'

'How about something fizzy?'

'Didn't you have enough of that last night?' he asked mildly, and she gave him a level look.

'I meant fizzy water, or cola or something. Not champagne.'

'Ah. Well, I have spring water.'

'Perfect.' She emerged from the kennel, he put the last of the tools away and then she remembered the parlous state of the fridge. 'Damn.'

'What?'

'I forgot to go shopping.'

He shrugged. 'We can go to the pub. It'll be a good test for Saffy. We'll leave her in here, sit outside at the pub and listen. If she barks or howls continuously, I'm sure we'll hear her.'

'I'm not sure I want to know,' Connie said drily, feeling a twinge of apprehension.

'Oh, man up. She'll be fine. She'd better be, after all we've done for her.'

Connie just raised a brow. 'Man up?' she said, trying not to laugh. 'Really?'

'Technical term.'

'I have met it.'

He grinned and threw her one of Saffy's toys. 'Here. I'll get her water bowl.'

She was fine.

They had a peaceful, undisturbed meal at the pub.

Undisturbed, that was, by Saffy. Connie, though, was ridiculously aware of James the entire time. His soft, husky laugh, the crinkles round his eyes, the bones of his wrist—there didn't seem to be a thing about him that didn't interest or absorb her.

And that was deeply distracting.

It was such a shame, she thought as she went to bed that night after shutting Saffy outside in her new quarters, that if she eventually had a child it wouldn't be his.

But the sudden ache of longing at the thought, low down in her abdomen, nearly took her breath away. She pressed one hand to her mouth, the other to the hollow, empty ache inside, and blinked away the tears that inexplicably stung her eyes.

No! She couldn't fall in love with him! Not really, truly in love with him, and that's what it was suddenly

CAROLINE ANDERSON 149

beginning to feel like. She couldn't let herself, she had far too much to lose. He would never be in it for the long haul, and she'd lose her heart, lose a friend she treasured, and lose her only chance to have a child. Because if she fell in love with him, truly, deeply in love with him, how could she ever consider having any other man's child inside her body, when all she longed for was his?

Far, far too late for common sense to intervene, she realised just what an incredibly stupid mistake this all was. She ought to cut her loses and go. But she couldn't leave, she thought desperately. Not while there was still hope. Maybe if she stayed, if they got to know each other better, explored this attraction, then at some point in the future maybe—

She was clutching at straws, dreaming up a happy-ever-after that could never be! She was deluding herself, and she really, really should know better.

She turned over, thumped the pillow into shape and made herself relax. She ached all over, not just in that hollow place inside that craved his child, and tomorrow was going to be hard enough without a sleepless night, so she slowed her breathing, tensed and relaxed all her muscles in turn, and finally fell asleep, only to dream of James.

He ended up on the sea wall again at stupid o'clock in the morning.

He'd crept out the front so he didn't disturb Saffy, and he was sitting there staring blindly out over the water and wondering what had happened to the amazing, relaxing properties of the waves because frankly they didn't seem to be working any longer.

Mostly because when he'd gone to bed, he could still

smell the lingering essence of Connie's perfume on the pillows, and his mind was in chaos.

He couldn't believe how much he wanted her. He told himself it was lust. He told himself it was just physical, she was a beautiful woman, it had been so long that frankly any half-decent-looking woman would have the same effect.

He knew he was lying.

It was Connie. He'd felt it for years, off and on, but because Joe had been there he'd managed to keep it down, keep it under control. Not now. Now, it was driving him crazy, and tomorrow he was going to go into work and change the rota so they didn't have to work together so much.

Or, more to the point, be at home together so much.

But first, he was going to see David and Molly about that picture of the marshes for the blank wall in his sitting room. At least clearing the room up ready for it would give him something to do for the day, even if he couldn't have the picture till the exhibition closed.

He got stiffly to his feet, stretched his arms out and groaned softly. He ached all over from the unaccustomed physical exertion of building Saffy's run.

He wondered if Connie ached, and immediately an image of him massaging her long, sleek limbs filled his mind, running his oiled hands up her back and round over those slender but surprisingly strong shoulders and then down, round her ribs, under her breasts—

He swore, quietly and viciously, stabbed a hand through his hair and headed back to the house. Sleep wasn't an option, he realised, so he went into the sitting room, unearthed the boxes of books and unpacked them, putting them on the empty shelves that had mocked him for the last two and a bit years.

Better, he thought, and it had only taken him a little over an hour. They weren't sorted, but they looked a lot better than they had, and he could always move them. And it was pointless spending a small fortune on a picture to hang it up in a room that was so obviously unloved.

He debated cleaning the room properly, but tomorrow would do. He'd dusted the shelves, put the books on. That would do for tonight. And anyway, he needed something to do tomorrow to keep him out of Connie's way.

Connie. Always it came back to Connie.

He gave in to the urge and went back up to his bedroom, lay down in the cloud-soft bedding and went to sleep, wrapped around in Connie's perfume. It was almost like lying in her arms...

'Wow, that looks amazing!'

She stood in the opening between the kitchen and the living space and stared in astonishment at the transformation. There were books on the shelves, he'd rearranged the sofas and it actually looked lived-in rather than as if the removal men had just walked out the door. 'What time did you get up?'

'Two,' he said, trying to ignore the pyjamas. 'I've been back to sleep since for a while.'

'I'm glad to hear it. Want a cup of tea?'

'Yeah, why not? Have I got time for a shower?'

'Sure. You won't be long, will you? I'll make it now.'

He'd like to be long. He'd like to be long enough that she went and got dressed into something he was less excruciatingly conscious of, but that clearly wasn't going to happen. He paused in the doorway. 'How was Saffy last night, by the way?'

'Fine. I've let her out, she's sniffing round the garden at the moment. Thank you so much, James. I actually had room to stretch my legs out.'

He laughed. 'Happy to oblige,' he said, and hit the stairs. 'Don't make it too strong, I've already had a lot.'

He had. There were three teabags lying on the side, and she picked them up and put them in the bin. He always did that. So idle. No. Not idle, she corrected herself, remembering how hard he'd worked yesterday. He just had odd little habits. She made the tea, wiped the worktop down and went into the sitting room to study it.

Saffy followed her, looked at the sofas and then at her, and lay down on the floor.

'Wise move,' she said, and Saffy's tail banged the floor.

'What's a wise move?'

'Saffy. She eyed the sofas.'

'Did you?' The tail thumped again.

'So where are you putting the picture?' she asked him.

'I don't know. I'm not sure yet. I can't have it till after the exhibition, so I thought I'd work out where I want everything else. The first thing I'm going to do is give the place a thorough clean, now I've got it more or less straight.'

'I'll give you a hand.'

He almost groaned with frustration. 'You don't need to—'

'Oh, come on, you spent all day yesterday making the run for Saffy. It's the least I can do. Here, drink your tea while I get dressed, and we'll get started.'

So much for his escape plan.

* * *

He went to the hospital in the afternoon, and savaged the rota.

He had to leave most of the coming week alone, but the following week onwards he chopped to shreds. He spoke to the other key people who would be affected, shifted whatever he could and managed to minimise their contact really quite successfully.

And if it all got too much at home, there was always a massive stack of admin with his name on it. He could always come back in. If necessary he could invent a few meetings.

He gave his desk a jaundiced look. Locked in the drawers for confidentiality were a stack of files.

So—Connie, or admin?

Admin won, which was testament to his desperation, and it only kept him going till six that evening, at which point he gave up. Six on a Sunday, when he wasn't even supposed to be working, was more than late enough.

He locked the files away, headed home and walked in to the smell of roasting chicken.

'Hey, smells good.'

'Saffy thinks so.'

She unravelled herself from the sofa and wandered through to the kitchen looking sun-kissed and delectable, and he had to forcibly stop himself from kissing her. 'So how's your day been?'

'Tedious. I had to rework the rota and do some admin. I've moved us around—we're really short of suitably qualified people in the next few weeks, so I've split us up a bit so one or other of us is there. I know it's not ideal, but I'll only be here or doing admin in the department, and it'll be better for Saffy.'

She nodded. 'OK. And if the offer's still open, I

might go and collect all the stuff that's in store and sort it out. You've only got me down part-time on the rota, haven't you?'

'Yes.'

'So when you aren't here and I am, I can go through it all. And I can have the kettle and toaster in the cabin, so that if it's raining I can make tea without coming over here.'

Except in practice she'd been over here all the time, and it had never been an issue—well, not for her. Still, it was an excuse to get the things and start to go through them, and maybe it was because of James dealing with his boxes, but she suddenly just wanted to clear up all the loose ends and get it sorted out.

'Are you sure?' he asked, watching her closely. 'I just remember going through Cathy's stuff. It can be a bit gut-wrenching.'

'I'm sure it can, but it has to be done, and I'm ready now.'

'Well, go for it. You can always stop and put it all away if it gets too much. And I won't charge you storage.'

He smiled, a wry quirk of his lips that said so much, and she felt warmed inside. He was such a good friend. She had to protect that friendship at all costs.

'Thank you,' she said humbly. 'So—roast, mashed, boiled or jacket?'

'Excuse me?'

'Potatoes. With the chicken.'

'Um—roast. Always.'

She smiled. 'Thought you'd say that. I'll put them in.'

It worked well.

He did a little more shuffling that week, and it ended

up panning out nicely, so that Saffy wasn't shut away for too many hours in her run, both of them had some personal time alone and there was enough company to make the place feel homely.

Actually, he realised, it was great. She'd got the stuff out of storage and started working through it, and everything was going fine. And since he'd washed his sheets, the hormones weren't such an issue, either. She didn't wear perfume at work or if they weren't going out anywhere, and life settled down into a regular and almost cosy routine.

And then he had a job application in from someone who sounded perfect. A woman with two children whose husband had taken himself off to another country with his second wife and left her literally holding the babies.

He phoned her, and she came in that afternoon to look round and impressed his socks off.

She wanted part time, her mother was in Yoxburgh, and she was going nowhere. She was young, younger than Connie, and it would be her first consultancy, but her CV and references were stunning. And she could start whenever he pressed the button. He just had to put it to the hospital board, get her a formal interview and it would all be set in motion.

It was like a dream come true—but it meant that he didn't really need Connie beyond the end of Andy Gallagher's paternity leave, and a bit of him felt gutted because he loved working with her.

But she wasn't there forever, he knew that. She wanted to go off and have her baby and start her new life somewhere else, and there was nothing here to keep her now.

Nothing except him, and he knew that didn't count.

He went home and found her sitting in a welter of Joe's possessions with Saffy snoozing on the floor at her side.

'How are you doing?' he asked, sitting down cross-legged on the floor opposite her and scratching behind Saffy's ears.

'OK. There's a lot of rubbish—paperwork that's meaningless now, irrelevant stuff about our army accommodation and so forth. I'll never need it, but it's got personal information on it.'

'Want to borrow my shredder?'

'Oh, please.'

He went and got it, and they spent an hour shredding documents. Then finally he called a halt.

'Stop now. I need to talk to you.'

She stopped, her heart hitching for some reason. He sounded so—serious? 'About?'

'I've had a suitable applicant for the job.'

'Wow.' She stood up on legs that trembled slightly, picked up the bag of shreddings and followed him downstairs, Saffy trailing after them. 'What's he like?'

'She. Very good. Divorced, two kids—twins. Dad walked. I interviewed her today.'

'And?'

'She's nice. Really nice. Open, friendly, efficient—little bit nervous, but that's to be expected. I need to get it rubber stamped, but we've been looking for someone for three months now without success, so I'm sure it won't be an issue.'

She nodded, trying to be practical, trying not to cry for some crazy reason. 'Good. Well, for you. For Andy, too. Takes away the guilt.'

'And you?'

She shrugged. 'I knew it was short term. I guess it's

just going to be shorter than I'd expected. I had hoped I'd have a bit longer to find a permanent job and somewhere to live, but I'm sure I'll find something. When can she start?'

'Now. She's free, so as soon as the formal interview's taken place and she's officially accepted, she can start.'

She stared at him across the kitchen, feeling the bottom drop out of her stomach. 'Oh. Right. So I haven't got time.'

'Well, you don't have to leave here, you know that, but the job will go. I'm really sorry. I honestly thought it would take months and I'm really grateful to you for what you've done.'

She shrugged, her shoulders lifting a little helplessly, and he felt a complete heel, but what could he do? It was only the truth. The job was taken, he didn't need her.

Not in that way, and he wasn't even going to think about the other.

'Don't worry about it. I'll be fine. I'll find a job, I always do. And I'll get out of your hair, just as soon as it's all rubber stamped and she's ready to go.'

'If you find something else you want to go to, if there's a job that comes up with your name on it, I don't expect you to give me any notice, Connie. You can leave whenever you like,' he said, and she felt her heart break a little more.

'Oh. Right. Well, I'll start packing.'

'But you haven't got anywhere to go to! I'm just saying, do it in your own time, don't worry about fitting in with me.'

'But you're right, there's nothing here, I might as well get myself out into the job market.'

'Connie, there's no rush. Sleep on it, give yourself time to work out what to do next.'

What's to sleep on? You want me out! Out of your home, out of your department, out of your life!

'Good idea. I'm tired. We'll talk tomorrow. Saffy, come on, James is going to bed.'

And she all but dragged the reluctant dog out of the door and down the steps and into her cabin. She got the door shut—just—before the little sob broke free, but it had a friend, and then a whole posse of them, and she shut herself in the shower room, turned all the taps on and sobbed her heart out.

Then she blew her nose, washed her face and put her pyjamas on.

She didn't need James. She could do this. She could still have a baby, still have her dream without the complication of knowing the father.

Simpler all round—except her dream had changed, and she'd realised that she didn't just want a baby, any baby. She wanted James's baby. And she wanted James.

God, what a mess.

She put Saffy out for a moment, and when she ran back in, she jumped straight up onto the bed, circled round and lay down in a perfect pattern of earthy footprints on the immaculate white bedding.

Tough.

Connie got into bed, shunted Saffy over a little and curled on her side, the dog behind her knees, and wondered what on earth she was going to do and where she was going to go.

She had no idea. She was out of options. The tenant in her house was there for the next six months, at least, and there was nobody else she could ask. Not with Saffy.

She'd have to get onto it first thing in the morning, try and find somewhere to go, somewhere to rent.

And a job?

God, it was all so complicated. It had been complicated since the day she'd agreed to have Saffy, and it just got worse. She needed a job, she needed a home and she didn't need James telling her she didn't need to work any kind of nominal notice period because he wanted her out of the house.

He hadn't said that, to be fair, but it felt like that.

And then she had a brilliant idea.

She'd apply for the job. Formally, properly. She'd find herself somewhere to live nearby, somewhere she could keep Saffy, and she'd go down the anonymous donor route, and then James would be close enough to help out if necessary, and she wouldn't lose his friendship, and it would be fine.

She just had to get him to agree.

There was no sign of her in the morning, and Saffy's run was hanging open.

Unlike Connie's curtains, which were unusually firmly shut.

He stood on the veranda and hated himself. It wasn't his fault that this woman had turned up when she had. It was nobody's fault. But it was his fault that they'd reached this point, that he hadn't given Connie a flat-out no right at the beginning so that she'd moved on with her life already.

And now she'd retreated into a cocoon, and he felt like the worst person in the world.

He made tea and took it over to the cabin.

'Connie?'

No reply, just a scuffle and the sound of Saffy's toe-nails clattering on the wooden floor as she came to the door.

'Connie? I've made you tea.'

He knocked and opened the door, to find her sitting up in bed, huddled in the quilt and watching him warily. She had her phone in her hands. Looking for a job?

'Are you OK?'

'Of course I'm OK. Put the tea down, I'll get it in a minute.'

Go away, in other words.

'Has Saffy been out?'

'Yes. I'm afraid she trashed the quilt cover.'

He glanced down and saw a crazy pattern of muddy pawprints all over it. 'It'll wash,' he said, although he doubted it, but the quilt cover was the least of his worries. Connie looked awful.

Tired, strained, her eyes red-rimmed, her back ramrod straight.

He put the tea down and left her to it, plagued by guilt and unable to change anything for the better.

He'd gone.

She'd hoped to catch him before he left for work, but he'd been too quick off the mark. Damn. She hadn't wanted him going to the hospital board before she had a chance to talk to him about it, so she took Saffy for a quick run, showered and dressed in work clothes and drove to the hospital.

'Anyone seen James?' she asked.

'He's not in the ED but he's around somewhere—want me to page him?'

'Please. Tell him I'm in the ED.' And hopefully it wasn't already too late.

The phone didn't ring. Had he not taken his pager? No, that wasn't like him. Just ignored it? Maybe he was in a meeting—with the chief exec?

He walked in, just as she was ready to give up.

'Connie. Hi. I gather you're looking for me.'

'Have you got a minute?'

'Sure. I'll just make sure Kazia's all right. We've got a patient with a head injury waiting for a scan but he's stable.'

He stuck his head into Resus. 'You all OK for a few more minutes?'

'Sure. No change.'

'Thanks, Kaz. Page me if you need me.'

He turned to Connie. 'My office, or do you want to get a coffee and sit outside?'

'Your office,' she said. She wanted this to be formal, in a way. A little bit official. And an office seemed the place to do that.

'OK.'

He led her in, shut the door and offered her a chair, then sat down opposite her. 'So. Talk to me.'

'I want the job.'

He felt his jaw sag slightly.

'Job?'

'Yes. The part-time consultant post in the department. I want to make an official application, and I want you to interview me.'

He sat back in his chair, fiddling with a pen to give him time, straightening the notepad, lining up the small ring-stained mat he used to protect the top of the desk.

'No,' he said in the end, because it was the only word that came to mind that wasn't unprintable.

'No?' She sat forward, her face shocked. 'Why no? I'm good, James. Whatever this other woman's got, I've got more, and I've thought it through. This is a sensible decision. I want a child, I have a dog already, I can't work full-time. You said you'd support me in my decision about the baby, and if I'm here in Yoxburgh, that makes it easy for all of us. I understand you don't want the fatherhood thing, that's fine, but I've thought it all through. I'll sell the house and buy one here, and I'll have a stable base, friends in the area—this is just the perfect answer.'

'No, Connie. I can't do it. I can't offer you the job because I've already offered it to the other woman. I offered it to her yesterday and I can't retract it. And anyway, I've spoken to the board and they've agreed. They're interviewing her now, as we speak. I'm really, really sorry.'

So was she. If only she'd thought this through sooner, mentioned it earlier—but she'd thought she'd had time, and she hadn't. Her time had run out, and it was over.

Just as well, perhaps. She'd get away, leave him behind her, start again. Good idea. Maybe one day it would feel like it.

She got to her feet, her legs like rubber, her eyes stinging.

'It's OK. It's not your fault. I understand. I hope it works out well. Goodbye, James.'

And she walked out of his office, through the department—why hadn't she agreed to coffee outside in the park?—and out of the doors.

Her frustration and anger at herself for not doing this in time sustained her all the way back to his house, and then she opened the gate to be greeted by Saffy wagging her tail, waiting to be let out of her run.

The run James had made for her out of the kindness of his heart.

Damn.

She let Saffy out, went into the cabin and started packing. There wasn't much, and it didn't take her long.

She took the kettle and the toaster, because she'd need them, and all her clothes and bits and pieces, and she stacked them as tightly as she could in the car.

Saffy's crate went in next, packed around with as much as possible, until she was left only with a box or two of things in the spare bedroom. She'd got rid of a lot of the stuff, and this was all that was left that was still unsorted.

Well, she wasn't doing it now. She was getting the hell out of here before James came home, because she really didn't think she'd be able to hold it together when she saw him again.

She'd been doing so well, and now she felt lost again. *Don't think about it!*

She scooped up the last two boxes, carried them downstairs and out to the car, and with a little repacking she even got them in. She could hardly see out of the car, but that was fine. She had wing mirrors. She'd manage.

Wherever she was going.

Where *was* she going? She had no idea, none at all, and it was already lunchtime.

Back towards Nottingham?

She had friends down in Cornwall, but that was too far and she couldn't expect them to help. But there was nobody in the world who'd tolerate Saffy in the way that James had.

Nobody else who'd build her a run and not mind when she stole the fillet steak or trashed the sheets with her muddy paws or ate his favourite trainers.

There was only one option open to her, and it broke her heart, but in many ways it was the right answer.

She'd leave Saffy with James.

CHAPTER NINE

HE HAD THE day from hell.

He couldn't leave, but Connie's face was etched on his mind and he was hardly able to concentrate.

What had he done? He could have told her about the other applicant, could have offered her the chance, but he'd wanted her out of his life because she was upsetting it, messing it all up, untidying it. He'd been trying to make life easier for himself, because the thought of having her working there with him indefinitely, driving him mad on a daily basis with her crazy pyjamas and her lace underwear, was unthinkable.

And now she was going, and he realised he didn't want her to. He didn't want her to go at all. And she'd said goodbye.

Hell. He had to go home to her.

He pulled his phone out of his pocket, called Andy and drummed his fingers until he answered.

'I need a favour. Is there any way you can cover for me? I need to go home urgently.'

'What, now? No, that's OK, I think. Lucy's here.' He heard him talking to Lucy, then he came back. 'That's fine. I'll come now. Give me ten minutes.'

'Thank you,' he said, but Andy had gone, without prevaricating or asking any awkward questions. Still, ten minutes was a long time and he just hoped to God nothing kicked off in the meantime which meant he couldn't leave.

He was there in five.

'I'll be as quick as I can,' he promised.

'Don't worry. Just go.'

'Thank you.'

He drove home on the back roads because there was less traffic, his heart in his mouth.

'Please be there, please be there, please be there—'

She was, her car on the drive, the door hanging open. He pulled up beside it and swore. It was packed to the roof with all her worldly possessions. Except Saffy. There was a crate-shaped hole in the back, but no crate, no dog, no sign of her.

She must be taking her for a last walk, he thought, but her keys were in the ignition, and his heart started to race.

Where was she?

The cabin was locked, the curtains open, the bed stripped. The house was unlocked, though, so he searched it from top to bottom, but there was nothing. No clue, no sign, no hint of what was going on. He even looked under the beds and had to stop himself from being ridiculous, but—where had she gone?

'Connie?'

He yelled her name, again and again as he raced through the house, but all that greeted him was silence. So he rang her, and her phone rang from the car. From her handbag, lying there in the gap between the two front seats, squashed in.

Had Saffy run off at the last minute? Unsure what to do, where else to look, he locked her car, pocketed the keys and went up onto the sea wall. Nothing. He could see for miles, and there was nothing, nobody.

Nobody with a sandy-coloured, leggy dog with dangling ears and a penchant for stealing, anyway.

He looked the other way, went up to his attic for a higher view of the river wall, but there was nothing there, either. All he could do was wait.

So he did. He made himself a cup of tea that he felt too sick to drink, took it out onto the veranda and waited.

And then he heard it.

A sob.

Faint but unmistakeable, from under him.

The kennel. Idiot! He hadn't searched the kennel!

He took the steps in one, crossed the run in a single stride and ducked his head through the entrance. 'Connie?'

'I couldn't leave her,' she said brokenly, and she started to sob again.

'Oh, Connie. Leave who? Why?'

'Saffy. James, where can I take her? How can I? I don't even have a home—'

Her voice cracked on the last word, and he squashed himself into the crowded kennel, dragged Connie into his arms and wrapped her firmly against his chest.

'Crazy girl. You don't have to go anywhere.'

'Yes, I do. I have to make a life. I have to start again, make something of my future, but I can't do it with this stupid great lump of a dog, so I was going to leave her here, because I thought, you promised Joe you'd take care of me, and he loved Saffy too, and I know you do, so I thought maybe you could look after her instead, but I can't leave her—'

The sobs overwhelmed her again, and he pressed his

lips to her hair and held on tight. His eyes were stinging, and he squeezed them shut, rocking her gently, shushing her, and all the time Saffy was licking his arm frantically and trying to get closer.

He freed a hand and stroked her. 'It's OK, Saffy, it's all right,' he said, his voice cracking, and Connie snuggled closer, her arms creeping round him and hanging on.

'Oh, Connie, I'm sorry,' he said raggedly. 'So, so sorry. I don't want you to go, and if I'd only known you wanted the job I could have done something, but I'm not letting you go anywhere like this. Come on, come out of here and blow your nose and have a cup of tea and we'll talk, because this is crazy.'

'I can't just stay here,' she said, still hanging on to him and not going anywhere. 'You don't need me, you don't want me...'

Oh, hell.

'Actually, that's not true,' he admitted quietly. 'I do.'

'You do?' She lifted her head, dragging an arm out from behind him to swipe a hand over her face. 'I don't understand.'

'Neither do I, but I know I can't let you go. I can't do what you came here to ask me. I've dug deep on this one, and one of the reasons I just can't give you a baby and then step back is because my feelings for you are very far from clear.'

She went utterly still. 'I don't understand.'

His smile felt twisted, so he gave up on it. 'Nor do I. I don't know how I feel about you, Connie. I know I want you. You have to know that, up front, but you're a beautiful woman and it's not exactly a hardship. But whether that has the capacity to turn into anything else, I don't know. We've both got so much emotional baggage and Joe may be an obstacle that neither of us can get over, but I just know I can't lose you forever without giving it a try, seeing where it takes us.'

She said nothing. She didn't move, didn't speak, just clung on to him, her eyes fixed on his face, but her breathing steadied and gradually some of the tension went out of her.

'Connie?'

She tilted her head up further, and in the dim light he could see the tear tracks smudged across her face.

'Can we start by getting out of here?' she said. 'It's all a little bit cosy and I'm not sure about the spiders.'

He gave a hollow chuckle and unravelled himself, standing up as far as he could and ducking through the doorway, and she followed him out, Saffy squashing herself between them, her eyes anxious.

Poor dog. She felt racked with guilt.

She put her hand down to Saffy and found his there already. He turned it, and their fingers met and clung.

'Did you say something about tea?' she said lightly, and he tried to smile but it was a pretty shaky effort. She didn't suppose hers was a whole lot better.

'If you like.'

'I like.'

'I'll make it. You go and wash your face. I'll see you in a minute.'

She looked awful. Her eyes were so red and puffy they were nearly shut, and her cheeks were streaked with tears and dirt from being in the kennel, and her clothes were filthy.

What on earth did he see in her? He must be mad. Or desperate.

No. He was single by choice. A man with as much

going for him as James wouldn't lack opportunity. And he wanted to explore their relationship?

She closed her eyes and sucked in a shaky breath. This was about so much more than just giving her a baby. This was everything—marriage, a family, growing old together—all the things she might have had with Joe, but had lost. The things he might have had with Cathy and their baby.

He was right, they had a hell of a lot of emotional baggage, but if they could make it work—

She let herself out of the cloakroom and went back to the kitchen.

'Out here,' he called, and she went and sat next to him, exactly over the spot where he'd held her while she'd cried, and Saffy leaned against their legs and trapped them there.

'Do you think she's telling us we can't go anywhere until this is sorted?' she asked, a little hitch in her voice, and James gave a quiet laugh.

'Maybe. Seems like a sensible idea.'

'Mmm.' She sniffed, still clogged with tears. 'So—what now?'

'Now? Now I suggest we unpack your car, settle Saffy back in and then I go back to work. I called Andy in, but I can't really leave him there for hours. Just—promise me you'll be here when I get back.'

'I'll be here. Where else can I go?'

'If you really want to, I'm sure there's somewhere. And for the record, I would have had Saffy for you. Not because of Joe, or you. Just for herself.'

Her eyes filled again and she blinked hard and cleared her throat. 'Will you please stop making me cry?' she said, and he hugged her, his arm slipping naturally around her shoulders and easing her up against his side.

'Oh, Connie, what are we going to do?'

'I don't know. I'm totally confused now. I thought you didn't want a relationship, I thought you were happy on your own.'

'Not happy,' he corrected softly. 'Just—accepting. I couldn't imagine falling in love like that again, and maybe I never will, but maybe it doesn't have to be like that. Maybe we're both so damaged that we can't ever love like that again, but it doesn't mean we can't be happy with someone else, someone who doesn't expect that level of emotion, someone who can accept our scars and limitations. Maybe it would only work with someone equally as hurt, someone who could understand.'

Which would make them ideal for each other.

Would it work? Could it work?

She took a deep breath. 'I guess there's only one way to find out.'

'Shall we unpack your car?'

'I'll do it,' she said. 'You go back to work. I won't go anywhere, I promise.'

He went—reluctantly—and she sat a little while longer, trying to make some kind of sense of the developments of the day.

She didn't even know how she felt about a relationship with him. It had seemed so unlikely she hadn't ever really let herself consider it, but—a couple? Not just an affair, but a real relationship?

She tried to get her head around it, and failed. Unrequited lust she could understand, but happy ever after? Could he do it? What would he be like as a partner? People who'd been single a very long time found it hard to be part of a couple, to give and take and compromise.

Could she? Joe had been away so much she'd been pretty self-sufficient. Could she cope with someone having a say in her life?

'I don't know,' she said out loud. Saffy lifted her head and stared up at her, and she rubbed her chest gently. 'It's OK, Saff. We'll be all right. We'll find a way.'

She wasn't sure how, if this thing with James didn't work, but it seemed they were still friends, at the very least, and she wanted to make sure that continued. It had to. Friends, she'd learned over the years, were infinitely precious. She only had a few, and James, it seemed, was one of them. The best.

She eyed her car. She ought to unpack it, really, but she'd stripped her bed and put the sheets in the washing machine; they were done, so perhaps she should hang them on the line before she started?

'Oh, Saffy, we're OK, the pawprints came out. That's a good job, isn't it?' Saffy wagged her tail, tongue lolling, and Connie shut her back in the run and emptied the car.

There was no point putting the stuff that had been in storage back in James's spare bedroom. There was so little left—had only ever been so little of any consequence, really—that she put it into the cabin with everything else.

And all the time there was a little niggle of—what? Anticipation? Apprehension? Excitement?—fizzing away inside her. Should she cook for him? If there even was anything in the fridge. She wasn't sure. She'd look later, she decided, after she'd sorted herself out, but by the time she'd unpacked her things, hung up her clothes, found her washbag and had a shower, he was home.

And the butterflies in her stomach felt like the images she'd seen of bats leaving a cave in their thousands.

* * *

She'd put her stuff in the cabin.

All of it, by the looks of things, because the car was empty and there was no trace of her possessions in the house. He went up to his bedroom to check, and it was untouched since he'd changed his clothes before he'd gone back to work.

He stood there, staring at it, and tried to analyse his feelings. Mixed, he decided. A mixture of disappointment—physical, that one, mostly—and relief.

His common sense, overruling the physical disappointment, pointed out that it was just as well. Too early in their relationship to fall straight into bed, too easy, too fast, too simple. Because it wasn't that simple, sleeping with Connie. Not after Joe.

Inevitably there would be comparisons. He knew that. He wasn't unrealistic. And he wasn't sure he wanted to be compared to his best friend. He didn't want to be better in bed, but he sure as hell didn't want to be worse.

He swore softly, sat down on the edge of the bed and stared at the picture of the estuary that Molly had painted here in this room.

The Eye of the Storm.

Was that what this was? The eye of the storm? The lull before all hell broke loose again in his life?

'James?'

He heard her footsteps on the landing, and went to his bedroom door. She was wearing jeans and a pretty top, and from where he was standing he had a perfect view of her cleavage. 'Hi. I'm just going to change, and then I thought we could go out for dinner if you like.'

'That would be lovely,' she said with a wry smile.

'I've just looked in the fridge and it's none too promising.'

He chuckled. 'Give me ten minutes. I'll have a quick shower and I'll be with you.'

A cold one. He retreated, the updraught through the stairwell wafting the scent of her perfume after him, so that it followed him back into the room. He swallowed hard. Damn his common sense. Just then, the other side of the coin looked a lot more appealing.

Dinner?

As in, supper at the pub, or dinner? Formal, dressy, elegant? Because jeans and a floaty little cotton top wouldn't do, in that case.

But he came down the stairs bang on time in jeans and a crisp white cotton shirt open at the neck with the cuffs turned back, and she relaxed. She didn't feel ready for a formal dinner. Not yet. Too—what? Romantic? Laden with sexual expectation?

'So—Chinese, Indian, Thai, Tex-Mex, English gastro pub or fish and chips out of the paper? You choose.'

She laughed, feeling another layer of tension peel away. 'Gastro pub?' she suggested. 'It's a lovely evening. It would be nice to eat outside, if we can. And if you want to drink, I don't mind driving, or we could go to the Harbour Inn and sit outside so we can walk.'

'We've done that, and I don't need more than one glass. I'll drive. There's a lovely pub just a few miles up the river. We'll go there. Have you fed Saffy?'

'Yes. She's ready to go in her run.'

He rubbed the dog's head. 'How is she? Has she settled down?'

'I think so. She was a bit clingy until I'd unpacked everything and put it all away in the cabin but then she was fine. Oh, by the way, I put the rest of the stuff from storage in the cabin, too, so your spare bedroom's yours again. There wasn't much, and it'll make it easier to sort out. I can pick at it, then.'

'Good idea,' he said, stifling the regret. 'Right, shall we?'

It was a lovely pub, as he'd said.

The setting was wonderful, down on the edge of the river bank and miles from anywhere, or so it seemed. The river was wide at that point, and there were lots of boats moored on the water.

'It's buzzing, isn't it?' she said, slightly surprised, and he smiled.

'Wait till you taste the food. It'll all make sense then,' he said.

'It makes sense now,' she pointed out. 'Look at it. It's gorgeous here.'

They sat outside at a picnic table, side by side, and watched the boats come and go, sipping their drinks and reading the menu and just chilling out. It had been a gruelling day for both of them, and the quiet moment by the river was just what they needed, she thought.

She scanned the menu again, her mind slightly numb with all that had happened, her concentration shot. 'I can't decide.'

'We can come again. It's not life or death, it's just food and it's all good.'

'But I'll just get food envy,' she said, and he thought instantly of the time he'd watched her eat that hog roast roll, the apple sauce squeezing out and dribbling down her chin.

'We could always share.'

'Dangerous.' Hell, had he really said that? He hoped

she hadn't heard—or caught the tiny eye roll he'd done at his impulsive comment.

Both.

She scrunched her lips up and gave him a wry grin. 'You're right. You might come off worst.'

'Never. I fight for my food.'

She smiled and put her menu down. 'Me, too. I'll go for the sea bream fillet on samphire.'

He put his menu down. 'I'll have the same. That way you won't be tempted.'

She pouted, and he chuckled softly, hailed the waitress and placed their order.

'Wine?'

'Oh—I'll have a small glass of whatever.'

'Two of the sauvignon blanc, then,' he said, handing back the menus, and he cradled his mineral water, propped his elbows on the table and leant against her.

She leant back, resting her head against his, and sighed.

'You OK?' he asked quietly. He felt her nod.

'Yup. You?'

'I'm OK.'

'Good.'

They sat there until their food arrived, in contact from shoulder to knee, feeling the way forward. From where he was sitting, it felt pretty good.

More than good.

And it smelt amazing—or, rather, she did. She'd put that perfume on again, and it had been teasing his senses ever since he'd got in the car.

He would have joined in, for once, but the only cologne he had was some Joe had given him for Christmas the year before he'd died. He hadn't opened it until now and it didn't seem like the time to break it out,

when he was contemplating seducing his widow. She'd
have to make do with clean skin.

'That was amazing.'

He smiled, his eyes crinkling at the corners. Funny
how she'd never really registered just how gorgeous his
eyes were. Not just the colour, that striking ice-blue with
the navy rim, but the shape of them, the heavy, dark
lashes, the creases at the corners, the eloquent brows.

They said so much, those eyebrows. She could often
tell exactly what he thought of something just from the
tiny twitch that gave him away. She'd seen it in the ED,
when someone had been trying to lie about how they'd
injured themselves. She could always tell if he thought
it was a pile of steaming manure.

And if he was troubled, or concentrating, they
crunched together, but in a different way.

So complex, the facial muscles. So revealing.

He glanced across at her as he fastened his seat belt.
'Will that still go round you?'

'Cheeky,' she said without rancour. 'It would have
been rude not to have a pudding. Anyway, I was starving. I hadn't eaten all day.'

'Really?' He shot her a quick glance, surprised, but
then realised he hadn't had much, either. And nothing since he'd spoken to her in his office that morning.

He drove her home, parked the car and looked at her.
'Coffee?'

'Is that *coffee* coffee, or go upstairs with you?' she
asked, hoping he'd say no.

Something happened to his brows, but she couldn't
quite work out what. 'That's *coffee* coffee,' he said,
firmly, and she felt her shoulders drop because all the
way home she'd been beginning to get tense.

She smiled, the tension sliding out of her like a receding tide. 'Yes, please. Can we have it on the sea wall?'

'Sure.'

They took Saffy, and as usual she sat in between them, her head on her front paws, hanging slightly over the edge of the wall. He lifted one of her ears and laid it across his thigh and stroked it rhythmically, and Connie chuckled.

'I swear, if a dog could purr,' she murmured, and he laughed softly.

'She's just a hussy. No wonder you couldn't leave her.'

'No. I wanted to burn my boats with you, but I just couldn't. Even if I'd left her, I couldn't have walked away. Not completely.'

'No. I'm glad you didn't.' He stopped stroking Saffy's ear and held out his hand, and she placed hers in it. His hard, warm fingers closed around it gently and he lifted it to his lips and kissed the back of it, drifting his lips over her knuckles.

It sent a shiver through her, a tingle of something electric and rather beautiful. Something she'd almost forgotten.

He turned his head slowly and she met his eyes, holding his gaze for an age. Their hands fell softly to his lap, and he straightened her fingers out over Saffy's ear, so she wasn't really touching him, but she was.

It was utterly harmless, totally innocent, and yet not, and the air seemed trapped in her chest so she could only breathe with the very top of it, just very lightly, a little fast.

His eyes fell to her cleavage, watching the rapid rise and fall, and then they dragged back up to meet her eyes again.

Even in the darkness, with only the soft light from the front of the cottage to illuminate them, she could see that his pupils had gone black. His mouth was slightly open, his chest moving in time with hers, and the tension was coming off him in waves.

She eased her hand out from under his and turned away, breaking the spell, and they sat there in silence, the heat simmering between them, and gradually their breathing returned to normal.

'So am I coming to work tomorrow?'

'You're down on the rota.'

'What time?'

He cursed himself inwardly for changing the rota so they never saw each other, but maybe, with the sizzle he'd just felt between them, that was just as well.

'Eight o'clock. I'm on from one till nine.'

'OK. Will you take Saffy for a run for me?'

'Of course I will.'

'Thanks.' She picked up her cup and turned her head to face him. 'I'm going to turn in now. Don't bother to get up. You take your time. I'll see you tomorrow. And thank you for a lovely evening.'

'My pleasure. Sleep well, Connie.'

And then, to his surprise, she leant over and kissed him. Just the lightest brush of her lips, not like the last kiss they'd shared but the first, and then she was gone, walking away, leaving his mouth tingling and tasting of regret.

She did sleep, to her surprise. She slept like a log, and woke in the morning feeling refreshed and ready for the day.

He greeted her on the veranda with a cup of tea and a slice of hot, buttered toast, and she ate it, said goodbye to Saffy and at the last minute leant over and kissed his cheek.

He hadn't shaved, and the stubble grazed her skin deliciously. 'See you later,' she murmured, and he nodded.

'Call me if you need to, if it gets too chaotic.'

'Are you implying I can't cope?' she asked cheekily as she went through the gate.

'I wouldn't dare,' he said, laughing, and watched her go.

Gorgeous, he thought, as she flicked her hair back over her shoulder and stuck her sunglasses on her head to anchor it. Utterly, unaffectedly gorgeous.

And if he'd thought that this was in any way going to be easier than ignoring his feelings, he was finding out just how wrong he was.

He sighed heavily. If only she hadn't been Joe's woman, he would have kissed her last night. She'd been all but hyperventilating when he'd brushed her knuckles with his lips, and if it hadn't been for Joe he would have slid his hand around the back of her neck and eased her closer and kissed her till she whimpered. And that would have been it, because this time they were stone cold sober and knew exactly where it was leading.

He sighed again.

So near, and yet so far.

They passed in Reception at lunchtime, him on the way in, her on the way out.

'Good shift?'

'Yes, fine. No problems.'

'Good. I'll see you later. Don't wait for me to eat, I won't be back till after nine.'

'OK. I'll have something ready for you.'

'Star.'

He winked. No kisses here, not in front of the others, she realised, and she was glad, really. This was all too new, too precious, too fragile. It could so easily go wrong.

She drove home, changed into her running gear and took Saffy out. Not for long, because James had taken her once already, but just for a gentle lope along the sea wall as a reward for being good shut up in her run.

Then she showered and made herself a sandwich and a cup of tea and went back into the cabin. Those last two boxes of stuff were all that was left, and she had time now to deal with them.

She put the tea down on the bedside table, took a bite of the sandwich and opened the first box.

Correspondence. All sorts of stuff, out of the top drawer of Joe's desk. She'd just emptied it out, stacked it all together and packed it, and she had no idea what it was.

A will, for one thing, she realised.

There had been a copy with the solicitors who'd done the conveyancing on their house, so in many ways it was redundant. She checked it, and it was the same, leaving everything to her.

Letters. Letters from his sisters, from his mother, from her, grouped together in elastic bands, kept out of sentiment. There had been more of those that had been sent home to her when he'd died, but she'd never looked at them. And then, leafing through them, she found two others she'd never seen before.

One to her, one to James.

To be opened in the event of his death.

Trembling, her fingers not quite brave enough to do this, she slit the envelope open, pulled out the single handwritten sheet and spread it out on her lap.

My darling Connie,

If you're reading this, then I guess it's caught up with me at last. I'm so sorry. I've been waiting for it for a long time now, dreading it, expecting it, hoping I was wrong, and I know you have, too.

I hope you're OK, that my family are taking care of you and making sure you're all right. I'm sure you're not, not really, but you will be. It takes time, but you'll get there, and when you do, I want you to go out and grab life with both hands.

You've been an amazing wife, a wonderful partner and a really good friend, loyal and supportive and understanding, even when you didn't agree with my choices. I'm just so sad that we've never had a family, that the baby I know you've longed for has never come, that I've let you down, but you'll have a chance now to find that happiness with someone else, and I want you to take it. Don't hold back because of me. I want you to be happy, to be a mother, if that's what you'd like, but I can't bear to think of you all alone without me, so don't be. Don't be sad, don't be lonely. If the chance for happiness arises, take it.

I've left a letter for James. Make sure he gets it. He promised me, the last time I saw him, that he'd take care of you when I died, and I know that whatever happens, he'll do that because he's that kind of person. I've always wondered, though, what would have happened to you two if he'd never introduced us. I know Cathy's death tore him apart. I don't know the details, but he's shut himself down and I know he's lonely, but I'm sure he could love again if the right person came

*along, and maybe you're the right person for him,
have been all along.*

*There's always been something between you,
some spark. I've noticed it sometimes and been
jealous, but why should I be, because I've been
the one privileged to share my life with you, and
I always trusted you both implicitly.*

*I know I shouldn't meddle, shouldn't match-
make, but I can't think of a single person more
worthy of you, no one I'd entrust your happiness to the way I would to James, and maybe
this would give you both a chance at happiness,
a chance to be parents, to have the family I know
you've both longed for.*

*I love you, my darling. Completely, unreserv-
edly, to the depths of my soul, and I always will.
But life moves on, and time heals, and I want you
to be happy.*

Goodbye, sweetheart.
All my love,
Joe x

She closed her eyes, the tears spilling down her
cheeks, and she let them fall. She didn't sob. She just
sat there while the tears flowed, his voice echoing in
her head as he said goodbye.

She was still sitting there motionless when James got
home, the sandwich long gone, stolen by Saffy when
supper didn't seem to be forthcoming.

CHAPTER TEN

She was in the cabin. He walked in and saw her, and something about her stillness alarmed him. He went over to her and sat down on the bed beside her, taking her lifeless hand in his.

'Connie?'

'I found a letter,' she said, her voice hollow. 'From Joe. There's one for you.'

She handed him the envelope.

'If it's anything like mine, you might want to read it on your own,' she said, and she folded the closely written sheet that was lying on her lap. It was smudged with tears, creased from the pressure of her hands, and she laid it gently down on the bedside table and got up and walked away.

Not sure at all that he wanted to read it, James slit the envelope.

Dear James,
I know you won't want to hear a load of sentimental crap, but there are times when it's necessary and this is one of them.

I asked you to take care of Connie for me when I died. If you're reading this, it's happened, and I hope she's giving you a chance to do that.

Whether she is or not, I know you'll be keeping an eye on her if only from a distance.

You've been the best friend a man could ask for. Too good to me, I've thought from time to time. You gave me Connie, for a start, and she's filled my life with joy, but I sometimes wonder if you cheated yourself when you did that. There's always been something there between you. I've seen you watching her, but I know I've always been able to trust you to do the decent thing, and I trust you now. I trust you not to use her, but I also trust you to love her if that's the way it goes.

I know you won't hurt her deliberately. I never have, but my choice of career and my inability to give her the family she's longed for have both hurt her deeply and it grieves me.

I know Cathy's death hurt you, too, very deeply, but maybe together you can find happiness. If not together, then I hope you both find it another way, because of all the people in the world, I love you two the most and I want you to be happy.

If it's right for you, then please feel free to love her as she deserves, as you deserve. You have my blessing.
Your friend
Joe

Hell.

He put the letter down, folding it carefully and putting it with Connie's, and then he got to his feet and went to find her.

She was on the sea wall, and she was waiting for him. He sat beside her, on the other side of Saffy, and she looked up at him searchingly.

'Are you all right?'

He closed his eyes because it hurt simply to look at her. 'I'll live,' he said, hoping it was true, because for the first time since Cathy had died, he really wanted to. 'How about you?'

She smiled a little wanly. 'Me too. What did he say?'

'I've left it on your bedside table.'

She turned to look at him again, her eyes searching in the dim light. 'Did you read mine?'

'No—God, no, Connie. Of course not.'

No. Of course he hadn't. It simply wasn't like him to do that.

'He wants me to be happy,' she said. 'And I think he's matchmaking.'

Beside her, she heard James huff softly. Not a laugh, not a sigh, something in between, a recognition of the character of the man they'd both loved and lost.

'I know he's matchmaking—or at least facilitating. He gave us his blessing, Connie.'

She nodded slowly. 'It makes a difference.'

'It does. It makes a hell of a difference. I've been feeling guilty, thinking of you as Joe's woman, but it's what he wants, if it's right for us. He wants us to be together. He's given us permission, Connie, handed us to each other and bowed out. I don't think I'd be that bloody noble.'

She laughed, the same little noise he'd made, something closer to a sob. She heard him sigh softly.

'Or maybe I was. When Cathy died I felt as if my life had ended. There was nothing in it, nothing worth having, and chasing round the world for God knows how long didn't seem to make it any better, so I came home and still there was nothing.

'And then you came into my life, bright and funny,

clever, quick-witted and warm—so warm. In another life, I would have grabbed the chance, but it was then, and I was broken, and so I introduced you to Joe. And I've never regretted it, before you ask. I loved seeing you together. You made him happy, and for that I'm truly grateful, because at the end of the day we're still alive and he isn't, and he deserved that happiness and so did you.'

She didn't say anything. She couldn't speak. She just sat there beside him, and their hands found each other over the top of Saffy's shoulders and clung.

It was pitch dark by the time they moved.

The sky had clouded over, the moon obscured, and he made her wait there while he went back to the house and turned on the lights.

She heard him stumble, heard the dog yelp and him swear softly, and then the lights were on and he was back there, holding out his hand to help her up.

She got stiffly to her feet, her body cold with lack of food and movement, and he led her back to the house, his arm slung loosely round her shoulders, holding her by his side.

'You're freezing. When did you last eat?' he asked, and she shrugged.

'I made a sandwich about three. I had a bite or two, then I opened the letter. I guess Saffy had the rest. I haven't fed her.'

He made a soft sound with his tongue and fed the dog, fed them both some toast slathered with butter and honey, and poured two glasses of wine.

'What's that for?' she asked, and he laughed, if you could call it that.

'Dutch courage?'

She blinked. 'Am I so scary?'

'You are when I'm going to ask you to come to bed with me.'

She felt her jaw sag slightly, and then she laughed. Softly at first, and then a little hysterically, and then finally she stopped, pressing her fingers to her mouth, tears welling, unbearably touched by his nervousness.

'Are you sure?' she asked.

'As sure as I can be. I don't know if I can love you like Joe wants me to, I have to tell you that, but, my God, I want to try, Connie. I've wanted you for so long, and you've been out of reach in every conceivable way, but now you're not, maybe, and I want you so much it hurts.'

She nodded. 'Me, too. I've always liked you, always felt I could trust you, known that you were decent to your bones, but just recently my body's woken up again and it's like I've seen you for the first time, only I haven't. I've always known you oozed sex appeal, it just wasn't aimed at me so it didn't register. But now...'

'Is that a yes, then?'

'It could be. Just—talking of conceivable...'

'Don't worry. I'm not going to get you pregnant, Connie. Not by accident. If and when we reach that point, it'll be by choice.' He smiled wryly. 'I went shopping yesterday, after I left work. Just in case.'

He drained his wine glass, stood up and held his hand out to her.

'Coming?'

She smiled. Not coquettishly, not the smile of a siren, but gently, with warmth. 'I hope so.'

Heat flared in his eyes, and he gathered her against his chest with a ragged sigh. 'Ah, Connie,' he whispered, and his lips found hers and he kissed her. Tentatively at first, and then more confidently, probing the inner recesses, his tongue duelling with hers, searching, coaxing until her legs buckled and she staggered slightly.

'Bed,' he said gruffly. 'Now.'

'Saffy,' she said, and he stopped, swore, shut the dog away with an extra biscuit and was back to her in seconds.

'The cabin's unlocked.'

He ran back and locked it.

It was closer, but the letters were in there, and this first time together they needed to be alone without the ghost of Joe smiling over them.

However graciously.

They ran upstairs hand in hand, right to the top, and then he stopped and turned her towards him and undressed her. He would have done it slowly but she was wearing that blue dress again and he lifted it over her head, leaving her standing there in that lace bra and the tiny, fragile little cobweb shorts that had tantalised him so much. He'd put on the bedside light, and its soft glow gilded her body and nearly brought him to his knees.

'You're wearing that raspberry red lace again,' he groaned, and she smiled, a little uncertain this time.

'It's comfortable.'

'I don't care. I think you've worn it long enough,' he said, and turning her away from him, he unfastened the catch of her bra and slid the straps off her shoulders, catching her soft, firm breasts in his hands as they spilled free.

He dropped his head against hers, his mouth raining kisses down the arch of her neck, over her collar bone, under her ear—anywhere he could reach. It didn't matter. Every brush of his lips, every touch of his tongue made her gasp and shudder. He slid his hands down her sides, but she pushed him away and turned, her mouth finding his as her fingers searched his shirt for buttons.

He was still in his work clothes, she realised. The shirt was nothing special, just a normal shirt, so she grasped the front of it and tore it open, buttons pinging in all directions. And then she giggled mischievously.

'I've always wanted to do that.'

'Have you?' he said, and took his trousers off himself, just to be on the safe side.

'Spoilsport.'

'Vandal.'

He kicked off his shoes, stripped off his boxers and socks and trousers in one movement and held out his hand.

'Come to bed with me, Connie,' he said, his eyes suddenly serious. 'I need to make love to you and I don't think I can wait any longer.'

She went with him, toppling into the bed in a tangle of arms and legs, hungry mouths and searching hands. So hungry. So searching.

So knowing. Knowing, clever hands that explored her body inch by inch. She'd thought he was in a hurry, but there was nothing hurried about his thorough exploration.

'James—please,' she begged, and he lifted his head and touched her lips with his fingers. She could taste herself on him, and she moaned softly, rocking against him.

'Please—now, please...'

He left her briefly, then he was back, his eyes glittering with fire and ice, his body vibrating with need.

'James,' she begged, and then he was there, filling her, stroking her, pushing her higher, higher, his body

more urgent, his touch more demanding, until finally
he took her over the brink into glorious, Technicolor
freefall.

His body stiffened, pulsing deep within her, and then
as the shockwaves ebbed away he dropped his head
into the hollow of her shoulder and gathered her gently
against his chest, rolling them to the side.

They lay there in silence for a moment, scarcely moving, and then he turned his head and kissed her.

'You OK, Connie?' he murmured, and she lifted her
head and met his eyes and smiled.

'I'm fine. More than fine. You?'

He smiled back. 'Oh, I'm fine, too. I'm so fine I think
I must be dreaming.'

'Not unless it's the same dream.'

He hugged her, then let her go and vanished to the
bathroom and left her lying there staring out of the roof
window at the night sky. The clouds had cleared, she
thought. There was moonlight on the side of the reveal
that had been in shadow.

He came back to bed and turned off the light, pulling her into his arms, and they lay together staring at
the stars and watching the moon track across the sky,
and they talked.

They talked about Joe, and Cathy, but about other
things, too. How he'd lost his parents, how she had,
what he should do with the garden, and about her career.

'I'm sorry I put you in a difficult position,' she said
quietly. 'I know you didn't have a choice, not if you'd
offered her the job. I just didn't want to hear it. I can't
afford to hear it, if the truth be told, because my money's running out fast and I need to work.'

'Not necessarily. Not yet, at any rate. If this works

for us, if we don't get sick of each other and decide we can't tolerate the other one's appalling habits—'

'What, like leaving a little heap of teabags on the side?' she teased, and he laid a finger over her mouth and smiled.

'If we don't get sick of each other, then it's not an issue. If we do, if one of us thinks it isn't working for them, then I'll support you until you find a job. Don't worry about the money, Connie. I promised Joe I'd look after you, and one way or the other, you're stuck with me.'

'Thank you.' She smiled tenderly, and leant over and kissed him, her lips gentle. 'I can think of worse fates.'

They both had irritating habits, it turned out.

He left the teabags in a heap, she was bordering on OCD with the arrangement of the mugs in the cupboard. Handles on the left, and God help anyone who put them away wrong.

She squashed the toothpaste in the middle, he didn't put the lid on.

But they muddled through, and the nights took away any of the little frustrations encountered along the road to adjustment.

Work was going well, too. Annie Brooks, the new doctor, had started, and Connie was doing only occasional shifts and researching career options and training Saffy in her free time.

The career thing was a bit difficult, because she didn't really know where she should be looking for a job.

Living with James was great, the sex was amazing, they seemed to get on fine at work—but emotionally he still hadn't given her a hint of his feelings, of how he thought it was going, of how their relationship might pan out long-term.

And she wanted to know. Needed to know, because she was falling in love with him, she was sure, and she didn't want to fall too far if he was going to pull the plug on them. She'd tried to hold back some of herself from Joe, but it hadn't worked. She thought it had, but then he died and she realised she'd been fooling herself. She wasn't going to let herself do the same thing with James.

And then one day towards the end of August they were down at the little jetty, and James was pointing out things on the other side of the river. Saffy was at his side, patiently waiting for him to throw her stick again, and then it happened.

One minute they were standing on the dock, the next a boat went past and sent up a wave that knocked Saffy off her feet.

She fell into the churning water and was swept out, right into the middle of the current.

'Saffy!' she screamed, and then to her horror James kicked off his shoes and dived in after her. 'Noooo!' she screamed. 'James, no, come back! What are you doing?'

He went under briefly, then re-emerged a little further downstream.

'He'll be all right, love. Tide's going out, and Bob's gone to fetch them.'

'Bob?'

'The harbourmaster. Don't worry. It'll be all right.'

Would it? She didn't think so. He went under again, and then came up, dragging Saffy by the collar, just as Bob got to him. Terrified, still unable to believe her eyes, she watched as Bob pulled Saffy's body into the boat.

'That's a goner,' someone said, and her breath hitched on a sob.

'Get him out,' she pleaded silently. 'Please, get him out.'

'He'll be all right now. He's got a rope wrapped round his wrist. Don't you fret.'

Fret? She was beside herself as the boat pulled up at the jetty and someone dragged James out of the water.

'Get the dog out of the boat,' he snapped, and hauling her onto the wet boards of the jetty, he pumped down hard on her chest. Connie fell to her knees beside him, numb with shock.

'What can I do?' she asked, and he met her eyes, his own despairing.

'Nothing. I'm going to swing her.'

And grabbing the big dog by the back legs, he lifted her up and swung her over the side of the jetty to drain her lungs.

Nothing happened for a moment, and then water poured out.

He dropped her back on the jetty, clamped her mouth shut and breathed hard down her nose. Her chest inflated, and he blew again, and then again, and suddenly she coughed and struggled up, and his face crumpled briefly.

'It's OK, Saffy,' he said gently, holding on to her for dear life. 'It's OK.'

But it was too much for Connie.

'No, it's not OK,' she yelled, losing it at last now she knew they were both safe. 'That could have been you lying there with filthy water pouring out of your lungs, scarcely breathing! I've lost one man with a death wish, I'm not going to lose another one. You could have told me you were an idiot before I let myself fall in love with you!'

And spinning on her heel, she ran back towards the cottage, tears of rage and fear and relief pouring down her face, blinding her so that she ran smack into something.

Someone?

'Connie?'

David. It was Molly's David, her blade runner, gripping her shoulders and holding her upright, and she fell sobbing into his arms.

'Connie, whatever's happened? I heard all the commotion—what is it? Where's James?'

'He went in the river,' she said raggedly. 'Saffy was swept in, and he went in after her.'

'Where is he?' he asked, starting to run.

'He's out, David. He's out of the water. He's fine. I'm just—so angry.'

'And Saffy?' he asked, coming back.

'I think she'll be all right. She didn't breathe. She had water in her lungs, and he got it out, but his stupid heroics—'

She broke off and clamped her mouth shut so she didn't make an even bigger fool of herself, but it was too late, apparently, because James was coming now, Saffy walking unsteadily at his side, and at the sight of him she started to cry again.

'Did you mean it?' he asked, stopping right in front of her. In front of everyone.

'Mean what? That I'm angry with you? You'd better believe it.'

'That you love me.'

The crowd went utterly silent.

'Well, of course I love you, you idiot,' she ranted. 'Why else would I put up with your teabags?'

He laughed, his face crumpling after a second. 'God knows, but I love you, too,' he said, then reached for her, dragging her up against his sodden chest and kissing her as if his life depended on it.

Against her leg she could feel Saffy shivering, and in the cheering crowd someone said, 'What was that about teabags?'

'Time to go home,' he said firmly, and tucking her under his arm, he walked slowly back, Saffy on one side, the woman he hoped to spend the rest of his life with on the other.

'We need to rub her dry and keep her warm,' he said, bringing towels for Saffy into the kitchen.

'Let me do that,' Connie said, taking a towel. 'You need a shower and some dry clothes on before you catch your death.'

'I'm fine. Call the vet. She'll need antibiotics after that.'

Saffy staggered to her feet again and went out onto the veranda and retched, bringing up more of the murky water, and then she came back, lay down beside them and licked his hand.

His eyes filled, and he blinked hard and rubbed her with a towel until she stopped shivering.

Connie was kneeling beside Saffy, keying a number into the phone and muttering about him catching his death of cold, and he sat back on his heels and looked at her. 'Can I ask you something?'

'What?' she said, holding the phone to her ear.

'Will you marry me?'

She stared at him, her jaw sagging slightly, and put

the phone down on the floor before she dropped it. 'Marry you?'

'Yes. You know, big dress, diamond ring, honey-moon, babies—'

Her heart started beating harder, so loud now it almost deafened her. 'Babies?' she asked, just to be sure she'd heard it right.

'Absolutely. Definitely babies. I can't wait.'

Her breath left her in a rush. 'Neither can I.'

'So—is that a yes?'

She laughed—or was it a sob? He wasn't sure, but she was in his arms, saying, 'Yes, yes, yes,' over and over again until he actually began to believe it.

'Good. We'll talk in a minute.' And he picked up the handset from the floor.

She stared at him, listening to someone saying, 'Hello? This is the vet surgery. Did you call?'

Oh, no! Had they heard? She felt hot colour surge into her cheeks, and he smiled at her, his eyes laughing. 'Yes. Sorry about that, we got a little distracted. Can you come out on a house visit, please? We've got a rather large dog who nearly drowned in the river. I think she needs looking at urgently.'

He gave them the details, hung up and tucked her in closer beside him. 'I'm sorry I scared you. Tell me you've forgiven me.'

'No, I won't,' she said, snuggling up to his side and ignoring the rank smell of river water that clung to his sodden clothes. 'I don't know if I ever will. I thought I was going to lose you, James. I was so scared.'

'I'm sorry. I didn't think. I just saw her go in, and I couldn't let her die. Not Saffy, not after all she's been through, all she means to you, to Joe. You would have been devastated. She's our family, Connie. And I knew the tide was going out. It's when it's coming in it's so dangerous, because the denser sea water sinks under the river water where they meet and it drags you under.'

'And if you hadn't known that? Would you still have dived in?'

He shrugged. 'I don't know. Probably not. I might have nicked a boat and gone after her, but even on an outgoing tide, the current's really strong. I do know it's dangerous. I'm not an adrenaline junkie, Connie, not like Joe. I want to grow old with you, and see our children graduate and have babies of their own. I have no intention of dying. Not now. Not now I've got something worth living for. Some*one* worth living for.'

Saffy lifted her head and laid it on his lap, and he stroked her gently. 'Poor old girl. Two someones.'

Connie leant over and pressed a kiss to the dog's now warm flank. 'Thank you for rescuing her. You're right, I would have been devastated if we'd lost her.'

'I know that. I'm sorry I frightened you.'

'Don't do it again. Ever.'

'I won't.'

'Good.'

Two hours later, after the vet had been and Saffy was declared fit enough to stay at home to recover from her experience, they were all upstairs in his bedroom.

Saffy was snuggled up on an old quilt on the sofa by the window, snoring softly, and James and Connie were in bed, emotionally exhausted but happy. They'd showered to get rid of the smell of the river water which by then had been clinging to both of them, and now they were lying propped up on the pillows watching Saffy's chest rise and fall and letting the drama of the day subside.

'I love you,' she murmured, and he bent his head and pressed a warm, gentle kiss to her hair.

'I love you, too. I've loved you for years.'

She turned her head then and looked up at him. 'Really?'

'Really. I didn't let myself think about it before but you've always been more to me than just a friend. That was one of the reasons I couldn't just say yes to giving you a baby the way you asked, because I wanted so much more. I wanted to do it properly, like this, in the context of a permanent loving relationship, and anything less just seemed wrong, as if it would cheat all of us.'

'Oh, James…'

She lifted her hand and cradled his cheek, touching her lips to his, and he eased her closer, deepening the kiss, feeling the warmth of her soothing him.

It was like coming home, and he couldn't quite believe it.

'So—about these babies,' he murmured against her lips, trailing a daisy chain of kisses over her cheek and down towards the hollow of her throat.

She arched her head back, the soft sigh whispering in his hair. 'Mmm—want to make a start?'

She felt his smile against her skin.

'You read my mind,' he said softly, and kissed her all over again.

* * * * *

A BABY BETWEEN FRIENDS

FRIENDS

KATHIE DENOSKY

This book is dedicated to my editor Stacy Boyd for allowing me to spread my wings and soar.

Kathie DeNosky lives in her native Southern Illinois on the land her family settled in 1839. Her books have appeared on the *USA TODAY* bestseller list and received numerous awards, including two National Reader's Choice Awards. Readers may contact Kathie by emailing Kathie@kathiedenosky.com. They can also visit her website, www.kathiedenosky. com, or find her on Facebook, www.facebook.com/ Kathie-DeNosky-Author/278166445536145.

One

Ryder McClain's temper flared as he stared at the five men grinning at him like a bunch of damned fools. Having spent their teen years together on the Last Chance Ranch, a home for boys that the foster care system had labeled lost causes, he loved all of them. In all ways except by blood, they were his brothers. However, at this moment, nothing would be more satisfying than to wrap his hands around their throats and throttle every one of them.

"I'm only going to say this one more time and then I expect you all to drop it," he said through gritted teeth. "I brought Summer Patterson to the party tonight because she's a friend who didn't have any other plans. Period. There's absolutely nothing going on between us."

"Sure, if you say so, bro." Jaron Lambert's skeptical expression indicated that he didn't believe a word Ryder had just said. "And I'll bet you still believe in the Easter Bunny and the Tooth Fairy, don't ya?"

"I'll give you all a hundred-to-one odds that the lady in question has other ideas," Lane Donaldson said, rocking back on the heels of his handcrafted Caiman leather boots. A highly successful, professional poker player, Lane used his master's degree in psychology to read people like an open book. In this instance, the man was definitely reading the wrong chapter.

"Yup. I'd say she's cut you from the herd and getting ready to measure you for a saddle," Sam Rafferty added, laughing. The only married one of his foster brothers, Sam and his wife, Bria, were throwing the party to celebrate the renewal of their wedding vows, as well as Bria's pregnancy. "You might as well face it, Ryder. Your bachelor days are numbered."

"You're just hoping one of us will join you in the pool of the blissfully hitched," Ryder said, blowing out a frustrated breath. "But as far as Summer and I are concerned, that's not going to happen—now or in the future. Neither one of us have any intention of being anything more than best friends. End of discussion."

Smiling, T.J. Malloy paused with his beer bottle halfway to his mouth. "Ryder, did you get kicked in the head by a bull at the last rodeo you worked? That might explain you not being able to see what's as plain as your hand in front of your face."

"Well, now, this makes things a whole lot easier for me," Nate Rafferty said, smirking as he turned toward the dance floor where Summer stood talking to Bria and her sister, Mariah. "As long as you're not interested, I think I'll just mosey on over there and ask the little lady to dance."

Ryder knew that his brother was baiting him, but without a second thought, his hand came down like a vise-grip on Nate's shoulder. "Don't even think about it, Romeo."

"Oh, so you *have* staked your claim," Lane said smugly.

"No, I haven't." Ryder's jaw was clenched so hard that he wouldn't be surprised if it took a crowbar to pry his teeth apart. "But Summer doesn't need Nate's brand of grief." He thought the world of his foster brother, but Nate Rafferty had a love 'em and leave 'em philosophy that had left a string of broken hearts across the entire Southwest and then some. "No offense, Nate, but you're the last thing she needs."

"He's got you there, Nate," Sam said, nodding. The only two biological siblings of the group, Sam and Nate couldn't have been more different. The older of the two, Sam had never even come close to having the wild streak that his younger brother Nate had.

Nate shrugged. "I can't help it if I love the ladies."

"You take your interest in women to a whole other level," Ryder said, shaking his head in disgust. "Leave this lady alone and we'll get along just fine. Cross that line and you and I are going to have one hell of a big problem, bro."

He chose to ignore the knowing looks his brothers exchanged and, in favor of doing them all bodily harm, walked away. For one thing, he didn't want to ruin Sam and Bria's reception by getting into a knock-down, drag-out brawl. And for another, he made sure he never raised a fist in anger to anyone for any reason. He had been down that road once, when he was a teenager, and the results had damned near ruined his life. He wasn't going to risk going down it again.

"Ryder?"

Turning at the sound of the familiar female voice, he watched the pretty blond-haired woman with the bluest eyes he had ever seen walk toward him. He and Summer had been best friends for the past few years, and although any man would be lucky to call her his woman, Ryder had avoided thinking of her as anything but his friend. Anything more between them and he would feel obligated to tell her the reason he had finished growing up at the Last Chance Ranch. That was something he didn't care to share with anyone and why he didn't intend to enter into a serious relationship with any woman. Some things were just better left buried in the past. Besides, he didn't want to take the chance of losing the easygoing friendship they had forged by becoming romantically involved with her. He suspected she felt the same way.

"Is something wrong?" she asked, her expression reflecting her concern.

Letting go of his anger, Ryder shook his head as he smiled at the petite woman standing next to him. "No, I just got tired of listening to my brothers' bull."

She smiled wistfully. "You're lucky. At least you have brothers to irritate you. I've never had that problem."

Ryder felt as guilty as hell. As aggravating as his foster brothers could be at times, there wasn't a doubt in his mind they would all be there for him no matter what—the same as he would be for all of them. They meant the world to him and there wasn't a day that went by he didn't thank the good Lord above that he had them in his life.

But Summer had never had anything like that. Over the course of their friendship, he had learned she was the only child of an older couple who, during her senior year in college, had been killed in the small plane her father owned. With their deaths, she had been left with no family at all.

"Yeah, they sure can be a thorn in my side sometimes." As the last traces of his anger dissipated, he grinned. "But I guess after all these years I don't have any other choice but to keep them."

She laughed. "Good idea, cowboy. But seriously, your family is great. I know some of your brothers from seeing them compete at the rodeos we've worked, but I'd never met Sam's wife and her sister. They're very nice and I think it's wonderful that you all have stayed so close over the years."

When Ryder noticed Nate eyeing Summer like a fox sizing up an unguarded henhouse, he shot his brother a warning glare, then asked, "Have you had a chance to dance yet?"

"Only the line dances," she answered, glancing at the dance floor Sam had his hired hands construct in one of the barns for the celebration.

"I thought I saw Sam's head wrangler ask you to dance a little earlier," he said, frowning.

"I suppose he was nice enough," she replied, shrugging one slender shoulder. "But I wasn't in the mood to dance then."

"Well, if you don't mind a cowboy with two left feet and the worst sense of rhythm this side of the Mississippi, I'd be honored to stand in one spot with you and sway in time to the music," he offered.

Her eyes filled with humor. "I thought all Texas cowboys took pride in sashaying around the dance floor doing the two-step or the stroll."

"You know me better than that, darlin'." As the band started playing a slow, dreamy country tune, he shook his head in mock disgust and placing his hand to her back, guided her out onto the dance floor. "This is one Texan who doesn't sashay, prance or shimmy anywhere. Anytime. Ever."

"I beg to differ with you," she murmured, placing her hands on his biceps when he rested his at her trim waist. "I've seen you when you're dancing with a two-thousand-pound bull. You have some pretty smooth moves, cowboy."

"That's because it's my job." He shrugged and tried to ignore the warmth of her soft palms burning his skin through the fabric of his chambray shirt. "If I don't get those old bulls to dance with me, a bull rider gets run over."

"Don't you have a degree in ranch management?" she asked. "I would have thought you'd be content to stay home and run your ranch instead of traveling around the country playing chicken with a bulldozer on hooves."

"Yup, I'm a proud graduate of Texas A&M." He put himself between her and a couple enthusiastically two-stepping their way around the dance floor in an effort to keep them from bumping into her. "But I have a good, reliable foreman I pay quite well to check in with me several times a day. He gives me a full report on how things are going, I tell him what I want done and he sees that it's taken care of. That frees me up to be out on the rodeo circuit saving knuckleheaded bull riders like Nate and Jaron."

As Summer gazed up at him, she frowned. "I don't think I've ever asked, but why did you choose to be a rodeo bullfighter instead of a rider?"

"One time when our foster dad, Hank, was teaching us all to rodeo, one of the training bulls got loose and tried to mow down Jaron. I didn't have a clue what I was doing, but I jumped in the arena and put myself between the two of them to keep that from happening. It turned out that I was pretty good at distracting a bull and getting it to chase me." He shrugged. "I've been doing it ever since."

"In other words, you like being a hero," she said, smiling.

Laughing, he shook his head. "Nah. I'm in it for the adrenaline rush, darlin'." It was an easier explanation than admitting that he had always felt compelled to protect others from danger at the risk of his own safety.

When the song ended, Ryder led her off the dance floor and after finding an empty table for them, made sure she was comfortably seated before he went to get them a couple of drinks. He frowned as he made his way to the bar. His arms still tingled where she had rested her hands, and for the life of him, he couldn't figure out why. That had never happened before. Had his brothers' ribbing put ideas in his head about Summer?

As he continued to ponder the strange sensation, he looked up to see his brothers watching with no small amount of interest. They all wore the same sappy, know-it-all grin, making him want to plant his fist in all of their guts.

Ryder was extremely grateful that their foster father had instilled a strong sense of family among the boys he helped guide through their troubled teenage years. As Hank Calvert always told them, once they were grown they would appreciate having each other and a little bit of history together that they could look back on since none of them had any other family to speak of. And that's the way Ryder felt…most of the time. But at other times—like right now—having brothers could be a real pain in the ass.

As Summer waited for Ryder to return with their drinks, she absently watched the dancers form a couple of parallel lines and begin to move in unison to a lively tune. She couldn't get over how much she was enjoying herself. Normally she turned down all invitations from the men she worked with, no matter what the occasion or the circumstances. But Ryder was different. They had been best friends from the time she took the job as public relations director for the rodeo association southwestern circuit, and for reasons she couldn't explain, she trusted him. He was honest, didn't play the games that most men did, and despite his above average height and muscular build, she didn't feel at all threatened by him.

Of course, that might have something to do with the way he had run interference with some of their more aggressive male coworkers when she first started working for the rodeo association. From the day they met, Ryder had made it a point to remind all of them that she was a lady and should be treated as such. He had shown her nothing but his utmost respect, and it hadn't taken long before they had developed an easy, comfortable relationship. And not once in all the time she had known him had he indicated that he wanted anything more from her than to be her friend.

Unfortunately, she couldn't say the same for a lot of the men she knew. Most of them fell into two categories—blatant flirts who made it clear what they wanted from a woman, and the seemingly harmless type who lured a woman into a false sense of security before revealing their true hidden agenda. It was the latter group that was the most dangerous. The flirts were easy to spot and, once rebuffed, usually moved on to set their sights on another female. But the men with hidden agendas were nothing more than predators hiding behind a facade of sincerity.

As she absently stared at the dancers, a shiver slithered up her spine. Regrettably, she had learned that lesson the hard way. But it was one she never, as long as she lived, intended to forget.

"Would you mind if I join you, Summer?" Bria Rafferty asked, from behind her. "After that last dance, I need a minute or two to catch my breath."

Turning to glance over her shoulder, Summer smiled at the pretty auburn-haired woman. "Please have a seat." She looked around. "Where's the rest of the clan?"

"Sam, Nate, T.J. and Lane are in a lively debate about the differences between breeds of bucking bulls and which ones are the hardest to ride." Bria laughed as she pointed to the other side of the barn. "And Mariah and Jaron are arguing again about whether I'm going to have a boy or a girl."

"What are you and Sam hoping to have?" Summer asked, smiling when Bria lowered herself into the chair across from her.

"I don't care as long as the baby is healthy," Bria said, placing her hand protectively over her still-flat stomach.

"What about your husband?" Summer was pretty sure she already knew the answer. "What does Sam want?"

The woman's smile confirmed her suspicions. "Sam says he doesn't care, but I think he's secretly hoping for a boy."

Summer smiled. "Isn't that what most men want?"

"I think it's because men want a son to do things with, as well as carry on their family name," Bria answered.

"Not to mention the fact that females of all ages are a complete mystery to most men and they'd rather not have to deal with raising a child they can't understand," Summer added.

Grinning, Bria nodded. "Well, there is that."

While one of her guests stopped to congratulate Bria on her pregnancy, Summer couldn't help but feel envious. Nothing would please her more than to have a child of her own—a son or daughter to love and to love her in return. She had been so lonely since her parents died that she craved that sense of belonging again, that connection with a family. Having a child of her own would help restore some of those ties and if the plan she had come up with over the past six months worked, she would accomplish just that.

"When is your baby due?" she asked as the guest moved on.

"In early spring." Bria glowed with happiness and Summer knew it had to be because she had just entered her second trimester. Ryder had mentioned that almost a year ago Bria and Sam had lost a baby in the early weeks of pregnancy—a baby they had both desperately wanted.

"It won't be too much longer and you'll know for sure whether you're having a girl or a boy." She hoped one day in the very near future to experience the joys of expecting a child herself and learning if she would be having a son or daughter.

"Sam and I have decided we don't want the doctor to tell us." Bria laughed. "But the closer it gets to having the sonogram, the more I think Sam is going to change his mind."

"Why do you say that?"

"He keeps asking me if I feel like I'm carrying a boy." The woman rolled her eyes. "Like I would know."

"Men just don't have a clue." Summer marveled at the misconceptions some men had. "If there's a bigger mystery to a man than a woman it has to be pregnancy."

Grinning, Bria nodded. "Exactly."

"Would you like for me to get you something to drink, Bria?" Ryder asked, returning to the table. He handed a soft drink to Summer, then set a bottle of beer on the table in front of the empty chair beside her.

"Thank you, Ryder. But I think I'm going to go see if Sam is ready to cut that humongous cake he insisted we had to have." Bria rose to her feet. "I'm pretty sure he wanted to support the old saying that everything is bigger in Texas."

Summer glanced over at the giant, four-tiered cake in the center of the refreshment table. "The cake is beautiful, but I have to agree with you. It's definitely worthy of the axiom."

"I hope you have plenty of room in the freezer," Ryder added, chuckling as he pulled out the chair and sat down. "From the size of it, I'd say you're going to have about half of it left over."

Nodding, Bria flashed a smile. "I won't have to make a birthday cake for any of you for at least another year. I can just thaw out some of this one, put a candle on it and sing 'Happy Birthday.'"

"She makes each of us a dinner and a cake for our birthday," Ryder explained as Bria walked across the barn toward her husband. "All of us that is except for Jaron. He's crazy for her apple pie, so she makes a couple of those for him and sticks a candle in the middle of them."

"I think it's wonderful that you're all so close," Summer said wistfully.

Having spent the past several years alone on her

birthday and holidays, she coveted Ryder's family gatherings. She was sure if he had known, he would have insisted that she join them. But she hadn't let on because she didn't want that, hadn't wanted to be reminded of all that she had lost. That was the main reason she had taken the job of the on-site PR person for the rodeo association. She was constantly on the move from one town to the next coordinating the many rodeos held throughout the southwestern circuit, and she was always so busy that she didn't have time to think of how lonely her life had become. She was, however, glad that Ryder had invited her to his family's celebration tonight. It made her more certain than ever that she had made the right decision to start her own family.

"Did your foster father celebrate with you all before he passed away?" she asked, curious to hear about how they had come together and bonded as a family.

"Bria made sure to include Hank and her sister, Mariah, in all of our get-togethers," Ryder replied. "Family is everything to Bria and we all appreciate that. It helps us stay close and in touch with what's going on with each other."

Watching Ryder from the corner of her eye, she admired him and his foster brothers for the change they had made in their lives and the tight-knit bond they had formed. They might have been brought together because of their troubled youth, but with the help of a very special man, they had all learned to let go of the past and move forward. Through dedication and hard work, all six of them had become upstanding, highly successful men, and in the process, they had remained just as close, if not closer, than any biological siblings.

When Bria and Sam finished cutting the beautiful Western-themed cake, then invited their guests to have some, Ryder rose from the chair beside her. "I'll go get us a piece of cake, then if you'd like we can dance a few more times before I take you back to the hotel."

"That sounds like a pretty good plan, cowboy," she said agreeably.

He had invited her to spend the weekend at his ranch, but she had decided against it, opting to stay in a hotel room in a nearby town instead. For one thing, speculation about their friendship had already surfaced with some of the other rodeo association contract personnel on the circuit, and she didn't feel the need to supply the busybodies with more fodder for their rumor mill. And for another, she wanted to discuss her future plans with Ryder on the drive back from the party. Depending on his reaction, staying at the Blue Canyon Ranch with him could become a bit awkward.

An hour later, after congratulating the Raffertys once again on their renewed nuptials and Bria's pregnancy, Summer let Ryder help her into the passenger side of his pickup truck, then anxiously waited for him to come around and climb into the driver's seat. This was the part of the evening she had anticipated for the past two weeks—ever since making the decision to ask for his help.

"Are you cold?" he asked, sliding into the driver's seat. "I can turn on the heater."

"No, I'm fine. But thank you for asking." There was

a little nip in the evening air, signaling that autumn had arrived, but she had been too distracted to notice.

"I hope you had a good time," he said, starting the truck and steering it down the long drive toward the main road.

"I really enjoyed myself," she reassured him with a smile. "Thank you for asking me to attend the party with you."

When Ryder turned onto the highway, he set the cruise control then turned on a popular country radio station. "You'll have to come back for one of our birthday get-togethers sometime."

"I'd like that," she said, realizing she meant it.

They fell into a comfortable silence and while Ryder drove the big dual-wheeled pickup truck through the star-studded Texas night, Summer studied his shadowed profile. If she'd had any doubts about her choice before attending the party with him, watching him throughout the evening had completely eradicated them. Ryder McClain was the real deal—honest, intelligent, easygoing and loyal to a fault. And it was only recently that she'd allowed herself to notice how incredibly good-looking he was.

With dark brown hair, forest-green eyes and a nice, effortless smile, he would be considered extremely handsome by any standards. But combined with his impressive physical presence and laid-back personality, Ryder McClain was the type of man most women fantasized about. His wide shoulders and broad chest would be the perfect place for a woman to lay her head when the world dealt her more than she felt she could handle. And the latent strength in his muscular arms as he held her to him would keep her safe and secure from all harm.

"Summer, are you all right?" he asked, startling her.

Slightly embarrassed and more than a little disconcerted with her train of thought, she nodded. "I was just thinking about the evening and what a nice time I had," she lied, unsure of how to start the conversation that would either help her dream come true—or send her in search of someone else to assist her.

"I can't think of any of our get-togethers when we haven't had a lot of fun," Ryder said, beaming.

"Even when your brothers irritate you like they did tonight?" she teased.

His rich laughter made her feel warm all over. "Yeah, even when we're giving each other a wagonload of grief, we still enjoy being together."

"From what you said earlier, I take it you were the one in the hot seat this evening?"

She was pretty sure she knew the reason they had been teasing him. Due to the demands of both of their jobs there had been very few occasions she and Ryder had been seen together anywhere but at one of the many rodeos they both worked. It was only natural that his brothers would speculate about their relationship, the same as their coworkers had done when she and Ryder started hanging out regularly at the rodeos they were working.

He shrugged. "As long as they're bugging me, they're leaving each other alone." Grinning, he added, "A few months back, we were all on Sam's case about what a stubborn, prideful fool he can be."

"Was that when he and Bria were having a rough patch in their marriage?"

"Yup."

"Do you always know that much about each other?" If he agreed to help her, she wasn't certain she would be overly comfortable with his family knowing about it.

"It's hard to hide things from the people who know you better than you sometimes know yourself," he acknowledged.

"So you don't keep any secrets from each other? Ever?"

"There are some things that we don't tell each other, but not very many." Turning his head to look at her, he furrowed his brow. "Why do you ask?"

She had purposely waited until they were alone in his truck and it was dark so she wouldn't have to meet his gaze. But the time had come to make her case and ask for his assistance. Considering the state of her nerves and the gravity of her request, she only hoped that she would be able to convey how important it was to her and how much she wanted him to help her.

"I've been doing a lot of thinking lately…" she began, wishing she had rehearsed what she was about to say a bit more. "Although I've never had a sibling, I miss being part of a family."

"I know, darlin'." He reached across the console to reassuringly cover her hand with his much larger one. "But one day, I'm sure you'll find someone and settle down, then you'll not only be part of his family, you can start one of your own."

"That's not going to happen," she said, shaking her head. "I have absolutely no interest in getting married, or having a man in my life other than as a friend." Ryder looked taken aback by the finality in her tone. They had never discussed what they thought their futures might hold and she was sure her adamant statement surprised him. Making sure her words were less vehement, she added, "I'm going to choose another route to become part of the family I want. These days, it's quite common for a woman to choose single motherhood."

"Well, there are a lot of kids of all ages who need a good home," he concurred, his tone filled with understanding. "A single woman adopting a little kid nowadays doesn't have the kind of obstacles they used to have."

"I'm not talking about adopting a child," Summer said, staring out the windshield at the dark Texas landscape. "At least not yet. I'd really like to experience all aspects of motherhood if I can, and that includes being pregnant."

"The last I heard, being pregnant is kind of difficult without the benefit of a man being involved," he said with a wry smile.

"To a certain degree, a man would need to be involved." They were quickly approaching the moment of truth. "But there are other ways besides having sex to become pregnant."

"Oh, so you're going to visit a sperm bank?" He didn't sound judgmental and she took that as a positive sign.

"No." She shook her head. "I'd rather know my baby's father than to have him be a number on a vial and a list of physical characteristics."

Ryder looked confused. "Then how do you figure on making this happen if you're unwilling to wait until you meet someone and you don't want to visit a sperm bank?"

Her pulse sped up. "I have a donor in mind."

"Well, I guess if the guy's agreeable that would work," he said thoughtfully. "Anybody I know?"

"Yes." She paused for a moment to shore up her courage. Then, before she lost her nerve, she blurted, "I want you to be the father of my baby, Ryder."

Two

Never at a loss for words, Ryder could only remember a couple of times in all of his thirty-three years that he had been struck completely speechless. At the moment, he couldn't have managed to string two words together if his life depended on it. Summer asking him to help her have a baby was the last thing he'd expected.

To keep from driving off into a ditch, he steered the truck to the side of the road, shifted it into Park, then turned to gape at the woman seated in the truck beside him. How in the world was he supposed to respond to a request like that? And why the hell was his lower body suddenly indicating that it was up for the challenge?

Shocked, as well as bewildered, his first inclination had been to laugh and ask her who it was she was really considering. But as he searched her pretty face, Ryder's heart began to thump against his ribs like a bass drum in a high school marching band. He could tell from the worry lines creasing her forehead that she wasn't joking. She was dead serious and waiting for him to tell her he would father her child.

"I know this comes as a bit of a surprise," she said, nervously twisting her hands into a knot in her lap. "But—"

"No, Summer," he said, finally finding his voice. "An unexpected gift or winning a few bucks in the lottery is a surprise. This is a shock that rivals standing in ankle-deep water and grabbing hold of a wire with a few thousand volts of electricity running through it."

She slowly nodded. "I'm sure it was the last thing you expected."

"You got that right, darlin'."

Ryder took a deep breath as he tried to figure out how to proceed. He knew he should ask some questions, but he wasn't entirely sure what he wanted to know first. What made her think that she wouldn't one day meet the right guy to change her mind about getting married and having the family she wanted? Why had she decided that he was the man she wanted to help her? And how did she figure she was going to get him to go along with such a cockamamy scheme?

"We're going to have to talk about this," he said, deciding that he needed time to think. Starting the truck's engine, he steered it back onto the road. "We'll stop by the hotel long enough for you to get your things and check out of your room. Then we'll drive on down to the Blue Canyon."

"No, I think it would be better if I stay at the hotel

instead of your ranch," she said, her tone adamant. "It might look like we were—"

"Seriously?" He released a frustrated breath as he glanced over at her. "You're worried about what people might think, but yet you want me to make you pregnant?"

"That isn't what I'm asking," she said, shaking her head. "I don't want you to *make* me pregnant. I'm asking you to put a donation in a cup for a clinical procedure in a doctor's office."

Ryder grunted. "Don't you think that's splitting hairs? The bottom line is, you'd be pregnant and I'd be the daddy."

"Oh, I wouldn't expect you to support the baby or help raise him or her," she insisted. "My parents left me more than enough money so that I never have to worry about taking care of myself and a child."

He barely resisted the urge to say a word she was sure to find highly offensive. Did she know him at all? She wanted him to help her make a baby and then just walk away like it was nothing?

Not in this lifetime. Or any other for that matter.

"Summer, we're going to wait to finish this conversation until after we get to my ranch," he said firmly. He needed time for the shock of her request—and the irritation that she didn't want him to have anything to do with his kid—to wear off before he was able to think rationally.

"No, I'd rather—"

"My housekeeper, Betty Lou, will be there with us so you don't have to worry about how things are going to look," he stated, wondering why she was so concerned about gossip. It wasn't like there wouldn't be plenty of that going around if he lost what little sense he had and agreed to help her—which he had no intention of doing. But he needed to get to the bottom of what she was thinking and why she was willing to risk their friendship to make her request.

He cleared his throat. "You'll have to admit that what you're asking of me is pretty massive, and we need to talk it over—a lot. Staying at my ranch until we have to take off for the next rodeo in a couple of days will give us the privacy to do that."

She didn't look at all happy about it, but she apparently realized that going to the Blue Canyon Ranch with him was her best chance of getting what she wanted. "If that's the only way you'll consider helping me—"

"It is."

He didn't want to give her any encouragement or mislead her into thinking he was going to assist her. But he needed to talk to her and make her see that there were other alternatives to have the family she wanted besides going around asking unsuspecting men to help her become pregnant.

She took a deep breath then slowly nodded. "All right. If you won't consider helping me any other way, I'll go to your ranch with you."

They both fell silent for the rest of the drive to the hotel and by the time she gathered her things, checked out and they drove on to the Blue Canyon, it was well past midnight.

"It's late and I don't know about you, but I'm pretty

tired," he said when he turned the truck onto the lane leading up to his ranch house. "Why don't we get a good night's sleep, then we can hash this all out after breakfast tomorrow morning?"

She nodded. "I suppose that would probably be best."

Parking in the circular drive in front of the house, Ryder got out and walked around to open the passenger door for her. "I guess before we go inside I'd better warn you. You'll need to steer clear of Lucifer."

"Who's that?" she asked, looking a little apprehensive.

"Betty Lou's cat," he answered, reaching into the back of the club cab for her luggage while she gazed up at his sprawling two-story ranch house.

"Oh, I won't mind being around him," she said, turning to smile at him. "I adore animals."

Ryder shook his head. "You won't like this one. I'm convinced he's the devil incarnate."

"Why do you say that?"

"He barely tolerates people." Ryder carried her bag to the front door, then letting them into the foyer, turned to reset the security system. "He hisses and spits at everyone who crosses his path, except Betty Lou. And there are times I think she walks on eggshells around him."

"You get chased by the biggest, meanest bulls the stock contractors can offer on a regular basis…and you're afraid of a house cat?" she asked with a cheeky grin.

Relieved that the awkwardness that followed her request seemed to have been put aside for the moment, he shrugged as he led her over to the winding staircase. "I know what to expect with a ton of pissed-off beef. But that cat is a whole different breed of misery. He's attitude with a screech and sharp claws. Sometimes he likes to lurk in high places and then, making a sound that will raise the hair on the head of a bald man, he drops down on top of you as you walk by." Ryder rotated his shoulders as he thought about the last time Lucifer had launched himself at him through the balusters from the top of the stairs. "He's sunk his claws into me enough times that I'm leery of walking past anything that's taller than I am without looking up first."

"Then why do you allow your housekeeper to keep him?" she asked when they reached the top of the stairs.

He'd asked himself that same question about a hundred times over the past several years—usually right after the cat had pounced on him. "Betty Lou thinks the sun rises and sets in that gray devil. She adopted him from an animal shelter after her husband died and when she took the job as my housekeeper, I didn't think it would be a big deal for her to bring him along with her. I like animals and besides, I'm gone a lot of the time anyway, so I don't have to be around him a lot."

"That's very nice of you," she said, sounding sincere. "But it's your house. You shouldn't have to worry about being mauled by a cat."

Ryder shrugged. "I don't see any reason to be a jerk about it when Lucifer means that much to her. I just try to steer clear of him as much as possible when I do make it home for a few days." Stopping at one of the guest bedrooms, he opened the door, turned on the light for her, then set her luggage beside the dresser. "Will this be all right? If not, there are five other bedrooms you can choose from."

He watched her look around the spacious room a moment before she turned to face him. "This is very nice, Ryder. Did you decorate it?"

Her teasing smile indicated that she was awaiting a reaction to her pointed question. He didn't disappoint her.

"Yeah, right. I just look like the kind of guy who knows all about stuff like pillows and curtains." Shaking his head, he added, "No, I hired a lady from Waco after I bought the ranch to come down here and redecorate the house."

"She did a wonderful job." Summer touched the patchwork quilt covering the bed. "This is very warm and welcoming."

"Thanks." He wasn't sure why it mattered so much, but it pleased him that she liked his home. "I bought it right after I sold my interest in a start-up company my college roommate launched while we were still in school."

"It must have been quite successful," she said as she continued to look around.

He grinned. "Ever heard of The Virtual Ledger computer programs?"

"Of course. They have a program for just about every kind of record-keeping anyone could want." Her eyes widened. "You helped found that?"

He laughed out loud. "Not hardly. I know just enough about a computer to screw it up and make it completely useless. But my roommate had the idea and I had some money saved back from working rodeos during the summers. I gave it to him and he gave me 50 percent of the company. Once it really took off, I sold him my interest in the company and we both got what we wanted out of the deal." He took a breath. "He has total control of The Virtual Ledger and I have this ranch and enough money to do whatever I want, whenever I want, for the rest of my life."

"Then why do you put yourself in danger fighting rodeo bulls?" she asked, frowning.

"Everybody has to have something that gives them a sense of purpose and makes them feel useful. Besides, I have to watch out for boneheads like Nate and Jaron." When she yawned, he turned to leave. "Get a good night's sleep and if you need anything, my room is at the far end of the hall."

Her smile caused a warm feeling to spread throughout his chest. "Thank you, Ryder, but I'll be fine."

Nodding, he quickly stepped out into the hall and closed the door behind him. What the hell was wrong with him? Summer had smiled at him hundreds of times over the past few years and he had never given it so much as a second thought. So why now did it feel like his temperature had spiked several degrees?

He shook his head as he strode toward the master suite. Hell, he still hadn't figured out why his arms had tingled where she rested her hands when they danced at the party. And why did the thought of her wanting him to be her baby daddy make him feel twitchy in places that had absolutely no business twitching?

* * *

When Summer opened her eyes to the shaft of sunlight peeking through the pale yellow curtains, she looked around the beautifully decorated room and for a brief moment wondered where she was. She was used to awakening in a generic hotel room where shades of beige and tan reigned supreme and the headboard of the bed was bolted to the wall. But instead of spending the night in a hotel as she'd planned, she had agreed to accompany Ryder to his ranch.

Her breath caught as she remembered why he had insisted she come home with him. After weeks of trying to find a way to bring up the subject and ask him to be the donor for her pregnancy, she had worked up her courage and made her request. And his answer hadn't been "no." At least, not outright.

He thought they needed to talk it over and although his insistence that they stay at his ranch had made her extremely nervous, she had agreed. She needed to reassure him that she would sign whatever document was needed to ensure that she would be solely responsible for the baby and that he would be under no obligation. She was sure that once he understood that, he would be more inclined to help her.

As she threw back the covers and got out of bed to take a shower, she thought about what Ryder would want to discuss first. He would probably start off with wanting to know why she didn't feel she would ever meet a man she wanted to marry. Or he might try to convince her that, at the youthful age of twenty-five, she had plenty of time and should wait to make such a life-changing decision.

Standing beneath the refreshing spray of warm water, she smiled. She might not have practiced the way she worded her request as much as she should have, but she was armed and ready with her answers for their upcoming discussion about it. She knew Ryder well enough to know he would try to talk her out of her plans, and she had painstakingly gone over the way she would explain her reasoning and how she would frame the responses she intended to give him. Once he realized that she was completely serious, along with the promise of a legal document relieving him of any commitment to support or help raise the child, surely he would agree.

Anxious to start their conversation, she toweled herself dry, quickly got dressed and started downstairs. Halfway to the bottom of the staircase, she stopped when she came face-to-face with one of the largest gray tabby cats she had ever seen.

"You must be Lucifer," she said tentatively. From Ryder's description of the cat, she wasn't sure how he would react to encountering a stranger in his domain.

She hoped he didn't attack her as she walked past. But instead of pouncing on her as she expected he might, the cat gazed up at her for a moment, then letting out a heartfelt meow, rubbed his body along the side of her leg.

Reaching down, she cautiously stroked his soft coat. Lucifer rewarded her with a loud, albeit contented purr. "You don't seem nearly as ferocious as Ryder claimed you were," she said when he burrowed his head into her palm, then licked her fingers with a swipe of his sand-papery rough tongue.

When Summer continued on down the stairs, Lucifer trotted behind her as she followed the delicious smell of fried bacon and freshly brewed coffee. "Good morning," she said when she found Ryder seated at the kitchen table.

"Morning." He rose from his chair as she entered the room, and Lucifer immediately arched his back and hissed loudly at Ryder. "I see he's still the same happy cat he's always been," Ryder said sarcastically as he shook his head. "Would you like a cup of coffee, Summer?"

"Yes, please. It smells wonderful."

"Just a little cream?" he asked. They had met for coffee so many times over the past few years, he knew exactly how she liked it. Just as she knew he always liked his coffee black.

"Yes, thank you." She smiled. "You know, I think Lucifer likes me. He rubbed against my leg and let me pet him when we met on the stairs."

"See, I told you it's just you he has a problem with, Ryder." The woman standing at the stove chortled.

"I don't know why." He looked as if he might be a bit insulted by her comment. "Most other animals don't seem to think I'm all that bad of a guy."

"Maybe you aren't home enough for him to get used to you," Summer suggested.

"Whatever." Shrugging, he walked over to take a mug from one of the top cabinets, then poured her some coffee. "Betty Lou Harmon, I'd like for you to meet my friend, Summer Patterson."

"It's nice to meet you, Mrs. Harmon," Summer said warmly as the older woman turned from the stove to face her.

"It's real nice to meet you, too, child. But don't go bein' all formal," the housekeeper groused, shaking her head. "You call me Betty Lou the same as everybody else, you hear?"

"Yes, ma'am," Summer said, instantly liking the woman. With her dark hair liberally streaked with silver and pulled back into a tight bun at the back of her head, her kind gray eyes and round cheeks flushed from the heat of the stove, Betty Lou looked more like someone's grandmother than a rancher's housekeeper.

Wiping her hands on her gingham apron, she waved toward the trestle table where Ryder had been seated when Summer entered the room. "You find yourself a place to sit and I'll get you fixed up with a plate of eggs, bacon, hash browns and some biscuits and gravy."

"I don't eat much for breakfast," Summer confessed, hoping she didn't offend the woman. She seated herself in one of the tall ladder-back chairs at the honey oak table. "Normally all I have is a bagel or toast and a cup of coffee."

"Well, you'd better eat a hearty meal this mornin' if you're goin' horseback ridin' down to the canyon with Ryder," Betty Lou said, filling a plate and bringing it over to set on the table in front of her.

"We're going for a ride?" Summer asked, crestfallen. She thought they were supposed to discuss her request.

"I thought I'd show you around the ranch," Ryder said, nodding as he brought her coffee over to the table. When Betty Lou went into the pantry, he lowered his voice and leaned close to Summer. "We'll have plenty of time to talk and no one around to overhear the conversation."

"We could have done that in my hotel room," she reminded him.

He raised one dark eyebrow as he sat back down at the head of the table. "For someone who is so concerned with appearances, you haven't thought of the obvious, darlin'."

Ryder's intimate tone and the scent of his clean, masculine skin caused her pulse to beat double time. "Wh-what would that be?" she asked, confused and not at all comfortable with the way she was reacting to him.

"How do you think it would look with us being alone in your room for several hours?" He shrugged. "I doubt anyone would be convinced we were just talking or watching television."

"Oh." She hadn't thought of that. "I suppose you're right."

"Now eat," he said, pointing to her plate.

"Aren't you going to have breakfast?" she asked, taking a bite of the fluffy scrambled eggs.

He took a sip of his coffee and shook his head. "I ate about an hour ago."

When she finished the last of the delicious food, Summer smiled at Betty Lou when she walked over to pick up the plate. "That was wonderful. Thank you."

The woman gave her an approving nod. "That should

tide you over until you eat the sandwiches I packed for the two of you."

"We won't be back in time for lunch?" Summer asked, turning to Ryder. "How far away is the canyon?"

"It's not that far." He gave her a smile that made her radiate from within. "But there's a creek lined with cottonwoods that runs through the canyon, and I thought you might like to have a picnic along the bank."

"I haven't done something like that in years," she said, happy that he had thought of the idea. Going on an outing like the one Ryder suggested was one of the many things she had enjoyed doing with her parents.

"You do know how to ride a horse, don't you?" he asked. When she nodded, he unclipped his cell phone from his belt. "Good. I'll call the barn and have my foreman get the horses saddled and ready for us."

A half hour later as he and Summer rode across the pasture behind the barns, Ryder watched her pat the buckskin mare she was riding. With the autumn sun shining down on her long blond hair, she looked like an angel. A very desirable angel.

He frowned at the thought. They had never been more than friends, and until his brothers started ribbing him about taking her to Sam and Bria's wedding vows renewal celebration, he had purposely avoided thinking of her in that way. So why was it all he could think about now? Of course, her making her plea last night for him to be her baby's daddy sure wasn't helping matters.

"I'm glad you thought of this, Ryder," she said, distracting him from his confusing inner thoughts. "I love going horseback riding. I used to do it all the time. But after I took the job with the rodeo association, I sold my parents' farm and all of the horses and I don't get to ride much anymore."

"Was there a reason you couldn't keep it?" he asked. She said she had plenty of money, so that couldn't be the cause of her selling everything.

She stared off into the distance like the decision might not have been an easy one to make. "With all the travel required for my job, it just didn't seem practical to hang on to it."

"I realize you have to arrive in a town a few days before a rodeo in order to get things set up for the media and schedule interviews for some of the riders, but couldn't you have boarded one of the horses and ridden on the days that you do make it home?" he asked, knowing that was what he would have done.

He could understand her not wanting to hold on to her parents' home without them being there. It would most likely be a painful reminder of all that she had lost when they were killed. But he didn't understand her not keeping at least one of the horses if she liked to ride that much.

"I don't go home," she answered, shrugging one slender shoulder. "I just go on to the next town on the schedule."

"You don't go back to your place on the few days we have off between rodeos?" They normally met up in the next town for the next rodeo and had never traveled together before. It appeared that although they were close friends, there was a lot that they hadn't shared with each other.

But he still couldn't imagine going for weeks without coming back to the ranch. Besides Hank Calvert's Last Chance Ranch, the Blue Canyon was the only place he had ever been able to truly call home. And a home of his own was something he never intended to be without again.

"I...don't have a place," she admitted, looking a little sheepish. "I know it sounds bad, but I couldn't see any sense in paying for the upkeep on my parents' home or rent on an apartment when I'd only be there a few days out of the month."

Reaching out, he took hold of the mare's reins as he stopped both horses. "Let me get this straight. You live out of hotel rooms and you don't have a place to call your own?" When she nodded, he asked, "Where do you keep your things?"

"What I can't pack into the two suitcases I take on the road with me, like furniture and family keepsakes, I keep in a storage unit in Topanga, California, not far from where my parents lived." When he turned loose of the buckskin's reins and they continued on toward the trail leading down into the canyon, she added, "It's much cheaper than paying to keep them in an apartment I'd never use."

Shocked by her revelation, he shook his head. "So for all intents and purposes, you're homeless."

"I guess it could be construed that way." She nibbled on her lower lip a moment as if she might be bothered by it more than she was letting on. "But as long as I'm traveling like I do, I don't mind."

"How long have you lived this way?" he asked, still trying to wrap his mind around what she had told him.

"About three years."

He had been friends with her all that time and not once had he suspected that she lived the life of a nomad. What else was there about her that he didn't know? And how the hell did she plan on taking care of a baby with that kind of lifestyle?

When they reached the canyon's rim, they fell silent as Ryder rode the bay ahead of her to lead the way to the meadow below. But he couldn't stop thinking about her lack of roots. Why did she want a baby when she didn't even have a home? What was she going to do with the poor little thing, raise it in a series of hotel rooms while they traveled from one rodeo to the next for her job? That wasn't any kind of a life for a little kid.

Ryder didn't know what her reasoning was, but he had every intention of finding out. He knew from personal experience that it was important to a kid to have a place to call home.

Leading the way to the spot along the bank that he had in mind for their picnic, he reined in the gelding. "How does this look?"

"It's great," she said, stopping the buckskin mare beside his horse. "There's plenty of shade." She pointed toward one of the cottonwoods. "And under that tree looks like the perfect place to put the blanket."

Dismounting the bay, he dropped the reins to ground-tie the horse, then moved to retrieve the rolled blanket he had tied to the back of the gelding's saddle, along with the insulated saddlebags holding their lunch. From the corner of his eye, he watched Summer jump down from the mare's back and start doing some stretches to loosen up after the ride.

He briefly wondered if she was having muscle cramps, but he quickly forgot all about her possible discomfort as he watched her stretch from side to side, then bend over to touch her toes. Her jeans pulled tight over her perfect little bottom caused his mouth to go as dry as a desert in a drought. When she straightened, then placed her hands on her hips to lean back and relieve pressure on her lower back, he sucked in a sharp breath. Her motions caused her chest to stick out and for the first time since he had known her, he noticed how full and perfect her breasts were.

Ryder muttered a curse under his breath and forced himself to look away. This was Summer. She was his best friend and he'd never thought of her in a romantic light. So why now was he suddenly taking notice of her delightful backside and enticing breasts?

Disgusted with himself, he shook his head and tucking the picnic blanket under his arm, finished unfastening the insulated saddlebags from the bay's saddle and carted everything over to the spot beneath the cottonwood that Summer had pointed out. His fascination with her feminine attributes was probably due to the fact that he hadn't been with a woman in longer than he cared to remember—and he'd have to be blind not to notice that Summer was a damned good-looking woman with a set of curves that could tempt a eunuch. He wasn't at all comfortable thinking of her in that way, but there was no denying it either.

As he set the saddlebags down and unfolded the blanket to spread it out on the ground, he gave some thought to his dilemma. He was a normal, healthy adult male who, like any other man, needed to occasionally get lost in a woman's softness. Once he got back out on the rodeo circuit, he needed to take a trip to one of the local watering holes in whatever town he was in and strike up a cozy little acquaintance with a woman who wasn't looking for anything more than a real good time. Maybe then he would stop having inappropriate thoughts about his best friend.

Three

Sitting beside the lazy little creek after finishing their lunch, Summer glanced over at Ryder's handsome profile. He really was one of the best-looking men she had ever known and she had a hard time believing it took her this long to realize it. Studying his features, she found herself hoping that if he agreed to help her, their child would look like him. But neither of them had brought up the subject of her request and the longer it took for them to start the discussion, the more uncertain she became. What if he refused to be the sperm donor?

He had all the attributes she wanted for her child and asking any of the other men she knew wasn't even a consideration. She didn't know them well enough to determine if they had the traits she was looking for, and truthfully, she didn't want to get that well acquainted with them. She didn't trust any man the way she trusted

Ryder and couldn't imagine anyone else as her baby's father.

"Have you given any more thought to helping me?" she finally asked.

"I really haven't thought about much of anything else," he admitted, turning to face her. "It's not every day that out of the clear blue sky a woman asks me to help her get pregnant." His expression gave nothing away and she had no indication of what he might be thinking.

"As I told you last night, you wouldn't be obligated in any way," she said, hoping to reassure him. "I'll be responsible for everything. You wouldn't even have to acknowledge that you were the donor."

"In other words, you don't want me to be involved at all in my own kid's life," he said flatly. Shaking his head, he added, "You of all people should know that's not the way I roll, darlin'."

The steely determination she heard in his voice surprised her. "I...well...I hadn't thought you would want—"

He held up his hand. "Let's back up. We can cover what would happen after you became pregnant a little later on. Right now, I have a few things I'd like to know."

"Of course," she said pleasantly. She was confident she could answer all of his questions. "What would you like to ask first?"

Ryder's piercing green gaze held her captive. "Why me?"

"You have all the qualities that I would want passed

on to my child," she said, not having to think about her answer. "You're healthy, physically fit, as well as physically appealing. You're also honest, loyal and other than my late father, you're the most trustworthy man I've ever known."

"You make me sound like a prize stud someone would want to cover their herd of mares," he said, shaking his head in obvious disbelief. "How long have you been thinking about this?"

"About six months," she admitted. Things weren't going the way she had hoped. He didn't sound as if he was all that receptive to the idea. "But I didn't seriously think of approaching you until a couple of weeks ago."

Nodding as if he accepted her answer, Ryder stared off into space for a moment before he asked, "Last night you told me you didn't want to wait to see if you change your mind about meeting a man you might want to settle down with."

"That's right." She shook her head. "I don't have any intention of ever getting married."

"Why?"

"As you know, I'm pretty independent," she said, reciting the answer she had rehearsed. "I don't want to lose that. I don't want to be dependent on a man or give anyone that kind of control over me."

He frowned. "Where did you get the idea that whoever you met would want to control you?" Shaking his head, he propped his forearms on his bent knees. "Most men I know admire independence in a woman. Me included."

"Maybe I should rephrase that," she said, thinking

quickly. "I don't want to give that kind of emotional control to anyone."

Staring at her for several long moments, Ryder asked, "Who was the bastard?"

His question startled her. "I…don't know what you mean."

"Someone had to have hurt you pretty bad to make you feel this way," he insisted. "Who was he?"

Ryder's assessment was hitting too close to the truth and she had to force herself to remain calm. "There wasn't anyone," she lied. "I've just never believed that I need a man in my life to validate my worth as a woman nor do I want to depend on him for my happiness."

"Okay," he said slowly. She could tell he wasn't buying her explanation, but before she had the chance to say more, he asked, "Why now? You're only twenty-five. It's not like your biological clock is ticking or the alarm is about to go off."

She took a deep breath. Her answer this time wasn't a lie or a half-truth. "I want to be part of a family again, Ryder. I want someone to love and be loved by in return."

"Ah, darlin'," he said, moving to wrap his strong arms around her. Pulling her to him, he gave her a comforting hug. "I know how alone you've been since your parents passed away, but do you really think having a baby will be the cure for your loneliness?"

"I really do," she said, feeling a bit confused by the fact that Ryder's embrace wasn't the least bit intimidating. Any other man giving her a hug would have sent her into a panic attack.

"What would you do about a home for you and the baby?" he asked, his tone gentle. "You can't raise a kid living in hotel rooms and moving from town to town every week."

His questions had her wondering if he might be seriously considering her request. "I intend to quit my job and buy a house. As I told you before, my parents left me quite well-off. Between their life insurance policies and the sale of the horses and ranch, I never have to work another day in my life if I don't want to." She exhaled slowly. "I'd like to be a stay-at-home mom until my baby is old enough for preschool. Then after my child starts school, I'll decide whether I want to find something to do part-time or continue being a stay-at-home mom." When Ryder remained silent, she leaned back to look at him. He appeared to be in deep thought and she hoped that was a positive sign he was going to help her.

"This is a big decision," he finally said, meeting her questioning gaze. "Let me think about it for a while."

"Of course," she said slowly. "But let me assure you, I don't expect you to do anything past being the donor. Like I said last night…you won't be obligated in any way for anything."

He continued to stare at her for what seemed like an eternity, then he rose to his feet and held out his hand to help her to hers. "I think it's about time we head back to the house."

When she placed her hand in his, a jolt of electric current streaked up her arm and spread throughout her insides. Summer frowned at the lingering sensation as she turned to pick up the blanket. What was going on with her? She wasn't interested in any man and especially not Ryder. He was her best friend and even if she had wanted to have a man in her life—which she didn't—she wasn't willing to jeopardize their friendship by starting something romantic. Sperm donation was one thing, involving emotions was another.

But as they rode back toward the ranch house, she couldn't stop thinking about the unsettling feeling that had coursed through her. Why was she suddenly more aware of Ryder as a man than ever before? And why, when he took her hand in his, did it feel as if something extremely significant had shifted in the universe?

While Summer helped Betty Lou finish up supper in the kitchen, Ryder stood by the window in his office, staring out at the sun sinking low in the western sky. He couldn't stop thinking about Summer's misguided idea that a baby was the solution to her loneliness.

It wasn't that he couldn't understand her wanting a family connection and the sense of belonging that came with it. He could. For the first fourteen years of his life, he had longed for the same thing as he was shuffled from one foster home to another. It wasn't until he was placed in the care of Hank Calvert and taken to live at the Last Chance Ranch that he learned what it felt like to have a home and be part of a family. But he was doubtful that her having a baby would make her feel like she was part of something like that again.

Normally, having a family meant having a built-in support system. But Summer wouldn't have that.

She would be the support system for the baby, but she wouldn't have anyone to help her. Who would be there to lend a hand with a fussy newborn when she got so tired she was about to drop in her tracks? Who would she lean on if, God forbid, the baby came down with a serious illness? That role was usually filled by a husband, a woman's mother or even her sister. Summer wouldn't have any of the three.

He wasn't buying into her claim that fearing the loss of her independence was the reason behind her not wanting to have a man in her life either. She had to know that in this day and time, most men were fine with a woman being strong and self-assured. And that wasn't the only thing that bothered him about their conversation.

Why did she believe that he wouldn't want to be part of his own kid's life? What made her think that if he lost what little sense he had and agreed to father her baby that he could just walk away?

He knew firsthand the effect a parent's abandonment had on a kid. He might have only been four years old when his mother left him in a hospital waiting room for the authorities to find, but her poor choice had a huge impact on his life. Aside from being raised by people who didn't care anything about him past the monthly check they received for housing him, the fallout of being shuffled from one unsuitable family to another had eventually landed him in enough trouble to be sent to the Last Chance Ranch. And although becoming one of Hank's boys had been the best thing that ever happened to him, the way he got there was something nobody would want for a kid.

Of course, Summer wasn't asking him to bond with the child and then leave to let her finish raising him or her. She didn't want him to be part of the baby's life at all. And that bothered the hell out of him.

Until Summer made her request, he had never given a lot of thought to having a child of his own. For one thing, he hadn't ever expected to get married. Finding a woman who understood his painful past and could overlook all that would be a tall order to fill. And for another, thanks to Hank's Cowboy Code, Ryder was old-fashioned enough to believe that you weren't supposed to put the cart before the horse. Getting married was what a man was supposed to do first, then start having kids. Not the other way around.

He couldn't help but smile fondly at the memory of his foster father sitting Ryder and the rest of his brothers down for lessons in manners and morality. Whether it was out of gratitude or they all wanted to emulate the man who had been there for them through thick and thin, Ryder and his brothers had learned their lessons well. A man always treated a woman like a lady, showed her respect and if he fathered a child, he owned up to his responsibility and helped the mother raise it.

He and his brothers all adhered to the Cowboy Code to this day—even Nate. He might be a ladies' man, but he was always respectful of women and limited his amorous activities to one woman at a time.

A knock on the door interrupted his thoughts. "Dinner is almost ready, Ryder," Summer called out to him.

Walking over to open the door, his heart stalled at the sight of her. With strands of her honey-blond hair escaping the confines of her ponytail and her cheeks colored a pretty pink from the heat of cooking, he didn't think he had ever seen her look lovelier.

"Lead the way," he said, wondering if he'd lost his mind. Why did he feel as if he had just run a footrace? Hell, he didn't get this out of breath when he played chicken with a ton of pissed-off beef.

As he watched her walk down the hall ahead of him, Ryder couldn't seem to stop watching the enticing sway of her hips. He gritted his teeth and forced himself to focus on the back of her head. Why, in the past couple of days, had he suddenly become so fascinated with her body?

He wouldn't even begin to entertain the idea of having something develop between them. For that matter, he wasn't willing to become romantically involved with *any* woman. He just couldn't bear the thought of falling for someone special and then seeing the revulsion and fear on her face once she learned the truth about him.

Entering the kitchen, he started toward his place at the head of the table, but Lucifer chose that moment to walk out from behind the kitchen island. As was his usual practice whenever he saw Ryder, the cat arched its back and let loose with a nasty hiss.

"Well, good evening to you, too, Lucifer," Ryder said cheerfully. He would have never believed he would be glad to cross paths with the disagreeable feline, but it had been just the distraction he needed to get his mind off Summer's shapely bottom.

"There's something about you that cat doesn't like," Summer said, crinkling her brow. "Maybe he's sensitive to your cologne."

Ryder shrugged as he sat down at the table. "He might be if I wore cologne. But since I don't, it can't be that."

"Do you have any idea why Lucifer reacts to Ryder the way he does, Betty Lou?" she asked, picking up a bowl of mashed potatoes from the island to set it on the table.

The older woman shook her head. "No, but he's been this way about Ryder ever since I started housekeepin' here four years ago." She walked over to place a platter of country fried steaks in the middle of the table. "I personally think Lucifer is bein' defensive because he's intimidated by Ryder's size." She grinned. "You gotta admit, Ryder's a long, tall drink of water."

"You might be right." Summer smiled as she poured them all glasses of iced tea. "Maybe Lucifer is just warning Ryder to look down and not step on him."

While the two women continued to speculate on why the cat found him so offensive, Ryder's thoughts turned to what he needed to say to change Summer's mind about pursuing her quest to get pregnant. Knowing her the way he did, he needed to be careful not to argue too strongly against her plans. If he did that, she just might end up more determined than ever to proceed with or without his help.

As an idea began to take shape, he waited until Betty Lou turned her attention to getting a pie out of the oven before he motioned Summer over to the table. "I've come to a decision," he said, careful to keep his tone low. "If you aren't too tired, we'll talk about it in my office after we eat."

An hour after Ryder told her he was ready to give her his answer, Summer followed him down the hall to his office. She didn't think she had ever been more nervous than she was at that moment. What if his answer was "no"? What would she do then?

When they walked into the thoroughly masculine room, he motioned toward the big leather armchair in front of his desk as he closed the door behind them. "Have a seat."

Lowering himself into the plush executive chair behind his big walnut desk, Ryder's smile gave her more hope than she'd had since making her request. "Before I agree, I think there are a few details that we need to discuss further."

"You're going to help me?" Her heart soared and unable to sit still she leaned forward. "Thank you, Ryder. You have no idea how much this means to me!"

He held up his hand as he shook his head. "I didn't say that, Summer. I said there would be things we would need to talk over before I agreed to anything."

"I thought I was pretty clear about my plans and your role in them." She had gone over everything so many times in her head, she couldn't think of anything she might have left out.

"You were very clear," he concurred. "But there are a few things that I would want in return for my donation to this cause of yours."

"What would that be?" she asked cautiously.

"You know all about my mother abandoning me when I was four years old and that I spent the rest of my childhood in the foster care system." When she nodded, he went on, "But I don't think I ever told you that I never knew who my father was." He shrugged. "For that matter, I doubt my mother did, either."

"What makes you think she didn't know your father?" Summer asked. "You were so little, maybe you just forgot her mentioning him."

"I don't think so." Shaking his head, Ryder sat back in his chair. "From what one of my caseworkers said just before I was sent to the Last Chance Ranch, my mother had been on their radar practically from the time I was born. Apparently at some point in their investigations, she had told the authorities she wasn't sure who had made her pregnant."

"I'm sorry, Ryder," she said softly. Having had a wonderful childhood with two loving parents, she couldn't imagine not having that security or the sense of identity that came with it. "But what does that have to do with you helping me?"

"I spent the first fourteen years of my life wondering who my father was and wishing that I had a dad to do things with like the other kids I went to school with. It wasn't until Hank Calvert became my foster father that I learned what it was like to have a real dad." He sat forward and placing his forearms on the desk, loosely clasped his hands in front of him. "If I agreed to father your child, I wouldn't want my kid going through that. I don't want him growing up wondering who's responsible for his existence and why his dad isn't around to take him places and do things with him."

"Are you telling me you want to be part of the baby's life?" She had been so busy assuring him that he wouldn't be obligated in any way that she hadn't considered Ryder might actually want the responsibility of helping her raise the child.

"Who knows? This might be the only kid I ever have," he answered. "But whether it is or not, I would want to be there for him or her like my biological father never was for me."

As Summer thought about what he said, she remembered the relationship she had with her father and how much it had meant to both of them. She had so many wonderful memories of things they had done together that she realized she wanted that for her child, as well.

"I would really like for you to be a part of the baby's life," she said, meaning it. She knew Ryder well enough to know that he would be a great father. "I just hadn't considered that you might want to be."

"Would you be agreeable to joint custody?" he asked, looking as if he thought his request might be a deal breaker.

"I haven't given it any thought," she answered truthfully. "But as long as we talk and agree on how to raise the baby, I don't think I would have a problem with it."

He raised one dark eyebrow. "You do realize that I would want equal time with him or her, don't you?"

"I'm sure we could work out something that we both find acceptable." They were best friends and got along quite well, so it shouldn't be that hard to arrange a suitable schedule. "Is that all?"

"No." He met her questioning gaze. "Where were you thinking about buying that house you mentioned?"

"I hadn't thought that far ahead, but I suppose I could buy a home anywhere," she said. With her parents gone and their property sold, there was no longer anything for her in California. "Why?"

Instead of answering her, he asked, "Would you be open to staying here at the ranch while you're pregnant and up until the baby is a year old, then finding a place close by?"

"I'm not sure that's a good idea, Ryder," she said, wondering how her simple request had suddenly become so complex. The longer they talked, the more complicated things became and the more concessions she was having to make.

"Actually, it's the perfect solution," he persisted. "If you stayed here at the ranch, I could experience the pregnancy with you, as well as go to your doctor appointments and whatever prenatal classes we need to take to get ready to become parents. Then once the baby is born, I could help out with its care during the first year. And when the time comes for you to find a house, being close by would make sharing custody a lot easier."

What he said made sense, but she wasn't ready to agree without giving it more thought. They might be best friends, but she wasn't sure she wanted to live with him for the better part of two years.

"Could I think about all of this for a little while?" she finally asked.

He smiled. "Sure. Take your time."

"Is there anything else?" Surely they had covered everything.

Ryder paused for a moment, then continued, "There's just one more thing…"

"I'm listening," she said, wondering what on earth there was left for him to ask of her before he agreed to help her.

"I don't think my making a donation in a cup is the route we should take for the conception." He shook his head. "I've got all the right equipment and trust me, darlin', everything is completely operational," he said, grinning. "Besides, I'd like to be able to tell our kid that we purposely got together because we both wanted him or her."

A knot started to form in the pit of her stomach. "Wh-what are you trying to say, Ryder?"

"If I'm going to help you, the conception would have to be natural."

"You mean, we would—"

"Make love," he finished for her.

"No!" Even she was startled by the vehemence in her one word answer. But there was absolutely no way she was going to bed with any man and especially not Ryder. He was her friend and she didn't want to lose their relationship.

"Then I guess the deal is off," he said, leaning back in his chair.

"Is there anything I can say to change your mind?"

she asked, knowing from his expression that it was unlikely she could convince him to see reason.

"No." He shook his head. "As far as I'm concerned, the means of conception is nonnegotiable."

She stood up to leave. "Then please forget that I asked for your help."

"I can't do that, darlin'." He shook his head as he rose to his feet. "That horse is already out of the barn and there's no way to get it back."

Staring at him a moment, Summer shook her head and hurried out of Ryder's office. As she marched up the stairs to the bedroom she had used since her arrival the night before, several emotions coursed through her. Naturally, she was disappointed. She wanted a baby and she wanted Ryder to father him or her. She was also a bit embarrassed that she'd had such a strong reaction to the idea of their having sex. He had no way of knowing that the very idea of having sex with any man came close to sending her into a panic attack. But more than that, she was angry.

As she'd stood in his office, staring at him as she tried to think of something to make him change his mind, it had occurred to her that she was the one having to make all of the concessions. It was true that most of what he had asked of her made sense. Given that he had never known his father, she could understand why he didn't want that for his child and even admired him for his willingness to be committed to being there for the baby.

But couldn't he at least consider her feelings on the matter? Why wasn't he willing to compromise on how the baby was conceived? Didn't he realize how far over the line that would be taking their friendship? Hadn't he considered that their relationship might not survive their being intimate?

A shiver ran through her and to her dismay it wasn't one of apprehension or panic. She frowned. Surely the unfamiliar sensation wasn't anticipation.

Shaking her head at the foolish thought, she grabbed her pajamas and headed into the bathroom for a quick shower. She needed to think of a way to get him to see reason. Unfortunately, all that kept running through her mind was the idea that Ryder was the only man she would even come close to considering making a baby with the old-fashioned way.

After Summer left his office like the hounds of hell chased her, Ryder sighed heavily and sank back down in his chair behind the desk as he thought about what had taken place. He had accomplished what he set out to do. He had successfully discouraged her from wanting him to father her child. So why didn't he feel good about it?

He hadn't wanted to crush her dream, but he honestly believed she wanted to have a child for the wrong reason. Having a baby simply because she wanted a connection with family again would be putting a lot of expectations on a kid that might prove hard for him or her to live up to.

Of course Summer would love the baby and the kid would love her. Ryder had no doubt about that. But he was of the opinion that a child should be wanted because of a desire to nurture and cherish it, not to be a remedy for loneliness.

But as much as her misguided reason for wanting a baby bothered him, something else bothered him more. What had caused her reaction when he mentioned conceiving a child the old-fashioned way?

Over the course of their friendship, he had seen her in several stressful situations and one of the many things he admired about Summer was her ability to remain calm and self-assured. She could handle a pressroom full of demanding reporters as easily as she applied her makeup. And last year, when one of the young bull riders had died from injuries sustained at one of the rodeos, she had immediately taken charge and somehow managed to keep the media satisfied without them hounding the family while they mourned the loss of their only son.

But he didn't think he had ever seen her thrown off balance the way she had been when he mentioned conceiving a baby by making love. Her confidence seemed to disappear before his eyes and a hesitancy that he would have never expected came over her.

Ryder scowled. Was the thought of making love with him that unpleasant? Or was she afraid of losing the comfortable friendship they had shared for the past several years?

Although he wasn't overly proud of himself for feeling the way he did, a small part of him had actually hoped she would agree to his terms. He had originally thought of his plan as a deterrent—a way to get her to give up on her idea that she wanted him to be her baby daddy. But just the thought of holding Summer's delightful body against his, of burying himself deep inside of her, caused the region south of his belt buckle to harden so fast it made him feel light-headed.

"McClain, you're one miserable son of a bitch," he muttered, rising from his chair and starting toward the office door.

Summer was his best friend, and for the life of him, he couldn't figure out what had changed between them over the past twenty-four hours that kept him in a state of semiarousal. He would like to blame his sudden unwarranted lust on her proposing the idea of him fathering her child. But he couldn't. Her hands on his biceps when they danced at the party had charged him up like the toy rabbit in one of those battery commercials—and that had been hours before she had asked him to help her become pregnant. And he had given up on blaming his brothers' teasing him about her as having any bearing on the situation at all. Hell, they had ribbed him countless times over the past several years about his relationship with her and not once had he started wondering what it would be like to sink himself so deep inside of her that he lost track of where he ended and she began.

His traitorous body tightened further and he made a beeline for the master bathroom and a cold shower. Maybe if he stood beneath the icy spray until he was colder than a penguin's tail feathers on an arctic ice floe, he would once again start thinking of Summer as his friend and stop thinking of her as the desirable woman who wanted him to help her make a baby.

Long after she heard Ryder walk past her room on his way to the master suite, Summer lay in bed staring at the ceiling. She couldn't stop thinking about what he said and how she had reacted to it.

She had been fine with almost all of his requirements. In fact, she decided that she liked the idea of sharing the responsibilities of raising their child with him. As protective as he was of those he cared for and as patient as she knew him to be, he would have been a great father. And she could understand him wanting her to live at the ranch with him during her pregnancy and for the baby's first year, too. He intended to be an involved father—going to doctor appointments and attending childbirth classes, as well as taking his turn at caring for the baby once it was born. She could even appreciate him wanting her to buy a home close to the ranch so that he could be with their child as often as possible. But his idea that they needed to conceive their child naturally was completely out of her comfort zone.

Shivering, she turned to her side and scrunching her eyes shut, she tried to block out the ugly memory behind her intimacy issues. She didn't like thinking about that night and the man who had violated her body and destroyed her trust in men. It gave him and the incident too much importance—too much power over her. Unfortunately, it had become a significant detail of her past and one that had shaped her future, as well as all of her future relationships with other men. At least all of them, that is, but her friendship with Ryder.

From the moment she met him, she had trusted Ryder. She wasn't sure why, but for some reason she had known he was everything he appeared to be—open, honest and respectful of women. The type of man her father had been. The type of man all men should be.

But as much as she wanted a baby, having sex with Ryder—a man she trusted more than any other—was something she just wasn't certain she could do. For one thing, she had avoided putting herself in a vulnerable situation with a man for so long that she wasn't sure she could do it again. And for another, up until the night she was raped, she had only been with one other man. That had been her freshman year in college, and although having sex with her boyfriend had been all right, their few times together certainly hadn't lived up to her expectations or sounded anything like the passionate encounters her roommate had talked about having with her boyfriend.

Turning to her back again, Summer opened her eyes to stare at the ceiling. She still wanted a child and it looked as if a sperm bank would be her only option. But did she really want to visit one in order to get the baby she wanted?

The thought still turned her off big-time. What if she couldn't find a donor that would be an acceptable substitute for Ryder? Or worse yet, what if she did and the guy lied about his medical history or his characteristics?

She knew there was a screening process that men went through before they were allowed to donate and that did give her some small amount of comfort. But the bottom line was—her baby would be fathered by a total stranger and that was something that made her extremely uneasy.

Upset by the idea of having to visit a sperm bank

and unable to sleep, Summer threw back the covers and got out of bed to walk over to the window seat. Sinking down onto the plush cushion, she drew her legs up to her chest and wrapped her arms around them as she stared out the window at the star-studded night sky. There was only one man she wanted to father her child and that was Ryder McClain.

Now that she knew that no other man would be an acceptable substitute, she had to decide if she could work up the courage to go through with his condition that the conception be natural. It would mean having sex with him, and even though it would only be for the purpose of becoming pregnant, she just wasn't sure she would be able to do it.

The thought caused an empty ache to begin to pool in her lower belly and she quickly stood up to pace the room. It had been so long since she experienced the sensation, she had almost forgotten what it felt like. But there was no mistaking it. Her mind might not be able to come to terms with his demand, but her body was more than ready.

Walking into the bathroom, she bent over the sink, turned on the cold water and splashed some on her face. Ryder was her friend, the only male she felt completely at ease spending time with. As she patted her face dry with a towel, she raised her eyes to meet the gaze of her image in the mirror. And although she wasn't the least bit comfortable with it, he was the only man who had made her feel the stirrings of desire in several years.

Four

The next morning as he brushed the shiny coat of his bay gelding, Ryder couldn't help but wonder if he had done irreparable damage to his friendship with Summer. He hoped with all his heart that wasn't the case.

When he suggested they make love in order for her to conceive, he had only meant to discourage her, not have her running for the hills. But he hadn't seen her since their conversation in his study yesterday evening and she hadn't even bothered coming downstairs for breakfast this morning. But for the life of him, he couldn't think of any other explanation for her absence.

He hadn't expected her to accept his terms and thanks to the ice-cold shower he had taken, his perspective had been restored. Although he realized her refusal had been for the best, he hadn't counted on his demands alienating her. The fact that she was avoiding him was testament to the fact that they probably had and it bothered him. A lot.

"Betty Lou said I'd probably find you here," Summer said, surprising him when she walked into the barn.

"I wasn't entirely sure you would ever talk to me again after our discussion last night," he said honestly. "You didn't join me for breakfast and I figured you were still pretty upset with me over our talk."

He continued brushing the bay to keep from giving in to the overwhelming urge to take her into his arms. That made no sense at all and he couldn't figure out why the feeling was so strong. Theirs had never been that kind of friendship.

She shook her head. "I'm not upset, but you did give me a lot to think about and I had a hard time going to sleep."

"So you overslept this morning?" he asked, relieved she wasn't mad at him, but wondering where the conversation was going.

Nodding, a frown wrinkled her forehead. "I haven't slept that late in years."

"You probably needed the rest." He unsnapped the lead rope he had used to tie his horse to the grooming post and taking hold of the halter, walked the bay gelding back into the stall. Closing the half door, he added, "I've seen you work some pretty crazy hours lately." A slight breeze blew a strand of her blond hair across her cheek and it took monumental effort on his part not to reach out and brush it aside.

"If you aren't too busy, do you mind if we talk a bit

more about last night?" she asked, sounding a little unsure.

His heart slammed against his ribs and the back of his neck tingled with apprehension. What could she want to talk about that they hadn't covered last night? And why did he suddenly want to wrap his arms around her and kiss away the uncertain expression on her pretty face?

Instead, he swallowed around the cotton coating his throat and nodded. "Sure. Would you like to go back up to the house or do you want to talk here?" When she looked around as if checking to see if they were alone, he added, "Don't worry. There's no one around to overhear what we say. My foreman took the men out to check the fences in the far pastures to make sure they're ready for winter."

"Here will be fine," she said as she walked over to sit down on a bale of straw.

He was happy that she was at least still speaking to him, but mystified about what she thought they needed to discuss further. As far as he was concerned, his stipulations had been quite clear and set in stone. She wasn't going to convince him to change his mind.

"What do you think we need to discuss?" he asked, crossing his arms and leaning back against the bay's stall across the wide barn aisle from her.

She took a deep breath. "I spent the majority of last night lying awake, thinking about your requirements and your reasoning behind them."

"And?"

"I agree with most of them." She picked up a piece

of straw and staring down at it began to shred it with her fingers. "I like the idea of the baby having two parents who will love and be there for it. And I also think it would be nice to have you go with me to doctor appointments and help with the baby's care once it's born."

He wondered when she was going to stop beating around the bush and get to the sticking point—the part about them making love in order for her to conceive. He didn't have long to wait.

"The only problem I had with your requests was the part about us having sex to make me pregnant," she said, her voice almost a whisper.

"I understand your refusal and I'm not in the least bit offended, darlin'," he answered. "You don't want to risk our friendship and I'm fine with that. I don't want to lose it either."

His breath lodged in his lungs when she shook her head. "That isn't what I was about to tell you."

Clearing his suddenly rusty throat, he asked, "What were you going to say?"

"I've thought a lot about it…and I believe our friendship is solid enough to withstand our having sexual intercourse for the purpose of conceiving a child."

It was the last thing he'd expected her to say, and he wasn't at all comfortable with his body's reaction at her mention of them making love. Just the thought sent a shaft of longing coursing through him at the speed of light and caused his body to tighten predictably. Removing his hat, he lowered it in front of him with one hand as he ran his other hand through his hair in an effort to hide his reaction to what she had just said.

Hell's bells! He thought he had a handle on things and the matter had been settled. Last night, he'd told her what he wanted in return for helping her get pregnant and she had found his demands unacceptable. That should have been the end of it. When had he lost control of the situation? And what the hell was he going to do about it now?

"You want a baby so much that you're willing to take that step?" he asked, still unable to believe what she had told him. "You're willing to make love with me until you become pregnant?"

She closed her eyes a moment, then nodding, she met his gaze head-on. "Yes. I'm willing to do whatever I have to do in order to have the baby I want."

"Okay," he said slowly. "Can I ask why you changed your mind?"

There was no hesitation when she nodded. "You have all the traits and characteristics—"

"Yeah, I'm the prize stud," he interrupted. "I got that before. What I want to know is what happened to change your mind between last night and now?"

"I realized that you're the only man I want to father my baby." She shrugged one slender shoulder. "You're my best friend and I·know you well enough to safely say that you'll be there for the baby no matter what. You'll love the child as much as I will and protect him or her from all harm."

He couldn't argue with her assessment of how he would feel about a kid. There wasn't a doubt in his mind that he would willingly lay down his life if that's what it took to keep it safe. For that matter, he would do the same for Summer.

"And you're completely comfortable with all this?" he asked, feeling like he might be lost somewhere in a parallel universe.

"Yes."

Ryder nodded as he stared off into space. Now what was he supposed to do? His plan had been to discourage her and it had been successful—last night. But now that Summer had changed her mind, he was trapped. He had given her his word that he would help her if she agreed to his terms and short of going back on it, he didn't see any other option but to honor his end of the bargain.

"I guess now all there is left to do is decide when you want to start trying to become pregnant," he finally said, clenching his fist into a tight ball in an effort to control his rapidly hardening body. Unfortunately, it wasn't working.

Squaring her shoulders, she rose to her feet. "I've given that some thought as well and I'd like to get started as soon as possible." Her cheeks colored a pretty pink. "We could start trying sometime today if that's all right with you."

It was all he could do not to groan aloud. A beautiful woman was standing in front of him, telling him that she wanted him to make love to her, and he was going to turn her down? His nobility only went so far and he was man enough to admit that he had reached the end of his.

"Sure," he said thickly as he pushed away from the bay's stall. Just the thought that they were going to make love sent a wave of heat straight to his groin, and he was glad she was too distracted to notice he was still holding his hat in front of jeans that were becoming way too snug at the fly. "I have some chores I have to take care of today, but this evening will be fine."

She nodded as she started to leave. "Now that things are settled, I'll go see if Betty Lou needs help with lunch." Stopping suddenly, she turned back. "By the way, do you wear boxers or briefs?"

"Boxer briefs." He frowned. "Why?"

"I'm not sure about those," she said, nibbling on her lower lip. "Until we're successful, you might want to start wearing boxers."

"Why?" Ryder knew he sounded like a damned parrot, but he couldn't figure out why she was so fixated on the type of underwear he preferred.

"Boxer shorts are less confining and enable more sperm production," she explained.

He laughed, releasing some of the tension that gripped him. "Don't worry about me, darlin'. Everything is in working order and since I sleep in the buff, I have no reason to believe that I won't have more than enough swimmers to get the job done."

"All right," she said as she turned to leave. "I'll trust that detail to you."

When she walked out of the barn, his smile faded and the reality of the situation set in. He and Summer were going to cross a line in their friendship and make love to have a baby. Un-freaking-believable!

If someone had told him three days ago that he would be consciously planning to make any woman pregnant, he would have laughed them right into the next county. But if they had told him that woman would be Summer Patterson, he would have readily told them that they were a few beers shy of a six-pack in the brains department.

A sudden thought had him cussing a blue streak as he jammed his hat back on his head. What were his brothers going to say when they found out about his arrangement with Summer?

He had no doubt that he would have their full support in whatever he did. But it would come with a pretty hefty price tag. Ryder knew as surely as the sun rose in the east each morning that he would have to endure endless ribbing and enough *I told you so's* to last a lifetime.

Picking up the brush he had used on the bay, he headed down the aisle toward the stalls at the end of the barn. His brothers' comments and jokes were just something he would have to cowboy up and deal with. As Hank always told him and his brothers, a man is only as good as his word and it should be as binding as any written contract.

Ryder tied the buckskin mare to the side of the stall and began brushing her dark golden coat. He felt like he was about to jump off a cliff into an unknown abyss, but he had made a promise to Summer and he would climb a barbed-wire fence buck naked before he reneged on it now.

After dinner, Summer helped Betty Lou clean up the kitchen, then slowly walked down the hall to join Ryder in the family room. She was as jittery as she could ever remember being, but she was determined to carry through with her plan. It meant too much to her to let anything stand in her way of having the family she wanted.

"Would you like to see a movie before we head upstairs to bed?" he asked, looking up from the show he had been watching when she entered the room. "There's a comedy you might like on one of the movie channels."

"I…um, no, I don't think so," she said, shaking her head. She'd had the entire day to think about what they were going to do and delaying it further would only increase her anxiety and could very well cause her to lose her nerve. She looked over her shoulder toward the kitchen to make sure Betty Lou had gone to her room. "If you don't mind, I'd just as soon go ahead and get started on our…little project."

He gave a short nod, then picking up the remote control, turned off the television and rose to his feet. "I went ahead and turned down the bed," he said, walking over to her. He paused for a moment before he reached up to touch her cheek with his forefinger. "Darlin', are you 100 percent sure this is what you really want to do?"

"Yes," she said as she fixed her attention on one of the snap closures on his chambray shirt. "Why do you ask?"

"Because you look like you're about to face a firing squad instead of going upstairs to make love with me," he said, frowning. He used his index finger to lift her chin until their gazes met. "You know it's okay if you've changed your mind. I'll understand and we'll go along like nothing ever happened."

The sincerity in his dark green eyes indicated that he really meant every word he said.

"No, I haven't changed my mind," she said decisively. "I just want to get this part over with so I can concentrate on looking forward to when the baby arrives."

His frown deepened as he placed his hand to her back and they walked over to the stairs. "You make it sound like you think making love with me is going to be about as pleasant as getting a tooth pulled."

"Not at all," she lied. "I'm just a little nervous. That's all." That was an understatement, she thought when they reached the top of the stairs and started down the hall. He might stir long dormant desires, but the thought of being intimate with any man was still extremely intimidating.

When she stopped to open the door to the bedroom she had been using, he shook his head. "I think it would be better if we go to my room."

A chilling trepidation streaked up her spine. "Why?"

He smiled encouragingly. "Betty Lou's room downstairs is on this side of the house, and I thought that you might not be overly comfortable with that."

"You're probably right," she said, forcing herself to continue on to the master suite at the end of the hall.

When they entered his bedroom and he turned on a lamp, she tried not to focus on the king-size bed and looked around at the Western decor. A blend of Native American artwork and Western wildlife prints graced the sage-colored walls, while colorful Navajo rugs brightened up the dark hardwood floor. The room was beautiful and perfect for Ryder. He was a Texas cowboy from the top of his dark brown hair to the soles of his big, booted feet and the room reflected that.

"Relax," he said, turning to face her. He reached out and put his arms loosely around her waist. "Just because we're doing this to make a baby doesn't mean it can't be fun, too."

This is Ryder. He's your friend. You can do this.

"I'm not sure about that," she said before she could stop herself. She wasn't certain if she was responding to his statement or answering herself.

"Don't worry," he said with a confident smile. "I'll make sure our lovemaking is enjoyable for both of us."

When Ryder lowered his head to lightly graze her lips with his, a jolt of awareness stronger than anything she had ever experienced instantly coursed through her. She told herself to take a step back, but when his mouth settled over hers to taste and tease, a delicious warmth began to pool in the pit of her stomach.

Lost in all the wonderful sensations swirling through her and unable to comprehend why she was experiencing them, it took a moment for her to realize that he had moved his hand to cover her breast. "Wh-what are you doing?" she asked, breaking the kiss.

"It's called foreplay, Summer." He kissed his way along her jaw to the side of her neck, then whispered in her ear, "Everything will be a lot easier and there's a better chance of success if we're both relaxed and ready to make love."

His warm breath feathering over her ear sent another wave of tingling heat crashing through her and caused her knees to wobble. "I hadn't thought it would be necessary," she said, wondering how she could feel excitement and apprehension at the same time.

Leaning back to look down at her, his dark green eyes held hers. "Are you a virgin, Summer?"

It was the last thing she expected him to ask. "No. Why?"

"Because I've never seen you this nervous," he said, pulling her to his wide chest. "How long has it been since you've been with a man?"

"I don't think that's relevant," she said, curious why her sexual experience, or lack thereof, mattered. "But if you have to know, I've only had sex a few times and that was my freshman year in college."

He nodded. "That explains why you're so tense. I'm betting the poor kid didn't have a clue what he was doing any more than you did. It wasn't all that good for you, was it?"

"No."

She decided to go along with his assumption. It was easier than admitting that her stress stemmed from the reprehensible act by one of the worst examples of his gender.

"I promise that it will be different for you this time," he said, bringing his hand up to thread his fingers through her hair. "I give you my word that I'll ensure your pleasure before I find my own."

Her heart beat double time. "D-don't worry about me. It's not necessary for me to—"

He shook his head as he started to tug the tail of her T-shirt from the waistband of her jeans. "I'm not a selfish man, Summer. Part of my satisfaction will be knowing that I've helped you find yours."

She closed her eyes. *You can do this. Just focus on your goal and you can do this.*

But when Ryder moved to lift the hem of her shirt to take it off her, she felt the hard evidence straining at his jeans and her nerves got the better of her. "I—I...can't," she said, beginning to tremble as she pushed away from him. "I can't do this. I thought I could...because I really want a baby. But I was wrong. I'm sorry. I just can't."

"Whoa! Slow down, darlin'," he said, releasing her shirt to place his hands on her shoulders. He stared at her for several long seconds. "Calm down and tell me what's wrong."

She tried to blink back a wave of tears as she stared into his concerned eyes. "I...just can't. I...want to. But I...can't."

Leading her over to the bed, he sat down and pulled her onto his lap. Cradling her to him as if she were a child, he held her close. "Talk to me, Summer. Tell me what's going on."

"I want a baby...but I just can't...do this, Ryder," she sobbed against his shoulder.

"It's okay, darlin'," he said, his tone gentle. "I give you my word nothing is going to happen that you don't want happening. Now, tell me what caused you to be so afraid."

"I was... I mean, I told him no," she stammered. "But he wouldn't stop."

She felt Ryder's body go completely still a moment

before he spoke in a voice so deadly quiet that it caused a cold chill to travel the length of her. "You were raped."

Unable to answer, she nodded.

"Was it your first experience?" he asked in the same cold tone.

"N-no. It was someone else." She took a shuddering breath. "I told him no, but we…were on a date. I'm not sure—"

"It doesn't matter if you were on a date or not," Ryder ground out, shaking his head. "No means no. If a man ignores that, then it's rape." His arms tightened around her. "When did it happen, darlin'?"

She hadn't talked about it with anyone. Not when the incident happened and not since. But apparently having suppressed it for so long, once she started talking about it, she couldn't seem to stop herself.

"It was at the end of my sophomore year in college. We were in a communication class together and he seemed nice enough. When he asked me out, I accepted." She shivered uncontrollably. "He turned out to be the worst mistake I've ever made."

"That's why you don't date and why you aren't interested in getting married, isn't it?" he asked, continuing to hold her protectively against him. "You're afraid of being intimate with a man."

"I've tried to get past my issues, but I'm not comfortable being alone with men," she said, swallowing hard. "I don't trust them."

"I'm a man and you've never had a problem being alone with me," he said, gently running his hand up and down her arm in a soothing manner.

"You're different," she said without hesitation.

He leaned back to look at her and she could tell his mock frown was meant to lighten the mood and make her feel a little better. "What do you think I am, darlin', a sexless old gelding?"

"No." For the first time since she'd agreed to his requirements, she smiled. "But you're my friend. I trust you."

His expression became serious. "And I promise that I'll never betray that trust, Summer."

Staring at each other for several long seconds, she finally said, "I still want a baby."

He nodded. "I figured you would."

"Where do we go from here? Will you still help me?" she asked, praying that he would.

"We'll talk more about this in the morning," he said evasively. "I just remembered that I promised my foreman the night off and I forgot to feed the horses."

"Do you need help?" she asked, disheartened that he had avoided answering her question.

"No." After setting her on her feet, he rose from the side of the bed, took her hand in his and led her out of the master suite. Then he walked her down to the room she had been using. "Sleep well, darlin'," he said, brushing her lips with his. "I'll see you in the morning."

Anger stronger than he had experienced in almost twenty years coursed through Ryder as he descended the stairs, grabbed a couple of cold beers from the refrigerator as he passed through the kitchen and stormed out of the house. He had done his best not to let Summer see the effect her telling him about the sexual assault had on him. For one thing, he didn't want to frighten her. And for another, the degree of fury that he felt toward the unnamed man had scared the living daylights out of him.

Entering the barn, he sat down on a bale of straw by the tack room and, popping the top on one of the cans, downed the contents. He knew the incident had taken place a couple of years before he and Summer had even met, but that didn't keep him from wanting to find the sorry son of a bitch and teach him a lesson he would never forget.

Ryder shook his head as he crushed the empty can, then tossing it aside, pulled the tab on the second can to take another swig of cold beer. Real men never took what a woman wasn't ready and willing to give. Period. When a woman told a man no, then he headed for a shower cold enough to cause frostbite, jogged until his shoes fell apart or bench-pressed a bulldozer if he had to in order to work off the adrenaline. And as far as Ryder was concerned, there were no excuses for doing anything else.

Feeling a little more in control, he leaned back against the barn wall. He hadn't liked lying to Summer about needing to feed the horses, but it couldn't be helped. He had needed the time and space to calm down and regain his equilibrium.

He couldn't help but remember another time when he had been filled with the same degree of anger and the consequences that he'd had to suffer through because of it. He had just turned fourteen and had been sent to live with a foster couple in Fort Worth. His foster mother had been real nice, but his foster dad had been a real piece of work. A functioning alcoholic, Pete Ledbetter held a job and to the outward eye everything was fine. But it hadn't taken Ryder long to realize that things weren't always as they seemed.

Pete usually stayed stone-cold sober during the day, but as soon as he got off work he started drinking and didn't stop until he passed out. Then he would sleep it off overnight, get up the next morning and the cycle would start all over again. But there were times before he passed out that Pete would turn into a mean drunk and made life a living hell around the Ledbetter home. Usually his wrath was directed at his wife and he left Ryder alone. Probably because even at the age of fourteen, Ryder was taller and more muscular than he was.

But the cycle was broken for good one fateful evening when Ryder came home after football practice and found Ellen Ledbetter sitting at the kitchen table nursing a black eye and a busted lip. She had told him that Pete was in a particularly nasty mood and that Ryder should make himself scarce until his foster father drank himself into oblivion.

Maybe his life would have turned out differently if he had listened to Ellen. But even at that young age, he had felt the need to protect those who were unable to defend themselves and when Pete walked in to take another swing at his wife, Ryder had stepped between them. The next thing he knew, Pete Ledbetter lay dead in a pool of blood on the kitchen floor, and Ryder was being handcuffed and hauled off to a juvenile detention center.

He took a deep breath and finished his beer. He had eventually been cleared of the involuntary manslaughter charge and sent to the Last Chance Ranch, but the incident had changed his life forever. From that moment forward, he had never raised his fists in anger at any time, for any reason.

He'd had no trouble keeping that promise to himself. Hell, he hadn't even been tempted to go back on it. At least, not until Summer told him about the man who raped her. Ryder knew beyond a shadow of doubt that if he could have gotten hold of the bastard, he would have torn him apart with his bare hands. And that bothered him.

But what scared him more was Summer finding out that he wasn't the person she thought him to be. How would she react if she discovered that the man she trusted above all others had caused another man's death?

Just the thought of watching the revulsion cloud her pretty blue eyes caused a knot the size of his fist to twist his gut. That's why he never intended for her to know about the incident. He couldn't stand the thought of losing her. And he had no doubt that's exactly what would happen if she learned the truth about him.

Five

When Summer finished helping Betty Lou make sand-wiches for a picnic lunch, she walked down the hall to Ryder's study. He had been busy making a list of things he wanted his foreman to take care of over the next week while he was working the rodeo with her up in Oklahoma. They hadn't had the opportunity to dis-cuss what had happened last night, but after telling him about the assault she'd done a lot of thinking and had a few things she wanted to talk over with him before they left the Blue Canyon Ranch.

The study door was open and, knocking on the door frame, she stepped into the room. "Ryder, I just finished helping Betty Lou make lunch for us. Do you have time to ride down to the canyon for another picnic?"

When he looked up and smiled, she caught her

breath. He was without a doubt one of the best-looking men she'd ever seen.

"That sounds like a great idea," he said, rising to his feet. He picked up a paper from the desk and walked over to her. "I need to drop this repair list off with my foreman anyway and while I'm down at the barn I'll saddle the horses." His expression turned serious. "I didn't want to ask this morning in front of Betty Lou, but are you feeling better?"

His concern touched her. "I'm fine," she said. "It seems that finally telling someone about what happened was a bit cathartic for me."

He frowned. "You hadn't told anyone? Why didn't you report the assault to the authorities?"

"Besides just wanting to forget that night ever happened, I wasn't sure they would believe me since I was on a date with him," she said, shaking her head.

Wrapping his strong arms around her, Ryder pulled her to his wide chest for a comforting hug. "That's a lot to have to carry by yourself for all these years. You should have told someone, darlin'."

"I guess I was…ashamed that I had been so naive," she said, hugging him back.

When he released her, he shook his head. "You didn't do anything to be ashamed of, Summer. It wasn't your fault and I don't want you thinking that is was."

Shrugging, she fell into step with him as they walked down the hall to the kitchen. "I suppose you're right."

"I know I am," he said vehemently. "Now, while I'm getting the horses ready, you pack the saddlebags and I'll meet you down at the barn."

An hour later as they dismounted the horses beside the lazy little creek on the canyon floor, Summer felt as if she had turned a corner in her life. She only hoped that Ryder would support her decision and still agree to help her.

"This seemed like a nice place the last time," he said, spreading the blanket in the same spot they had picnicked a couple of days before.

"I love that the trees are just beginning to change colors," she murmured, looking around at a few golden leaves on the cottonwood trees. "I think autumn is the prettiest time of year."

"We'll have to come back in a couple of weeks," he said as he lowered himself onto the blanket. "Just about every tree in this canyon will be a bright gold."

"I'll look forward to it." She couldn't help but feel heartened by the fact that he was making plans for them to come back together in the future. "I'm sure it will be beautiful."

While they ate, they exchanged small talk about the upcoming rodeo they would both be working and some of the plans Ryder had for the ranch. Summer enjoyed hearing about the projects he wanted to undertake, but couldn't seem to get her mind off what she needed to discuss with him.

Deciding that there was no easy way to start the conversation, she took a deep breath. "Last night after you left the house to feed the horses, I did a lot of soul-searching," she admitted as she gathered the remnants of their lunch. "And I still want a baby."

He planted his feet at the edge of the blanket and

rested his arms on his bent knees. "That's what you said last night."

"Are you still willing to father my child?" she asked, mentally holding her breath as she awaited his answer.

"I gave you my word and that hasn't changed," he said. "But I won't hold you to our having to make love for you to become pregnant. If you'll make the appointment with your doctor, I'll go get cozy with a specimen cup." She could tell it wasn't in the least bit appealing to him, but he was willing to do it in order to keep her from feeling uncomfortable, as well as honor his commitment to her.

She nibbled on her lower lip a moment before finding the nerve to tell him what she had decided the night before. "Actually, that isn't what I want you to do."

One dark eyebrow rose in question as he slowly turned his head to stare at her. "What are you saying?"

"I'm tired of being afraid, Ryder," she said, knowing it was true. "I'm not sure how this is going to sound, but I want to be a whole woman again. If you're willing, I'd like for you to help me get over my fear of intimacy." She could tell from the look on his face that he was thoroughly shocked by her proclamation. "I think that can be accomplished if we have sex in order to conceive."

"Darlin', I can understand you wanting to go through with having a baby," he said quietly. "And I get that you don't want to be afraid anymore. But are you really sure about this?"

"Yes."

He remained silent for several long moments before he spoke again. "You do realize that it's probably going to take more than one lovemaking session for you to become pregnant?"

She nodded. "I'm aware of that, but I started thinking about something you said when you first agreed to help me…and I realize artificial insemination isn't what I want."

"I say a lot of things, but that doesn't mean I'm always right," he admitted.

"But in this case, you were," she insisted. "You told me that you would like to be able to tell our child that we purposely came together because we wanted him or her, not because a doctor intervened with a clinical procedure." She smiled. "I think it will mean more to our child when he or she is old enough to understand."

He hesitated for a moment before he asked, "Do you still want to get started right away?"

She didn't have to think about her answer. "Yes."

"Then I think instead of you staying in a hotel room, from now on you should stay with me in my camper," he said, meeting her startled gaze. Ryder was one of the many cowboys and rodeo personnel who preferred to travel with their own accommodations, rather than rent a hotel room.

"There's only one drawback to that," she countered. "Everyone will think that we've taken our friendship to the next level."

It took her by surprise when he laughed out loud. "What the hell do you think they'll say when they find out we're having a baby together?"

"I really hadn't thought much about that," she admitted.

"You know how close rodeo people are," he said pointedly. "Word will get around. It's not something we can hide, nor do I intend to try. When your pregnancy starts to show, I'm going to proudly tell people that I'm the daddy, not make it seem like it's an accident from our sneaking around."

What he said made sense. But she had avoided rumors of anything going on between them for so long that old habits were hard to break.

"All right," she said, realizing he was probably right. She didn't want people to think their child was the mistake of a clandestine affair, either. "I guess that settles everything."

Ryder surprised her when he shook his head. "Nope. There's one more thing that we haven't covered."

"What would that be?" For the life of her, she couldn't imagine what there was left to be decided after their countless conversations on the subject.

"We're going to start acting like we're a couple," he stated.

"You mean as if we've fallen in love?" Things just kept getting more and more complicated by the moment.

"It's easier to go with that, than it is to try and explain everything." He leaned over and briefly pressed his lips to hers. "Besides, that's what people are going to think anyway. We might as well go along with it."

"Does that mean we'll be openly affectionate toward each other?" she asked, liking the way his kiss made her tingle all over.

"Yup. That's what people do when they're...involved."

She furrowed her brow. "Do you think we can be convincing?"

"Let's see," he said, lowering his head.

He kissed her again, but this time it wasn't a chaste brushing of the lips between two friends. This time it was the kiss of a man asking a woman to trust him, asking her to let him show her that intimacy didn't have to be feared.

Closing her eyes, Summer forced herself to relax and experience his gentle caress. She knew without question that if she asked him to stop, he would do so in a heartbeat. But that wasn't what she wanted. She wasn't entirely certain why, but for the first time in years, she needed to feel like a real woman again, instead of the frightened female she had become after the assault.

Ryder teased her with his tongue until she parted her lips on a sigh, then slipping inside, he gently explored her tender inner recesses. She didn't even try to stop herself from melting against him. She had avoided men for so long that she had forgotten how nice it was to feel safe in a man's arms, to feel cherished.

"I don't think we'll have any problems convincing anyone that we've taken our friendship to the next level," he said, easing away from the kiss.

"There isn't anyone around right now for us to impress," she said breathlessly. "Why—"

"I thought we could use the practice." His wide grin sent a wave of goose bumps shimmering over her skin. "Besides, I decided you needed to be reminded that kissing is just plain fun."

He rose to his feet, then held his hand out to help her

to hers. Summer didn't even think to hesitate before she placed her hand, as well as her complete trust, in his. They had crossed a line in their friendship, and there was no going back now. The only thing left to do was move forward and see where this latest twist in their relationship took them.

When he and Summer rode the horses back into the ranch yard, Ryder groaned inwardly at the sight of his brother's truck parked beside his own. What was Lane doing here?

"It looks like one of my brother's is going to be the first one to learn about the new development in our friendship," he said as they dismounted and led the horses into the barn.

"Do you think he'll be convinced?" she asked, unsaddling the buckskin mare.

Ryder laughed, releasing some of the tension building across his shoulders. "The other night at Sam and Bria's party, I couldn't convince any of my brothers otherwise. So, no. I don't think we'll have a problem getting him to believe there's something more going on between us." As an afterthought, he added, "But it wouldn't hurt to test-drive our show of affection toward each other."

"In other words, you don't want me freaking out when you put your arm around me?" she asked.

"Or when I kiss you in front of him," he said, nodding.

Summer looked thoughtful for a moment. "That's

why you were irritated with your brothers at the party, wasn't it? They were speculating on our relationship."

"Yup." He led the horses back into their stalls, then draping his arm across her shoulders, started walking them toward the house. "And you can bet by supper tonight, Lane will have reported back to every one of them and let them know that their speculations were right on the money."

She grinned. "Wouldn't you do the same if you discovered something about one of them?"

He laughed as they climbed the steps to the back porch. "Darlin', I wouldn't be able to dial the phone fast enough."

When they entered the kitchen, Lane was seated at the table having a cup of coffee with Betty Lou. "Hey you two, I was beginning to think I was going to miss seeing you," he said, rising to his feet. Nodding at Summer, he added, "It's nice seeing you again, Ms. Patterson."

"Please, call me Summer. And it's nice seeing you again, too, Lane." She smiled at Ryder. "While you visit with your brother, I think I'm going upstairs to take advantage of the Jacuzzi before I help Betty Lou with dinner."

Ryder pulled her to him and covered her mouth with his. He told himself the kiss was for his brother's benefit, but as Summer's lips clung to his, he knew that was a bald-faced lie. The kiss they had shared under the cottonwood tree had left him aching to kiss her again and he couldn't resist seizing the opportunity now.

"I'll see you in a little while, darlin'," he said against her soft lips.

As Summer left the room, he turned back to Lane and almost laughed out loud. For a professional poker player who prided himself on his ability not to show any emotion, Lane was failing miserably. He looked like he had just been treated to the business end of an electric cattle prod. For that matter, so did Betty Lou.

"What?" Ryder asked, feigning ignorance.

The first to recover, his housekeeper got up from the table and walking up to him, patted his cheek. "I'm glad to see you finally woke up," she said, grinning from ear to ear. "You and that little girl are gonna make a real fine couple. The way you always talked about her whenever you came home from a rodeo, I knew it was just a matter of time before you realized there was more going on between the two of you than just being good friends."

When Betty Lou walked on past him to enter the pantry, Ryder turned to see his brother grinning at him like a damned fool. "What's up, bro?" he asked, already knowing he was about to face an inquisition.

"Why don't we grab a couple of beers and go into your office for that visit?" Lane asked, pointing toward the hall. "You can tell me once again that you and Summer are just good friends and I can tell you that you're full of bullroar and buffalo chips."

"I can already tell you're going to be a jerk about this, aren't you?" Ryder groused as he got them both a cold beer and they headed toward his office.

"Oh yeah. But you wouldn't expect anything less from me," Lane shot back. He lowered his lanky frame into the armchair in front of Ryder's desk. "If you had the chance, you'd do the same thing to me or any of the other guys."

Grinning, Ryder nodded. "You bet your sweet ass I would."

Lane took a swallow from his beer bottle. "So what's the story with you and Summer?" He gave Ryder a knowing look. "Since Betty Lou was just as surprised as I was, I take it that you two just started dating?"

Ryder propped his booted feet on the edge of the desk, then crossing his legs at the ankles, leaned back in his desk chair. "We just started thinking of each other as more than friends in the past couple of days." Frowning, he added, "Apparently you guys saw something that night at the party that I didn't because we didn't start talking about taking things up a notch until we were on the way back here."

His brother nodded. "I watched her watching you and I could tell friendship was the last thing on her mind."

"Okay," Ryder said, holding up both hands in surrender. He wasn't about to tell Lane that she'd had something on her mind all right. She had been sizing him up as a prize stud, instead of the romantic encounter his brothers all thought. "I was wrong and you all were right. Does that make you happy?"

"You have no idea how much," Lane answered glibly. "The next time Bria has a family dinner for all of us, you can expect to be the one in the hot seat."

"When you leave here, you won't even make it to the main road before you tell the rest of the guys about this, will you?" Ryder asked, knowing it was already as good as a done deal.

Lane laughed out loud as he shook his head. "You know good and well that finding out something like this has got to be shared. And the sooner, the better."

Ryder knew that if he asked Lane not to tell their brothers, he would keep the confidence. Being a licensed psychologist, Lane knew how to listen and keep his mouth shut. But as much as he dreaded the ribbing he would take from his brothers, Ryder realized it was the best way to get the word out that he and Summer had taken their friendship to the next level and would set the stage for her becoming pregnant.

"Enough about me, what are you up to?" Ryder asked, realizing it was time to change the subject.

"After you two left the party the other night, Bria decided that we all needed to take some cake home with us and I volunteered to bring yours by on my way to Shreveport," Lane replied, checking his gold Rolex. "And that reminds me, I need to get on the road so I can get to the casino and get checked in."

"Are you playing in another big tournament this week?" Ryder asked.

"Not this time." Frowning, Lane set his half-empty beer bottle on the desk. "It's the damnedest thing. Last week, I got a written invitation to a private game with Ben Cunningham."

Ryder recognized the name of one of the most famous players in the world of professional poker. "I thought Cunningham retired."

"So did I." Lane rose to his feet. "But I'm not going

to turn down the chance to play a game with arguably the best player in the history of poker."

"I don't blame you," Ryder said, following his brother down the hall to the kitchen. "It's not every day you're invited to play with a legend. Good luck."

"Thanks, but you know I don't rely on Lady Luck. She's too fickle. I'd much rather use my skills. At least that way I have a fighting chance of winning." Turning to Betty Lou standing at the counter cutting up vegetables, Lane touched the wide brim of his black Resistol. "Betty Lou, you take care and if you have any problems with this big lug, just give me a call. I'll line him out in short order."

"You and whose army?" Ryder laughed, following Lane out to the porch.

"You're working a rodeo at one of the county fairs up in Oklahoma this weekend, aren't you?" Lane asked, his easy expression turning serious.

Ryder nodded. "Why?"

"Nate and Jaron are planning on competing in the bull and bareback riding events. You might want to keep an eye on Nate," he said, starting down the steps. "He's not quite up to par these days."

"What's up with him?" Of all his brothers, Nate was the last one to take life too seriously and Ryder couldn't imagine anything bringing him down for very long.

"That little nurse he's been seeing down in Waco broke things off with him the day after the party and he's not taking it very well," Lane explained.

"Wounded pride?" Ryder asked, a little surprised by the news. To his knowledge, it was the first time that

Nate had been dumped. Normally, he was the one initiating a breakup when things looked like they might be getting too serious.

"I'm not so sure," Lane answered. "There was something about the way Nate looked when he talked about her that led me to believe he had started feeling more for her than he had any other woman."

"I'll be sure to keep an extra close eye on him," Ryder promised as Lane walked to his truck.

Watching his brother's truck disappear down the driveway as Lane headed toward the main road, Ryder felt his protective instincts come to full alert and made a mental vow to be extra vigilant during the bull riding event. Being around the rough stock while nursing a broken heart wasn't a good mix. They had all learned that firsthand a few months back when Sam had been run down by one of the meanest bulls his rodeo stock contracting company had to offer. The accident had ultimately led to his brother and Bria working out their marital problems, but Ryder would just as soon not see another one of his brothers sustain a life-threatening injury as a result of a romantic breakup.

"I'm getting too old for this," he muttered as he turned to go back inside the house.

But as long as he had breath in his body, he knew he would do whatever it took to keep his family safe from harm. And that included Summer and their as-yet-to-be-conceived child.

Summer had just finished packing her luggage for the trip with Ryder when the sound of him bellowing like an outraged bull came from somewhere downstairs. As she rushed out into the hall the sound of glass breaking, accompanied by his guttural curse, sent her running to see what had happened. Her heart thumped inside her chest as fear began to course through her veins. What on earth could have happened? Was he hurt?

"Will somebody get this damned cat off me?" Ryder shouted when she found him at the bottom of the staircase.

He was twisting around like a whirling dervish as he tried to reach behind him where Lucifer clung to the middle of his back. The cat screeched and hissed almost as loudly as the rapid-fire curse words Ryder continued to spew out.

"Hold still," Betty Lou commanded, hurrying in from the kitchen. Stepping around the shards of a shattered vase that Ryder and Lucifer had knocked off a console table, she carefully tried to disentangle the cat's claws from the fabric of Ryder's shirt. When she finally lifted the cat from his back, she motioned for Summer to step in. "While I get Lucifer calmed down and clean up this glass, see what you can do about smoothing Ryder's ruffled feathers."

"Are you all right?" Summer asked. "Did you get cut by the glass when the vase broke?"

"No, I'm fine." He scowled. "I swear that cat hates me. And I'm beginning to return the feeling."

"Take off your shirt," she said, noticing some drops of blood dotting the back of it. "Your back is bleeding."

"I'm okay," he insisted, rotating his shoulders. "It's just a few scratches."

"I'm not going to argue with you, Ryder." Why did men have to be so darned stubborn about these things?

"Really, darlin', it's no big deal," he said.

Losing patience, she took him by the hand to lead him up the stairs. "Any time there's a break in the skin, it could become infected. We need to put antibiotic ointment on those scratches."

"I don't see what all the fuss is about," he complained as they entered the master suite and he turned on the bedside lamp. "But if you insist, there should be something in the medicine cabinet in the bathroom."

"Take off your shirt while I go get the ointment," she commanded.

When she found the tube and returned to the bedroom, she stopped short at the sight of Ryder with his shirt off, sitting on the end of the bed. In all of her twenty-five years, she didn't think she had ever seen a more beautiful specimen of a man in his prime. She'd felt the rock hard strength he had been hiding behind his chambray shirts when he held her, but nothing could have prepared her for the perfection of his well-defined chest and finely sculpted abdominal muscles.

She'd known he was in excellent physical condition. He had to be, considering the agility and athleticism required for his job as a bullfighter. But she had never given a thought to how all that would translate to his physique. With his broad shoulders, rippling abs and bulging biceps, he had a body most men envied and women wished their significant other had.

"Summer, are you all right?"

Embarrassed that he had caught her staring, she nodded. "I was wondering if I should go back for bandages."

"No." He shook his head as he turned for her to put the ointment on his back. "I really don't think I need the salve either, but if it makes you feel better, go ahead and put some on the scratches."

"I thought you said you always look up to see where Lucifer is before you walk past the stairs," she said to distract herself. The feel of his warm, firm skin beneath her fingertips caused a pleasant tingling in the pit of her belly and she could swear the temperature in the room had gone up by several degrees.

"Normally, I do make sure I know where he is." Ryder shrugged. "I guess I was distracted about getting things ready so we can take off early tomorrow morning."

"How early is early?" she asked, capping the tube of ointment.

"It's a good six hours' drive up to the fairgrounds where the rodeo is being held, so I'd say we better leave around four or five in the morning." Turning to face her, he smiled as he reached to pull her down onto his lap. "Don't you have to be there by noon?"

"I have to…set up interviews with the local newspaper and…radio stations." With all that bare masculine skin pressed against her side, she was having a little trouble catching her breath. "But that seems awfully… early to be leaving."

"You normally fly when you leave one town to go to

the next one on the rodeo schedule." He grinned. "Road trips take a little longer."

It had been so long since she had traveled by car between the many cities and towns on the circuit, she had forgotten they would need extra time. "I'll be sure to set my alarm," she said, starting to get up from his lap.

He tightened his arms around her to hold her in place. "Don't worry about it. I'll just roll over and wake you."

Her breath lodged in her lungs as she stared at him. She had thought they were going to wait until she stayed with him in his camper before they started trying for her to conceive. But as his green gaze held hers, she realized it was probably for the best that she hadn't had time to anticipate their first time together. There was a very real possibility that if she knew too far in advance her anxiety level would go sky-high and she would lose her nerve again.

Taking a deep breath, she nodded. "I'll go get my pajamas."

"I've been thinking about how to go about getting you past some of your fear," he said slowly. "And I think a compromise is in order."

She wasn't entirely certain she was going to like what he had to say next. But before she could ask what he had in mind, he told her.

"I mentioned that I like to sleep in the buff and you apparently like to be covered up from neck to ankles." He gave her a smile that curled her toes inside her cross trainers. "I'll wear underwear to bed and you can wear your panties and one of my undershirts."

Her heart fluttered wildly. "How is that going to accomplish getting me past the fear of having sex?"

"Before we go any further with this, let's get one thing straight, darlin'." He shook his head. "We aren't going to be having sex. We're going to make love."

"It's the same thing, isn't it?" she asked, frowning.

He hugged her close. "Sex is nothing but mechanics." His tone was so low and intimate it sent shivers of anticipation up her spine. "Making love is two people coming together to bring each other pleasure and to enjoy the shared experience."

She doubted that would be the case for her, but she wasn't going to argue with him. She was still trying to get past the idea of both of them sleeping in the same bed with so little on.

"You still haven't answered my question," she said, finally finding her voice. "How is sleeping in the same bed and wearing so little going to get me past my fear?"

Kissing the top of her head, his deep chuckle seemed to vibrate all the way to her soul. "What do people normally wear when they're making love?"

"Nothing," she said automatically.

He nodded. "And I'm betting that thought bothers you. A lot."

"I...um...well, it does make me a little uncomfortable thinking about it," she admitted.

"Don't you think that us wearing at least a few things to bed would be easier for you in the beginning than if we wore nothing at all?" he asked.

Being naked together wasn't something she had allowed herself to think about before and she wasn't sure she wanted to now. "You're probably right."

When he used his index finger to lift her chin until their eyes met, he asked huskily, "Do you still trust me, Summer?"

She didn't have to think twice about her answer. "Yes."

"Then let's try this." He smiled. "If it doesn't work, then we can always make that appointment with your doctor."

Setting her on her feet, he stood up and, walking over to the dresser, opened one of the drawers. "Here," he said, handing her one of his white cotton undershirts. "While you change and get into bed, I'll go downstairs and turn off the lights."

As she watched Ryder leave the room, she knew he was giving her the time to come to terms with his reasoning. And she had to admit his idea made sense. But as she went into the master bathroom to put the ointment back into the medicine cabinet and change into his undershirt, she wasn't overly confident that it would work.

Hurrying to take off her clothes and put on his shirt, she had just crawled into bed and pulled the comforter up to her chin when Ryder walked into the bedroom and closed the door. "Did Betty Lou get the pieces of the vase cleaned up?" she asked. "I should have helped her with that."

He nodded. "She had everything cleared away and was giving Lucifer a cat treat when I got down there." He shook his head as he sat on the side of the bed to take off his boots. "Can you believe it? He uses me as a scratching post and then gets some kind of reward for doing it."

She appreciated Ryder talking as if they were holding a conversation over coffee instead of getting ready to sleep together. It helped keep her mind off what was about to happen.

"Did you want Betty Lou to give you a cat treat?" she asked, unable to stop a nervous giggle.

Looking over his shoulder at her, he grimaced. "I'm glad to hear you're having a good laugh at my expense." He stood up to remove his jeans. "But you forgot one thing, darlin'."

"Wh-what's that?" she managed to get out as she watched him shove the denim down to his ankles.

"There's this thing called retribution," he said, kicking the garment aside, then turning to stretch out on the bed beside her. Grinning, he reached for her as he added, "And I happen to know just how to even the score."

Apprehension coursed through her a moment before Ryder moved his fingers over her ribs and she dissolved into a fit of laughter. "St-stop," she shrieked as she tried to get away. No match for his strength, she gasped for breath. "Why did I ever…tell you…I'm…ticklish?"

"I don't know, but I'm glad you did." His grin faded as his fingers stilled and his green eyes darkened to a forest-green. "I'm going to kiss you, Summer."

Her pulse sped up as he slowly lowered his head. But the moment their lips met, she eyes drifted shut and she lost herself in the kiss. Moving his mouth over hers, the tenderness and care that he took exploring her brought tears to her eyes. Every time he kissed her it was as if he reaffirmed his commitment to help her get over the assault that had held her prisoner for the past several years.

Using his tongue, he coaxed her to open for him and when she did, the touch of his tongue to hers sent tiny charges of electric current skipping over every nerve ending in her body. But instead of stroking her inner recesses as she expected, he engaged her in a game of advance and retreat as if daring her to do some exploring of her own. As she tentatively followed his lead, she felt his big body shudder when her tongue entered his mouth to taste and tease.

Lost in the heady feeling of being in charge, it took a moment for her to realize that his hand was moving along her side. When he paused at the underside of her breast before cupping its weight in his palm, she caught her breath. The cotton undershirt he had given her to put on was the only barrier between her hardened nipple and his calloused hand, but instead of causing the panicked feeling she expected, a delicious heat began to pool in the pit of her stomach.

The delightful sensations might have continued had she not moved her leg and come into contact with the hard evidence of his arousal straining at his boxer briefs. Her heart skipped a beat and breaking the kiss, she waited to see what happened next.

To her surprise, instead of taking things further, Ryder continued to chafe the tip of her breast as he gave her a brief kiss. Then, removing his hand, he whispered close to her ear, "Don't worry, darlin'. I'm in complete control."

"Are you… I mean, are we going to—"

He held her close as he rolled to his back. "Not tonight."

She couldn't understand the sudden tangle of emotions coursing through her. On one hand, she was relieved that they weren't going to make love. And on the other, she was slightly disappointed. It was the disappointment that she found so confusing.

"Why not?" she asked before she could stop herself.

"Because you're not ready," he said, reaching over to turn off the bedside lamp.

"But you are."

"It doesn't matter." His low chuckle as he pulled the comforter over them caused warmth to spread throughout her chest. "We won't be making love until we're both ready." He pressed a kiss to the top of her head, pillowed on his shoulder. "Now, I suggest you get some sleep because morning will be here before you know it."

Long after she heard Ryder's soft snores, Summer lay awake thinking about his plan to help her overcome her fears. He wasn't going to rush her. He was giving her the time she needed to get used to the idea of sleeping in the same bed with him, used to having him hold and touch her. She knew it had to cost him some measure of physical discomfort, but he was willing to suffer through whatever it took to help her. An unfamiliar emotion began to spread throughout her chest at the thought. How many men would take that kind of care with a woman? Be that understanding?

Feeling more safe and secure than she had in years, she snuggled closer to him. He was her best friend and if she hadn't known that before, she certainly did after his honorable gesture.

But as she started to drift off into a peaceful sleep, her last thought was that she and Ryder had passed a turning point in their relationship—one that neither of them had seen coming and there was no way of reversing now.

Six

"Nate, you look like you don't know whether you lost a horse or just found a halter," Ryder said, spotting his brother leaning against the outside of the arena fence. Normally the most carefree of his brothers, Nate didn't appear to have his head in the game and that could spell disaster for a bull rider. "What's up?"

"Nothing," Nate answered, looking up. He replaced his serious expression with a smile. "I've just been mentally reviewing what I know about the bull I drew for today's round. That's all."

To the outward eye, most anyone would think Nate was shooting straight with them. Ryder knew better. There was a shadow in his brother's eyes that he had never seen before, and Nate's easy expression looked forced.

Lane had been right. There was more going on with

Nate than a case of wounded pride over being dumped for the first time in his life.

Ryder claimed a space along the fence next to his brother and, leaning back against it, folded his arms across his chest. "You want to talk about it?"

"Nope." To his brother's credit, Nate didn't try to deny there was more going on with him than thinking about the bull he'd drawn.

He hadn't expected his brother to open up to him and it wasn't Ryder's style to push the issue. "You know I'll have your back out there. But just in case, keep your mind on business or turn out and call it a day. There's no sense in either one of us getting hurt if you're not up for this."

His suggestion that Nate have the bull released into the arena without riding him when it came his turn, produced the result Ryder had been looking for. Determination had replaced the shadow in Nate's gaze.

"Like hell I will," Nate retorted, shoving away from the fence. "I've never turned out and I'm not about to start now." Squaring his shoulders, he gave Ryder his familiar cocky grin. "You better take your own advice and be a little more careful, brother. You're the one with the sexy lady waiting on you when the round is over."

"Talked to Lane, did you?" Ryder asked. He had expected Nate to mention the new development between himself and Summer at some point.

Nodding, Nate reached behind his thigh to buckle his leather chaps, then did the same with the other leg. "Yeah, Lane was in charge of holding the money for the pool."

"So what was the bet and which one of you won?"

Ryder wasn't the least bit surprised that his brothers had been making wagers on his relationship with Summer. They all made bets with each other on just about everything. Always had and probably always would.

"The bet was a hundred bucks each on how long it would take for you to wake up," Nate answered, laughing. "Jaron won."

"What did I win?" Jaron asked, walking over to join them.

"The pool where you all bet on when I'd wake up and realize Summer is more than my best friend," Ryder said, shaking his head. "So what's the next bet?"

"When the two of you tie the knot," Nate and Jaron both said in unison.

"I've got Thanksgiving," Jaron said, grinning.

Nate nodded. "If you could just hold out until Christmas, I'd appreciate it. I could use the money for Christmas presents."

"I hope you aren't holding your breath for either one of those dates," Ryder grumbled as he turned toward his camper to change into his bullfighting gear. "You'll both turn blue and pass out before that happens."

As he walked the distance to the designated camping area where he'd parked his trailer, he hoped that his talk with Nate helped his brother regain his focus. Otherwise, Nate would end up in a heap on the ground about two jumps into his eight-second ride, and Ryder would be responsible for saving his tail end from being run down by a ton of ornery beef.

Quickly changing into his protective undergear and

the uniform supplied by one of the rodeo association's sponsors, Ryder tied his running cleats, then grabbing his black Resistol, headed back to the arena. That's when he spotted Summer with her electronic tablet, directing photographers where they could safely stand for their action shots.

Watching her, he would be the first to admit she was pretty damned awesome. Every rodeo she coordinated ran like a well-oiled machine and there wasn't a doubt in anyone's mind who was in charge. She was the epitome of self-confidence and had no trouble ordering around men twice her size. That's why it had come as a shock to learn that her strength and self-assuredness didn't extend to her personal life, as well.

He couldn't help but wince when he thought about his role in helping her regain her courage in that particular area. For the past few nights, he had lain awake with his arms around her and his body urging him to sink himself into her softness. But he had promised they would both be ready before they took things to the next level. And he wasn't about to betray that trust, no matter how much his body ached.

Fortunately, he didn't think it would be much longer before she was comfortable enough with him to make love. If her snuggling against him at night was any indication, she trusted him without hesitation. And as far as he was concerned, a woman placing her complete trust in a man was what made the difference between making love and just having sex.

"Hey, cowboy," she said when she looked up to find him watching her. "Are you ready to dance?"

He nodded. "Yup. Dances With Bulls at your service, ma'am."

She reached up to brush a piece of lint from his black shirt. "I'm glad the rodeo association opted to have bull-fighters wear these jerseys and athletic shorts. The job you do is too important for you to dress like a clown."

"Yeah, I guess it's hard to take a guy's job all that serious when he's wearing more makeup than most women," he said, grinning.

"Well, now that you mention it, that is a factor," she chuckled. Then her expression turned serious. "Please be careful, Ryder."

When the announcement came across the PA system that bull riding would be the next event, he leaned down and pressed his lips to hers. "Don't worry, darlin'. I understand those old bulls better than I do most people."

Turning, he jogged into the arena and, taking his position beside the chute gates, focused on the task at hand. He could give more thought to Summer's uncharacteristic plea for him to be careful after he'd done his job. Right now, he had over two dozen cowboys, including two of his brothers, counting on him to protect them from animals that had nothing more on their minds than making roadkill out of the person who had the audacity to try to ride them.

"Good luck," he called when he noticed Jaron was in the first group of riders.

"Thanks," his brother answered with a wave of his hand. "I'm going to need it with this one."

With his adrenaline level at its peak, Ryder stepped in when Jaron successfully rode his bull for the full eight seconds. Deftly dodging the animal's sharp horns, he ensured that his brother had time to sprint to the fence and out of danger before he lured the bull to the open gate leading out of the arena.

"Thanks, bro," Jaron said, jumping from his perch on the fence to gather his bull rope and wait for his score to be posted.

"All in a day's work," Ryder replied, grinning as he exchanged a high five with his brother.

As the afternoon wore on, he and the other bull-fighter working the event managed to distract one angry bull after another and keep the riders protected from getting stomped or gored. With only one bull rider left to ride in the day round, Ryder watched Nate climb on the back of Freight Train, a big, black bull known for running over whoever had the misfortune to get in his way.

He hoped Nate's mind was on taking care of business, but when his brother nodded that he was ready and the gate swung open, Ryder knew immediately that Nate was in serious trouble. His balance was off and when the bull went into a flat spin, Ryder's gut clenched as he watched Nate slide down into the well. Being on the inside of the spin was one of the most dangerous places a bull rider could find himself, and to make matters worse, Nate's hand was hung up in the bull rope.

Without a thought to his own safety, Ryder jumped into action, and while the other bullfighter tried to divert the angry animal out of the spin, he ran alongside the bull and worked on the rope to dislodge Nate's hand. Thankfully, Nate had managed to regain his footing when the bull stopped spinning and switched directions to chase the other bullfighter. But when Ryder finally managed to free his brother from the rope, Nate dropped to his knees, making him completely helpless if the bull decided to turn his attention back to the man who had tried to ride him.

"Get up and haul ass, Nate!" Ryder shouted as the bull turned toward him.

Slapping the bull's nose to keep its attention on him, Ryder continued to taunt the animal until he was certain Nate had made it to safety. Only then did he and the other bullfighter maneuver the bull toward the open gate leading out of the arena and back to the holding pens.

Angry with Nate for even attempting the ride when his mind was elsewhere, Ryder was glad that the events were over for the day. Jogging out of the arena, he had every intention of finding his brother and giving him a good tongue-lashing for putting them both in more danger than was necessary.

"Thank goodness you made it out of there without getting injured!" Summer cried, running up to him.

Ryder stopped when he noticed that she was trembling. His problem with Nate's carelessness forgotten, he took her into his arms and hugged her close.

"I'm fine, darlin'." Leaning back to look down at her, he brushed a lock of her honey-blond hair from her creamy cheek. "You've seen me in a lot worse situations than that one. What was there about this time that scared you?"

"I'm not sure, but..." Frowning, she paused for a moment like she might be as surprised by her reaction as he was. "…it seemed to take forever for you to free Nate and for all of you to make it to safety."

"But we made it just fine," Ryder assured her. He looked around as he searched for his brother. "Although, when I get the chance, I've got some choice things to say to Nate that he's not going to be all that fine with."

"I think he and Jaron are already on their way to the training room to gather their things," she said. "Will he be competing tomorrow?"

Ryder nodded. "I'll catch him then." He gave her a kiss, then stepped back. "Right now, I'd better go get a quick shower and change before the barbecue and dance."

"I'll be waiting." Her sweet smile and the promise in her cornflower-blue eyes caused heat to coil low in his belly.

As he turned toward the camping area, one thought kept running through his mind. He was in real trouble if all it took to rev up his libido was one little smile. He had another endless evening ahead of him, holding and kissing her without being able to make love to her.

Ryder shook his head as he entered the camper and went straight to the small shower to turn on the cold water. "It's going to be a long night," he muttered as he stripped out of his uniform and stepped under the stinging spray. He sucked in a sharp breath. "One hell of a long night."

One of the many things Summer liked about her job was the fact that nearly every rodeo had a barbecue and dance after the Saturday events. It didn't matter what town they were in, tables were always piled high with all kinds of food, the scent of burning mesquite hung on the crisp night air, and the live band, although not always the best, played with enough enthusiasm no one cared. Tonight was no different, except for one little detail. Tonight she wasn't with Ryder as just his friend. They were acting like a couple.

Amazingly, no one had appeared to be all that surprised by the change in their relationship status. Not even when they arrived together hand in hand or when they chose a table off to themselves.

After dining on some of the most delicious food she could ever remember, she and Ryder watched the band tune their guitars and adjust their microphones in preparation for the dance to begin. When she glanced up, he was smiling at her.

"Do you have any idea how pretty you are?" he asked, covering her hand with his where it rested on the table.

Her heart skipped a beat at his compliment and the feel of his warm, calloused palm against her much smoother skin. It caused a pleasant tingling to spread throughout her body. "Thank you." She smiled. "You clean up real nice yourself, cowboy."

Her breath caught when she realized they were actually flirting with each other. Was this part of Ryder's plan? Were they role-playing for the benefit of one of their coworkers?

Looking around, she didn't think so. There wasn't anyone they knew close enough to overhear their conversation. Frowning, she realized that for her, their flirting had felt very real.

Before she could speculate further on the matter, he stood up when the band started playing a slow number and held out his hand. "Can I have this dance, darlin'?"

As she stared up at him, her pulse began to race. Like a lot of Texas men, Ryder called all females "darlin'," whether they were one or one hundred. He had called her that from the first time they met and she had never given it a second thought. But this time there was something about the tone of his voice and the look in his eyes that made his use of the word extremely personal. This time, he actually meant it as an endearment. And instead of upsetting her as it might have a week ago, it made her feel incredibly special.

Confused, she placed her hand in his while she tried to process what might be happening between them. He helped her to her feet, then leading her out onto the dance floor, took her in his arms and pulled her to him. Without thinking twice, she wrapped her arms around his waist and it felt like the most natural thing in the world to rest her head against his broad chest.

When they had danced at Sam and Bria's party, they had both been mindful to keep a respectable space between them, to keep things companionable. But tonight there wasn't anything platonic about the way Ryder held her or the way she leaned against him.

As they swayed in time to the music, it felt as if the world was reduced to just the two of them and she had never felt as content as she did at that moment. For the first time in longer than she cared to remember, she felt

as if she was where she belonged. That in itself should
have scared her as little else could. But it didn't. She
knew without question that Ryder would never do anything to harm her, either emotionally or physically. He
was her safe haven.

Not even the feel of his hardening body pressed snug-
gly to her stomach frightened her. Instead, it made her
feel as if the blood in her veins had been turned to warm
honey and created an aching feeling in the most feminine part of her.

"Are you doing okay?" Ryder whispered close to her
ear. "I'm not scaring you, am I?"

For the past several nights as she lay in his arms,
she'd felt his body harden with desire and not once had
he tried to press for them to make love. Leaning back
to look up at him, she shook her head. "I trust you more
than I've ever trusted anyone…and I doubt there's anything about you that would frighten me."

When the song ended, he stared at her for endless
seconds. "Do you want to stay and dance some more?
Or do you think you're ready to go back to my camper?"

There was a spark of need in his eyes that stole her
breath. If she hadn't already felt the evidence of his desire, the look in his dark green gaze would have been
enough to let her know that he wanted her. And with
sudden clarity, she realized he was asking if she was
ready for more than just returning to his trailer for the
night. He was asking if she was ready to make love
with him.

She took a deep breath, then another as she searched
his face. With Ryder she was safe and there wasn't a

doubt in her mind that if she said she wasn't ready, he would accept her decision. But was that what she wanted?

"I think I am ready to leave," she finally said, nodding.

Ryder closed his eyes a moment, then giving her a kiss that caused her head to spin, he took her by the hand and led her through the crowd. "There's Nate with Jaron over there," she said, pointing toward the dessert table. "Didn't you say you wanted to talk to him?"

"Yeah, but taking Nate to task in front of a bunch of people isn't my style," Ryder replied, as they walked across the rodeo grounds toward the camping area. "I'll wait until I can get him alone tomorrow before I chew on his sorry hide." He raised her hand to his mouth to kiss it. "Besides, I have other things on my mind right now."

When they reached his fifth wheel trailer, he unlocked the door, then helped her up the steps. The deluxe camper had more amenities than any hotel room and she could understand why Ryder preferred taking his accommodations with him. It truly was a home away from home. And a very luxurious one at that.

When he closed the door and secured the lock, he turned and immediately reached for her. "You do know I was asking if you felt ready to try making love again?" he asked, raining tiny kisses along the side of her neck.

His warm breath feathering over her skin sent shivers of excitement coursing the length of her and caused her knees to feel as if they were made of rubber. "Y-yes."

"I don't want you to feel rushed, Summer." He reached up to cup her face in his hands. "Are you sure?"

She nodded. "Yes."

His smile sent her temperature soaring. "If at any time you need to slow down or want to call a halt to things, tell me."

"I will."

Lowering his head, he gave her a kiss that sent tiny electric charges skipping over her nerve endings and caused heat to gather in her lower belly. Then, without a word, he took her by the hand and led her up the steps to the bedroom at the front of the camper.

"Aren't you going to turn on the light?" she asked when he knelt to remove her boots, then pulled off his.

"Not unless you want me to." His low, sexy tone caused her insides to feel as if they had been turned to warm pudding. "I want whatever makes you the most at ease with what we're doing."

She nodded as he wrapped his arms around her and hugged her close. "I think I'm good with the light off... for now."

"That's fine, darlin'." He kissed his way from her cheek, down her neck to the fluttering pulse at the base of her throat. "I'm going to take my clothes off first," he murmured against her skin. "Then I'll take off yours."

She briefly wondered why he was telling her everything he was about to do. Then it dawned on her that Ryder was making sure there were no surprises, as well as giving her the opportunity to stop him if her insecurities got the better of her. Her chest tightened with emotion at the lengths he was going to in order to help her overcome her fears.

Neither of them spoke as he removed his shirt and jeans, then reached for the pearl buttons on the front of her pink silk blouse. When his fingers brushed her collarbone as he worked the tiny disks free, she shivered. No other man's touch had ever caused her to feel the excitement or anticipation that Ryder's did. And she knew as surely as she knew her own name that no other man's touch ever would.

Her heart skipped several beats and she struggled to take a breath. Was she beginning to fall for him?

It went without saying that for the past few years she had been closer to him than she had been with any other man. And there was no doubt that she was extremely fond of him. But what she felt now was different and went beyond mere friendship.

"Darlin', I'm going to take off your blouse and unfasten your bra," he whispered, causing her to abandon her unsettling speculation.

When he slowly brushed the pink silk from her shoulders, then released the front clasp of her bra to slide the straps down her arms, he gently pulled her to him. The slight abrasion of his hair-roughened flesh against her overly sensitive nipples sent a need like nothing she had ever known coursing through her.

"O-oh…m-my," she stammered, wrapping her arms around his waist when her knees threatened to give way.

"Are you still doing okay?" he asked, kissing her bare shoulder as he reached between them to unsnap her jeans and slowly slide them down her thighs.

"Mmm…yes," she managed as she kicked the denim aside.

Waves of heat coursed from the top of her head to the tips of her toes when he wrapped his arms around her and covered her mouth with his. His firm lips moved over hers with such tenderness she thought she just might melt into a puddle at his feet. But when he coaxed her to open for him, the feel of his tongue as he stroked hers, the tender care he took as he explored her thoroughly, caused the heat inside of her to tighten into a deep coil of need.

The feeling intensified when he ran his hands down her back to cup her bottom and pull her into the cradle of his hips. The only barriers separating them were his cotton underwear and her lace panties.

"You feel so…good, darlin'." His tone was raspy and it sounded as if he had as much trouble drawing in oxygen as she was having. "Do you need for me to slow down?"

"N-no. I'm fine."

"I'm going to take the rest of our clothes off," he said, raining tiny kisses from her forehead to her chin.

Unable to make her vocal cords work, she simply nodded.

Ryder quickly pushed his boxer briefs down his long legs and kicked them aside, then reaching out, placed his hands at her waist and slowly slid his fingers under the elastic at her waist. Her breath caught at the slight abrasion of his calloused palms skimming over her hips and down her thighs as he lowered her panties.

Stepping out of them, she could hear the beating

of her own heart when he drew her to him. The sudden heat of his hard masculine flesh against her softer feminine skin sent a shock wave of desire all the way through her.

She had expected a moment of panic, but it never came. There was nothing frightening about feeling Ryder's body aligned with hers. Having her breasts crushed against his chest, feeling his hard, hot arousal snug against her lower stomach only caused the need inside of her to intensify.

"Why don't we lie down?" he suggested, swinging her up in his arms to carry her over to the bed. He placed her in the middle of the mattress as if she was a precious gift, then stretched out beside her. "I want you to be completely comfortable with everything we do, Summer." When she started to tell him that she was, he placed his index finger to her lips. "That's why I'm only going to take things so far. I'll make sure we're both ready to make love, then I'm going to let you take control."

"What do you mean?" she asked, confused.

Giving her a kiss hot enough to melt metal, he lightly touched her cheek. "I've seen you flinch a couple of times when I lean over you to kiss you good-night. I think you'll feel more at ease if you're the one on top of me instead of the other way around."

What he said was true. She still felt extremely vulnerable lying flat on her back.

"You don't mind?"

His low chuckle sent a wave of goose bumps over her entire body. "Darlin', you know I'm not an insecure man." She could just make out his wide grin in the darkened room. "Lovin' is lovin' whether I'm on bottom, on top or standing on my head."

Summer smiled. "That last position might be a little difficult."

Shrugging, he brushed her lips with his. "If that's what it takes to make you happy, then I'd give it my best shot."

Her heart swelled with emotion. "Ryder McClain, you're a very special man," she whispered, touching his lean cheek with her fingertips.

"Nah, I'm just a guy trying to help out his best friend," he said, running is hands over her bare back.

His calloused palms felt absolutely wonderful on her sensitized skin, but having him mention their friendship bothered her. And she wasn't entirely certain why. But as he continued to touch her, she gave up trying to pin down the reason she found it unsettling. At the moment, having Ryder's hands on her bare skin was creating far too many delicious sensations within her to concentrate on anything but the way he was making her feel.

When he lowered his lips to hers, she gave herself up to the mastery of his kiss and forgot about anything but the man holding her to him. As his mouth moved over hers, he slid his hand from her back to the underside of her breast, then cupping her, used his thumb to gently chafe the hardened tip. Tiny electric sparks skipped over every part of her and she couldn't have stopped her moan of pleasure if she'd tried.

"Does that feel good, Summer?" he asked, raining

kisses down her neck to her collarbone, then the valley between her breasts.

"Y-yes."

He continued to tease her with his thumb for a moment before kissing his way down the slope of her breast to take her into his mouth. His tongue against her tight flesh caused stars to burst behind her closed eyes and she was certain that if he continued much longer she would surely burn to a cinder.

"Y-you're driving me...crazy," she gasped.

"Darlin', it's only going to get better," he murmured as he moved to take her hand in his. Guiding her to him, he whispered, "I want you to touch me. I want you to see that there's nothing threatening about a man's body."

Doing as he commanded, she tentatively ran her palm over his hard flesh, then the softness below. She felt him shudder with need, but he didn't stop her exploration and made no demands of her.

"Now I'm going to touch you," he said, his tone tight, but nonthreatening.

When he found her, the coil inside her lower body tightened to an almost unbearable ache. "P-please, Ryder."

"What do you want, Summer?"

"You."

Giving her a quick kiss, he rolled to his back and pulled her on top of him. "I'm all yours, darlin'."

True to his word, he was handing her control and making sure she wasn't threatened by his much larger body hovering over hers, pinning her down, trapping her. His concessions caused a deep emotion she didn't dare identify to fill her chest as she straddled his lean hips.

When he helped her guide him to her, she closed her eyes as she slowly took him in. She didn't think she had ever felt more complete as she did at that moment. It was as if she had finally found a part of herself that she hadn't even realized was missing.

Placing his hands at her hips, he helped her set an easy pace as she began to rock against him. Her body quickly responded to being at one with him and all too soon she felt herself reaching for the completion they both sought.

"I'm going to touch you again, darlin'," Ryder said, sliding his hand between them.

The moment he stroked the tiny nub of sensation, the tight coil inside of her set her free and wave after wave of intense pleasure flowed through her. A moment later she felt Ryder go completely still, then with a low, raspy groan he wrapped his arms around her and released his sperm deep inside of her.

Collapsing on top of him, Summer felt as if their souls had touched and she knew in that moment why his calling her his friend bothered her. Ryder was more than her friend, he was the man she was falling for.

Seven

The following morning, Ryder watched Summer from across the pressroom as she sat in on an interview a reporter from a national magazine was doing with Nate. A top contender for the Champion All-Around Cowboy title, his brother's outgoing personality and quick wit were exactly what the rodeo association was looking for to promote their upcoming national finals.

But as proud as Ryder was of his brother and his accomplishments, his main focus was on Summer. She was amazing and without a doubt the most captivating, desirable woman he had ever met. What he couldn't get over was why he had been immune to her charms before. How could he have been so blind?

When they had returned to his camper from the dance last night, he'd half expected for her to decide that she wasn't yet ready to make love. And although he hadn't looked forward to it, he had been fully prepared to endure a shower cold enough to freeze the balls off a pool table.

But Summer had surprised him and they had shared the most mind-blowing night of lovemaking he had ever experienced. He had done everything he could think of to make her feel as comfortable as possible, and with the exception of wanting the light off, she had been fine. She had even seemed to forget that they were making love for the purpose of conceiving a baby. For that matter so had he. All he'd been able to think about was the woman in his bed and how she excited him in ways he could have never imagined.

He frowned as he mulled that over. When had he lost sight of wanting to help Summer with her request of having a baby and simply started wanting her?

He had come to terms with the notion that their friendship had been permanently altered. That had happened the first time he had kissed her. In all of his thirty-three years, he'd never tasted lips so sweet or as soft as Summer's.

But what bothered him the most about the whole damn thing was that he could very well be helping her get over her fears of intimacy only to have her meet another man she decided she could settle down with. Then where would he be? He would not only lose his best friend, he would forfeit the right to make love to the most exhilarating woman he had ever known.

He tried to tell himself that it didn't matter since they really had no future together. Besides the fact that he didn't want to saddle any woman with his past, how could he tell Summer that the man she thought had such a high degree of integrity was a miserable fraud?

The thought had Ryder getting up from the chair he had been sitting in to amble out of the pressroom into the hallway. What the hell was wrong with him?

He wasn't interested in taking their relationship any further than they already had. So why did he have a knot the size of a football twisting his gut at the thought of Summer finding out about his past or moving on with her life in the arms of another man?

"Bro, you look like you got hold of a persimmon that wasn't quite ripe," Nate said, striding up to him as he walked out of the pressroom. "Are you all right?"

"Yeah, but you're not going to be if you pull another stunt like the one you did yesterday," Ryder shot back. It was easier to focus on his brother's lack of concentration yesterday in the bull riding event than it was to think about what he could never have with Summer. "If your head isn't in the game, don't climb on the back of another bull and risk getting into a wreck that might get you hurt real bad or worse."

Nate had the good sense not to argue. "I'm sorry about yesterday. But don't worry, bro. I've got things under control now." He grinned. "You know it's hard to keep me down for very long."

"Already turning on the charm with another unsuspecting woman, are you?" Ryder asked, relieved to see that Nate was more himself than he had been the day before.

"Nope." Nate shrugged. "I've decided to take a break

from the ladies for a while and focus on winning the All-Around."

Ryder frowned. Lane had been right; there was a lot more going on with Nate than a case of wounded pride. He must have fallen pretty hard for that nurse he'd been seeing if he was willingly giving up female companionship in favor of a rodeo title.

Before he could caution his brother further, Summer's hand on his arm stopped him. "Ryder, when you get time, I need to talk with you before the events start," she said, giving him a smile that caused his jeans to feel like they were a couple of sizes too small in the stride.

"Sure thing, darlin'." He turned back to Nate. "You know I'll have your back out there this afternoon. But remember what I said and pay attention to what you're doing."

"Will do," Nate said before he walked down the hall toward the training room.

"Is he all right?" Summer asked.

"I think so." Ryder put his arm around her shoulders and started back toward the pressroom. "Now what do you need to talk to me about?"

When they entered the empty room, she closed the door behind them. "I just wanted to tell you to be safe out there this afternoon," she said, wrapping her arms around his waist.

Hugging her close, he nodded. "I'll make sure of it. I have plans for tonight."

"Really?"

He lowered his head to brush her perfect coral lips

with his. "Oh yeah. I think we should skip the dance this evening and go to bed early."

"You're already sleepy?" The twinkle in her blue eyes indicated that she knew better.

"Darlin', when we go to bed tonight, I seriously doubt that sleeping will be on either of our minds," he murmured, kissing her until they both gasped for breath. "Are you doing all right? You should have woke me when you got up this morning."

"I couldn't be better," she said, rising on tiptoes to kiss his chin. "And you were sleeping so peacefully, I couldn't bring myself to wake you. Your job is so much more physically demanding than mine, I wanted you to rest."

"So now you're taking care of me?" Other than his brothers and his foster father, Hank, no one had ever bothered to look after his well-being.

She looked thoughtful for a moment, then nodded. "You're so busy watching out for everyone else, you need someone to take care of you."

Before he could respond, a knock on the pressroom door caused Summer to pull from his arms. When the door opened, a man holding a microphone like it was some kind of trophy walked in. "Excuse me, but would either of you know where I could find the PR guy?"

The man inquiring looked to be somewhere around his own age and a little too slick and sure of himself. "Who wants to know?" Ryder asked, taking an instant dislike to the man.

"I'm Chip Marx from Live Eye News," the fellow answered, managing to look down his nose at Ryder even though he was a good six inches shorter than Ryder's six-foot-two-inch frame.

He acted like they should immediately recognize him and his name. Besides finding the guy irritating as hell, it didn't mean squat to Ryder.

"I'm Summer Patterson, the regional rodeo association's public relations director," she said, extending her hand. "What can I do for you, Mr. Marx?"

The little weasel's demeanor changed immediately. "Well, now, this is a pleasant surprise," Marx said, flashing a bleach-toothed grin as he took her hand. He didn't shake it, but continued to hold on to it. "I can tell I'm going to enjoy doing this story after all."

Ryder watched Summer tug her hand free before reaching for a copy of the press release she had prepared. "Here's the information you'll need. If you have any questions, let me know. Since this is the last day and most of the cowboys are already getting ready to compete, I doubt that I'd be able to arrange an interview with one of them." She nodded cordially at him. "They usually take off to make the trip to the next rodeo as soon as the events are over with on the last day."

"Oh, this isn't for this week's dog and pony show," he said, laughing as he shook his head. "I'm here to do an advance story on the rodeo next week down in New Mexico. I'd also like for my cameraman to get some footage of the cowboys doing whatever it is they do."

"All right," Summer said, sounding reluctant. Ryder could tell she didn't like the guy any more than he did. "I'll arrange for a couple of seats in the VIP area. It's closer to the arena action. You should get some pretty good footage of the events from there."

"We would rather follow you around and get some of the behind-the-scenes stories." Marx pointed to his cameraman just outside the door. "He can get some video of the animals as well as the cowboys preparing for their rides."

"That isn't going to happen, Mr. Marx." Ryder had seen that look of determination on Summer's face before. She was the one calling the shots and wasn't about to let the guy dictate to her what he was going to do. "For one thing, this is a rodeo. It's not a 'dog and pony show.' And for another, you don't tell me what you're going to do. I tell you. The reason for that is to ensure your safety as well as that of the crew behind the chutes. Now if you can accept those terms, I'll be more than happy to arrange for you to get your story. If you can't, then our business here is finished."

Ryder had never been more proud of her. He had seen her deal with pushy reporters before, and he could have told Marx his dictatorial tactics wouldn't work. But watching her tell the man in no uncertain terms that she was in charge was a lot more enjoyable.

The guy didn't look the least bit happy, but apparently realizing Summer wasn't going to budge, he shrugged. "Well, I suppose we could get whatever footage we need from the VIP section." He flashed his practiced grin. "Would it be possible to get an interview with you after the events are over?"

"That could probably be arranged," she answered slowly. "But it will have to be brief."

"That's fine," Marx said. "I'll get what I can today and then set up something with you for next week's rodeo."

"I'll call the VIP attendant and have your seats waiting for you," Summer said, dismissing the man.

Marx looked like he would like to say more, but instead turned and walked out without so much as a thank-you. "Someone needs to teach that jerk some manners," Ryder said darkly.

"I've dealt with his type before," she replied, shrugging as she reached for her cell phone.

Ryder checked his watch. "While you make that call, I'll go get changed." He gave her a quick kiss. "I'll see you in a little while, darlin'."

"Be careful," she said, looking a little worried.

"Always am," he assured her.

During the bull riding event, Summer was too nervous to watch Ryder play tag with a ton of bovine fury. It was completely ridiculous, considering she had seen him do it almost every weekend for the past three years. But that was before he'd held her, kissed her, made love to her.

Busying herself with clearing out the pressroom to keep her mind off what was happening between them, an ominous announcement over the loud speaker caused a chill to snake up her spine and sent her running toward the area behind the chutes. The medical trainers were calling for an ambulance to enter the arena. That meant someone had been injured. And it was serious if they weren't bringing the rider back to the training room for evaluation before sending him on to the hospital.

Searching for Ryder, her heart felt as if it stopped beating completely until she spotted him kneeling beside a rider lying facedown in the loose dirt on the arena floor. Weak with relief, she looked around to make sure the fallen rider wasn't one of his brothers.

"Who is it?" she asked the chute boss.

He named one of the younger cowboys, then added, "The kid fell forward on Sidewinder's first jump out of the gate and knocked himself out. If it hadn't been for Ryder, that boy would have been a goner for sure. As soon as he hit the dirt, Ryder fell on top of him to protect him from getting kicked or stomped."

"Is Ryder okay?" she asked, holding her breath. On several different occasions she had seen him put himself in jeopardy to protect a cowboy who had no chance of protecting himself.

"I think he might have been shook-up when Sidewinder butted him in the side, but that's about it," the man answered. "He might be a little sore in the morning, but his Kevlar vest should have kept him from getting a couple of cracked ribs."

Once she learned that the young cowboy had regained consciousness and would be transported to the hospital for a CT scan and observation, the bull riding resumed and Summer had to wait until the rest of the event was concluded before she could approach Ryder. It felt like an eternity. She needed to talk to him and see for herself that he was all right.

As she impatiently paced the area behind the chutes,

she tried to figure out why she was so anxious…why she was more upset by his bravery than she had ever been before. She had always known it was his job to put himself between the cowboys and the dangerous bulls. He was one of the best and hundreds of men had Ryder to thank for saving them from serious injury and, in some cases, for saving their lives.

But the stakes had been raised and she had a feeling she knew why. She had always been fond of him, but this time she was seeing his acts of heroism through the eyes of a woman who was falling harder for him than she had any other man.

Summer took a bolstering breath as she acknowledged her feelings. She had suspected her feelings for him had developed into something much deeper than mere friendship after they made love last night, but she had refused to think about it. She had told herself not to jump to conclusions—that it was probably just the afterglow of their lovemaking she was experiencing. She knew now that her feelings went far deeper than that.

"Darlin', if you don't stop pacing, you're going to wear the dirt down to bedrock," Ryder said from behind her.

Turning, she hurried over to him and threw her arms around his neck. "Are you all right?"

His arms immediately closed around her. "I'm fine. Old Sidewinder just gave me a couple of nudges to tell me hello."

Suddenly angered by his casual dismissal of what had been a very serious situation, she stepped away from him. "Don't you dare say it was nothing, Ryder

McClain! You could have been hurt or worse. What if that stupid bull had stepped on you?"

"Whoa! Where's this coming from?" He looked confused. "You know it's my job to save riders. Hell, you've seen me do it at least a hundred times over the past few years."

"That was before," she protested, knowing she was overreacting but unable to stop herself.

He frowned. "Before what?"

She couldn't tell him that she had fallen for him. "We'll talk about this tonight," she said before turning to walk back to the pressroom. "I have to get things packed up and ready for next weekend."

"I'll help you," he said, falling into step beside her.

Out of the corner of her eye, she saw him glance at her several times as if trying to figure out what had gotten into her. She knew beyond a shadow of doubt what the problem was, but how was she supposed to explain that for the first time, instead of seeing him as a friend and coworker putting himself in danger, she had been watching through the eyes of a woman who was on the verge of falling head over heels in love with him? She hadn't fully come to terms with it herself and he probably wasn't expecting to hear it anyway.

"Did you get the interview with that little weasel over with?" he asked.

"Oh rats! I forgot all about that." How could a day start out to be so good, then turn into a royal headache so fast?

When they entered the pressroom, she sighed. Chip Marx was waiting for her.

"I was beginning to wonder if you were going to stand me up," he said, his smile barely hiding his impatience.

"I'm sure you can understand that when we have a rider taken away by ambulance it's a serious matter," she said, doing her best not to lose her temper with the man. "My first priority is to get accurate information about the cowboy's injuries and assess whether I need to notify his family or make a statement to the media."

"Of course." He didn't look at all as if he understood or cared. "Why don't we do a dinner interview? That way I'll have your undivided attention."

When Summer glanced at Ryder, she caught her breath. He looked furious. And she couldn't blame him. She was angered by the man's insensitivity, as well. He hadn't even bothered to ask if the injured rider was going to be all right.

"I'm sorry, but I won't have time to talk with you after all, Mr. Marx."

"Please, call me Chip," he said, his tone suggestive.

He gave her a grin that she was sure he'd stood in front of a mirror practicing—probably for years. If he thought it would win her over, he was sadly mistaken.

"As I told you, I don't have time…Chip." She hadn't meant for his name to come out sounding as if she said a dirty word, but at the moment she really didn't care.

"You have to eat anyway," he insisted. "It might as well be with me."

She'd just as soon dine with a snake. "Thank you, but I meant it when I said I don't have time. Now, if you'll excuse me, I have to get the rest of the pressroom shut down and ready to move on to the venue in New Mexico."

The man didn't seem to grasp the concept that she wanted nothing more to do with him and, stepping forward, took hold of her arm. "Surely you can—"

"The lady says she doesn't have time," Ryder interrupted, moving in to wrap his hand around the man's wrist and remove it from her arm. "Now, I suggest you take Ms. Patterson at her word and find another story."

She had only heard Ryder use that deadly tone one other time. The night she had told him about being raped.

Ryder must have applied pressure to the man's wrist because Chip Marx let out a yelp and winced in pain. "You can't do this." He glared at his cameraman. "Don't just stand there! Get footage of this. I'll need it when I sue this goat roper for assault."

The cameraman glanced from Marx to Ryder, then back to Marx. "You're on your own, Chip," he said, turning to walk out of the room. "I didn't see a thing."

Summer had never seen Ryder look as dangerous as he did at that moment and she couldn't say she blamed the cameraman for bailing on the arrogant reporter. Calling a cowboy a "goat roper" was extremely insulting and not at all wise when the cowboy in question had a vise-grip hold on your arm.

"It's all right, Ryder," she said, hoping to defuse the situation. "He was just leaving, weren't you, Mr. Marx?"

Before the reporter could answer, Ryder nodded toward the door. "You'd better take her advice, Marx. Otherwise, you'll force me to kick your ass. Since I'm still wearing cleats, something tells me that would make the experience doubly painful. And just so we have things straight…I'd better not catch you bothering Ms. Patterson again." Turning the man loose, he finished, "Because if you do, you'll be picking your bleached teeth up off the floor. Are we clear on that?"

His face beet-red, Chip Marx turned to rush from the room. But apparently as stupid as he was arrogant, he turned back for one parting shot. "This isn't over."

"Yes, it is," Ryder said, taking a step forward. The man fled as if he was being chased by the devil.

"Thank you, Ryder, but I'm sure I could have handled that situation myself," she said, reaching for a stack of brochures. She wasn't at all sure, but she didn't want him to know just how vulnerable she had felt.

He shook his head. "I know you're capable of taking care of most things like this, and I'm fine with that. But when that lowlife put his hand on you…" His voice trailed off for a moment before he took a deep breath and cleared his throat. "I'm not going to apologize because I'm not sorry I stepped in." Turning, he walked to the door. "And just so you know. As long as I have breath in my body, no man will ever treat you the way that bastard just tried to do and get away with it."

Long after Ryder left, Summer stared at the empty doorway. For the past several years, she had dealt with pushy reporters who thought they could bully or charm her into doing what they wanted and she'd never had a problem putting them in their place. But until today, none of them had ever crossed the line and put his hands on her.

She shuddered as she finished packing the small container with brochures and picked it up to leave. The only man's touch that didn't make her want to shrink away in revulsion, the only man she ever wanted to touch her, was Ryder.

Her heart skipped a beat as she acknowledged her feelings. She had tried to avoid putting a name to how her relationship with him had evolved. Acting as if they were a couple was only supposed to have been roles they were playing for the benefit of their coworkers and his brothers in preparation for the baby they were going to have together. But there was no sense in evading any longer what she knew in her heart was true. Even if she didn't feel she could reveal to him how she really felt, she could at least admit it to herself. She had fallen in love with Ryder McClain.

Ryder leaned up against the side of the arena, waiting on Summer. After leaving the pressroom, he had decided to make sure that Marx was long gone and wouldn't give her any more trouble. And he had no doubt that if given the chance, the man was stupid enough to try putting the moves on her again. Pushy little weasels like Marx thought they were God's gift to women and couldn't get it through their thick heads that they weren't adored by every female they came in contact with.

He sighed heavily. The last thing he had wanted was for her to see him lose his temper. And he'd been damned close to doing just that. Fortunately, for her sake as well as Marx's, Ryder had been able to keep a tight rein on his control.

He couldn't have cared less that the man had insulted him. As far as he was concerned, Marx's opinion of him didn't matter one way or the other. But when he grabbed Summer's arm, Ryder had damned near come unglued. It had taken every ounce of restraint he had in him to keep from knocking the jerk into the middle of next week. Unfortunately, he couldn't guarantee that the next time he would be able to stop himself. And that bothered him almost as much as Marx putting his hand on Summer.

"I thought you left to go back to the camper to shower and change clothes," Summer said, stopping in front of him as she left the arena.

"Nope." He shoved away from the wall to take the small box she carried. "I thought I'd stick around to carry this for you."

As they walked across the fairgrounds toward his camper, they fell silent. He hated the awkwardness and figured she was still upset that he hadn't let her handle Marx on her own. But he had told her the truth. As long as he was around, no one would ever lay an unwelcomed hand on her.

Stowing the container in the outside cargo area of the fifth wheel, he unlocked the door and helped her up the steps. "As soon as I shower and get changed, we can go to the barbecue if you'd like."

"I thought you wanted to stay in this evening," she said, frowning. "I was going to make some sandwiches for us."

"After that run-in with Marx, I wasn't sure you'd want—" Stopping himself, Ryder shook his head. "Never mind. Whatever you want to do is fine with me."

She stared at him for several seconds, then surprising the hell out of him, moved closer to wrap her arms around him. His arms automatically closed around her to hold her close.

"Today was the first time since I started this job that I felt threatened," she said, her voice trembling. "I didn't want to admit it, but when Chip Marx took hold of my arm, I was actually afraid."

"Summer, I was right there with you." Ryder leaned back to look down at her. "You've got to know there's no way in hell I'd ever let him do anything to you."

She nodded. "I know that. And I wasn't upset with you for stepping in to stop him. I was mad at myself for allowing him to frighten me." She shuddered against him. "But he gives me the creeps."

"Forget about Marx. He's not worth the time and trouble to give him a second thought." He kissed the tip of her nose. "Now, while I go take a shower, why don't you make those sandwiches."

"I can do that," she said, her sweet smile sending his hormones racing around like the steel bearings in a pinball machine.

He swallowed hard and forced himself to climb the steps to the upper level of the camper. "I'll only be a few minutes."

Showering in record time, he wrapped a towel around his waist and walked into the bedroom. He stopped short at the sight of Summer wearing nothing but his T-shirt and her panties.

Her cheeks turned pink as she grabbed her robe and held it in front of her. "I thought your shower would take a little longer."

"Nope."

"Since we aren't going out...I thought I would change into something more comfortable," she said hesitantly. Her gaze drifted to his bare chest and she reached out to lightly touch the small white scar just below his left pectoral muscle. "I didn't notice this the other night when I put ointment on the scratches. What happened?"

Ryder clenched his teeth at the surge of heat caused by her fingertips caressing his skin. "I got hooked by a bull about ten years ago."

"You weren't wearing your Kevlar vest?" she asked, stepping closer. She rested her palm over the scar and he felt like he'd been branded.

The light herbal scent of her hair and her soft touch caused his body to harden and he had to clear his throat before he could answer. "It didn't happen at a rodeo. I was helping Hank move one of his herds and a bull got loose. When it started to charge him, I figured I had a better chance of dodging it than he did because I could move a little faster."

She raised her eyes to meet his and the spark of desire he detected in the blue depths robbed him of breath. "You're a true hero, Ryder McClain."

Taking the robe from her other hand, he tossed it aside then took her in his arms and pulled her close. "Summer, I'm flattered that you think I'm such a nice guy. But I didn't do anything more than any other man would have done in the same situation."

"You're my hero," she insisted, gazing up at him.

As they stared at each other, Ryder felt guilty as hell. He didn't deserve her admiration, but he couldn't tell her that the man she held in such high regard wasn't what she thought he was.

To distract her from saying something else that would only end up making him feel even worse than he already did, he lowered his mouth to hers. The sweet taste of her lips quickly had him forgetting about anything but the woman in his arms and how much he wanted her. Considering that the only things keeping him from having all of her against him was the towel around his waist and the thin cotton T-shirt and panties she had on, it was no wonder his lower body had come to full alert.

When she raised her arms to wrap them around his neck and leaned more fully against him, he half expected her to bolt at the feel of his arousal pressed to her soft stomach. But to his immense satisfaction, instead of pulling away, her lips parted on a sigh. Encouraged by her response, he deepened the kiss to coax and tease.

"Darlin'...I think...we'd better...slow down," he said when he broke the kiss to nibble his way along her jaw to the delicate shell of her ear. "I give you my word that nothing is going to happen unless you want it to, but I'm hotter than a two-dollar pistol on Saturday night and want you now more than I've ever wanted anything in my entire life."

"But it's not…dark yet," she said, looking a little unsure despite the blush of desire coloring her cheeks.

Ryder laughed, releasing some of the tension that gripped him. "Our bodies will fit together just as well in the daylight as they do in the dark."

"I'm well aware of that, cowboy," she retorted, giving him a look that suggested he might be a little simple-minded. "But when it's dark it's not as easy to see…" Her voice trailed off and her cheeks turned a deeper shade of pink.

He could have told her that although his T-shirt covered her from neck to midthigh, it was still thin enough for him to see the silhouette of her delightful curves and the shape and size of her perfect breasts. But he wisely kept that bit of information to himself. Although she had become a little more comfortable with intimacy in the past few days, she still had a couple of lingering issues.

"Do you still want to make a baby with me, Summer?" he said huskily.

"Yes. But—"

"And do you still trust me?" he asked.

She nodded. "Of course."

He gave her a quick kiss. "I give you my word on this, darlin'. I won't see any more of you than what you want me to see."

Eight

Ryder's heated look sent a wave of goose bumps shimmering over her skin as he swung her up into his arms, then placing her in the middle of the bed, reached for the towel at his waist. Scrunching her eyes shut, Summer waited until she felt him stretch out beside her and pull the sheet over them.

Opening her eyes, she turned onto her side to face him. "You certainly aren't shy about your body."

"Nope." He smiled. "Most guys aren't hung up with modesty issues like women are."

"I wonder why?"

He reached out to take her in his arms. "Do you really want to talk about the lack of inhibitions in men right now?"

The hunger in his eyes stole her breath and she suddenly wasn't sure what he had asked her. When he covered her mouth with his, she decided it really didn't matter. All she could think about was the way Ryder was making her feel.

Less than a week ago, she had thought she was immune to desire and passion. But Ryder's kiss, his gentle touch and the concessions he had made for her peace of mind, had not only convinced her that her trust was well placed, it created a need in her stronger than she had ever dreamed possible.

Parting her lips, she welcomed him slipping his tongue inside to explore her with a thoroughness that sent a delicious warmth coursing throughout her body. But when he slowly glided his hand down her thigh to the hem of the T-shirt she was wearing and lifted it as he brought his hand back up to cup her breast, the heat inside of her coiled into a pool of deep need.

"Look at me, Summer," he whispered close to her ear. When her eyes met his, he smiled. "I'm going to take off this shirt and your panties now, darlin'."

A shiver of anticipation made its way up her spine as he swept the T-shirt up and over her head, then reached for the elastic at her waist. Not once did his gaze waver from hers and by the time the scrap of satin and lace was sent to join the shirt over the side of the bed, she realized that Ryder had kept his word. He hadn't so much as glanced at her body. She loved him even more for his integrity and the understanding he had shown for her self-consciousness.

Her heart skipped a beat and she closed her eyes as she felt her love for him blossom. She was no longer making love with her best friend in order to have a baby. She was making love with her soul mate—the man she had fallen hopelessly in love with. She had even forgotten all about their coming together for her to become pregnant.

But apparently he hadn't lost sight of the reason behind the intimacy they had shared last night and were about to share again. Why else would he have mentioned it?

She sighed. If he was still focused on their goal, that meant his feelings for her hadn't developed into anything more than what they had always felt for each other—a deep abiding friendship and a wealth of mutual respect.

Before she could give the matter more thought and come to terms with the fact that Ryder might not ever feel anything more for her, his fingers grazed her cheek. "What's wrong, Summer?"

When she opened her eyes, he was propped up on one elbow, staring down at her, his expression reflecting his concern. Reaching up, she cupped his lean cheek with her palm. "How could anything be wrong?" she asked, evading his question. "My best friend and I are about to make a baby."

He stared at her for endless seconds, as if trying to determine the real reason behind her heartfelt sigh, then lowering his lips to hers, gave her a kiss so tender it caused tears to flood her eyes. Ryder might be a giant compared to her petite frame, but he was the most gentle man she had ever known.

As he deepened the kiss to tease and explore her with feathery flicks of his tongue, his hand moved along her side and down her thigh. Caressing the back of her knee for a moment, he skimmed his palm back up to the apex of her thighs. Parting her, his touch caused her body to hum with an energy that threatened to consume her.

Lost in the delightful sensations he aroused in the most feminine part of her, it took a moment for her to realize that he was lifting her leg to drape it over his hips. "Ryder?"

"We're going to make love face-to-face, Summer. You need to see that it's me making love to you, not some selfish bastard taking what he wants." He kissed her bare shoulder. "I want to watch the moment I bring you pleasure…and I want you to see me when you help me find mine."

Her chest swelled with emotion. Ryder was an incredibly compassionate man. He had vowed to help her get over her intimacy issues, and he was doing everything he could to reassure her that she was safe in his arms.

Before she could find her voice to tell him how much his consideration meant to her, he moved to align their hips and she felt his blunt tip poised to enter her. His green eyes darkened as he captured her gaze with his and he slowly pressed forward. Feeling herself become one with the man she loved, seeing the tender passion on his handsome face as he filled her was utterly breathtaking.

With their eyes locked, he slowly began to move within her. Neither spoke as their bodies communicated in ways no words could ever express and all too soon, Summer felt the coil of need inside of her begin to tighten as she moved closer to the pinnacle. Her body ached to hold on, to prolong the moment of being one with Ryder, but he deepened his thrusts and she suddenly felt herself trembling from the pleasure rushing through every part of her. Unable to stop herself, she closed her eyes as she savored the exquisite feelings of unbridled fulfillment.

Ryder suddenly went completely still for a moment. Opening her eyes to focus on the man she loved with all her heart and soul, Summer watched as he found the satisfaction of his own release. A groan rumbled up from deep in Ryder's chest as his big body shuddered against her and he filled her with his essence.

For the next several days when he wasn't in the open-air arena at the fairgrounds just outside of Albuquerque saving some poor rodeo rider's hide from being stomped on by a bull, Ryder found himself hanging around the press tent. He liked watching Summer do her job. She was nothing short of a miracle worker when it came to dealing with schedule changes and any number of other problems that arose at the last minute. He had watched her put together press kits and arrange a goodwill trip for some of the cowboys to a children's wing in one of the hospitals, in addition to coordinating interviews with the media so they could get their stories and photographs without being in harm's way.

Walking up behind her, he wrapped his arms around her waist and pulled her back against him. "Do you have any idea just how incredible you are, Summer Patterson?"

"Incredibly tired is more like it," she sighed, leaning back against him. "I haven't been getting a lot of sleep lately."

He turned her to face him. "Is that a complaint?"

Her sweet smile sent his temperature sky high. "Not at all, cowboy. I've just recently discovered how relaxing nighttime activities can be."

Laughing out loud, Ryder pulled her to him for a quick hug. "We can always skip the barbecue and dance tonight and turn in early."

"I'm actually looking forward to the party," she said, snuggling closer. "After tonight I won't have to worry about the possibility of running into a certain pushy reporter who has a problem taking 'no' for an answer."

"Has old Chip contacted you?" he asked, hoping like hell the man had the good sense to look elsewhere for a story. He didn't like any man who tried to get a woman to bend to his will, but the behavior Chip Marx had displayed bordered on harassment and Ryder wasn't about to tolerate it.

"No, I haven't heard from Mr. Marx and I doubt that I will now. Since everything is drawing to a close today, he's missed his chance to find something to report." She rose up on tiptoe to kiss his lips. "Thanks to you, I'm pretty sure he got the message."

"He'd better," Ryder said, then reluctantly took a step back. "I need to go change and get ready to tango with a bunch of bovines."

"Be careful and save some of those dance moves for tonight," she said, smiling as she turned back to straighten a display of promotional items.

As he left the tent and headed toward the trailer, Ryder couldn't help but grin. Summer had conquered most of her intimacy issues, and although she was still hung up on how much they saw of each other in the bedroom, she seemed completely comfortable making love with him. In fact, she had even initiated their lovemaking last night.

His easy expression faded and he couldn't help but wonder what would happen once she became pregnant. Would he continue to have the privilege of holding her every night, to be able to make love to the most captivating woman he had ever met? Or would they try to return to the easy friendship they had enjoyed before?

He shook his head as he let himself into the trailer and gathered his bullfighting gear. He didn't see any way in hell they could go back. Not when he knew how responsive she was to his touch, how when they made love he felt like he had finally discovered the other half of himself.

Sucking in a sharp breath, he stood as still as a marble statue. Had he fallen in love with Summer? Was that why he couldn't imagine his life going on without the sweet intimacy they shared?

With his heart thumping against his ribs, he cursed his foolishness and finished getting ready to do his job. He wasn't in love with Summer. She was his best friend and the woman he was trying to make a baby with. He had the same needs as any other normal, red-blooded male and after a long dry spell without the softness of a woman, it was only natural that making love to her every night was influencing his emotions.

He stood up to leave the trailer and go back to the arena. And if he kept outlining all the reasons why he was starting to feel the way he did about Summer, he just might start to believe them.

Ryder held her hand as they walked to the pavilion where the after-rodeo barbecue and dance were being held. Truth be told, Summer didn't think she had ever been happier. Since beginning their physical relationship, she had started feeling like a woman again and not the skittish female who shuddered at the thought of being alone with a man. It was empowering and she loved the cowboy walking beside her for the special man he was and for helping her heal the emotional scars she hadn't thought she could ever overcome.

"I don't know what you're thinking, but it must be pretty nice," Ryder murmured, leaning down close to her ear in order to be heard above the live band.

"Why do you say that?" she asked, unwilling to reveal her feelings before she knew for certain he felt the same.

"Because you look like you know something nobody else knows and you can't wait to share it," he said with a wide grin.

"Maybe I do." She loved the intimate teasing and playfulness that had developed between them over the past couple of weeks.

"Want to let me in on the secret?" he asked, looking as if he already knew what she might be thinking.

"Not yet."

She actually had more than one secret, but she wasn't

going to jinx either one of them by talking about them too soon. She was certain that she loved Ryder and she would eventually tell him when the time was right. But her other secret was one that would take a trip to the drugstore and the purchase of an early pregnancy test to confirm. She was only a couple of days late, but due to the fact that her cycle had always been quite regular and she hadn't had any of the premenstrual symptoms she normally experienced, she was almost positive they had already been successful in conceiving.

"Let's dance," she said, tugging him toward the dance floor when the band started playing a slow tune.

When he took her in his arms, Summer leaned against him and realized that she was never more content than when they were holding each other. And knowing him the way she did, she had a feeling Ryder just might be feeling the same way.

"While I go get us a couple of drinks, why don't you find a table, darlin'?" he said when the dance ended.

Kissing his chin, she grinned. "You've got a deal, cowboy."

When she spotted an empty table in a secluded corner of the pavilion, Summer started toward it. She liked the idea of being able to talk with Ryder and not have to worry about being overheard. But as she made her way along the edge of the crowd, she stopped short when an imposing figure stepped out of the shadows and into her path.

"Well, imagine meeting you here," Chip Marx said, his speech slurred. He had obviously had too much to drink and, if the sarcastic expression on his face was any indication, he wasn't a very nice drunk.

"Good evening, Mr. Marx," she responded, attempting to step around him.

He caught her by the wrist to stop her. "Hey, where you going?"

A cold chill slithered up her spine. But she wasn't going to let him see that he was frightening her. Arrogant jerks like Marx fed on fear and intimidation. If she could keep from it, she refused to give him that kind of power over her.

"It's none of your business where I'm going," she said, pulling her arm back in an attempt to break his hold.

He tightened his grip and her hand began to ache from having the circulation cut off. "Where's your friend?" he asked, glancing around. "I'll bet you're not nearly as high-and-mighty when the goat roper isn't around."

"Number one, I don't appreciate you insulting Ryder," she said, stalling for time. Chip Marx was inching them away from the crowd and closer to the shadows where no one could see what he was up to. "And number two, he should be returning with our drinks at any moment. Do you really want him to see you with your hand on me again?"

"Too late," Ryder said from behind her.

A mixture of relief and dread coursed through her. She was relieved that Ryder had arrived before the man had a chance to drag her into the shadows, but if she had thought his voice sounded dangerous the first time

Chip Marx had grabbed her, it was nothing compared to the deadliness in his deep baritone now.

"Ryder, I'm sure Mr. Marx was leaving," she said, hoping to avoid a confrontation.

"No, I wasn't," Marx said, showing that he was every bit as stupid as she suspected. "And I'm not going to let the likes of him keep me from getting to know you better."

Marx suddenly released his hold on her and, shoving her to the side, took a swing at Ryder. Easily dodging the man's doubled fist, Ryder's punch was forceful, accurate and very effective. Chip Marx fell to the dirt like a discarded rag doll and as Ryder had promised the man the first time he grabbed her, two of his once sparkling white teeth, now bloody and broken, lay on the ground beside him.

Ryder immediately took her in his arms. "Are you all right?"

Nodding slowly, she hitched in a breath as she stared down at Chip Marx. She didn't like seeing anyone hurt, but she had no doubt that if Ryder hadn't arrived when he did, Marx would have dragged her off into the shadows and… She didn't even want to think about what he might have done.

"I was frightened, but I didn't want him to see it. I'm glad you showed up when you did." Glancing up, Summer wasn't prepared for the look of abject misery on Ryder's handsome face. "Are you all right?" When he remained silent as he continued to stare down at Marx's limp body, she started to become alarmed. "Ryder?"

It took a moment for him to finally look at her. "I

didn't want to have to do that," he said, his voice rough with emotion.

Summer shook her head. "He really didn't give you a lot of choice."

"We saw the whole thing and Summer's right, bro."

Looking up at the sound of the male voice, Summer was glad to see Nate and Jaron jogging toward them.

"It isn't your fault there's no cure for stupid," Jaron said, kneeling beside Marx. He took off his black Resistol and fanned it over Marx's face to help bring him around. "It was a case of punch or be punched, Ryder."

"I agree," an unfamiliar voice said. As Summer watched, a security guard hurried over to join them. "Are you all right, ma'am?"

"I'm fine," she answered.

"I saw the whole thing and it was self-defense. Plain and simple." The uniformed man shook his head as they watched Marx begin to stir. "When I saw him accost this little lady, I was trying to get over here to intervene, but I couldn't get through the crowd fast enough." The older man looked directly at Ryder. "To tell you the truth, I admire your restraint, son. If the bastard had grabbed my woman the way he did yours, I'd probably still be pounding on his worthless hide."

"We probably need to call the police and make a report," Ryder said, taking a deep breath. Nothing any of the other men had said seemed to be able to ease the morose expression on Ryder's face.

"Don't worry about it," the security guard said, pointing to a camera mounted on one of the pavilion rafters. "I've got the whole thing on tape and you can give me your name and where you can be reached in case the police get involved." He chuckled. "But it's my guess that once this fellow is fully conscious and he sees the video I'm going to show him, he won't be all that eager about getting the police in on this. If he does, he's going to be facing assault charges for man-handling the lady."

Once Ryder had given the guard the information he asked for, he turned to her. "Are you ready to go back to the trailer?"

Summer didn't have to think twice about her answer. "Yes."

Her concern increased when she glanced at Nate and Jaron. They looked just as concerned as she was.

"We'll talk to you when we meet up at the rodeo in Las Cruces a few days from now," Nate said, helping Jaron haul Chip Marx to his feet. "Hang in there, Ryder. You didn't have a choice."

As she and Ryder walked the short distance to the camping area, Summer realized that he was still deeply affected by the incident and didn't seem to be able to shake it off. "Are you all right?" she asked when he unlocked the door and they entered the trailer. "Please talk to me, Ryder."

"I'll be okay," he said, reaching for her after they both had removed their boots and left them in the hall-way. He held her close as if she were a lifeline and it scared her more than his obvious anguish over the in-cident. "I don't want you to be afraid of me, Summer. I swear with everything that's in me that I'd die before I ever hurt you in any way."

Leaning back, she cupped his lean cheeks with her palms. "It never crossed my mind that you would."

Sensing that he wouldn't allow himself to believe her, she tried to think of something that would convince him of her unwavering trust in him. Unable to think of anything she could say to persuade him, she took him by the hand and led him up the steps to the bedroom. Words might not be adequate enough to prove her confidence in him, but actions might.

When they stopped at the side of the bed, Summer turned on the bedside lamp. "Ryder, I need you."

"Summer, I don't think this is a good idea..."

"I do," she said, reaching to unbutton her turquoise blouse. "If you won't believe me when I tell you how much faith I have in you, then I'm going to show you."

All things considered, she was a bit surprised by the strength in her own voice. But as she stared up at Ryder, she realized it was true. She not only needed to show him that there wasn't a single aspect of their relationship that she wasn't completely sure of or comfortable with, she needed to help him restore his faith in himself.

As she removed the silk garment and reached for the front clasp of her bra, she watched a spark of hunger ignite in the depths of his green eyes. "Darlin', I don't want you doing something that you aren't ready for."

"I've never been more ready for anything in my entire life," she said, sliding the straps of the silk and lace down her arms.

Rewarded by his rough groan, she looked up to see that the spark in his eyes had ignited into a flame of deep need. Quickly unzipping her jeans before she lost her nerve, she slid them and her panties down her thighs, then stepping out of them, shoved them in the direction of the rest of her clothes.

Summer had thought she might feel some degree of apprehension, but as she stood before Ryder, an emotion unlike anything she had ever experienced before began to fill her. She wasn't just showing him her trust and faith in him, she was laying herself bare both physically and emotionally. She loved Ryder with all her heart and soul and she needed for him to know it.

"You're beautiful," he said, his voice filled with awe.

Reaching for the snaps on his shirt, she made quick work of the closures, then shoved the chambray off his shoulders and tossed it on top of her clothes. "So are you, cowboy," she said, placing her hands on his warm flesh.

He closed his eyes and took a deep breath. When he opened them, he stepped back to take off the rest of his clothes, then reached over to pull her into his arms. The feel of his hard body pressed intimately to hers caused Summer's knees to give way and she had to hold on to his biceps to keep from melting into a puddle at his feet.

"I don't want to scare you, but I need you more right now than I need my next breath," he said, his voice raw with desire.

Without thinking twice, Summer got into bed and held her arms up in invitation. "Make love to me, Ryder."

When he lay down beside her, he immediately wrapped his arms around her and covered her mouth with his. There was a desperation in his kiss, an urgency that she ached to ease.

Moving his lips over hers, then down to the slope of her breast, his mouth closed over her beaded nipple. Writhing with pleasure, she tangled her fingers in the sheets as the sensations he created inside of her threatened to consume her. She felt as if she might burst into flames from the wave of heat sweeping through her when he slid his calloused palm over her abdomen to the most feminine part of her…and she knew she needed him as desperately as he needed her.

"Please make love…to me…Ryder," she gasped as she reached to find him. Stroking him, she wanted him to feel the same excitement, the same hungry anticipation that swirled within her.

She watched him close his eyes and swallow hard as he struggled for control. But when he started to pull her on top of him, she shook her head as she kissed her way down along his strong jaw to his chest, then the thick pads of his pectoral muscles.

"I want to feel you…surround me," she said, lying back against the pillow.

A groan rumbled up from deep in his chest as he nudged her knees apart and settled himself over her. Without hesitation, Summer guided him to her and as she enveloped him with her warmth, her heart felt as if it might burst from the overwhelming emotion filling her. She loved him with every fiber of her being and knew without question that she always would.

When Ryder began to move against her, she welcomed the feeling of his larger body covering hers, making her feel as if she truly had become part of him. But all too soon the urgency of their passion took control and she found herself poised on the edge. Apparently attuned to her needs, he increased the rhythm and depth of the pace he'd set and she suddenly felt herself released from the tension holding her captive. Pleasure, sweet and pure, flowed from the top of her head to the soles of her feet and when Ryder surged into her one final time, it felt as if their souls united.

When he collapsed on top of her, she held him to her and in that moment, she knew without question that she was forever his.

"Are you all right?" he asked as he levered himself to her side.

"I've never been better," she said truthfully. She wanted to tell him she loved him, but she wasn't sure he was ready for that. Instead, she snuggled against him and sighed with contentment. "That was absolutely incredible."

"You're incredible," he said, kissing her until they both gasped for breath.

He held her tightly to him and they were both silent for some time before he finally released her. Clearing his throat, his gaze didn't quite meet hers when he spoke. "I almost forgot to tell you. I got a call from my foreman this afternoon just before the bull riding event. You're going to have to go on to Las Cruces without me. I have to head home tomorrow."

The finality in his voice had her sitting up to tuck the sheet under her arms to cover her breasts. "Is something wrong at the ranch? Is Betty Lou all right? Do you need me to go back with you?"

"No. Betty Lou is fine. It's just ranch stuff. I can handle it." He sat up on the side of the bed and reached for his clothes. "The first thing in the morning, I'll arrange for a charter flight to take you down to Las Cruces."

Her heart seemed to come to a complete halt. "Do you have any idea when you'll be coming back to work?"

Shaking his head, he got to his feet to pull up his jeans. "No."

"Ryder, what's going on?" she asked, tugging the sheet loose to wrap around her as she got out of bed. She had never seen him so stoic or as unwilling to talk to her.

When he turned to face her, she detected a sadness in his eyes that sent a chill up her spine. He quickly shuttered the emotion, replacing it with a look of determination. "Do I really have to spell it out for you, Summer? It was nice while it lasted, but this is over. We're over."

She stared at him in total shock for a moment before she shook her head. "What brought this on? Surely that run-in with Chip Marx—"

"I've changed my mind," he said, cutting her off. "I won't be able to help you with your plan to have a baby after all."

She couldn't believe what was happening. How could everything have fallen apart so fast? And why?

"Don't I even deserve an explanation?" she asked, fighting to keep her emotions under control.

She needed to keep her wits about her in order to

think. Something was going on with him, but for the life of her she couldn't think of what it might be.

"Let's face facts, darlin'. I'm just not cut out to be a daddy and we were only fooling ourselves thinking that I was." He started toward the door. "But now that you've overcome your fears, I'm sure you'll be able to find someone you can settle down with and have a whole houseful of kids."

"Is that…what you really want?" she asked, following him. She hated that she couldn't keep the anguish out of her voice.

"Sure, darlin'." He smiled, but there was a sadness about it that brought tears to her eyes. "Remember? I'm your friend. All I've ever wanted was for you to be happy."

"Where are you going now?" she prodded, desperately trying to think of some way to get him to open up and tell her what was really wrong. She certainly wasn't buying his story that he had changed his mind. He couldn't have made such tender, exquisite love to her and not have it mean anything.

"I'm going out for a while," he said, descending the steps into the main part of the camper. "I don't know what time I'll be back, so don't bother waiting up."

When she watched the door close behind him, Summer felt as if a band tightened around her chest. Why was Ryder shutting her out? Why wouldn't he talk to her?

Tears streamed down her cheeks as she retraced her steps up to the bedroom and sat on the side of the bed. She had never seen him like this. He wasn't the same man she had known and been best friends with for the past few years, the one she trusted above all others. The cowboy she loved.

The man who had just broken her heart was a complete stranger to her.

Nine

Ryder stopped grooming the bay and propped his forearms on the gelding's back to stare at the brush in his hand like it might hold a solution to his problems. After he dropped Summer off at the airport, he had called the rodeo association office and taken an extended leave from his contract commitment with them in order to regain his perspective. But he had been home for a week and his mood still hadn't changed for the better. He was miserable and apparently, without even trying, he was making those around him just as unhappy as he was.

It wasn't that he was irritable and lashed out at anyone. That wasn't his style. Hell, most of the time he tried to keep to himself, either in his office or by taking a ride down to the canyon. But Betty Lou had been hard to avoid. She'd quit at least three times yesterday and once today because she said he was too depressing to be around. Even Lucifer seemed to sense something was wrong and instead of hissing and spitting at him, the cat had rubbed up against Ryder's leg a couple of times as if trying to console him.

But there was nothing anyone could say or do that was going to change the facts. He was here at the Blue Canyon Ranch and Summer was out somewhere on the rodeo circuit. Without him.

Telling her that things were over between them and that he had changed his mind about having a baby with her had been the hardest thing he'd ever had to do in his entire life. But when he lost his temper with Chip Marx and knocked the guy out, it had scared the living hell out of him. All he had been able to think about was the last time he'd thrown a punch in anger. Pete Ledbetter had died because of it and although Ryder had only meant to defend himself and his foster mother, his actions had ended up killing the man. And even if it had been an accident, there was no excuse for it. No one had the right to take another's life.

He wasn't overly proud of the way he handled things that night with Summer either. After punching out Marx, he had realized that he had to let her go, had to let her find happiness with a man who didn't have the kind of baggage he would carry for the rest of his life. But he'd ended up being selfish. He'd had to make love to her one last time before he stepped aside to let her get on with her life, needed to store up one more memory of making love to the woman who would always own him heart and soul.

When his cell phone rang, Ryder groaned. Summer

hadn't tried calling him, but his brothers had. In fact, all five of them had called him at least once a day and sometimes more than that after they learned he had taken a leave of absence from his bullfighting duties on the rodeo circuit.

He knew Nate and Jaron had spread the word about the unfortunate incident and they were all concerned about him. They knew the hell he'd gone through as a teenager as he came to terms with Pete Ledbetter's death and his fear of something like that ever happening again. But as much as they meant to him and as close as they all had been since their days at the Last Chance Ranch, they were the last people he wanted to talk to. He didn't need to hear them tell him that he was making a mountain out of a molehill—or that he was selling Summer short by not telling her about his past and letting her decide for herself what was best.

The bottom line was, he knew he'd done the right thing. They would do well to respect that and leave him alone.

When the phone chirped again he checked the caller ID. His housekeeper probably wanted to tell him she was quitting again.

"What's up, Betty Lou?"

"I think you better come up to the house," she said, sounding a little shaky.

He immediately tossed the brush aside and started toward the barn's double door. "What's wrong?"

"We've got a bit of a situation that you're going to have to handle," she said evasively. "You'd better get up here to the house, pronto."

He'd never heard Betty Lou sound so distressed. "I'm on my way."

The first thing he did as he sprinted across the barnyard was check to see if there was smoke billowing from the house. There wasn't. At least the house wasn't on fire. Then he wondered if Betty Lou had somehow hurt herself. She might have cut herself with a knife while making supper or fallen off the little step stool she used to reach the top shelves in the pantry.

All sorts of disasters ran through his mind and by the time he reached the house, Ryder took the porch steps two at a time. "Betty Lou, are you okay?" he shouted as he jerked open the kitchen door.

Instead of finding Betty Lou bleeding profusely or cradling a broken arm from taking a fall, all five of his brothers sat at the kitchen table, their coffee cups raised in an obviously staged greeting. "Ah, hell," he muttered, glaring at them. He hadn't seen even one of their trucks. If he had, he would have taken off in the opposite direction. "Where did you park?"

"On the other side of the equipment shed," Nate said, grinning.

"We figured you couldn't ignore us if we used the element of surprise," Sam added.

"That was my idea," T.J. chimed in, looking particularly proud of himself.

"And you went along with it, Betty Lou," Ryder accused. "I should fire you for being a traitor."

Unconcerned, Betty Lou shrugged as she turned to stir a big pot on top of the stove. "You can't. I already quit this morning."

"Why don't we get out of Betty Lou's way and go into your office?" Lane suggested, rising from his chair at the table.

"I'd rather not," Ryder said even as he followed his brothers down the hall.

"You know why we're here don't you?" Jaron asked as they filed into the room.

"Yeah, you've dropped by to give me hell over breaking it off with Summer," he said, lowering himself into the chair behind his desk. "But I didn't expect you all to turn it into an intervention."

"It wouldn't have been if you'd taken any of our calls," Sam said as he took a seat on the leather couch.

Fortunately, the office was big enough that the decorator included a couch, as well as the two armchairs in front of his desk. Or maybe in this case, that was unfortunate. There was more than enough room for all of his brothers to sit comfortably while they pointed out the error of his ways.

Glowering at them, he shook his head. "While I appreciate your concern, there's no reason for it. I'll be okay."

"Can it, bro," Jaron spoke up. "If you'll remember, Nate and I were there. We saw how the incident affected you."

"That arrogant bastard didn't give you a choice," Nate added. "He started it and all you did was end it. You were only defending Summer and yourself."

"Yeah and any one of us would have done the same thing," Sam agreed. "If some son of a bitch tried anything like that with Bria, I'd probably have done a whole lot more than just knock out a couple of his teeth."

"A real man doesn't treat a woman like that." T.J. shook his head adamantly. "The jerk needed to be taught a lesson."

"Yeah, but I'd have given anything not to have to be the one teaching the class," Ryder groused.

"How do you feel about what happened?" Lane asked, looking pensive.

Ryder glared at his brother. "Put your psychology degree away, Donaldson. I don't need analysis. I'll be fine."

"Take it from me, you won't be okay until you've talked about it with Summer," Sam advised. "I had to learn my lesson the hard way. Don't be me, Ryder. Don't wait until it's almost too late and you come close to losing her."

Ryder stared at his brother. Sam's stubborn pride had damned near cost him and Bria their marriage and it wasn't until Sam had been injured in an accident that he woke up and realized how much he had to lose. But he and Summer weren't married and it would be easier for him to do the right thing and walk away from her now than it would be later on. He couldn't bear telling her about his past and then watch disillusionment fill her pretty blue eyes when she realized that he wasn't the man she thought him to be.

Before he could set Sam straight and remind him that their situations were different, Lane looked him square in the eye. "Ask yourself what the outcome would have been if you hadn't intervened—both times. Could you have lived with yourself if you'd stood by and let Ledbetter beat his wife to death? Could you have watched Marx while he manhandled Summer and done nothing to stop him?" Checking his watch, he rose to his feet. "I hate to cut this short, but I have an appointment." Turning to the others, he added, "And I believe we've given Ryder a few things he needs to think over."

Watching his brothers file out of the office, Ryder grimaced. One thing about it, his brothers didn't pull any punches. No matter how painful the truth was, they were nothing if not honest with each other.

But they didn't know the whole situation. They weren't aware that Summer had an unshakable belief that he was something he wasn't. She was convinced that he was forthright and incapable of doing any real harm to anyone. The thought of having her find out differently made him feel sick to his stomach.

He would give everything he had to be that man for her. But he couldn't and nothing he could say or do was ever going to change that. He couldn't go back and rewrite his past any more than he could stop the sun from rising in the east each morning.

Unable to sit still, he stalked out of the office and headed back to the barn to saddle the bay. As he rode out of the ranch yard and across the pasture toward the canyon, he knew in his heart that he'd done what was best for her.

His run-in with Marx had turned out all right and had that been the only time he'd had to raise his fists to defend someone, he might feel differently about things.

But he loved Summer too much to saddle her with his youthful mistakes…and a past that he couldn't erase.

Several hours after his brothers left the ranch, Ryder sat beneath the cottonwood tree and watched the breeze cause ripples in the lazy little stream as he tried to figure out what he was going to do with the rest of his life. He couldn't go back to playing chicken with a ton of pissed-off beef. Eventually his and Summer's paths would cross at some rodeo and it would kill him to see her with another man. And there wasn't a doubt in his mind that's exactly what would happen. She was too pretty, too vivacious and full of life not to have a string of men just waiting for the chance to gain her attention.

Leaning back against the tree, he stared up at the gold-colored leaves. His brothers had meant well when they advised him to tell Summer about his past and leave it up to her to decide what was best. But they didn't understand. They had all been in trouble for one thing or another, but robbing a store or running a con game wasn't the same as being responsible for someone's death.

Lost in his own misery, it took a moment for Ryder to realize that someone was approaching on horseback. It was probably one of his men coming to check on the pasture conditions at the far end of the canyon he decided as he got to his feet.

When he looked up, his heart lurched as he watched Summer ride the buckskin mare over beside his bay gelding. Dismounting, she ground tied the horse, then started walking toward him.

"What are you doing here?" he asked, not entirely sure he wasn't dreaming.

From the determined expression on her pretty face, he could tell she was angry. "You owe me an explanation…and I'm not leaving until I get it."

It was all he could do not to take her in his arms and kiss her senseless when she sauntered up to stand in front of him. But that would only further complicate matters. And God only knew everything was complicated enough.

"I don't know what you think I need to explain." It was a barefaced lie. He knew damned good and well what she wanted to know, but it wasn't something she would want to hear.

"Give me a break, cowboy," she said, propping her hands on her shapely hips. "I thought friends were honest with each other."

He took in some much-needed air, then slowly released it. "I'm sorry, darlin', but I don't think I can be your friend anymore."

Her pretty blue eyes narrowed. "Why not?"

"I think you already know the answer to that," he hedged. Why couldn't she just let it go?

"Don't assume that I know anything for certain." Her stubborn little chin was set and he'd seen that expression on her lovely face one too many times not to know that hell would freeze over before she gave up. "I was confident we were best friends and now it appears that's over. I want to know the reason why you ended our friendship. You owe me that much."

Lowering himself to sit at the base of the tree, he shrugged. "We crossed a line and made love."

"I'm well aware of that," she said, sitting on the grass in front of him. "In fact, we crossed that line several times."

"Dammit, Summer, I know how irresistible you are, how responsive," he said, taking off his hat to run his hand over the tension building at the back of his neck. "I can't go back to seeing you every day and not being able to make love to you."

"Who said you had to?" she pressed.

"The deal was that we would make love until you became pregnant," he stated flatly.

"That's true, but that was before," she said, shrugging.

Good Lord she was driving him nuts and she probably didn't even realize it. Or maybe she did and she was determined to make him pay for his transgressions.

"Before what?"

Her expression softened. "Before we fell in love."

She couldn't have shocked him more if she'd tried. "You think we're in love?"

"No, I don't think we are," she said, shaking her head. "I know we are. And I'm here to find out why you're trying to throw away what we have together."

He closed his eyes against the gut-wrenching pain knifing through him. She loved the man she thought he was, not who he really was. In that moment he knew she'd forced his hand and he was going to have to tell her the one thing that would end things between them for good.

"Summer, I'm no good for you," he said, feeling like he had the weight of the world resting on his shoulders. "I'm no good for any woman."

Her honey-blond ponytail swung back and forth as she shook her head. "That's a bunch of garbage. You're the most honest, trustworthy man I've ever known."

"No, I'm not." He took a deep breath. "I haven't been honest with you. I've got a past and it isn't a pretty one, darlin'. You're better off not knowing what I've done."

She met his gaze head-on. "Why don't you tell me about it and let me be the judge of that?"

A knot formed deep in his gut. He was about to see the confidence in her eyes turn to disillusionment and then revulsion. But it was the only way he could convince her that she would be better off without him in her life.

"You know I was a foster kid and finished growing up at the Last Chance Ranch." When she nodded, he swallowed hard. "Do you really want to know why I was sent there?"

"Yes, if that will explain why you think you're not good enough to be in a relationship with me when we both know we're in love."

"I killed a man." Just saying the words caused the knot to twist painfully. "I didn't mean to, but I did."

Her sharp intake of breath made him feel like a piece of his soul had been ripped apart. "My God, Ryder. What happened?"

Telling her about his drunken foster father and the man's habit of beating his wife, Ryder stared down at his balled fists. "When he started to take another swing at my foster mother, I stepped between them. That just pissed him off even more and he drew back to punch me. Because he was drunk he wasn't as steady on his feet and when my fist landed along his jaw, he fell backward." Ryder took a deep breath as the memory of old Pete lying on the floor in a pool of blood ran through his mind. "He hit his head on the kitchen counter, and the next thing I knew he was dead and I was being hauled off to jail and charged with manslaughter."

"That's why you reacted the way you did after that confrontation with Chip Marx, isn't it?" she guessed.

He nodded. "That brought back a lot of bad memories."

"Oh, Ryder, I'm so sorry you had to go through that," she said, surprising him when she rose to her knees to put her arms around him. "But you're being too hard on yourself. Don't you see that the altercation with Marx wasn't your fault any more than it was with your foster father? Both times you were only defending yourself."

"It doesn't bother you that a man died because of me?" he asked, unable to believe she could accept what he'd done.

"Yes, I'm bothered that it happened, but not for the reason you're thinking," she said, cupping his face with her soft palms. "I'm disturbed by the idea that the man tried to hurt you and because of that you've been left feeling that you've done something terribly wrong." She kissed him lovingly. "Yes, it was tragic that the man died, but it was an accident. It's in the past and there's nothing you can do to change that. Don't you think you've punished yourself long enough?"

Wrapping his arms around her, he held her close as he felt a drop of moisture trickle down his cheek. "I can't forget what happened."

Her arms tightened around him. "I'm not saying you should forget. I'm telling you that you didn't do anything wrong and that it's time to stop blaming yourself for the choices other people made. You need to accept and forgive yourself for an unfortunate accident that was out of your control."

Ryder felt free for the first time in years. He wasn't responsible for the actions of others, and although he regretted what happened all those years ago, Summer was right. He needed to look forward instead of living his life regretting the past.

"Did you mean it, Summer?" he asked suddenly.

She looked confused. "What?"

"You said we fell in love." He looked into her crystalline blue eyes. "Do you really love me, darlin'?"

Her smile caused his chest to swell with emotion. "Absolutely. I love you with all my heart and soul, Ryder McClain. You're my best friend and the love of my life. That's something else that you need to accept that's never going to change."

A lump the size of his fist clogged his throat. "Thank God! I love you more than life itself."

Kissing her until he thought they both might pass out from a lack of oxygen, he asked, "Will you marry me, Summer? I want to be the man you go to bed with every night and wake up with every morning. My family will be yours and we'll start our own with a whole houseful of babies." He smiled. "I give you my word, you'll never be alone again. I'll be with you until the day I die."

To his relief, there wasn't a moment's hesitation in her answer. "Yes." Her smile was the sweetest he had ever seen. "But there's something I need to tell you, cowboy."

Holding her to his chest, he kissed the top of her head then the tip of her nose. "What's that, darlin'?"

"I'm thrilled I'll finally be part of a big family," she said, giving him a watery smile. "And just so you know, you were right about those swimmers."

Ryder frowned. "What are you talking about?"

"We've already started on that houseful of babies," she said, grinning.

He felt his heart come to a complete halt, then start thumping hard against his ribs. "You're pregnant?"

"I haven't seen a doctor yet, but the test I bought at the pharmacy says I am," she said, nodding.

He couldn't stop grinning. "It looks like Bria's sister, Mariah, and Jaron will have two reasons to argue about babies and whether they'll be boys or girls."

When she touched his cheek, he felt like the luckiest man in the entire world. "I love you, cowboy."

"And I love you, darlin'." He rose to his feet, then held out his hand to help her up. When she placed her hand in his, he felt as if he'd been handed a rare and precious gift. "Let's go back to the house. We have a few phone calls to make."

"Your brothers?" she asked.

He laughed. "I can't remember the last time I knew something about myself that they didn't know first."

Epilogue

"I'm telling you, they'll both be girls, Jaron Lambert," Mariah insisted.

Jaron stubbornly shook his head. "And I'm telling *you,* they're going to be boys."

Ryder stood with his brothers, watching Mariah and Jaron debate the gender of the babies Summer and Bria were going to have. "Do you think it's crossed their minds that we might have one of each?"

Sam shrugged as he took a swig of beer from the bottle in his hand. "I doubt it. I don't think it matters to either one of them what sex the babies are. They just like to argue."

"So who's next?" T.J. asked, grinning like a fool.

"Next for what?" Nate asked, distracted. He had his eye on a willowy redhead across the dance floor, and

Ryder was glad to see that his brother had finally gotten over that little nurse up in Waco and was moving on.

"The next to get married, genius," T.J. shot back.

"My money is on you and that neighbor of yours, T.J.," Lane said with a grin.

"I keep telling you, I'd rather go buck naked for eight seconds on a porcupine than to take up with the likes of her," T.J. said, shaking his head. "She's still letting that stud of hers jump the fence and get with my mares."

Ryder blocked out his brother's complaints about his neighbor and the horse she couldn't seem to keep at home as he scanned the crowd, looking for his wife. When he spotted her in that gorgeous white wedding gown, he caught his breath. He doubted there would ever be a time that the sight of her didn't have that effect on him.

"It might be you, Lane," Ryder said, checking his watch. Another hour and it should be socially acceptable for him to take his bride and leave the wedding reception to start their honeymoon.

"Getting married isn't part of my life plan," Lane quipped. "The ranch I won last month in that poker game in Shreveport is as close to settling down as I intend to get."

They all looked at Nate for a moment. His attention had already turned from the redhead to a curvy brunette.

"That's a sucker bet if I ever saw one," Lane said, laughing.

"While you all carry on about who the next will be to take dip in the marital pool with me and Sam, I'm going to dance with my wife," Ryder announced, turning to walk across the dance floor.

When he approached Summer, her smile caused his body to tighten and he wished like hell they were already on that island in the Caribbean where they were spending their honeymoon. "Could I have this dance, darlin'?"

She placed her hand in the crook of his arm as she smiled up at him. "This one and all of the dances for the rest of my life."

"That's sounds like a good idea to me," he murmured, taking her in his arms. When she rested her head against his chest, he kissed her forehead. "Are you happy, Summer?"

"I've never been happier, Ryder." Leaning back to look up at him, the love shining in the depths of her eyes sent his hormones into overdrive. "You've given me every one of my dreams."

"And you've given me every one of mine, darlin'." He grinned. "All except for one."

"Which one is that?" she asked, clearly intrigued.

"As beautiful as you look in your wedding gown, when you were walking down the aisle toward me, all I could do was stand there and daydream about the moment I get to take it off you," he whispered close to her ear.

She shivered against him and he knew she was looking forward to starting their lives together as much as he was. "I've been dreaming about you doing that, too." Smiling, she kissed him tenderly. "I love you, cowboy."

"And I love you, darlin'." Grinning, he took her by

the hand and started toward the door. "Now, let's go somewhere a little more private and I'll see what I can do about making both of our dreams come true."

* * * * *

MILLS & BOON®

18 bundles of joy from your favourite authors

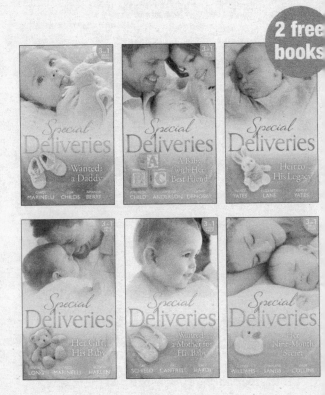
Get 2 books free when you buy the complete collection only
www.millsandboon.co.uk/greatoffers

SPECIAL DELIVERIES_0916

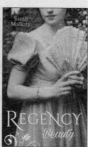

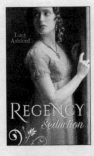

MILLS & BOON®

Why shop at millsandboon.co.uk?

Each year, thousands of romance readers find their perfect read at millsandboon.co.uk. That's because we're passionate about bringing you the very best romantic fiction. Here are some of the advantages of shopping at www.millsandboon.co.uk:

Get new books first—you'll be able to buy your favourite books one month before they hit the shops

Get exclusive discounts—you'll also be able to buy our specially created monthly collections, with up to 50% off the RRP

Find your favourite authors—latest news, interviews and new releases for all your favourite authors and series on our website, plus ideas for what to try next

Join in—once you've bought your favourite books, don't forget to register with us to rate, review and join in the discussions

Visit **www.millsandboon.co.uk**
for all this and more today!